MoonDust

Falling From Grace

By Ton Inktail

This is a work of fiction. Names, places, characters and events are either fictitious, or used fictitiously. Any resemblance to actual events, locations, organizations or persons, alive or dead, is entirely coincidental and unintended.

For the fox who told me it was broken,
The dachshund who showed me how to fix it,
And the lioness, rat, war horse, and squirrel who made me care.

Also, a big thanks to all the people who gave their time and effort along the way:

My beta readers Ember, Kish, and Ruth who pinned down themes and helped tie up more loose threads than a cheap rug.

The crew over at critiquecircle.com deserve much thanks as well: Conni, EK, Jason, John, Laurel, Rick, Sharon, and all the others. Without their willingness to put up with my sloppy revisions and an angsty, complaining caribou, this book would be nowhere near as good as it is. I can't thank them all enough, and any errors I've managed to include are despite their diligent efforts.

Much appreciation also to my cover artist, Katrin, for making the book look as good on the outside as I hope it is on the inside.

1

HOME

The moon hung low over Ankara, a blood-red eye blinking as clouds of smoke drifted across the city. Machine gun fire chattered in the distance, and the stench of burning oil rode a hot desert breeze.

Imogene clutched her rifle, ears flicking at every sound. Her gaze darted back and forth over the bare asphalt separating her checkpoint from the perimeter fence. In the six months she'd been here, no one had breached that three-metre wall of concrete and razor wire. But tonight the fighting sounded close.

Sharing her sandbagged dugout, Ralph looked as nervous as Imogene felt. He was a transgenic caribou-human hybrid like herself, and easy to read. Mostly human in outline, he had thick brown fur and a ruggedly handsome deer-like face. His long ears twitched where they stuck out of his helmet, as did the white-furred tail below his waistband. He leaned with his elbows propped on the sandbags, his two combat-booted hooves lost in the shadows beside her own.

With him that twitchy, Imogene would normally make a joke about attracting flies. But not tonight. Tonight, it was enough to survive. To make it another day closer to being shipped home. That's all that mattered.

The cough and growl of engines yanked her attention towards the outer gate. The troops there opened the barrier, and a string of tan trucks entered. Their crimson diamond patterns marked them as ambulances, but Imogene's stomach clenched anyway. What better way to get inside the base with minimal inspection?

The vehicles sped towards Imogene and the bunker-like hospital crouched behind her position. They pulled into a tight semi-circle around the entrance she and Ralph guarded. Medics spilled out of the ambulances, some supporting limping soldiers, others pulling stretchers from the rear compartments. A meerkat hybrid on a stretcher screamed as they moved him.

Imogene flattened her ears against his cries, but the tension left her shoulders. Just more wounded. No threat. She set down her rifle and left the dugout's shelter. With five ambulances, they might need extra hands.

More medical staff emerged from the hospital, brushing her aside in their rush to meet the incoming casualties.

A long-tusked boar from the nearest ambulance labored towards the entrance, then stumbled, falling sideways into Imogene. His hands locked on her shoulders, and she stiffened. His grip tightened, his body hot and close and reeking of fear. He grunted something, the weight of him pulling them both towards the pavement.

"Steady, steady." Imogene wrapped an arm around him, struggling to stay upright.

Two medics sprinted forward and grabbed the boar before Imogene collapsed. They took him away, half-carrying, half-dragging him into the hospital.

Imogene stared after him. His warmth still pressed into her. She reached up to her chest. Her hand came away sticky with his blood. Her nostrils flared and she backed away from the stream of wounded still trailing by. She edged past Ralph, deep into the shadowy safety of their dugout, then closed her eyes and tried not to throw up.

※ ※ ※

"Man, that oinker got you good, huh?" Ralph's voice echoed off the tile in their barrack's washroom.

"Yeah." Imogene glanced at his reflection in the mirror, then dunked her jacket into the sink again, scrubbing harder. The water took on a pink tinge, but the stain had already set. As indelible as the memory of the boar's pain and fear.

Ralph's boots squeaked as he came closer. "At least neither of us are career. They won't send us outside the wall."

"So, just the mortars to worry about?" She wrung out the jacket and slipped it on, covering the auburn fuzz where her pelt had been shaved to offset the desert heat. The cool damp would be a welcome change for the few minutes while the jacket dried. "Or wondering if tonight is the night the riots turn into a full-on coup? Or why we're even in this gods-blasted country?"

His leathery nose wrinkled. "Then think about something else. You hear from Steve?"

A little spark of lightness kindled in her chest. Thinking of Steve always did that, even as his messages grew less and less frequent. But she'd gotten one yesterday. A good one.

"His discharge went okay," she said. "He's back in Helsinki, and getting things cleared with his dad for that job he promised me."

Ralph's muzzle bobbed in a nod. "That's good. You're lucky to have him, guy who can get you a job and all. Dunno what I'll do when we're cut loose."

Imogene offered a sympathetic grunt. She'd felt bad turning down Ralph's early romantic advances. Doubly now, since Steve was getting her a job, and Ralph's prospects back in Sweden were so slim. She looked down, and the rusty stain of the boar's blood caught her eye. Was he okay? He'd made it to the hospital, but that wasn't always a guarantee. There weren't guarantees for anyone here.

She tried to turn her thoughts back to Steve, but they twisted sideways to why she wasn't with him. How her seasickness ruined his plan to get them both assigned to the same ship. Steve was home already, while her transfer to the infantry added months to her enlistment. They should have done their service together in a safe, climate-controlled berth. Instead, she was here with Ralph, sweating and hoping a stray mortar shell didn't send her home in a box.

Her ears wilted, and she wrapped her arms around the sudden emptiness in her middle. "Gods, I wish I was home."

"Hey there, hey." He pulled her into an awkward, brotherly hug. "We'll make it. Only four more weeks. We'll get through this together."

His strong arms closed around her, and her fear ebbed. He wasn't Steve, but he was a friend—and here when Steve wasn't. She returned his embrace, wishing she dared believe him.

The boar's blood still stained Imogene's jacket a month later as her hooves clicked down onto the tarmac of the air station north of Helsinki. Bright sun and cool air washed over her, and the scents of springtime growing things filled her with a feeling of home.

A line of other soldiers deplaned with her, mostly in their late teens like herself, but no one she knew. She and Ralph had parted ways in Berlin.

All she'd dreamed about for the past year was her compulsory service to be over, but now that it was, a hole had opened up in her chest. One shaped like Ralph and their squadmates, and the challenges they'd overcome. Strange, to feel loss over something she'd never wanted.

She frowned a little, then took a breath of the fragrant, smoke-free air and let the worry fade. She was home. There was no hole big enough to swallow the pleasure of reuniting with her family. And with Steve.

She'd only heard from him once more after the message that he'd gotten back to Helsinki. Nothing for almost two weeks now. He said everything was fine, but what else did anyone ever say? Imogene gnawed her lip. Hopefully his antler suppression drugs weren't giving him trouble again. A lumpy forehead didn't bother her, but he'd never admit to his body doing something outside his control.

The others filed away from the aircraft, and she followed. The inner security fence came into view between two hangars, along with a colorful mass of families waiting beyond the wire mesh. Imogene walked faster, then broke into a trot. Her gaze darted over the crowd, dismissing hares, wolves, otters—there! Her mother's brown head bobbed amid the sea of smiling, waving fur.

She charged past the bored MPs at the gate, dropped her duffel, and threw her arms around her mother.

"Mom!"

Her mother staggered, but pulled her closer. "Oh, honey, I'm so glad you're home."

Imogene buried her nose in her mother's chocolaty neck ruff, drawing in her warm, familiar scent. "Me too, Mom. Me too."

They held like that for a long, wonderful moment, then her mother pushed her out to arm's length, dark brown eyes looking Imogene up and down. Her mother's smile tightened, and her hands trailed up to the fuzzy stubble where Imogene's own ruff should have been.

"Gods, your fur...was it this short when you called?"

Imogene snorted. As if she'd detour after her vid call in Berlin to get a trim. "It'll grow back. I'm just glad it's coming up on summer here." She pulled her mother into another hug, then broke away to reclaim her duffel. Sliding her free arm around her mother, she steered them along with the other families towards the city bus idling at its kiosk.

Her mother took the window seat, arranging the folds of her light yellow dress around her. "So, I thought we'd head back to the apartment, and then once you're settled, we could walk down to the waterfront or something."

The bus lurched into motion, and Imogene sat down quickly. "Actually, I kind of wanted to go see Steve now."

"Oh. Okay." A pleased smile flitted at the corners of her mother's muzzle. "They have me working odd shifts at the plant, but I'm off the rest of today. You two can have lunch, and then you and I can get caught up over dinner."

"Spaghetti?" Imogene pricked her ears hopefully. "With real sauce? The stuff on base all had meat in it, and I'm so sick of just noodles and butter."

Her mother patted Imogene's knee. "Spaghetti it is. Say about six o'clock? That will give you and Steve plenty of time."

Lunch, a peaceful stroll in the park, maybe a discreet detour into one of the abandoned buildings along the waterfront... Heat rose into Imogene's ears. She looked away and cleared her throat. "Heard anything from Josh?" Her younger brother had started his UNA compulsory service two months ago.

"Right after you called, actually. He got his assignment: some little ship, UNS *Spokane*. In the Pacific Fleet."

Her mother's tone dropped on the last, and Imogene winced. The Unified Nations of America didn't control the Pacific nearly as well as the Atlantic or Arctic oceans.

"It's still Navy, though," Imogene said. "He'll be safe. It's not like Turkey where the Pan-Asians can funnel in supplies and let the nationalists do their fighting for them."

"No, thank the gods." Her mother shook her head. "I just wish the bloody pandas would leave well enough alone."

Pandas? Imogene blinked. Her mother never used species slang, either for the Pan-Asians or the UNA. At least she hadn't before Imogene went away.

Imogene leaned closer so their shoulders brushed. "It's okay, Mom. I'm okay, and Josh will be too."

She turned their conversation to the less stressful topic of her mother's birdwatching until the bus reached the stop nearest their apartment. Then she rode on alone, past the weathered stone buildings of downtown, before getting off to walk the last two blocks to Steve's office.

Should she call him? The thought bubbled up, but she pushed it away. Surprising him would be more fun. He'd look confused for a moment, then smile and sweep her into his arms. She'd help him finish whatever work he had, then they'd head to the little sidewalk cafe by the park. Warm May sun shone down out of a cloudless sky—perfect for an open-air lunch.

Helsinki's harbor district bustled around her, cute yellow forklifts scuttling about like crabs, fishing boats bobbing at their docks, pigeons flapping in the bombed-out building where she'd had her first kiss...

The memories of Steve set butterflies loose in her stomach. The normal happy ones, as well as a few nervous swallowtails. She looked down at her camouflage fatigues. Civilian clothes would have been better. Something tight, to show off her hips and chest. But that would've taken time. Time she could be with Steve, healing the rift their separation had opened.

A maritime-scented gust ruffled what fur the base stylists had left her. She let her ears droop and smoothed her auburn headfur with one hand. Even if her current style was more recruiting poster than glamor magazine, it wouldn't do to arrive looking mussed.

Mussed could wait until after they'd kissed.

Fixing that thought firmly in mind, she climbed the three granite steps to the front door of Clausen and Sons Frozen Seafood.

Steve stood in the outer office, talking with someone hidden behind his broad shoulders. He turned when the chimes above the door jingled. A head taller than Imogene, and with darker fur, he was a caribou like herself. She drank in the sight of him, of his sharp gray eyes widely spaced over a strong muzzle, and his well-muscled legs leading up to a trim waist. A suit coat hid the soft creamy fur of his chest, except a tantalizing tuft peeking out through his unbuttoned collar. No sign of antler buds or anything else amiss.

He blinked at her, startled expression giving way to an uneasy smile. "Imogene, I wasn't expecting you...here." Rather than wrap her into a hug, he just stood there, fidgeting with a sheaf of papers.

The butterflies in her middle flapped harder. He must be nervous too, but why didn't he seem happier to see her? She should have stopped to find one of her dresses. The green one. He'd always liked it.

"I thought I'd surprise you." She fought the urge to smooth her fur again, and took a few steps closer. "I don't suppose that job we talked about is still available?" Not that he'd have given it away to anyone else, but it seemed a safe topic to ease the tension.

His muzzle tightened and he looked down at his papers. "Actually, I'm afraid the position has been filled."

Imogene felt her own smile falter. She tried to meet his eyes, but he avoided her gaze, looking anywhere in the cluttered office except at her.

"Dad might need someone out in the warehouse. Cindy? Can you pull up the personnel file?" Steve moved to stand beside the person he'd been talking to earlier, a voluptuous young rabbit behind the secretary's desk. He peered at her computer screen, and Imogene's jaw tightened at the familiar way his hand found the rabbit's shoulder. The same way he'd once found *her* shoulder.

The rabbit looked uncertainly over at Imogene, then up at Steve. "I don't see any openings, Stevie—I mean, Mr. Clausen."

He finally met Imogene's eyes. "I'm sorry, Imogene. I'd like to help you out, but with the Pan-Asians making war noises, and this latest downturn, we just can't take on unnecessary people. I'm sure you understand."

Imogene's stomach turned to ice. She was unnecessary, and this rabbit wasn't? She glared at Steve, then down at the secretary. Was that a Navy service pin on the rabbit's lapel? Imogene's gaze darted back to Steve. He wasn't wearing it, but she knew he had a matching pin. Probably even with matching ship's names.

"I think I understand, Steve. I understand just fine."

Silence filled the office, then Steve cleared his throat. "Still, it's good to see you again. We'll have to get together and catch up...sometime."

Imogene clenched her teeth behind a polite smile. "Yeah. Sometime. Thanks anyhow."

She made it out the door and far enough down the street to put Steve's building out of sight before she came to an uncertain stop. Standing in the middle of the sidewalk, she stared out at the harbor, then up into the pale blue sky. Her chest tightened, and despite the cool breeze, she struggled for breath.

This wasn't supposed to happen. All her plans, not just for the afternoon, but the rest of her life—and he hadn't even bothered to tell her. Didn't think she was worth telling. If she'd accepted Ralph's advances, she would have told Steve. That was only fair, wasn't it?

Her eyes started to water, and she mouthed a silent curse. She wanted to be angry. At Steve, or the compulsory service that pulled them apart, or the rabbit who stole him. Even at herself. Anger would feel good. But all that came was pain, and a terrible, gnawing uncertainty about what else in her life might be no more than lies and stardust.

2

LUNA CORPS

Imogene stared up at her mother's apartment building. Old and gray, it rose to ten stories of utilitarian serviceability. Of the four buildings that had surrounded a small park, only it survived. Two others were rubble, while the fourth clawed at the sky with broken, concrete fingers.

Most of Helsinki was like that. Twelve years after the Unified Nations of America "liberated" the city, the cleanup effort was far from complete. Especially away from the wealthy neighborhoods. Imogene couldn't remember what it was like before the UNA. Derelict buildings and mounds of broken concrete seemed the natural state of things.

Rather than risk the lumbering and temperamental elevator, she pushed open the door to the stairwell. Someone had spray painted it with a rough version of the Finnish Freedom Front's logo while she was away.

Annoying, but at least the vandalism offered a distraction from the pain Steve had left churning in her gut.

She frowned at the entwined triple-F, then sighed and started to climb. What point was there in resisting the UNA when that would only open the door for the Pan-Asian Federation to return? Neither superpower gave a tail flick for the locals, and there was no chance Finland could stand against them alone.

Most people here understood that, and knew enough to accept things and move forward. Unlike in war-torn Turkey.

Or was that a trap, too? During the PAF era, her father had done his best to move forward. He'd died fighting in the Pan-

Asian Defense Force, and left her mother with two kids and no way to provide food or shelter. Her mother had worked hard to get them a place even this nice. Now that Imogene was done with school and free of the military, she wanted to help.

Their door recognized her implanted ident chip on the third hand wave and let her in. She almost wished it hadn't. Her mother was bound to ask about Steve, and Imogene didn't know what to think, let alone say.

In the living room, her mother's dark brown fur clashed with the threadbare violet sofa. She set aside a datapad and looked up. "I didn't expect you back so soon. Was Steve busy?"

"Yeah." Imogene slumped into an armchair. "Him and his rabbit bimbo."

"What?"

Imogene's ears wilted. "I should have expected it. I didn't tell you, but we...sort of drifted apart. I figured we could work things out after I got back, but now, it's not looking like it."

"Oh, honey, I'm so sorry." Her mother leaned forward to squeeze Imogene's hand. "I know you really liked him."

"Yeah." Tears welled up again, and she bit her lip. "I guess maybe I shouldn't have."

Her mother made a noncommittal noise and smoothed the fur on the back of Imogene's hand.

It would be so easy to break down and unload all her confusion and grief. But doing that wouldn't change anything, except maybe to make her feel better—and her mother worse. Imogene forced those painful feelings back into the cage where they belonged. She'd deal with them later, on her own time and terms.

She took a deep breath and let it out in a sigh. "Anyway, now I need to find some other job."

"I suppose." Her mother sat back on the sofa. "If you want, I can try to get you something at the plant."

Imogene suppressed a grimace. Replacing some broken robot on a fish packing line wasn't quite what she had in mind.

"I thought you said they were cutting everyone's hours already?"

"I have a few favors built up. Maybe enough to get you in despite that." Her mother frowned, counting something off on thick-nailed fingers. "You don't really need a job. Things are a little tighter than they were, but we'll manage."

Imogene's mouth tightened. Unnecessary, just like she was to Steve. Not that her mother meant it that way, but Imogene *wanted* to be useful.

Before the sting could deepen, her mother rose and pulled Imogene up beside her. "Why don't I help you dig out your old clothes and we'll go down to Kaivopuisto?" she named the waterside park Imogene had always loved. "The trees are all leafing out, and we can have pear pie and ice cream. It's your first day back, so we should do something special."

Imogene's pelt grew out from its short desert buzz in the weeks that followed, restoring the face in her mirror to the slightly plain, broad-nosed, green-eyed deer in all her family photos. Thank goodness, too. Shaved fur was for punks and jocks.

The maple leaves in the park had grown as well, spreading to knit an emerald canopy beneath a cloudless mid-morning sky. The sweet scent of lilacs filled the air. Birds chirped, wild rabbits nibbled at the grass, and Imogene couldn't bring herself to enjoy any of it.

Her continued failure at job hunting saw to that. She'd even accepted her mother's help at the fish-packing plant, but apparently it took more than favors to get a job.

Sitting slumped on a park bench, she tried to ignore the smell of the drunk sleeping two benches over. To ignore the wolf pawing through the garbage beside a long-unemptied trash can. To ignore the latest message from Ralph, saying he'd given up looking for work and reenlisted. Navy, at least, so he should be fairly safe.

She wished for the thousandth time since returning that she'd picked something other than demolitions for her military specialization. At least if she'd gone in for motor pool she'd have a chance. More people would pay you to fix a car than to blow one up. So far, the only place to even accept her application was the government job service. After seeing her qualifications, the clerk offered her a welfare application, too.

She wasn't ready for that. Not yet. There had to be someone who wanted her somewhere. She just had to keep looking. That's what she told herself, but the future was fast becoming a topic she didn't want to think about.

She stood and walked deeper into the park, trying to lose herself in the comforting lilac haze.

A burst of children's laughter erupted beyond a hedge, and Imogene smiled. *They* knew what to do with a beautiful summer day. She rounded the corner, saw where they were playing, and her hopefulness drained away.

Two felines and a skunk took turns throwing rocks through the doorway of an abandoned air-raid shelter, listening with glee to the echoing splashes.

The skin crawled beneath Imogene's fur, but she couldn't look away.

There'd been a shelter twelve years ago, too, under the army hospital where her father worked. And water.

Memories of the UNA invasion flooded up from the dark corners of her mind. Of fear, and the thick musk of too many bodies crammed into too little space. Of ice-cold water rising, lapping at her hooves. Her knees. Her chin. Then the screams and smoke outside, the acrid taste of terror and confusion as she searched for her father. And then finding him—

Imogene shook her head sharply. Yet another topic she'd rather not think about.

She turned her back on the children and their games. The tight-packed buildings of the city center crowded just beyond the trees, frowning down and daring her to resume her search.

Three rejections and a "don't call us, we'll call you" later, she stood on a corner, waiting for the light to change.

Across the street stood the Unified Nations of America Armed Forces recruiting office. She'd walked by countless times in the past weeks, but this was the first she really looked at it.

Unlike the rest of downtown, the six story building was freshly painted, and no obvious bullet holes marred the blue walls or elegant 19th-century trim. But that wasn't the building's most eye-catching feature.

Large posters covered the facade, each cycling through a collection of images. Jungles, deserts, tanks and helicopters, men and women from a dozen species—all determined, confident. And everywhere the red and blue circle crest of the UNA.

One image of a dead gray landscape drew her gaze.

A dozen armored soldiers crouched in the shadow of their personnel carrier, while above, a jagged ridgeline cut the blue-white disc of Earth. Clean slate-gray plains spread out in all directions, stark and beautiful beneath the stars. The display shifted, and three menacing tanks plowed across a dusty, crater-specked valley. Then a handsome panther stood in full lunar body armor, helmet under one arm, gauss rifle cradled in the other. Another shift, and the panther posed shoulder to shoulder with his grinning squadmates beside an armored vehicle.

Imogene forced her gaze down to the pavement. Propaganda. It was all propaganda. There was a reason the lines of people waiting at the job service didn't reenlist, and she'd seen it first hand. Been smeared with it, and seen it carried screaming into triage.

But that was Army Infantry. There weren't any belligerent natives on the moon. No pawns for the UNA and Pan-Asian

Federation to push back and forth at each other without declaring the open war neither side wanted.

And there was a grain of truth behind that panther's plastic smile. It had felt good to be a part of something this past year. She didn't think of herself as a joiner, but that sense of common purpose and belonging had been real.

She looked up again, but the panther was gone, replaced by the slogan "Together, we can make a difference."

A warm, coppery taste came into her mouth, and she realized she was biting her cheek. It was time to accept what some part of her had known for weeks now.

No one really wanted her here.

She could stay with her mother, scrape by from one welfare payment to the next, but that was a shabby sort of life. No, if she wasn't wanted here, then she'd go somewhere else.

Before she could talk herself into waiting, she crossed the street and pushed open the recruiting office door. Inside, only two desks were occupied, and no customers but herself.

The grizzled brown otter nearest the entrance watched her cross the lobby and offered a wide smile. "What can we do for you?"

"I want to sign up."

"Excellent." His long whiskers twitched. "Which branch did you compulsory with? Or do you want to switch? Navy's the best money now. There's a two thousand credit signing bonus if you put in for Pacific Fleet or Maritime Infantry."

Imogene's stomach clenched. Her one, very brief, stint at sea had been enough. She'd scrubbed decks and learned sea-shanties, but mostly she'd vomited. It didn't take much of that to get her transferred elsewhere.

"No, thanks. I'm thinking infantry. Luna Corps."

The clerk lifted an eyebrow at the last. "Stars in your eyes, eh? Luna Corps is the best of the best, but there's extra med-tests, and a minimum twelve-year hitch with no guarantee you'll get off-world. Still interested?"

Imogene hesitated. Twelve years was a long time. She'd be thirty before the contract expired. She hadn't even known she'd be here this morning; how could she guess what she wanted that far into the future? And what if she ended up in one of the radioactive or ice-covered hellholes Luna Corps took care of here on Earth?

But staying home wasn't an option. Whatever made her look at that poster was in control now, and she knew with the certainty of a rat fleeing a sinking ship that she had to go.

"Yep. I'm sure."

The clerk smiled again, clicking his teeth for extra emphasis. "Good choice. Fill these out and sign 'em. You'll have to go over to the Air Corps hospital for the tests. I can make an appointment for today, if you'd like."

"That would be great." Imogene accepted the datapad he held out to her.

She found a seat and filled out several screens' worth of forms, then let the datapad's bio-scanner watch her retinas while she signed on the dotted line. She was committed now, unless the medics found something wrong.

When she returned the datapad, the clerk gave it a cursory glance. "Looks good. I've got you scheduled over at the base for three-thirty. You know how to get there?"

Imogene nodded.

He reached over his desk and shook her hand. "Best of luck then, Soldier."

Fifteen kilometres north of the city proper, Helsinki-Vantaa Air Station squatted in the midst of a heavily bombed industrial district. Scrubby trees and brush grew up through the rubble, doing their best to hide the burned-out shells of factories and warehouses. The air station itself was kept clear, and the buildings behind its multilayered perimeter fences were in good repair.

The city bus took her as far as the second checkpoint, and from there it was a short walk to the hospital. Taller and cleaner than the one she'd guarded in Turkey, it was lower and more strongly built than the old one where her father had worked—and died.

At least the UNA had torn down the PAF hospital's ruins and started fresh. The white concrete and glass held no painful memories.

The receptionist directed Imogene to a small waiting area where a handful of other people sat. One by one they were called back until only she remained. Then it was her turn to be poked, prodded, and finally released back to the vacant waiting area to fret while her extra lab work was done.

Would she pass, or be found as unacceptable here as everywhere else? And would that be a bad thing? Her thoughts kept circling back to that twelve-year contract. And her mother. Lunar duty was far safer than the ground forces, but her mother still wasn't going to like it.

A tall ferret with a lieutenant's rank tabs on his collar entered the room. He glanced at a datapad, then up at her. "Imogene Haartz?"

"Yep." She rose from her chair, too tense to stay still.

"The bad news is you're gonna die. Good news is you might get to do it on the moon."

Imogene's heart fluttered. For good or ill, there was no way out now.

"Everything checks out, then?" she asked.

"Yep. Welcome to Luna Corps, Private."

"Yes, sir." She straightened, clasping her hands behind her back.

He consulted his datapad again. "You're lucky too, straight up to Luna, no messing around down here. We've got a cargo plane heading south tomorrow. You can hitch with them as far as Berlin."

Imogene blinked. "Tomorrow?"

"Oh-six-hundred." He cocked an eyebrow at her. "Unless you need more time to get your affairs in order?"

She blinked again. They were that desperate for recruits? But what did she have to gain by waiting? The extent of her "affairs" so far had been pulling her civvies from storage. "No, I think I can manage."

"Good. Show up early so they can cut your travel papers." He tapped a quick entry into the datapad. "One standard duffel of personal stuff, and be sure to leave room for your new fatigues. Any questions?"

Imogene shook her head.

"Right then." He checked his chronometer. "You've got about fifteen hours. Make the most of it."

Her mother wasn't home when Imogene returned to the apartment. Part of her was glad for the extra time before breaking the news, while another part just wanted to get it over with.

Too keyed up to sit still, she put the nervous energy into packing and tidying up. That didn't take as long as she'd hoped, so she moved on to preparing dinner. Vegetarian spaghetti, with extra oregano and garlic since her brother Josh was off in the Pacific somewhere and couldn't complain. She'd just turned the sauce down to simmer when her mother returned.

"That smells wonderful." Her mother's ears perked from their weary half-droop, and she took another sniff. "Just let me get cleaned up first."

Imogene gave her a head start on the shower before starting the noodles. The boiling water frothed and bubbled, roiling under its own pressure.

They made small talk through the first part of the meal while Imogene worked up her courage.

"So," she said into a lull in the conversation, then rushed onward, "I signed up for Luna Corps today."

Her mother flicked one ear in amusement. Then she glanced up at Imogene and set down her fork. "You're serious?"

"Yeah." Imogene projected more certainty than she felt. "I've never quite known what I wanted to do, but this feels right."

"Right? It feels right?" Her mother's tone left no doubt what she thought of it.

Imogene frowned. Compared to her usual brooding, the decision was impulsive, but that didn't mean it was wrong. What had all that planning gotten her, anyway?

"It's not an unreasonable choice," she said. "After all, Father was a soldier."

Her mother's lips compressed to a hard line. "And it got him killed."

Imogene's ears went limp and she looked down at her plate. "I know."

A long quiet crept past, then her mother sighed. "Well, don't worry about it too much. Tomorrow we'll go down to the recruiting office and get things straightened out." She picked up her fork and speared a chunk of onion.

The words slithered into Imogene's folded ears. They'd get things straightened out. As if this were some childish indiscretion. Her jaw bunched. All her life's plans might be collapsing lately, but this was one course of action she could follow through. She forced her ears up and met her mother's eyes.

"It's too late. I'm shipping out tomorrow."

Her mother's eyes widened. "Tomorrow?"

Imogene nodded. "Early."

The pain on her mother's face sent guilt trickling through Imogene's veins.

"You realize you're leaving to fight for the people who killed your father?" Her mother's mouth turned down at the corners. "Isn't it bad enough they've stolen you and Josh away for their beastly Year's Service? And now you're running off to help them? Willingly?"

Imogene winced. Flags and labels didn't mean much, but betraying her father's memory unsettled her. Had his allegiance to the Pan-Asian Federation been more than a matter of convenience? There wasn't much difference between the PAF and UNA as far as Imogene could see, but had he felt that too?

"It's a job, Mother, and one I happen to be good at." That last wasn't exactly true, but her scores *were* good enough to get her accepted. Luna Corps didn't take second-rate people. "Do you really think Dad would have wanted me to lie around leeching off UNA charity?"

"I know he wouldn't want you to get hurt or killed." Her mother looked down, blinking back what might have been tears. "I...I'm sorry. But whatever you say or think, I *know* this is a mistake." She pushed back from the table and retreated into her room.

Imogene stared at the crimson sauce covering her plate. The image blurred, and she closed her eyes against the water filling them. What if her mother was right? What if this was the biggest blunder she'd ever make? But all the paperwork had been signed, and her commitment made. The clean gray expanse of the moon and that handsome panther's smile still called her.

She rose and started clearing the table.

It might be a mistake, but it was one she had to make.

3

FREEFALL

In the dead dark hours between yesterday and tomorrow, Imogene's alarm roused her from an uneasy sleep. Fixing breakfast made enough noise she must have woken her mother, but the door to the older caribou's room stayed shut.

Imogene lingered over breakfast, hoping her mother would come out to say goodbye. Her toast grew cold, and then the bus appeared in the distance. Stuffing the toast into her mouth, she snatched up her duffel, and with a last glance around the familiar apartment, hurried down to the street.

She reached the base by five, and by six-oh-five, rode south in the belly of a cargo plane. The roar of the drive fans filled her ears, but couldn't drown her thoughts any more than the reek of scorched grease took away the bitter taste in her throat.

Would it have killed her mother to say goodbye? It wasn't fair to leave things like this. Not to either of them. Heat crept into her face and ears. That was right: it wasn't fair to *either* of them. Imogene could have asked for that deferment the ferret offered. Stayed long enough to patch things up. Maybe she should have. But why did *she* have to be the one to bend? It wasn't her irrationality causing problems.

A frustrated snort broke from her muzzle. She didn't want that anger or guilt, but no matter how hard she pushed them away, one or the other sprang right back.

The engines changed pitch and she looked out to see land beneath them once more, damp woods and fields rising up from a carpet of mist.

After some delay finding her way out of the freight section of the Berlin airport, she rode a series of maglev trains south and west. Trying not to brood, Imogene concentrated on the changing scenery. Deep green forests and croplands blurred past, giving way to the yellows and tans of Iberia. The final train sped across the ruined sea level control barrier at Gibraltar and into the deserts of northern Africa.

There, tunneled into the jagged peaks of the Atlas Mountains, lay Toubkal Spaceport. One of four major launch sites under UNA control, Toubkal's 500 kilometre-long linear induction catapult kept up a steady stream of traffic into low Earth orbit.

Imogene's middle tightened. The catapult was basically a large-bore electric cannon. Was the distance she was about to put between herself and all her earthly problems really worth becoming a caribou-shaped artillery shell?

The maglev sped alongside a landing field where returning spacecraft were towed back into the mountain like so many beached whales, then the train plunged into a tunnel of its own.

Deep underground, she detrained into a vaulted chamber where herds of people milled about on loading platforms. Her nose twitched, dropped into the middle of a three-way battle between desert heat, musky sweat, and the cold, sterile air pumped out by the ventilation system.

While supposedly a joint facility, the gray uniforms of Luna Corps outnumbered khaki fatigues ten to one. Of course that didn't count the dozens of support personnel in their rainbow of jumpsuits and coveralls. There was no telling from which branch they hailed.

At the processing center, Imogene claimed her new fatigues. No boots were offered, which suited her just fine. Ugly and uncomfortable footwear was useless on the moon where everything was either indoors or required a spacesuit.

Looking at herself in the dressing room mirror, she gave her short tail a sassy flick and smiled. The gray camo didn't complement her coloring like the khaki had, but it spoke volumes about its wearer. Luna Corps was the best of the best. And presuming she made the cut in training, that meant *she* was the best.

Her shuttle was already boarding when she found it, and she got only a brief glimpse at the sleek, white craft before it swallowed her. The passenger cabin looked much like conventional aircraft she'd ridden: two seats on either side of a narrow aisle and small, oblong windows.

Reassured by the familiarity, Imogene settled into an empty row near the middle. Once the four-point harness was snugged across her lap and shoulders, she sat still and tried not to think about why the restraints were needed. She'd gulped the motion-sickness tabs handed out as they boarded, but the prospect of being shot from a glorified cannon tied her stomach in knots.

"This your first time up?"

She startled and looked up into a pair of golden, feline eyes. Their owner smiled down at her, his tawny brown ears perked forwards.

Imogene's ears drooped. "Does it show that much?"

"Yep." He slid gracefully into the seat beside her. "But don't worry—I've only been up once myself, and I held on so tight I nearly broke the armrest. It's really not so bad, just a steady pressure pushing you back until we clear the launch tube, a little bump, and then it's smooth sailing." He bent to cram his duffel under the seat.

"That's what I keep telling myself, but my guts just won't listen."

"You'll do fine." The feline won his battle with the duffel and settled back into his seat. "I'm Victor Vidal, by the way." He gave the name an odd pronunciation, rolling the R and reminding her of old, dead languages from before the Unification.

"Imogene Haartz." She extended a hand, which he shook. His firm grip hinted at a controlled strength.

Her gaze followed the outlines of a well-muscled body beneath his gray uniform. A small red and blue corporal's insignia pinned to his collar drew her attention up to a regal, long-whiskered face. She couldn't quite place his species. Caramel brown fur spoke for puma, but faint spots and rosettes suggested leopard or jaguar.

She was about to ask him about it when a loud tone filled the cabin, followed by the bored voice of the pilot asking everyone to fasten their harnesses and remain seated.

The shuttle lurched into motion, and Imogene clutched the armrests.

"Don't worry, we're just taxiing into position," Victor murmured. "They'll give us a countdown before the launch."

"Right, right." She forced herself to relax. "You know, I'd feel a lot better about this if they didn't call the launcher a railgun."

"There are other names for them, but most of them are just as bad," he offered.

Not wanting to dwell on those other names, Imogene looked out the window. They'd joined a short line of similar shuttles waiting before the launch tube's airlock. Luna-bound launches were only practical for a short period each day, and the space port operated at fever pitch to get as many shuttles airborne as possible.

At last it was their turn, and a metallic thump and jerky stop announced their shuttle had coupled with the launch armature.

As promised, a ten second countdown flashed across overhead displays, and some of the more adventuresome—or crazy—passengers chanted along with it. Imogene tensed, braced for a resounding "Zero!" she would never hear as the passengers' final cry vanished in the crackling roar of the railgun.

A giant, invisible hand reached out and smashed Imogene into her seat.

Intellectually she knew what was going on. A high-voltage arc between their shuttle and the twin rails induced a magnetic field which pushed the shuttle down the airless launch tunnel at something close to four Gs of acceleration. She also knew it should take less than ninety seconds to reach full speed.

Crushed back into the suddenly rock-hard seat and struggling for each breath, it felt like an eternity.

A tremor ripped through the cabin as they shot through the launch tube's plasma windows, hitting progressively thicker atmosphere before soaring into the desert sky. Her breath came easier as the pressure reduced, only to be forced out again as the shuttle's engine roared to life, making up the remaining velocity needed to reach orbit.

The sky faded from cobalt through turquoise and pale cyan to the velvet black of space. The sound of the wind fell away, and the shuttle stabilized, back in the element for which it was designed. The quiet lasted only a moment before a scattering of cheers and whistles washed over the passengers.

Imogene realized her hands were still locked on the armrests, and eased them loose. Her arms floated strangely without Earth's gravity, and a smile spread across her muzzle. Then the full force of the feeling hit her and she clamped onto the armrests again, trying not to be sick.

Several rows ahead, a young white rabbit's ears laid back while he vomited into a small sack. His black lab seatmate patted him on the shoulder, looking on with a uniquely canine expression mixing both sympathy and tongue-lolling amusement.

"*Pobre conejito*," Victor murmured, eyes also on the rabbit.

Imogene glanced over, but let his cryptic utterance pass. Outside her window, the majestic blue arc of Earth was sliding from view. The shuttle continued climbing, and she watched avidly until the last scrap of the sapphire planet disappeared.

"Please remain seated," a voice said over the intercom. "We're less than thirty minutes out from the Luna-2 transfer station, and will be maneuvering. You get up, and you'd better hope your injuries are limited to bruises. The last person who got blood on my upholstery was sent back to Earth. Without a ship."

Beside her, Victor made a disappointed noise. "Figures. Waste of zero-g if you ask me."

"Oh?" Imogene glanced around the crowded compartment. "Can't blame them; flailing around in here you'd be sure to hurt someone." Her stomach was settling, but staying seated sounded like a very good idea.

"Yeah." He frowned for a moment, then chuckled. "How about this?" He pulled a pen from the front of his uniform and set it down in midair, half a metre before his muzzle. It stayed there, tumbling slowly around its center of gravity.

Imogene couldn't take her eyes off the spinning pen. It was the sort of stupid trick she'd seen on countless documentaries, yet here, in person, it was mesmerizing.

When the pen came horizontal again, Victor tapped it with one finger, sending it floating her way. He flashed her a dazzling white smile with his pointed teeth, and Imogene felt a flutter in her middle that had nothing to do with the gravity.

Suddenly self-conscious, she looked back to the pen, then tapped it towards him. She misjudged the angle, but Victor caught the writing implement before it escaped, and returned it to a gentle tumble between them.

"Trickier than it looks, huh?" he said. "I'd dearly love to try floating and spinning myself."

Imogene nodded, sneaking a look at his shining golden eyes. "We'll have to when we change shuttles. And I've heard the Luna ones are bigger, maybe you can try it then." Something occurred to her and her brows knotted. "I thought you said you'd been up before?"

"That was just a little sub-orbital hop."

"Oh. Then you're new to Luna Corps, too?"

"Afraid so. No picking my brain for easy answers." He laughed.

Imogene chuckled too, letting her gaze slide over him again. His uniform pegged him as infantry, and if he were new as well, they might end up in the same unit. In fact, she hoped they would. After eleven months waiting for Steve, then finding out she shouldn't have, Imogene wasn't sure she wanted to spark up a new relationship. But Victor seemed nice, and he was certainly handsome.

The spindly struts and walkways of the Luna-2 transfer station came into view. Little atmospheric shuttles weren't economical for long distances, so passengers and cargo shifted into larger ones for the trip out to the moon.

The assemblage of habitat modules, solar arrays, and docking ports floated nearer. A dozen sleek white shuttles clustered around one pylon, while three larger, blocky craft occupied another.

Their shuttle joined the others with a muffled clank. The airlock hissed open, and the pilot's voice came over the intercom.

"That's it folks. Be sure to collect your belongings, and any small children you may have brought along as a snack. Quick tip for any dirtpaws: pull your duffel out *before* unfastening your seat-belts, and then keep a grip on the railing. If you're still here after I finish the shutdown checklist, I'll give you a hand. I'm not gentle. Don't be here."

This obviously wasn't the first trip for most of the passengers, and they moved out with a minimum of delay. That left Imogene and the dozen or so other "dirtpaws" to fumble in the microgravity.

Victor had the sense to wait for the regulars to clear the aisle, but the minute they did, he was up. Ears pricked forward and long tail waving in an attempt to keep nonexistent balance, he floundered out into the aisle. Grasping at the seats and railings, he turned back to Imogene with a wide grin.

"Come on." He waved her up. "The swimming's fine, and you don't want to be here when the pilot shows up, do you?"

"I suppose not." Tentatively, she unfastened her restraints and rose. Rose right off the floor. Her stomach lurched and she clutched at the seat in front of her. The nausea urged her to hold still. But Victor was waiting. Swallowing hard, she looped her duffel's strap around one shoulder and drifted towards him.

Swimming. If she pretended she was swimming, it wasn't so bad.

She clung to one of the ceiling rails, going hand over hand and letting her hooves trail along behind. Victor used the matching rail, and helping each other, they made it through the airlock and into the space station. More railings and a vertigo inducing tangle of shafts and corridors—and shafts that turned into corridors—led to the loading area for their lunar transport. Inside the larger craft, relief filled Imogene at the sight of a basically normal passenger cabin with proper walls, ceiling and floor.

"I hope they let us up this time," Victor said once they were both strapped into their seats. "It's like base jumping without needing to land."

"They'll have to." Imogene cast a look over the vacant seat beside her and on towards the refresher stalls at the end of the compartment. "It's twenty-three hours out to Luna, after all."

"Right, right." He drummed his hands against the armrests, obviously eager to float away again.

Closing her eyes, Imogene concentrated on the feel of the straps holding her tight against the seat. Hopefully the one-sixth gravity on the moon would be enough to keep her inner-ears happy. The Air Corps medic said it would be fine, but after her weak stomach got her kicked out of the Navy, she worried anyway.

"Mind if I sit here?" someone asked from the aisle.

Imogene opened her eyes and turned to see the white rabbit who'd been motion-sick hovering beside her. He didn't look likely to repeat the performance, so she offered a small smile. "I guess not. But then your friend won't have space to join you." She nodded back to where the black lab was stuck behind a slow-moving bear.

"We're not exactly friends," the rabbit said, pulling himself down into the vacant aisle seat. "That's why I want to sit here."

"Oh." She glanced at the lab again, seeing him now seated beside—and speaking enthusiastically at—the bear, who looked like she'd rather be anywhere else. "I see." She turned back to the rabbit. "Anyhow, I'm Imogene, and this is Victor."

"Alexei," the rabbit supplied. "But don't let me interrupt you."

"No trouble. I was just about to ask Victor where he was headed once we get to Luna?" She raised an eyebrow at the golden feline.

"I'm not sure," he said. "My orders end at the Santbech spaceport, saying I'm to meet some Sergeant Hendricks."

Imogene's heart beat faster. Those were her orders as well. Could she and the handsome feline be assigned to the same squad? That would make pursuing a relationship so much easier...

"Really?" she said. "That's mine, too."

"And mine makes three," Alexei put in. "I wonder if this Hendricks is in charge of sorting out new arrivals? It'd be a hell of a coincidence if all three of us were going to be in his squad."

Imogene sighed. Alexei was probably right. Still, arriving at the same time increased the odds of Victor being in the same unit, if maybe not the same squad. She stole another glance at the golden feline. Twelve years wouldn't be so long if she was spending it with someone like *him*.

4

ARRIVAL

Victor snored.

It was more of a purr, actually, and Imogene paused to listen to the soothing vibration before opening her sleep-crusted eyes. His muscular frame filled the seat beside her, and with him asleep, she let her eyes linger on his plush golden fur and the strong lines of his jaw and muzzle.

A louder snort broke the rhythm of his breathing and he shifted in his seat. He didn't wake, but Imogene yanked her gaze away in a guilty start.

On her other side, Alexei had his datapad out and was reading. There didn't seem to be much else to do, so she followed his lead. Her own datapad flashed its cheerful, wild-flower-bedecked welcome screen, then brought up the latest news and entertainment offerings.

Pan-Asian Federation advances in the Pacific; breakdown in negotiations for UNA military aid to Australia; shocking new photos of Seymour Raff in bed with his ex-wife's current husband; rumors Australia was joining the PAF in return for promises of home rule; proof the living human found in Appalachia was a hoax.

The list went on and on, but right now Imogene didn't have the patience to sift out the handful worth viewing.

She canceled out of the public grid and logged into her UNA military account. The wealth of new technical manuals that came with her lunar posting promised to be far more interesting than celebrity gossip. In addition to the "how to pee in a spacesuit" type material, her demolitions specialty granted access to several more esoteric documents.

Papers on blast physics in low-pressure environments, tabulations of radiation profiles and energy release curves—none of it really useful to a rank and file trooper, but fascinating just the same. She tried to enjoy the details, but Alexei had started up an entertainment vid that kept drawing her eyes away.

A dramatization of the Unification Wars, the vid focused on the valor and heroism of the transgenic soldiers, glossing over the fact they were counted as chattel and had no choice but to fight. That wasn't the only creative liberty taken, but it rankled Imogene the most. True, she hadn't known her grandparents, let alone the great-grands who'd been forced to war, but it still served the humans right their own bio-weapons got loose and their animal slaves were the only ones immune.

Of course the vid covered that too—slanted to show the noble humans passing on the torch of civilization to their worthy successors. It even made a half-hearted nod to the hoarding of medical supplies that split the Unified Nations of America from the Pan-Asian Federation.

Just as the evil PAF were about to betray their UNA allies by demanding an even share of antiserum, a tone sounded over the transport's intercom. Alexei folded up the datapad and stuffed it in his duffel.

The tone came a second time, then the voice of a crewman advised everyone fasten their restraints and prepare for landing at Santbech.

A distant rumble and gentle tugging at her harness signaled the start of landing maneuvers. The transport turned, and pure white light flared outside Victor's window.

Looking past him, Imogene gasped.

Almost blinding in its brightness, the silver disc of the moon crept across the star-studded blackness. What had seemed a smooth orb from the planet below now revealed itself as a scarred and tortured wasteland. Impact craters hundreds of kilometres across competed with jagged mountain ranges, all painted in shades of gray.

"Pretty forbidding place," Alexei said, also peering out the window. "Where are we landing?"

"Santbech's under Mare Nectaris," Imogene answered without taking her eyes off the spectacle.

"Which is exactly where?" Alexei asked.

She and Victor both turned to stare at him.

"You signed up for Luna Corps without even looking at a map?" she asked.

Alexei frowned. "Why bother? North is panda country, south is ours. All the Latin names are unpronounceable anyway."

"True." Imogene flicked her ears, then looked back out the window. "You see the big, very dark patch? That's the Sea of Tranquility. Panda country. Lighter stuff around it is the highlands. Now south, there's a smaller dark bit, which is Nectaris. That's ours, and Santbech's on the south side of it."

A roar from the main drive cut off further conversation. The deceleration burn crushed Imogene back into her seat and kept her pressed there as the transport rode its tail rockets towards the lunar surface. A saw-toothed gray ridge rose in the distance as they sank into the wide basin of Santbech Crater.

Imogene jerked forward against her restraints as they touched down. The computers might know how to kill the main engine and kick the transport into a horizontal orientation just before landing, but they sure didn't do it smoothly. At least the moon's one-sixth gravity kept the maneuver from turning into an outright crash.

Weight returned, Luna affectionately tugging the new arrivals into a gentle hug. Imogene's muzzle quirked at her own whimsy, but that didn't lessen the excitement tingling under her fur. She peered out Victor's window, soaking in the first-hand view of another world.

Low hills surrounded the landing field, barren and gray and ramping up into the towering walls of the kilometres-deep crater. A few small buildings specked the landscape, but she knew most of the base lay below the crater's central peak.

True to her prediction, the transport rolled forward and descended through a blast-proof door large enough to swallow a house. The sloping tunnel beyond twisted and forked before opening into a cavernous hangar. Techs in blue pressure suits swarmed over one of the parked transports, like cleaner-fish on a huge, brick-shaped shark.

Their own transport halted, and a few moments later, the long-awaited announcement came that they were free to depart.

Imogene began digging her luggage out from under the seat, but Victor put a hand on her arm.

"Hold on a minute. It's gonna take everyone up front a while to get cleared out. We may as well take it easy till they do."

"I suppose so." Imogene freed her duffel with a yank, then let it rest between her knees.

Alexei did likewise. Once the aisle cleared, he rose to his paws—and promptly overbalanced. Cursing, he soared head-first over the next seat to sprawl half in and half out of the aisle.

"Are you okay?" Imogene straightened more slowly, with a firm hold on the seatback.

"Yeah." He growled another curse and pulled himself up again. "This is worse than no gravity at all. Just enough to trick you into thinking it's normal."

She mumbled something agreeable, although privately she'd take one-sixth gravity over none any day. Up was up, and down was down, and her stomach and inner ears felt much better for the distinction. Keeping her motions to a cautious shuffle, she followed Alexei to the front of the cabin.

The boarding tunnel let out into a white-walled staging area where the other passengers hopped and shuffled. Most of them seemed to know where they were going, and the crowd thinned rapidly as they left on foot or riding small electric carts.

Only one of the people recruiting passengers onto carts was a sergeant, and he turned Imogene's group away with a distracted "Hendricks? Nope."

Soon only the three of them remained, along with one other private: a silver lynx standing by one wall. The feline straddled her duffel, with paws spread and hands clasped behind her in parade-ground-perfect posture.

After watching her a few minutes, Imogene strode over. "Looking for Sergeant Hendricks?"

"That's right." The lynx flicked her black-tufted ears in acknowledgment. "My orders are to wait for him here."

"Ours, too." Imogene nodded to include Victor and Alexei.

"So we're squadmates then?" The lynx unbent enough to turn and face the others as they moved closer. Her yellow slitted eyes prowled over Imogene, then locked on Victor. "Lauren Porter." She offered the name to him with a wide smile.

Imogene frowned. It took a moment to recognize the prickly feeling in her throat as jealousy. Ridiculous, since she had no claim on Victor, but there nonetheless.

They introduced themselves, with Imogene adding an, "Any idea when the sergeant might get here?"

"No," said Lauren. "Orders say wait, so that's what we'll do."

And they did. A cart piled high with blue-suited techs rolled past, but that was the only sign of life.

"I don't think anyone's coming," Imogene finally said. "Do you suppose one of us should go look for him or something?"

Victor shrugged and Alexei nodded, but Lauren's ears folded back. "That's not what's in the orders," she said. "You go wandering off, you'll miss him. Show some discipline. He'll come for us."

Imogene glanced down at her chronometer. "It's been almost an hour. What if he forgot, or is waiting at a different gate? Someone around here has to be able to look up his comm-code, and I'm going to go find them."

Most of the other passengers had gone right, so she went that way too. The clack of her hooves against tile echoed off the white walls and ceiling.

After passing six more deserted boarding areas, Imogene began to wonder if Lauren had the right idea. She kept over-balancing in the low gravity, and the exaggerated care needed to stay upright made even the modest distance between boarding gates seem like an all day trek.

She was about to stop and rest when the soft whine of a cart coming up behind made her turn. A polar bear with a private's rank tabs drove, her tall, solidly-built frame making Lauren look almost childlike beside her.

"There she is." Lauren pointed at Imogene, and the polar bear stopped the cart next to her.

"Sorry for the delay." The polar bear smiled, pulling black lips from a set of very large teeth. "The sarge is busy, so he sent me to pick you up. I'm Fiona Whiting, and since you're the last one on the list, you must be Imogene, right?"

"Yep." Imogene returned her smile. "Thanks for finding me."

Lauren rolled her eyes. "Like we had a choice. Now if you're done ignoring orders, we can get going."

Hunching her shoulders, Imogene climbed into the rear of the cart beside Victor and Alexei. At least the Sergeant wasn't the one to pick them up. Making him chew her out for wasting time wouldn't leave a good first impression.

🐾 🐾 🐾

"Here we are." Fiona pushed open a door in one of the spoke tunnels radiating out from the hub of their wheel-shaped housing block. "Barracks G-nine-oh-seven."

Imogene glanced around the pastel blue room, taking in the rows of dark-gray bunks and silver lockers. "Not too shabby. I expected something a lot more cramped."

"I've seen worse," Fiona said. "We've got refreshers and showers through that door on the right. Once you all get settled, I figured we'd meet up with the rest of the squad on the rec-deck."

Imogene and the others fanned out to claim bunks, and Imogene picked one in a corner. There wasn't any real privacy to be had, but it was better than nothing.

Back in the corridors, they passed other pedestrians. Mostly low ranking infantry, decked out in the same lunar gray camo fatigues Imogene and her companions wore. A few wore jumpsuits of various colors, indicating the cooks, mechanics, and other support personnel who kept everything running smoothly.

"Just how many people live here?" she asked after they passed through a particularly thick clump of grease-smeared technicians.

"It varies," Fiona said. "G block will hold about four and a half thousand, and we're as full as I've ever seen it. For the whole base, maybe fifty thousand?"

"That many?"

Fiona's wide shoulders rolled in a shrug. "Santbech is a regional headquarters. Biggest UNA base between Tycho and Far Side, and only a few hundred klicks behind the lines. But here's our first point of interest."

The polar bear stopped to wave at a large, white-paneled corridor. "This runs about a klick to the north tactical block, and comes out right between the garage and a bunch of weapons ranges and storage tunnels. That's where we'll be spending the next couple weeks while you guys get up to speed on lunar operations and equipment."

"Weeks?" Lauren's tufted ears flicked back. "We've all been through Basic, and another nine months real service. The equipment up here can't be that different, can it?"

"It is mostly similar," Fiona said. "The main thing is the gravity. Everything feels and acts different here. It takes a while to get used to."

"I hear you there." Victor nodded. "I sure don't want to get in a fire fight while I'm still tripping over my own paws."

Lauren looked over at him and her ears perked up. "You're right. That's a good point."

Imogene snorted. If she was any judge, the lynx wouldn't be so fast to agree with anyone but the handsome corporal.

Fiona led them on, pointing out the large mess hall, then ascending a flight of stairs to the block's main recreation center. Inside, the wide, well-lit passages gave way to dim, twisting alleys. Walls textured to look like old brick crowded in on either side, while above, a nighttime city sky cast murky, yellow light.

After enough disorienting corners to leave Imogene half-believing they really were in an Earth-side bar district, the alley opened out into a courtyard. Tiny artificial stars twinkled from the vaulted ceiling, and stairways led up to a balcony overlooking the plaza.

"Quite the place, huh?" Fiona gestured at the colorfully lit entrances of several eating and drinking establishments.

"It is at that." Imogene cast her gaze over the bustling walkways between the planters.

"There are arcades and shops upstairs, and down here it's mostly clubs and bars," Fiona said. "Come on, I think I know where our guys are."

The watering hole she led them to proved to be more of a lounge than a club, with warm lighting and soft music.

Imogene's ears pivoted to listen, but she couldn't place either the genre or instruments. The lively rhythm lent an extra bounce to her careful, low-gravity stride.

"There they are." Fiona stepped up beside two privates at the long, wood-topped bar. "Ryan Sanders." She indicated a light-brown ground squirrel.

Ryan looked like he'd still be the shortest person in the room even if he stood on his chair. He gave them a timid smile.

"And Bruce Andersen." Fiona nodded to the rust-colored stag beside Ryan.

Tall and lean with an attractively wide nose, Bruce sat with his elbows propped on the bar behind him. Despite his redder fur and warm brown eyes, he reminded Imogene uncomfortably of her ex-boyfriend. Then he spoke, and his accent destroyed whatever similarity she'd felt.

"Howdy." The greeting rolled off his tongue, not quite a drawl, but not far from it.

Fiona rattled off everyone else's introductions, and Bruce's gaze followed. He paused on Imogene, and she felt his eyes travel from her dark hooves up to her bright green eyes before he hurried to catch up with Fiona.

"A pleasure to meet you all," Bruce said. "Why don't you guys order your drinks while Ryan and I push some of those tables together?" He rose to his hooves and overbalanced in the light gravity. A quick grab at the bar steadied him, and he set off purposefully towards a pair of unoccupied tables.

"If any of you want alcohol, you'd better make it count." Fiona leaned over the counter and waved for the bartender's attention. "Since we're on duty tomorrow they'll have flagged our accounts and won't sell you more than one."

The mournful looking basset hound barman came over and began taking orders. Imogene passed her right hand over his scanner so it could read her ident chip, then took her ale and headed for their table. She slid into a seat beside Victor and across from Bruce.

The stag caught her eyes and smiled. "So, you guys just got in?"

"Yep." Imogene nodded. "What about you?"

"A couple hours ago. We got a night launch out of Mexico."

Victor glanced over. "Torreon or Oaxaca?"

"Torreon," Bruce said. "You from around there?"

"Sometimes. Mostly farther south—"

Imogene didn't see what happened next. Someone yelled, and the next thing she knew, a round, black-and-white-furred body slammed into their table, sending up a fountain of spilled drinks.

She jerked back, which in the low gravity toppled her chair over backwards. Her yelp joined with other exclamations and the sound of glass and furniture hitting the floor.

Thankfully, the gravity also kept the fall from hurting much. She rose, sparing a quick thanks for whatever luck directed the flying drinks away from her new uniform.

A barrel-chested panda sprawled in the middle of her recovering squadmates, tangled in with the legs of the fallen table and chairs. Imogene cast a quick look around to see what had sent him crashing into them, but saw nothing unusual. Probably just drunk.

"That's a nasty fall you took," Victor said, helping the panda to his paws.

"Fall nothing, some fucker tripped me." The panda's narrow-eyed gaze darted around the wall of onlookers. "Come on out, if you've got the guts for a fair fight!" He raised a fist, but no one came forward. He turned back towards Victor. "Fuckers, the lot of 'em. Sorry about the mess."

He was about to leave when Fiona heaved herself up from behind the toppled table. Something resembling a smile twisted its way onto the panda's muzzle, and his black ears perked forward. "Hey, Fi, long time no see."

"Oh gods." Fiona's ears flattened. "What do you want, Jared?"

"Nothing much." His quasi-smile matured into a full-blown leer. "Why don't we go someplace more private and we'll, uh, *talk* about it?"

"I don't think so." Fiona bared her impressive fangs. "Remember what happened last time? I'm not sure what they'd bust you down to now... What's lower than private?"

"You bitch!" His fur bristled, and he took an angry step towards her.

Victor slid between them, followed a moment later by Bruce and Alexei.

"I think the lady made herself clear," Victor said. "How about you just call it a night?"

Jared's fists clenched, and Imogene tensed, ready to wade in if things turned ugly. The panda took one more step, then turned and pushed his way out into the crowd.

"Fuckers. The whole fucking bunch of you!"

The front door slammed behind him, and the onlookers dispersed as the prospect of live entertainment evaporated.

"Sorry about that." Fiona looked around apologetically before turning back to Victor. "And thanks."

"*De nada.*" The big cat gave a dismissive flick of his tail.

Bruce righted Fiona's chair, then helped Victor with the table. "Who was he and what's his problem anyway?"

"It's kinda complicated," Fiona said. "His name's Jared Chey, and he was a corporal in my old unit. Won't take no for an answer, and for some reason thinks he's hot stuff."

Imogene snorted at that. Bears weren't her type, but even if they were, the chunky panda wouldn't get a second glance.

Fiona's lip twitched. "I know, right? Anyhow, he kept pushing, and I ended up having to beat the snot out of him in one of the back corridors. With his record, nobody even questioned my side of it. I thought they sent him back to Earth after that, but I guess not."

Lauren's yellow eyes narrowed. "What I wanna know is what a panda's doing up here anyway."

"That's a damn good question," Alexei agreed. "I know they can't keep them out of the Earth-side forces 'cause of the compulsory service, but Luna Corps is supposed to be career only."

Imogene blinked, marshaling a counter argument, but Bruce beat her to it.

"Don't be stupid." The stag's ears lay back in disgust. "Just because wild pandas used to live in east-Asia doesn't make every transgenic panda a PAF sympathizer."

"But you can't deny there's a bloody lot more of them over there," Lauren shot back.

"Whoa, let's just calm down." Imogene put a hand on the lynx's shoulder, which she immediately shrugged off. "Is that jerk really worth fighting over?"

"Right," Bruce said. "I for one am not letting some yahoo —of any species—mess up my first day on Luna. Now, what say I go sweet-talk the barkeep into replacing these spilled drinks?"

Dubious more alcohol would be forthcoming, Imogene watched as the barman first shook his head, then reluctantly nodded. She also saw Bruce pass his hand over the credit scanner again, and resolved to split whatever the charge had been. Keeping the peace was everybody's job.

"So, Fiona," Victor said in a slightly raised voice, gesturing with his renewed glass of tequila. "You've been here awhile. What are we likely to have in store for us tomorrow?"

"First day's usually orientation, but with the PAF shelling today they'll probably push us through faster, so who knows?"

Imogene's ears pricked forward. "Wait, what shelling?"

"You didn't hear?" Fiona asked. "They plastered some fly-speck in the Pacific. Fuji? Fiji? Last I heard, we were pulling back and letting 'em keep it."

Victor started growling at "Fiji", and her last words drove him into an outright snarl. "Letting them keep it? Cowards!"

Imogene glanced over at him. Their tiny base on Fiji wasn't more than a line in the sand. Hardly worth Victor's agitation. "At least it's not strategic," she offered. "There's no shortage of islands down there."

"It's the principle of it." Victor's frown deepened. "Both my parents died taking that useless rock, and now we're rolling over and giving it to the blasted Pan-Asians. It's not right."

Sympathy panged in Imogene's heart. When her father died, she'd at least had Josh and their mother. How much worse must things have been for him? She leaned towards him, infusing calm certainty into her voice. "Don't worry, I'm sure we'll take it back. Sometimes to advance, you have to retreat."

"Maybe so." The big feline knocked back the remainder of his drink. "But damn if I have to like it."

5

TOOLS OF THE TRADE

The barracks door opened with a soft whoosh, rousing Imogene from her sleep. Light from the hallway silhouetted a tall, thin figure briefly before the overhead glow panels snapped on.

"All right, people! Time to rise and shine," a deep voice barked out. "We've got a lot to do today, and some of it may even get done. I want to see each and every one of you up and ready to move inside of five minutes."

The lithe Dalmatian wearing a sergeant's uniform strode into the middle of the room.

Already sliding out of her top-level bunk, Imogene's hooves struck the tiles before he finished speaking. She ducked around him and beat the morning rush on the refreshers. She relinquished the stall to a sleepy-looking but fully dressed Fiona and hurried to don her own uniform.

"Right then." The Sergeant's piercing blue eyes followed Alexei as the last member of the squad stumbled out of the refreshers. "I am Sergeant Robert Hendricks. I'll be in charge of your training, and may end up shipping out with any of you who survive the cull, so you'd better keep on my good side. Now, we're going over to the north tactical block to get you people geared up."

Imogene fell into a loose double file with the others and followed the Sergeant into the corridor.

In the row ahead of her, Alexei whispered to Victor, "What's he mean, survive the cull?"

Victor's muscular shoulders rippled in a shrug. "People who don't make the grade get sent dirt-side. You didn't think they filled the Rad Brigades with volunteers, did you?"

Alexei's ears flattened, and Imogene's stomach twisted. People in Rad units usually didn't live to reenlist. The radioactive wastes along the Volga saw to that.

She cleared her throat. "I thought Luna Corps also ran the penguin stations, and some of the extreme desert units?"

Victor glanced back at her. "Right, but that's mostly for lunar troops rebuilding muscle tone between deployments up here." His golden eyes flicked from her hooves to muzzle. "Arctic species like you and Fiona might get picked for penguins, if you're lucky. But the best bet's just to make the grade and stay here."

Imogene's tail twitched. In the back of her mind she'd been counting on an antarctic posting as a backup, but what Victor said made sense. Command would reserve the safest jobs for the most valuable troops. But it was too late to back out now. She'd just have to make sure she didn't wash out.

After leaving the housing area, the white-walled corridor seemed endless. Despite the low gravity, or perhaps because of it, Imogene's legs began to ache. Finally, they passed through a heavy blast door and into the north tactical block. Sergeant Hendricks didn't slow down, and struck out confidently into the maze-like complex.

Walls of bare lithcrete—lunar dust fused solid with microwaves—arched over the wide passages. Utility and communications conduits festooned the dark gray panels, and the floor was scored by decades of abuse by heavy equipment. Flatbed freight haulers roamed the passages, sometimes forcing Imogene's party aside to let them pass. Side tunnels came every twenty metres, most of them partitioned off with lithcrete around a single vehicle-sized doorway.

Their first destination was a quartermaster's depot, where the squad received weapons and were measured for pressure-suit armor. From there, they went straight to an indoor firing range. Another squad was still shooting when they arrived, and Sergeant Hendricks used the extra time to drill them on their new weapons.

"...And that's it for the book," he concluded his "*basic operating procedures for the LAR-M87 rifle*" speech with a swish of his tail. "Now some practical advice. In this gravity, your perceived recoil is going to be harsh, even with the rifle's built-in compensators. You'll start off firing prone, so you don't fall over, and it should always be your preferred position. Now, let's get started." He led them into one of the storerooms behind the firing line.

Imogene glanced over the racks of loaded magazines and power packs. Without a rifle, the ferro-uranic slugs were harmless, and the same type of power packs served all manner of other devices, so there was no need for special storage or security. All of them were painted an obnoxious shade of dayglow orange, though, probably to discourage accidental theft.

"Everybody, earplugs, then two mags of six-millimetre and a power pack each." The Sergeant's voice floated over the crowded room. "Fiona, Ryan, the specialty stuff's here at the back."

As the largest member of the squad, Fiona carried their heavy machine gun, while the ground squirrel Ryan toted a sniper rifle. Imogene and the rest had assault rifles—Victor and the Sergeant's embellished with under-barrel grenade launchers.

The rubber padding of the firing position gave slightly under Imogene as she lay down and snapped her magazine into place. At the far end of the range her target waited: a set of pale blue concentric circles hovering in midair. The effect worked by lasers ionizing small pockets of atmosphere, turning the air itself into a monochrome plasma display. Having bits of plasma floating around made the technology too dangerous for most uses, but it was perfect for targets—never filling with holes or needing to be replaced.

Imogene centered her sights on the innermost glowing ring and squeezed the trigger.

The rifle emitted a low electric whine, drowned out by the crack of the bullet breaking the sound barrier. Both were lost in her surprise as the rifle kicked heavily into her shoulder.

The shot buried itself into the catchment berm with a puff of dust, and the range computer painted a small spinning circle to show where it had passed—a full two metres left of the target.

Imogene winced. The computers kept track of every shot, adding them to the statistics in her file. The same statistics that would determine if she stayed here or ended up in irradiated Russia. She laid her ears back and lined up on the target again. It took a while to learn a new weapon's quirks. Whoever set the acceptance standards had to have factored that into their equations.

At least she hoped so.

By the time her second magazine ran dry, she could consistently hit within the outermost ring of the target. That counted as a success in her book. The projectiles were optimized for use in vacuum, after all, and had accuracy problems in atmosphere.

She ejected the magazine and power pack, then retreated from the firing line. She stood back to watch Ryan and a few of the others still shooting.

The fuzzy little ground squirrel squeezed off shot after near-perfect shot, seemingly without any effort, and Imogene's ears went limp with chagrin. Some of it could be chalked up to his higher-powered weapon, but there was no question his skill would keep him safe from the cull.

Two positions over, Victor finished his own shooting and came to join her. He watched Ryan for a moment, then leaned towards Imogene. "And that's why he gets a marksman's rifle and we don't. Must have been born with his eye on the scope and a finger on the trigger."

"It's remarkable all right." She looked up at him. "But you were doing pretty well yourself."

"A rifle's a rifle." He hitched one shoulder, then turned his luminous amber eyes fully onto her. "Besides, I haven't had much to do but practice lately."

"Oh? No carousing and chasing women?" She flicked her ears at him playfully.

Victor chuckled. "I'll admit there was some of that, too. But it's not much fun when you know you'll be leaving it all behind. What if you met that special someone dirt-side, then got stuck up here for the next twelve years?"

A trickle of excitement ran up Imogene's spine. So the handsome corporal *was* available. "I don't know, there seem to be some pretty special people up here."

"I suspect so." He gave her a wink, then returned his attention to Ryan. "But time enough for that after training. Those PAF *cabrones* won't be happy with just Fiji or even Australia. There's a showdown coming, and it's our duty to be ready for it."

"You really think they'll try to take Australia?" she asked.

"All that coal and uranium? And only a stone's throw from China? It's a perfect hedge against any disruption of their lunar operations."

Imogene nodded. The moon had a number of strategic military and industrial uses, but producing refined fuels for nuclear and antimatter reactions were the largest. If full-on war broke out again, having a dirt-side energy reserve might well tip the balance.

Before she could counter with the mutual aid treaties between the UNA and Australian governments, Sergeant Hendricks barked for attention. Ryan had finished shooting, and formed up with the others in a line.

The Sergeant pulled a datapad from his breast pocket and strode down the line, reading off their evaluations. "Alexei, acceptable—barely. Lauren, acceptable. Fiona, acceptable."

Imogene chewed the edge of her tongue. Of course Fiona was safe. The polar bear hadn't just arrived like the rest of them.

The Sergeant moved closer. "Bruce, acceptable. Ryan, very acceptable. Victor, acceptable. Imogene, unacceptable."

Her heart stopped.

The Dalmatian looked up from his datapad, cool blue eyes meeting hers levelly. "They cut dirtpaws some slack, but that's slack you gotta pick up. You want to stay here, get your scores out of the gutter."

Imogene's chest tightened and her knees went weak. How did she always manage to be found lacking? She jerked her muzzle in a nod she hoped wasn't too stiff. "Yes, sir."

He eyed her a moment longer, then rolled the datapad into a cylinder and turned to face the whole squad. "All right, let's get some grub, then get back at it. Some bureaucrat's idea of acceptable doesn't mean jack out in the dust. Exceptional is the only acceptable I know."

Imogene's nerves were still jangling as she moved through the mess hall's serving line. She skipped over the vile-looking processed ham and heaped her plate with salad, steamed vegetables and rolls, then followed her squadmates to an unoccupied table.

Alexei arched his eyebrows at her as she set down her tray. "A lot of veggies there. You miss the meat bin?"

She glanced at her food. She wasn't a vegetarian, exactly, but her brother was, and after he converted their mother, Imogene had more or less given meat up too.

Alexei was still eying her, so she shrugged.

His eyes narrowed. "Don't tell me you're one of those freaks who won't eat meat because 'we're all animals too' or some rubbish?"

An acidic reply about just how many animals—and what parts—were in the hunk of processed "meat" he was eating rose to her lips, but she bit it back. A table full of meat-eaters wasn't the place to trot that out. Especially not after the cold shoulders it earned her in Turkey.

She shrugged again. "I just don't like ham."

"Good." The white rabbit stuffed another forkful into his mouth. "Something wrong with a person who won't eat meat."

Lauren leaned across the table towards him, lips parting to show pointed teeth. "So you wouldn't mind eating, say, rabbit?"

Alexei grinned. "Done it. Tastes like chicken."

Disappointment flitted across Lauren's silver features, but beside her, Bruce nodded.

"Rabbit's dry, though," the stag said. "Now venison, that's good eating. Not factory food like this stuff." He poked the slab of pink flesh on his tray. "Back home we had some wild white tails that'd hang out in the woods behind our farm. Best steak I ever had."

That led to a bragging match between the men about who had eaten the weirdest foods. Glad the focus had shifted off of her, Imogene tucked into her lunch.

Back at the firing range, she maintained her mediocre hit-ratio, but couldn't improve on it. She spent about half a magazine before one particularly wide miss made her snarl a curse.

Lying on the next firing pad, Ryan looked over and caught her eyes. "Try shifting your left hand forward and aiming lower," he said in a voice soft enough the others' earplugs would keep them from overhearing. "The recoil dampers make it ride up more than the ones back home."

Imogene adjusted her grip and put her next shot into one of the intermediate rings. She glanced back over at Ryan and smiled. "Thanks. Any other tips?"

He shrugged, a shy smile tugging at the corners of his muzzle. "Dunno. You seem kinda tense. Try to loosen up, and don't fight the recoil. Be ready for it, but not afraid of it."

"All right, thanks."

Sergeant Hendricks had barked similar advice at her as he prowled back and forth behind his subordinates, but all he'd done was make her more nervous. Short and fuzzy Ryan reminded her of her brother before he'd put on his growth spurt. It was easy to accept suggestions from him.

She filled her lungs and let the air out slowly, trying to exhale her tension along with it. Relaxing sounded easier than it was, but as the session went on, her shooting did improve.

When the Sergeant read off the scores, her effort earned a gruff, "Better, but not better enough. Keep after it."

Imogene clenched her teeth and nodded.

From the firing range, Sergeant Hendricks led them back out into the maze of tunnels, headed for their squad's assigned armory.

Following along, Imogene rubbed her right shoulder. It ached after all day shooting. The gravity was another annoyance. She'd gotten to the point where she'd forget it wasn't normal, and the moment she did, stumble or drop something. Her squadmates fumbled too, but at least they had better rifle scores to compensate.

Washing out frightened her, but what more could she do to improve? Her mother's parting words echoed through her mind. Had signing up been a terrible mistake? She struggled to shake off the feeling, reminding herself how exotic and exciting this all should be. It almost worked, especially if she kept her thoughts—and eyes—on Victor.

The armory proved much like the other tunnels, a wide corridor with metal mesh cubicles along either side, each large enough for a squad's worth of equipment. Two-thirds of the way down the passage, Sergeant Hendricks stopped and swiped his right hand over one of the door locks. It opened to reveal a narrow space, almost completely filled with plastic crates.

The Sergeant shook his black and white spotted head. "Looks like our armor got here ahead of us."

Victor whistled. "That was fast."

"One thing you'll find up here, Luna never sleeps," said the Sergeant. "Let's crack 'em open so you can try it on and make sure it fits."

While Imogene and the others sorted out which box held whose suit, the Sergeant stepped back. "I planned to go over this tomorrow, but I'll give you the short version now. It's all pretty similar to the nuke-bio-chem suits you used dirt-side. The computer's a little more advanced, to control the closed circuit environmental stuff, and they have better armor."

"How much better?" Victor asked.

"A lot. It'll stop most small arms, and any stray micro-meteoroids. The low gravity lets the designers really pile it on."

Imogene found the crate with her serial number scrawled across its label and pulled off the lid.

Like so much else on the Moon, the armor inside was a flat gray, mottled with lighter and darker patches. The only exceptions were the reflective silver faceplate and the blue rank insignia shining proudly upon each shoulder.

She gazed down at the suit, her weariness and regrets sliding away. It looked just like the armor on the recruiting poster. Better even—it was hers. She glanced over at Victor, unpacking his own armor. He wouldn't look quite as good in it as the poster's elegant black-furred panther, but again, the fact he was here and real more than made up for that. He looked up, and the grin he shot her was definitely better than the poster's. She smiled back, then set to work.

With one hand against the wall for balance, she worked her right hoof into the suit's combined boot-leggings. Her leg slid in easily, but her pants bunched up against the thick padding. She pulled her hoof out and tried again, with similar results.

Beside her, Lauren was having the same problem.

Fiona glanced up from helping Ryan open his crate and lumbered over to them. "Here now, you'll never get in that way. These are meant to be worn right over the fur. You can keep your underthings since we won't be suited up long, but the rest's gotta go."

Imogene glanced towards the squad's male contingent. They were all focused on their new armor, none paying the women any special attention. Bruce had already stripped to his boxers, and a flick of his short white tail drew her eyes to his firm, brown-furred thighs. Her ears warmed and she looked away. Not many people survived their compulsory service with modesty intact, but it wasn't polite to take advantage of the fact.

She shucked out of her own uncooperative pants and stepped into the armored leggings. They fit snugly around her, and she stomped to settle herself into the hoof-style boots. With the light gravity and gentle pressure of the padding, it felt almost like being waist-deep in water.

Lauren stamped her boots and scowled. "I don't like it. My toes are all squished together."

"At least you don't have to stuff your tail into a metal tube." Victor cast them a woebegone look from where he was engaged in that very task. "I envy you short-tailed girls right about now."

Fiona snorted, her dark lips pulling back in a grin. "You're lucky it's a standard leg-side sheath. I was talking with a lemur from special forces, and he told me about the fancy free floating sheaths they use for extra balance climbing cliffs and stuff. Now, a leg-sheath doesn't need any padding or to fit tight, since it just follows the leg and your tail's free to drift around inside. But when you make it a separate appendage it needs padding like the rest of the suit, and then you have to shove your tail down past all that padding...backwards."

Her three listeners shivered. Imogene hated forcing her short tail through the holes in everyday garments. To stuff a metre or more of caudal appendage through a tiny tube would take true dedication. Or psychosis.

"I'd thought about trying for special forces someday," Victor said as the last of his tail disappeared into the suit. "Now, though, I don't know." He gave another exaggerated shiver.

Imogene chuckled and turned back to her own armor. It wasn't difficult now she had the knack of it. Torso, arms, gloves, all snapped together with reassuring clicks.

She twisted the helmet into the torso's collar, and an eerie blue glow illuminated the faceplate with a heads-up display. A flashing icon in the upper left invited her to activate the eye tracking interface that controlled the suit's comm and other systems. Careful not to blink at it, she left the computer to its own devices.

A few tentative steps showed the suit's range of motion was actually rather good. With a little practice, she could move comfortably, if not quite with the same dexterity. The added mass helped, bringing her total weight closer to Earth-normal.

And it was dead sexy. She took a dozen steps down the corridor, then turned to watch her squadmates, admiring the matching gray camo and mirror finished faceplates. Knowing she looked just as sleek and deadly made her smile.

Then the others started to take their armor off, and she hurried to do the same.

"Any problems?" The Sergeant glanced around at his subordinates. "No? Let's get your gear stowed, then. The two front lockers are for me and Corporal Vidal, then I want the rifle team on the right and the specialists on the left."

Imogene was pleased to see Victor's front locker was on the left, where her demolitions specialty landed her as well. But Lauren grabbed the locker next to his before she could, leaving her to take one between Lauren and Bruce.

"So." She turned to Bruce. "I'm demolitions, Victor's got the grenade launcher, and Ryan's our sniper. That makes you comms? Or medic?"

"Medic," the stag confirmed. "Although if you get hit out there, odds are you'll be dead before I have a chance to patch you up. Probably for the best, too. Blood makes me queasy." He gave a cheerful wink.

Imogene closed her eyes and grimaced. "Reassuring. You have a great bedside manner."

"I try." He flashed her a smile, then turned back to his equipment.

"*I* would be comms," Lauren said. "And information services. If you need a computer gimmicked or code cracked, you talk to me."

"Good to know." Somehow, Imogene was glad it would be Bruce and not Lauren sewing her back up. The silver feline oozed an arrogant self-confidence Imogene really didn't want to test. Especially with her own blood and guts in the balance.

6

THE GREAT OUTDOORS

Back in the barracks, Imogene massaged her calves and let the others have first crack at the showers. How long would it take her muscles to get used to the low gravity's different demands? Right now some proper weight sounded very tempting, even if it meant being sent dirt-side to get it. Maybe she could *ask* for an antarctic posting? Doing that before actually failing the cull might keep her out of the Rad Brigades.

She watched her dry squadmates dwindle, replaced with new, slightly damp versions. Soon only she and Victor were left, and the big cat waved her to precede him.

Like the other fluids she'd encountered so far, the water in the shower acted strangely. It felt almost sticky, and flowed sluggishly down her soft brown fur and towards the drain. It seemed to work well enough otherwise, and after letting the spray drizzle over her for a moment, she set to work with shampoo and conditioner.

Several wet minutes later, she squeezed the excess water from her pelt and moved to the full-body drying unit. This was the big brother of the dryers found next to washbasins: a blower with ultraviolet and infrared emitters to quickly dry, and to some extent sanitize, wet fur.

Bruce and Lauren waited in the barracks, but the rest had already left. Imogene ignored them for now and rummaged in her locker for a set of fresh clothing.

"So," Bruce said, his eyes seeking hers when she finished dressing. "I'm not sure where the others went, but we're waiting for Victor to finish up before going over to the mess hall. Care to join us?"

"Sounds good." She ran a brush through her fur a few times, then pulled out her datapad to wait.

An unviewed message from her brother blinked in one corner. She tapped it, and his brown-furred features appeared, backed by the familiar pin-ups and battleship gray wall of his berth.

"Hey, Imogene." Josh flashed that goofy grin he'd never grown out of. "Congrats on the Luna Corps! Dad always said we were a pair of space cadets. He would have been proud." He paused, eyes unfocusing just a little before snapping back to the camera. "Things here are pretty much the same. I finally got off the galley crew and into maintenance. Better hours, but I'm gonna miss getting first crack at the leftover deserts."

Imogene chuckled as his ears drooped dramatically.

"I talked to Mom earlier." The mirth lurking around his muzzle faded, and Imogene dropped her gaze to avoid meeting his recorded eyes. Leaving her mother's address off the message she'd sent last night probably hadn't been very mature, but it certainly felt good at the time. If her mother didn't approve of her occupation, why should Imogene keep her updated on it?

"She didn't get your message, so I sent her a copy. I know you and her aren't seeing eye to eye, and I don't really agree with her, but I wish you'd try and make nice. She missed you a lot when you went south, and since I had to leave she's been all alone. It's...hard for her."

He ran his tongue over his lips. Imogene bit down on hers. She wasn't the one being unreasonable, but somehow it was still her job to fix things.

Josh took a deep breath and his expression brightened. "Anyhow, bring me back a moon rock, and take lots of pictures. I never recovered after you told me Space Rangers was only a kid's vid show. You owe me big, and I intend to collect." He waggled his ears and leaned forward to end the recording.

Imogene folded the datapad in half and stuffed it under her pillow.

He was right. He was always right about those sorts of things. She glowered at the pale blue pillowcase and the offending device it concealed. Reluctantly, she pulled the datapad out and flipped it open. She glanced over at Bruce and Lauren. The tiny directional speaker would have kept Josh's message private, but they'd hear anything Imogene recorded.

What would she say, anyway?

Victor emerged from the showers, and she pushed the datapad back under her pillow. A message to her mother shouldn't be rushed. Or public.

Her eyes drifted to Victor, his fur still damp and clad only in loose-fitting shorts. She'd been too preoccupied to notice when they tried on their armor, but now she admired his muscular back and shoulders. The faint markings on his face were much more pronounced along his spine and flanks. Definitely some leopard or jaguar ancestry there. The dark tip of his tail bobbed hypnotically as he hummed a few off-key fragments from a popular song.

Imogene realized she was staring and jerked her gaze away. It wasn't like she'd never seen an attractive man shirtless before, but something about the well-built, outgoing feline set butterflies tickling and fluttering deep in her middle. She glanced back and found him fully clothed.

He tamed the fur of his head and face with a few hand swipes, then arched his eyebrows at his squadmates. "Shall we then?"

"We're waiting on you." Lauren gave him a solicitous ear flick and pushed off from her bunk.

"So you are." He grinned and followed her out into the corridor. "And most kind of you to do so."

Frowning, Imogene hurried after and stretched her stride to come abreast of Victor. Ahead, Lauren did a poor job of adapting a tail-swishing sashay to the low gravity. Imogene stayed by his side, making sure her elbow brushed his whenever someone passing the other way gave her an excuse to edge closer.

No way she was letting the lynx out-flirt her.

Crammed solid with a riot of furry bodies, the mess hall buzzed with conversation. The main dish tonight was suspiciously regular sized and shaped chunks of chicken, covered in gravy and accompanied by mashed potatoes and steamed green vegetables.

Imogene hesitated over the chicken. Alexei wasn't here to needle her about avoiding it, but after being singled out earlier she didn't want to draw more attention to herself. She picked up the spatula, pretending indecision about just which piece she wanted.

Behind her in line, Bruce leaned forward. "Don't think of it as meat," he murmured. "After all the processing it probably isn't anyway. One step up from jello."

Imogene snorted, but shoveled one of the brick-like chicken things onto her tray regardless. Somehow eating it didn't seem as bad if the stag knew it was rubbish, too. Besides, doing yet another thing that would annoy her mother felt perversely satisfying.

Finding an empty table took some searching, and just as they located one, a group of Armor Corps troops bustled by going the other direction. A raccoon with a sergeant's tabs knocked into Victor's elbow. The jostle sent his food skidding to the edge of his tray and about half his water sloshing onto the table.

"*Maldita sea!*" Victor steadied his meal, then quickly tossed a napkin onto the spreading puddle.

"Sorry there," the raccoon said. "Just the water, though? Good. Sorry." He gave a guilty half-wave and hurried to catch up with his friends.

Victor set the tray down and sat with a sigh. Imogene slipped in next to him before Lauren could, leaving the lynx and Bruce to sit across from them.

Lauren took a bite of potatoes, then pricked her ears at Victor. "What did you say when he bumped you? I didn't quite catch it."

"Oh." His whiskers slicked back. "I said 'gods dammit'."

"That's not what it sounded like," Imogene said. "Was it even Standard?"

"Ah, no. It's old Spanish."

"I thought so." Bruce's tone held a note of surprised respect. "You speak old Spanish?"

"Not as well as I'd like." Victor looked down at his napkin and pushed it around the puddle. "But a reasonable amount, yes."

Imogene cut into her chicken and took a bite. Mealy and empty tasting, but the salty gravy covered that. She swallowed quickly and glanced over at Victor. She hadn't marked him as the scholarly type, but only egg-heads bothered with the dead languages anymore.

"Why'd you learn it?" she asked.

"It's a family tradition. My father taught me, his own taught him, and once I have children, I will teach it to them."

"Oh." Imogene tried to think of anyone she knew with a similar tradition, but couldn't. "How does something like that get started?"

Victor shrugged. "My great-grandfather was one of the first transgenics and spent a lot of time in Central America. You know the ancient humans there worshiped jaguars? Even had warrior societies dedicated to them."

He smoothed the fur on his right cheek, running fingers over the faint spots and rosettes. "Great-grand was a powerful warrior, and met some of the natives' descendants. Picked up some of their religious ideas. Nothing against Pragmatheism, but I think it's important to have some connection to the past. Something personal you can pass on to your offspring."

Imogene nodded, not sure she understood. For a cat to follow some jaguar cult sounded almost narcissistic, even if it was tied in with family.

Across the table, Bruce set down his glass. "How do you figure on having kids anyway? Stuck up here, anyone you're likely to meet will be career Luna Corps too. Who'd take care of the kids?"

Victor chuckled. "I take it you're not from a service family. My parents were both active duty Maritime Infantry. There's extra leave for people with young kids, and a really great creche system. If your performance rating is high enough—and mine and my mate's will be—you get priority choosing your post between lunar deployments. McMurdo has a really nice family housing area."

Bruce flicked his ears. "Still, with the rotation schedule here, that's what? Four months a year with the kids?"

"About. No worse than the submarine branches get," Victor said.

"Or boarding school," Lauren offered. "I actually got along better with my parents after going away. Makes the time with them more special."

Imogene chewed her mealy chicken, trying not to frown while she thought. Children weren't something she'd really considered. What would a family with Victor be like? A little feline boy from him, and a caribou girl—or maybe just felines. Propagating genetic material didn't matter much to her, and it obviously meant a lot to Victor. She pictured them together somewhere with grass and maple trees, laughing, playing tag.

Not an unpleasant prospect, but the certainty with which Victor was set on it troubled her a little. That and the importance he put on his hypothetical partner's performance rating.

"How do they calculate performance ratings?" she asked. "Is it the same as the cull scores?"

Victor nodded. "Pretty much. I think there's less target practice and more general competency stuff thrown in. Especially if you see combat."

Which meant she might have half a chance at a decent score. Assuming she didn't wash out before she could show "general competency". She swallowed another mouthful of chicken and shook her head. "I just wish the cull had less target practice."

Victor turned, ears cupping towards her. "Hey, *chiquita*, don't worry. I'm sure you'll make the cut." He gave her shoulder a gentle punch.

A whiff of his hot sandy musk reached her, and warmth radiated out from where he'd touched her. She smiled up at him, letting her ears cant back just a little. The amber glow in his eyes was all the encouragement to make herself acceptable she could ever need.

Arched and about ten metres wide, the tunnel from the tactical block up to the surface was long. Very long. The base was under a mountain, but Imogene hadn't realized just how *far* under. She and her squadmates marched for what felt like kilometres before a tight corner brought them to the vehicle-sized airlock.

In the lead, Sergeant Hendricks hit the green open button, then turned to face his squad. "All right everybody! Visors down and check your pressure and power readings. There's hard vacuum on the other side of the lock, and I don't want to end up scraping anyone's brains off the inside of their helmets. Check and re-check, and if anything's not green, let me know."

Imogene slid her faceplate down, and it locked with a soft click. Her heads-up display showed green: ninety-nine percent power, and suit-pressure fifty millibars above the corridor outside. The suit kept a reserve of compressed air so it could check for proper sealing, and to make up for incidental losses from eating or other bodily functions.

"Any problems?" His tinted visor hid Sergeant Hendricks' face, but his voice came clear over the comm. "No? Then let's head out."

Two full-size surface crawlers could have fit in the airlock, and before they reached the chamber's far end, the inner door closed behind them. The air recovery pumps hummed, and the pressure dropped. It took a minute or two for the system to reclaim all the air it cared to, then the outer door lumbered open. A puff of dust swirled out with the last dregs of atmosphere, and Imogene's outside pressure gauge fell to zero.

"Everyone still good? No leaks?" Sergeant Hendricks asked again.

A chorus of affirmatives answered him, and he nodded. "Onward and upward then."

They passed through an open blast door thicker than Imogene was tall, then around another corner.

The tunnel emerged near the foot of a ridge, high enough to overlook the humpy floor of Santbech Crater. The grayish-white mountains of the crater's rim rose a dozen kilometres to the east, gleaming in the setting sun. Closer at hand, premature darkness shrouded the landscape. Without atmosphere to scatter the light there was no dusk here, and shadows were sharp-edged and absolute.

Floodlights lit a courtyard around the tunnel mouth, but beyond its berm of rubble, blackness ruled.

Coming to a stop just outside the tunnel, Imogene drank in the stark, alien vista. With no distracting color or foliage, the textures of rock and dust leapt out, drawing her eyes to the distant crater rim. Crags and smaller craters showed sharp details with none of the distortion or haze present on even the clearest Earth days. And above the mountains—her gaze slid upward and her heart skipped a beat. Perfect velvet blackness filled the sky, strewn with more gem-bright stars than she could ever hope to count.

Her mother was wrong. All her own doubts were wrong. The ache in her legs, the twelve-year commitment, everything —it was all worth it to stand here and feel the gravity, and know this was no vid-clip.

A muffled "wow" from Ryan pulled Imogene's attention down to where the squirrel stood looking north.

She followed his gaze and gasped.

Glowing blue and white, the majestic sweep of Earth sailed just above the jagged horizon. Night shrouded the right half of the sphere, but the left shone as an azure crescent, swirled with milky white clouds.

Lost in the terrible splendor, she couldn't say if it was minutes or only seconds before the Sergeant's dry chuckle rattled over the comm.

"Quite the view, huh?" the Dalmatian asked. "Don't worry; it'll be there day in and day out, and by the time your deployment's over you'll be dying to see an honest blue sky."

He was just as wrong as her mother. That view could ever get old. Imogene took one last look, then returned her attention to the Sergeant.

"Turn on your headlamps, everybody," he said. "The trail's not bad at the start, but you'll need 'em higher up." He set out in the long, bounding gait that was most efficient on the moon, where you had the space to use it.

The Sergeant had said they'd take it easy this morning. If this was easy, Imogene didn't want to see hard. The trail started off well enough, a well-trampled path through the dust, climbing gently into the foothills. Then it entered a murderous switchback up a narrow draw, and dust gave way to tamped gravel and rocks.

Imogene and the others stumbled frequently, which she supposed was the point. The low gravity ruined a lifetime of experience, and the sooner they rebuilt muscle memory, the better.

At last the trail left the ravine and cut cross-slope to a rocky knob. Sergeant Hendricks stopped in the saddle between it and the main ridge. "Take ten, people, and hydrate. You'll have sweated more than you think."

The squad spread out. Several comfortable looking boulders littered the knob, and the boot-prints leading to them marked this as a popular rest stop.

Intent on keeping her footing, Imogene hadn't noticed how high they'd climbed. The puddle of light around the tunnel where they'd started was tiny, and the line of tanks now entering looked like toys. Far away across the uneven floor, the crater walls rose in towering ramparts to dwarf the central peak their squad was climbing.

"Are we going on to the top?" Ryan pointed to where the trail continued upwards.

"Not today," said the Sergeant. "It gets cliffy up ahead, and I don't trust you bunch not to trip over your own paws."

Ryan sighed. "I suppose. I'd love to go higher, though."

"You're actually enjoying this?" Lauren asked.

"Sure. The gravity screws with your balance, but it's useful too: we must be six hundred metres up, and I'm not even winded."

The lynx snorted. "You squirrels really are nuts."

"I don't know," Alexei cut in. "I haven't done much climbing, but it might be exciting. Battling to the top and standing on the very summit—"

"Squirrels *and* rabbits then."

Imogene ignored them and pulled a tube of water from her armor's thigh pocket. She snapped it into the coupler below her visor and wrapped her lips around the helmet's built-in straw. Above, the stars shone bright, and she watched them while the others talked.

When they returned to the valley floor, the Sergeant set them to practice other forms of motion. Running, jumping, belly-crawling—everything from basic training had to be relearned and adapted for their new environment.

They went back inside for lunch, but then suited up again for an afternoon on the outdoor rifle range.

This was more like the ranges Imogene had used dirt-side. Without atmosphere for the laser targets to ionize, rows of old-fashioned steel cut-outs dotted the gray hills, leading away from the firing line.

After collecting their ammunition allotment, the Sergeant gathered them behind the firing positions. "So, you all got the scenic tour this morning. Luna's beautiful and exotic as anything. And she's dangerous. Stop and pretend you're a bullet. There's no air friction here, not much gravity, nothing to slow you down. What happens if you miss what you're aimed at?"

He looked around at his subordinates for a moment before Alexei shifted. "You keep on going?"

The Sergeant's helmet jerked in a nod. "Damn right you keep going. You go a long, long way, and you don't lose any of your killing power. Ricochets are deadly too, so this range is the one and only place you will fire your weapons outdoors during peacetime. You see that ugly frog-shaped thing with the googly eyes?" He pointed to a large dark-green piece of equipment crouched on a nearby ridge. "That is the little brother of the base defense screen. His name is LIDD—Laser Intercept Deflection or Destruction—and he is your new best friend. Watch."

The Sergeant raised his rifle and aimed into the black sky.

Imogene looked up. There shouldn't have been anything to see, but a split second after he squeezed the trigger, a blinding flash burst amid the stars. Imogene blinked, the after-image blending with the now dimming trail of superheated gas where the bullet had been vaporized.

Sergeant Hendricks lowered his weapon. "Anything going fast in the wrong direction gets zapped. Now take your positions and get busy."

As the squad fanned out towards the firing line, Alexei's voice came over the comm. "So if they've got something that can shoot down bullets, why don't they just build one into our suits?"

Victor snorted. "Lasers drink power, never mind the heat buildup and aiming issues. The smallest portables are the size of a house, and cost more than a brigade of tanks."

"And we all know how many infantry a single tank is worth," Sergeant Hendricks added with a wry chuckle. "Leave the tactics to the brass and concentrate on your shooting. So far only Ryan and Fiona are scoring well enough to pass the final cut."

Imogene gritted her teeth at that. Alexei and the others were at least meeting the training goals. If the white rabbit needed to concentrate, she needed a miracle.

Unlike the indoor range, the targets here were at a variety of distances and elevations. That actually made it seem easier to her; each shot was a little puzzle, like finding the best places on a bridge to plant demolitions charges. The spinning rings and lasers inside felt more like an arcade game.

She did pretty well on the closer targets, and even some of the mid-range ones. The armored shoulder of her suit made the recoil easier to handle, and keeping Ryan's tips on stance and grip in mind helped. She could never keep as good a count in her head as the range computers would, but a little flicker of pride warmed her chest as her hit ratio crept slowly upward.

That flicker guttered and threatened to go out at the end of the session as the Sergeant worked his way down the line to her. His silver faceplate hid any expression as he stopped in front of her.

"Imogene, acceptable. By exactly one point."

The wash of relief swept away any bitterness at his addendum. She was good enough. And she'd been getting better towards the end. She could do this. She *would* do this.

7

HART THROB

Imogene spent the following day with the demolitions department, learning how best to blow things up in vacuum. Without air to transmit shock waves, a lot of conventional devices were less effective. But by the same token, you could stay much closer to a blast—so long as you accounted for shrapnel and radiation.

She drank it all in, pleased to talk shop with people whose eyes didn't glaze over. When she finally returned to the barracks, she found it empty. A note scrawled in what might have been Fiona's handwriting indicated the rest of the squad had left for the recreation deck.

The dusky alleys of the rec-deck were busy as ever. The music in the taproom was less exotic tonight, but the long-eared basset hound still stood behind the bar, polishing a glass while he waited to be of service.

Imogene didn't see her squadmates, and walked over to check the few booths she couldn't see from the entrance. Sending one last glance over the taproom, a rust-brown stag waggled his ears at her. Her eyes had slid over him in her search for a group, but now she cringed for not recognizing Bruce.

He sat crossways to the bar, one elbow propped next to a mug of some dark beverage. He smiled as she came over, and gestured to the stool beside him. "Have a good time blowing things up?"

She slid into the offered seat and gave a crooked smile. "Good time, yes, blowing things up, no. I asked, but apparently the neighbors complain about the noise."

"I bet." Bruce chuckled.

She glanced around, making sure she hadn't missed any other squadmates. "Looks like I'm a little late for the party, huh?"

"So it would seem," he said. "The rest relocated to the arcade upstairs so Alexei and Lauren could settle who was the better tank driver."

"And yet, you're still here…"

"Aw, from what I've seen of those two, there'll be rematches till one or the other passes out. I'd rather relax here than watch them fight inside a computer."

The barman had been hovering nearby, and Imogene ordered a pint of light ale before replying. "So you're not big on computer games, I take it?"

"They're okay." He settled into the stool's padded backrest. "Just seems like there's enough fighting to go around without doing it for fun, you know?"

"My mother always said that, but I never quite believed her. Not until the last couple months, anyway."

"Oh?" Bruce arched his brows.

"I was posted in Turkey. They kept us greenies in the secured areas, but we'd see patrols coming back all shot up, and hear what it was like out away from the base. Makes you think sometimes."

"It sounds like it." His smile faded. "If you were feeling that way, why sign up for another hitch?"

Something in the earnest way he asked made Imogene want to tell him the truth, about breaking up with Steve and her apparent uselessness to every other possible employer. At the last moment, she bit the words back and flicked her ears. "Well, it's a job, and somebody's got to do it. Also, I like the security; the Armed Forces always take care of their own. Always. That's not a bad feeling to have these days.

"But what about you?" She raised her eyebrows and glanced over at him. "You can't have seen much action in Mexico."

"No, just guarding munitions dumps out in the desert." His leathery nose wrinkled in distaste. "If I never see another scorpion or cactus, it'll be too soon. That's half the reason I put in for Luna. No bugs."

The corner of her mouth quirked upwards. "There is that. What about the other half?"

"Oh, the usual. Adventure, excitement, the romance of space. I'd always dreamed of going out to the stars, and this is about the only way someone like me is getting off-planet."

"I can go along with that. My little brother went through the whole Space Rangers phase. He grew out of it, but I guess some must have rubbed off on me."

"And here we are." He cast a meaningful look around the taproom. "Two Space Rangers in a cantina on a desolate, airless planetoid. I don't see any fantastic aliens, but maybe they've just stepped out or something. Who says dreams don't come true?"

Imogene snorted, and they both sipped their drinks in silence as a group of blue-jumpsuited mechanics settled in a few seats over.

"What does he want to do now?" Bruce asked after a time.

Imogene cast him an inquiring glance. "Who?"

"Your brother, now that he's not going to be a Space Ranger."

"Oh. He's doing his compulsory service in the Navy, but after that he's gonna try and go back to school to be an architect."

"Sounds nice," Bruce said. "I always wanted a brother, but all I got were three sisters and a pet dog."

"They're overrated. Especially the younger ones." She flopped one ear to show she didn't really mean it, and set her empty mug on the bar. "Have you eaten yet? I was going to hit the mess hall, then get some sleep."

He downed the last of his drink and stood. "Yes, actually. But I'll come keep you company."

One level down in the mess hall they were serving sandwiches with egg salad and some rather limp-looking greens.

After collecting her portion, Imogene turned away from the counter and spotted Victor sitting alone with his back to them. His long, fluffy tail wrapped elegantly around his left ankle, and her gaze followed it up to his trim waist and broad shoulders. A warmth crept into her face and she suddenly wished Bruce had stayed in the bar. Then again, maybe some perceived competition would intensify Victor's interest in her.

She took her tray and sat down across from the big feline. "Mind if we join you?"

Victor blinked, then smiled. "Not at all. And here I was pitying myself as the last one to get his supper."

Bruce slid in beside Imogene. "Where did you and the Sergeant disappear to anyhow?"

"Practicing with my grenade launcher." Victor folded his ears. "If you think the gravity screwed up your aim with rifles, you don't even want to know what it did to grenades."

"Bad, huh?"

"Not if you're the one I'm trying to hit."

Both Bruce and Imogene snorted.

"I'm sure you'll figure it out," Imogene said. "You strike me as the more than slightly competent type."

His whiskers twitched. "Well, thank you. I guess we'll see if I can live up to that."

The pleased look in his golden eyes made Imogene's heart beat faster and sent a half-dozen replies scrambling towards her tongue. None of them seemed terribly grown-up or intelligent, so she just smiled and turned back to her food. The egg salad was excellent, just zesty enough without becoming hot.

Victor followed her example and munched through his soggy greens before looking up. "Did you hear about the military aid package for Australia?"

Imogene shook her head. "Only that it was hung up in red tape."

"It went through. They didn't talk details, but some of our rapid deployment units are already digging in around the big cities."

Bruce whistled. "We're sending troops? Not just equipment?"

"That's what they said. They're giving the PAF two weeks to withdraw from Australia's outlying possessions, or we're gonna kick 'em out."

"Somebody's spoiling for a fight." A worried frown ruffled the fur of Bruce's forehead. "The media are saying this, or the military?"

Victor shrugged. "It was a government press conference. It's all over the grid if you want to see for yourself."

"I will, later."

Victor shrugged again and took a huge bite from his sandwich.

Imogene poked at her egg salad, finding it suddenly less appetizing. Neither the PAF nor UNA had any real claim on Australia, but both coveted the nation's resources. It and the Ross Sea oil fields frequently topped lists of potential flashpoints for the next PAF-UNA war.

"This is going to void the Oceania Treaty, isn't it?" she asked.

Bruce's muzzle tightened. "If we've sent troops, it already has. The only question now is what the PAF plan to do about it."

🐾 🐾 🐾

"Grasp it firmly and pull." Victor looked down at Imogene as he spoke. "But smoothly. Don't jerk."

She shifted her grip and moved closer. "I don't want to hurt you, though." She glanced up into the powerfully built feline's golden eyes.

"Don't worry, you won't."

With a nod, she tightened her fingers and pulled. Her ears swung forward in surprise as she felt him sliding towards her, then past, to fall slowly onto the padded floor of the gymnasium.

"Good." He rolled back up to his paws. "I think you've got a feel for the leverage now. Give it another few passes and we'll try out the next throw."

Around them, the other members of the squad sparred, relearning the subset of unarmed combat deemed useful on the moon. There wasn't a great deal of it, but Imogene had never enjoyed hand-to-hand and was struggling.

Of course the fact she was struggling was what had gotten her paired with Victor, so it wasn't all bad. He moved with all the grace she lacked, and had taken to lunar martial arts like an otter to water. If only this excuse to be close to him hadn't come coupled with something she was bad at.

"I don't see why we have to bother with all this," she said. "It's not like we're going to be this close to anyone without our armor and weapons. Shouldn't we be practicing with them?"

"You never know. And it is good exercise." He waved Imogene towards him. This time he twisted when she threw him, and somehow managed to pull her down on top of him.

The firmness of his muscles against her sent an electric tingle down her spine, and heat flooded her cheeks.

"Besides, wrestling with you is more fun." He wiggled his eyebrows.

"Oh?" She flicked her ears at him, lingering a moment longer than she needed to before rolling off of his chest. Gods, he smelled good. Warm sandstone and musk.

His fatigue jacket pulled tight over well defined shoulders and biceps as he pushed up onto his paws. "Yep." He extended a hand and hoisted her to her hooves. "Now keep your center of balance farther back this time, so I can't pull you down."

A few throws later, the instructor broke up the squad's practice, pairing them off against members of another unit.

Imogene sized up the brown and white rat he picked for her, hoping she wasn't about to be made into mincemeat. To her relief, the rodent proved almost as incompetent as herself. They traded a clumsy series of textbook grabs and blocks until Imogene fumbled and ended up with her muzzle stuffed in the rodent's armpit and her wrist pulled high between her shoulder blades.

"Ah!" she yelped. "I think you got me."

The rat let go instantly, her round ears folding as she scurried back. "I didn't hurt you, did I?"

Imogene flexed her arm, wincing as the muscles and joints returned to their preferred ranges. "I'll live."

She turned, looking to where Victor's bout continued. He and his otter opponent were the only ones still fighting. Everyone else stood in a loose circle around them, and Imogene moved in for a better view. The two men grappled, occasionally throwing each other to the mats, but never managing a decisive grip or "kill" worthy blow.

"That's it! Toss him, Daniel!" Imogene's opponent called. The otter's other squadmates started shouting encouragement too, and Imogene added her calls to the tumult. "Go, Victor!"

His eyes darted towards her for a split second, and he grinned before launching himself back at the otter. They tussled, then moved apart. The otter sprang into what looked like a flying tackle, and Victor braced to take the impact of his smaller opponent.

With a move like something out of a bad martial arts vid, the otter twisted into a midair somersault. His paws lashed out, and rather than absorbing the force, Victor flew backwards. His breath went out in an audible whoosh, and when he landed near Imogene's hooves, he stayed down.

"Well, that's enough of that," Sergeant Hendricks said into the sudden silence. "Looks like you cubs all need some practice. Don't let size fool you like that. Up here it's technique that counts. Now, let's get some chow."

Helping Victor to his paws, Imogene heard him growl something in Spanish. The glares he shot first at the Sergeant then at the otter were all the translation she needed.

"Hey," she said softly, squeezing his hand. "Nobody wins all the time."

His ears perked slightly, and his golden eyes met her own. "I know." He gave her a tired smile. "Thanks."

The tawny feline returned her squeeze, maintaining their hold as the squad filed out into the brightly lit corridor.

🐾 🐾 🐾

Last to take her shower again, Imogene emerged to find only Ryan still in the barracks. The diminutive ground squirrel was rearranging his locker, and paid no attention while she dressed and brushed her fur.

Grooming complete, Imogene was about to close her locker when a gleam of silver amid the jumble caught her eye. The corner of her datapad stared back up at her, and she squirmed under its gaze. She didn't want to try and find something polite to say to her mother, but it would only get harder the longer she put it off.

She sat cross legged on her bunk, back propped against the wall, and opened her datapad's recording program.

"Hi, Mom. Sorry I didn't talk to you sooner, things here have been...busy." She gave an apologetic ear-waggle, then launched into some highlights from training, and getting used to the gravity over the last week.

"...and of course Alexei got the jello all over the front of his shirt. Everyone else had left, so Fiona and I helped him clean it up. She's the polar bear who's been up here before and sorta looks out for the rest of us. Most of the people in my unit seem pretty nice, actually. Especially Victor. He's a corporal." She substituted his rank for the "puma" she'd been about to say. Best not to bring the cross-species thing up when her mother was already on edge.

"We haven't had much free time with training and all, but he's awfully nice, and I think he likes me." The memory of his hand enfolding hers and his warm scent flooded back, bringing heat into her cheeks and ears. She twitched her ears, making sure the camera couldn't see the insides where her flush might show.

"We're really too busy to worry about that sort of thing, though. Lots of training. In fact, I kinda need to go get dinner now before it gets too late. I hope everything's...good with you. And say hi to Josh for me, if he calls." She managed to dredge up something close to a happy smile, then ended the recording. She flicked her mother's address into the recipient box, then sent the message off into the grid.

Both her news feeds and in-box looked to be overflowing, but nothing from Josh or their mother, so rather than deal with the messages she stuffed the datapad back in her locker.

Ryan was still fussing with his locker, rearranging sports and outdoorsman pinups stuck to the inside of the door. He looked up when she approached.

"You wouldn't happen to know where Victor and the others got off to?" Imogene asked.

He tilted his head to one side, then shook it. "Lauren and some others went to the bar. But I think Victor went off on his own."

"Hmm, thanks." Imogene smiled.

"No problem." He was already turning back to his locker.

Since she had no real idea where to look for Victor, Imogene headed to the bar that had become the squad's off-duty headquarters. It was standing room only inside, and she edged her way through the crush towards their usual table. About halfway there her ears pricked at the sound of her name. The scrap of conversation came from the direction of the bar, and she changed course to investigate.

"Oh come on! He was just being polite." Lauren's voice cut through the bustle of the crowd. "You saw how she couldn't keep her hands off him. It's not even like she's his girlfriend or anything."

Alexei snorted. "Neither were you, last I checked."

"Not yet maybe, but I'm not about to let some red-nosed reindeer steal him."

Imogene bit her lip. She could see Lauren and Alexei alone at the bar, but hung back, using a boisterous group of techs for cover.

Lauren took a long pull from her mug, then thumped it down on the bar. "Besides, you know how important family is to him. He'd never get anything out of a deer like her but manure."

"So being feline, you must be purr-fect?" Alexei chortled at his own joke.

"Funny, bunny." Lauren's ears laid back. "She's not good enough for him, even if she was a cat. Second-rate tag along material if I ever saw it. She just better stay out of my way."

Imogene didn't wait to hear the rabbit's reply.

Her vision swimming with tears, she pushed to the door and stumbled over the threshold. Outside, a steady stream of pedestrians washed around her while she stared down at the fake sidewalk. Someone bumped into her, and she mumbled an apology, then let the flow of traffic carry her away.

The housing block's circular layout was perfect for aimless wandering. A never-ending arc of corridor, filled with an equally inexhaustible supply of purposeful, mostly happy people.

Imogene tried not to think as she walked among them, but couldn't block out the echo of Lauren's words. The lynx was hardly unbiased, but what if it was true? Luna Corps wasn't supposed to take second-rate people, but then Imogene knew she'd never been more than passable at anything. What if they just needed warm bodies?

She didn't know, and there was no way to find out, but the questions nibbled away at her.

Eventually her wanderings brought her to the mess hall. She waited in line, but found she'd lost her appetite. Most of the chicken casserole went in the waste bin, and Imogene went back to the empty barracks. She performed the motions of tooth brushing and hoof cleaning, then crawled into the comforting darkness of her bunk.

8

BLACK AND WHITE

The metal target swung as the bullet hit, and Imogene allowed herself a grim smile. It might not have fur or yellow eyes, but the target was the right shade of silver-gray. Her imagination could supply the rest.

"Nice shot, Imogene," Sergeant Hendricks' voice came over the comm. "Finally hitting your stride, eh?"

"Something like that." She shifted her aim to the next target, farther up the hillside.

Even without picturing Lauren's face on the targets, she would have been enjoying this. There was something distinctly satisfying about sending the heavy steel targets swinging with a solid hit, even if she couldn't hear the distant ring of metal against metal.

She emptied the rest of her magazine with care and determination. They'd been shooting most of the day, and she knew she was improving. Acceptable wasn't good enough for her. Not anymore.

Imogene reached for a fresh magazine, but found she'd already used her allotment. The others were still shooting, and she retreated from the firing line to observe.

Watching them lay in the dust wasn't very exciting, and her attention drifted to contemplating the frosty reply message she'd gotten from her mother. All the words seemed encouraging enough on the surface, but the tone and little barbs about being thankful this message "got through" left no doubt her mother wasn't ready to let their argument go.

Envisioning her mother feeling alone and betrayed set guilt creeping in around the edges of Imogene's mind, but she refused to let it dig its hooves in. This was her life, not her mother's, and despite the trouble with Lauren, she wanted to be here.

And if she wanted to *stay* here, she couldn't let stress tie her up into knots.

She took a deep, calming breath and turned her gaze first to the barren, monochrome landscape, then up to the star-specked sky. Despite the growing familiarity, it was still the most beautiful thing she'd ever seen. Earth had waxed full, and now shone as a turquoise marble amid the blackness. The sun had set days ago, and without its glare the other stars burned bright and steady.

Their colors struck her the most. Blues and whites and oranges—they'd never seemed so vivid from Earth. She searched for constellations, but the carpet of glowing pinpricks refused to order itself into any pattern she knew.

"See any you'd like?"

She looked down to find Bruce watching her, and answered him over the same private comm channel. "Maybe. How about that bright yellow one above Earth?"

The stag's visor turned from her up towards the sky. "Alpha Centauri? All right."

"I thought Alpha Centauri was a southern star."

"It is. Santbech is in the moon's southern hemisphere."

"Oh." She frowned up at the stars. That would explain why she couldn't find any constellations. "Does that mean we can see the Southern Cross?"

"Yep, a bit higher and to the left." He pointed. "I didn't know you were interested in astronomy."

"Only a little. One of the kids in our building had a tele-scope, and it was a good excuse to goof around on the roof at night."

"I'll bet." Bruce chuckled. "Santbech has a really nice observatory left from before the military took over. You should come check it out with me sometime."

Attention still lost amid the stars, Imogene nodded. "Sounds like it might be interesting."

"All right, people, that's enough for today." Sergeant Hendricks broke in over the squad channel. "Make sure your rifles are locked down, and let's get back inside."

The Sergeant let them go earlier than usual, and while she showered, Imogene planned how she could use the extra time to best advantage with Victor. But he'd vanished by the time she was done, so she joined Ryan and Fiona. They wanted to check out the shops on the second level of the recreation area, which Imogene had been curious about herself.

The first three venders proved disappointing. Mostly snacks or health and grooming supplies, and all standard items. She wasn't sure what she'd expected, but to find all the familiar corporate logos on the moon was a let down.

The fourth was better, with racks of decidedly non-regulation clothing, cases of cheap jewelry, and shelf after shelf of what Imogene could only label Tourist Junk. Ryan and Fiona headed straight for the clothes, and Imogene drifted along in their wake.

"How about this one?" Fiona took out a silky, emerald dress and held it up to Imogene. "It'd really bring out your eyes."

"Yeah?" The thin material felt slick between Imogene's fingers and picked up the light. "Not very practical, though. It'd be a shame to have something like this and no reason to wear it."

"Well, I can think of at least one stag who'd like to see you in it."

Imogene blinked. "Who? Bruce? We're just friends."

"Right," Fiona drawled. "So when he stares at your tail all through target practice, he's just being friendly?"

"He did?" Imogene's cheeks grew warm under her fur. "Well, that's his problem then, not mine."

"It's no use," Ryan said to the white bear. "She's got her eye on something bigger and with sharper teeth."

Fiona held the dress up to Imogene again. "Oh? I'm sure Victor'd appreciate it too. It's such a lovely color for you."

Imogene blushed harder and her short tail gave an involuntary twitch. She looked down at the dress to cover her embarrassment. It *was* a nice color, but the midriff baring cut wasn't her style. Besides, if she was any judge, Victor cared more about whether you could hold up your end of a firefight than what you wore. She hung the garment back on the rack.

"I don't really want more clothes now. Maybe once we know where we're posted and get settled in." She did her best then to hurry the other two along towards the safer shelves of souvenirs.

"Moon cheese!" Ryan squeaked. He grabbed a foil packet with an odious wedge of green cheese pictured on it. "You can't go wrong with cheese."

Imogene picked up another packet. "I don't know. Should something that color be edible?"

"Moon rocks then?" He pointed to a rack of gray stones, each laminated to a small plaque.

Fiona rolled her eyes. "And what do you think we've been crawling through outside? You could fill your whole duffel with moon rocks, and the only people who'd care are the ones who had to lift it."

They continued to browse, Ryan gathering up an armful of odds and ends. Imogene picked out a tablet of stationery with "From Luna, with love" emblazoned across the lower margin. She hadn't learned how physical mail service worked to and from the moon yet, but Josh would get a kick out of it. Pinning a moon-letter up next to his berth's porthole might buy her time to find him some more unique space souvenir.

After settling with the cashier, they walked out onto the balcony overlooking the recreation center's courtyard. The synthetic sky glowed with its perpetual twilight, while below, planters and park benches broke up the pedestrian traffic.

Ryan looked at his chronometer, then at his companions. "Want to see if the rest are at the bar yet?"

Imogene's ears perked up. Shopping was okay, but the possibility of meeting with Victor was better.

Fiona shrugged and led the way towards the nearest stairway to the courtyard.

When they were about a quarter of the way down, the black and white bulk of a panda appeared at the bottom. Jared glanced up at them, and a grin split his muzzle. Imogene grimaced as he shifted direction to intercept.

He stopped in front of them. "Going somewhere, Fi?"

Fiona growled and tried to go around, but he blocked her again.

"Is that a 'no'?" He cocked his head and leered.

Fiona crossed her thickly muscled arms over her chest. "Look, how many different ways do you need me to say I'm not interested?"

"What about all those times you sat with me in the mess hall?"

She scoffed. "Once. And that was only because I felt sorry for you."

Jared's nostrils flared and his muzzle bunched. "Fucking sorry? For me?"

"I got over it, if that makes you feel better."

"Yeah?" He rocked forward, thrusting out his jaw. "Keep telling yourself that."

Imogene planted her fists on her hips and took a step forward. Fiona could probably take care of him if things got physical, but a little intimidation never hurt. Ryan caught on too, and moved up on Fiona's other side.

Jared's gaze darted between them, then back to Fiona. "Go on then." He shifted aside just far enough to clear a narrow passage. "I'd hate to keep you from whatever pathetic fuck you feel sorry for today."

Fiona snorted and pushed past him, Imogene and Ryan following close behind.

Inside the bar, the dim light and upbeat music flowed over Imogene, soothing her rattled nerves. Alexei waved at them from the far end of the bar, and they walked over to join the lanky white rabbit.

"Well, that's one," Imogene said, settling onto the stool next to Alexei. "Any idea where the rest are?"

"Upstairs playing air hockey. Said they'd be down after Bruce and Victor broke their tie."

Ryan and Fiona sat beside Imogene, and the basset hound barman came to take orders.

The drinks arrived just as a pretty brown rabbit slid into the empty seat between Alexei and the end of the counter. She ordered a beer, then turned to Alexei. "Haven't seen you around before. New here?"

From the corner of her eye, Imogene saw him give a polite smile.

"A couple of days, yeah."

"I thought so. Want to come sit with us?" She flicked her eyes towards another table from which a vixen watched intently.

He followed her glance, then looked back. "Maybe some other time."

"You sure? We'd make it worth your while." She put a hand on his shoulder, tracing her fingers down to his elbow.

"I bet you would, but I'm waiting for some friends."

"All right." She picked up her drink and slipped off the stool. "But if you change your mind..." She wobbled her ears at him, then sidled away.

After giving her a good start, Alexei leaned forward to peer around Imogene. "Hey, Ryan, come sit over here and help keep the bimbos at bay."

Ryan snickered. "That'd just encourage them to sit on your lap."

"True." Alexei cast an appraising eye over the ground squirrel. "You look pretty light. You sit on my lap. That'd keep everyone away."

Ryan returned his survey, then snickered again. "Nope, never on a first date. Besides, you've got knobbly knees."

He did sit next to Alexei, though, and Imogene tuned out their conversation as it degenerated into a debate over which Tank Commander sim had the best gameplay and graphics.

The bar was filling up, and the crowd more clamorous than usual. There was a sharpness to the atmosphere, an electric current no one quite knew what to do with, and so they laughed and cursed and yelled that little bit louder to compensate.

By the time Victor and the others arrived, there wasn't an empty seat to be found.

Imogene got up, ostensibly so they could make a tighter group in the noisy crowd, and used the excuse to stand between Lauren and Victor. Lauren's ears flattened, but Imogene ignored her, turning to Victor instead. The muscular feline's tawny fur was ruffled, and his gray shirt had come untucked from his waistband.

Forcing her attention back to his face, Imogene arched her brows. "So, did you win? Looks like you worked up quite a sweat."

"About even, actually." He gave her a toothy grin. "I think Bruce was ahead by the end."

Imogene glanced over at the stag, who shrugged.

"You'll have to wait for me next time." She mock-frowned up at Victor. "I haven't played in a while, but I used to be pretty good."

"I'll be sure to do that." Victor glanced towards the entrance then, where angry shouts had broken out over the general buzz.

Probably some minor argument. But rather than dying down, the disturbance multiplied, propagating like wild fire through the crowd. Imogene's ears folded against the jumbled assault, but she picked out two words: "Australia" and "PAF".

The taproom's music cut off, and the seldom-used display screen above the bar flickered to a news broadcast. There was too much crowd noise to hear what the red fox on screen was saying, but the burning buildings behind him didn't look good.

The image shifted to a map of eastern Australia, with angry arrows in the PAF's emblematic green and gold stabbing in from the ocean. A few icons appeared and changed color, then the scene cut to a shaky hand-held shot of a UNA Navy vessel, belching black smoke as it sank into blue-green waters.

Imogene's breath caught. Where in the Pacific had Josh said he was? South somewhere, but she didn't know where. Her eyes darted over the people splashing in the waves, frantic for her brother's face.

9

STARLIGHT, STARBRIGHT

Imogene couldn't tell if any of the survivors were Josh. Furred heads bobbed in the water, too tiny on the bar's screen to identify. Edging forward, she stared up at the display anyway, gnawing her lip. It couldn't be Josh's ship. It just couldn't.

A hand found her shoulder and Bruce asked, "You said your brother was Navy?"

"Yeah." She didn't look away. That dark head on the left—was it a caribou?

"What class of ship?" he persisted.

She folded her ears. What difference did that make? "A destroyer. UNS *Spokane*."

"Good." Bruce patted her shoulder. "He's good then. That's a troop transport."

Imogene blinked at the screen, looking at the ship rather than the survivors. It wasn't much like the pictures Josh sent. The tension in her chest eased, but it was still all too easy to imagine him in one of those tiny orange life rafts.

The view cut again to the burning city.

"Fucking pandas," Lauren snarled.

On Imogene's other side, Victor nodded. "At least now we'll get to stand up to them. This treaty crap is well and good with a reasonable opponent, but the only thing PAF'll understand is a boot in the teeth." Venom laced his tone, and his eyes shone with a hard gleam.

Imogene shifted uncomfortably. Right now she had no sympathy for people who'd go around sinking ships, but the easy way her squadmates demonized the Pan-Asians felt wrong. She couldn't remember her father well, but she knew being a PAF soldier hadn't made him a bad person.

Alexei snorted. "You know what the real problem is? We should have kept after them in '82. Pushed 'em all back to China and built a wall around 'em."

"Who knows?" Lauren said. "Maybe this time we can finish things ourselves."

"You think so?" Alexei's ears pricked forward.

Lauren glanced up to where the city still blazed. "Sure. They keep pushing, it's all the excuse we need to start another offensive. Crazy fucking pandas."

Those three words summed up the conversation that followed. Imogene hid behind her ale and didn't speak. At least in Turkey her squadmates' animosity had only targeted the rebels trying to kill them, not a whole nation. This open hatred for people they'd never met unnerved her almost as much as the news of war.

After a time, Bruce edged closer and murmured in her ear, "You want to get out of here?" His gaze flicked to Lauren and Alexei. "Unless you're enjoying the conversation?"

She looked up at him, then over at Victor. The feline hadn't said much after his first comment, just nodded occasionally when something halfway reasonable broke the flow of vitriol. To leave him here with Lauren rankled. But neither of them were making any romantic headway at the moment, and escaping the anger-filled taproom sounded good.

She nodded to Bruce, and the two of them slipped away into the crowd.

The subdued hum of the courtyard was a shock after the bedlam inside. A wave of cooler air came with it, and she sighed.

"Feels better, doesn't it?" Bruce took his own deep breath of the fresher air. "Too many people in there getting too worked up over things they can't control."

Imogene let her ears perk from their half-fold. "Yeah. Not my idea of fun, anyway."

"Mine, either." The stag's warm brown eyes met hers. "I was thinking about going up to the observatory, but if you'd like company we can do something else."

She blinked. She'd only been thinking of getting out of the bar, not what doing it with him might imply. Fiona's remark about him watching her tail whispered through her ears, and she licked suddenly dry lips.

She did like Bruce, as a friend, but did he want more than that? And if he did, was it her responsibility to push him away? As long as she didn't do anything more than friendly, it was his job to manage whatever expectations he might have. Wasn't it?

Returning alone to their empty barracks was depressing, and the observatory *did* sound interesting.

"Sure," she said. "I'd like to see it before we ship out."

"All right." He smiled and led her from the recreation center towards the nearest stairwell. The other pedestrians thinned as they descended, until on the lowest level the white-walled passages were empty. They circled the hub's ring corridor towards the parking area where Fiona had left the cart on the day they arrived.

A muffled shout echoed over the omnipresent hum of ventilation equipment. Three gray-clad figures came into view a dozen metres down the curving corridor, clustered around a fourth who lay slumped against the wall.

Concern pricked at Imogene, and she hastened her pace.

The three looked up at the clack of her and Bruce's hooves, then moved off in the other direction.

As they drew closer, the fourth person rose, letting the wall take most of his weight. He turned towards them, and an all-too-familiar face made Imogene's jaw clench. She and Bruce stopped a length or so short of Jared.

"So—" He paused to wipe blood from the corner of his muzzle. "You came to get your piece of panda too, huh? Come on then!" He shoved off from the wall and raised his fists.

Imogene's pulse quickened, and she took a step back, settling into a wider stance.

Beside her, Bruce stood his ground. "Are you hurt enough to need help?"

"From the likes of you?" Jared spat, but the red-laced glob fell short and spattered on the white floor. An angry growl escaped him, and he lurched forward. "Just get out of my way." He pushed around them, limping on his left leg.

Impassive, Bruce watched him out of sight, then flicked his short tail. "Poor bastard."

"Yeah?" After his performance on the stairs, Imogene couldn't help thinking he had it coming. Some of that must have colored her voice, because Bruce shot her a sideways look. Her conscience panged, and she cursed silently as they resumed their trek.

Row after row of electric carts greeted them in the dimly-lit parking area. Most everything a soldier needed was within walking distance of their barracks, but for longer trips, the carts came in handy.

Plus they were cute. Beige and about thigh-high, the sociable little things could always be found huddled together outside briefing rooms or office areas, taking comfort in the presence of their kindred while patiently awaiting their owners' return.

They picked a small four-seater, and Bruce guided it out into the tunnel system.

After the first three junctions, Imogene gave up trying to understand where they were. The tunnels had plenty of signs, but the one for Housing Block H with arrows pointed both directions was too much.

Marked simply "Summit", the passage Bruce picked settled into a steep spiral. The cart whined in protest, but bore them upwards until at last the tunnel leveled out.

"Well, here we are." Bruce stopped in a wide spot beside a doorway. "We have to climb the last few stories on our own, I'm afraid."

She followed him off the cart and into a rather dingy corridor. "We're at the top of the mountain, then?"

"What's left of it. They flattened off quite a bit to make room for radars and the defense screen projectors. But the telescope survived. No one takes care of it, but it's not exactly off limits, either, according to the tech who showed it to me."

A tickle of nervous excitement crept up Imogene's spine. The last time she'd done something not strictly allowed was sneaking out of the barracks back in Basic to steal some time alone with Steve.

Ahead, a metal staircase switchbacked crazily up into darkness. Bruce ducked behind the stairs and threw a manual cut-off switch hidden in the shadows. The lights in the stairwell flickered on.

"Remind me to shut that off again when we come down," he said. "It doesn't pull much power, but no point drawing attention if we don't have to." He gave her a conspiratorial wink and started to climb.

Fourteen flights of stairs later, Imogene was thankful both for the low gravity and her hard hooves. The stairs were the cheap expanded mesh type that quickly lost favor when shoe-loving humans went extinct.

"This is where the imager data comes out." Bruce stepped through a submarine-style door and waved towards a tangle of computer terminals beneath a larger wall screen. "We can go look out the window at the telescope if you're into the nuts and bolts, but this is where the exciting stuff happens."

Imogene glanced around the cramped room with its dirty, off-white walls. "We don't get to look through the lens or something?"

"Ah, no." He chuckled. "Not unless you want to suit up and stand around in vacuum. Give me a minute to get the dome open, and we'll see what we can see." He settled into a workstation and roused it from its slumber.

Imogene dragged one of the mismatched chairs up on his left and sat. The wall screen snapped to life, showing a black field with fuzzy blobs that resolved themselves into the bright dots of stars.

"There we are." Bruce leaned forward to the console once more. "Anything in particular you'd like to look at?"

"How about Earth?"

"All right." His long, brown-furred fingers skittered over the console, and the view began to shift.

Stars drifted from right to left, then an arc of cloud-dappled blue pushed them from sight. The telescope panned over the ocean and came to rest without ever showing land.

"The Pacific must be towards us." Bruce wrinkled his leathery nose. "Let's zoom out a bit..."

The view blurred, then cleared again to show the whole planet taken up with white and blue. Only a few scraps of North America and the Far East showed around the lower edge.

Imogene sighed. "Not a good day for Earth-gazing I guess. Unless you like water."

"Maybe we can manage anyhow." He sent the view zooming in towards the Gulf of California.

They spent the next half-hour working north, past the half-flooded LA Crater and on to San Francisco. It was too foggy to pick out individual buildings, but the telescope was more than capable of showing the giant structure spanning the bay's mouth. Monolithic and gray, the Golden Gate Barrier reared up out of the blue waters. Twin to the ruined dam she'd crossed on the train near Gibraltar, this one was still doing its job: holding back time and tide to their 20th-century levels.

Farther north, clouds blanketed the Pacific Northwest, while Asia was just peeking out from the veil of night. Towns and cities twinkled in the dark, strung like glowing beads on the gossamer threads of rivers and coasts.

Then there was Australia. Black, sooty smoke boiled up at several points along the coast, thinning to gray as it swept over the sea. They panned across the outskirts of a burning city, and both Imogene and Bruce fell silent. Vehicles too small to identify crawled through the streets.

Something darted in from the east, and a flash of yellow-white dazzled the camera. When the screen cleared a heartbeat later the vehicles and houses were gone, replaced with billowing dust and smoke.

"Damn." Bruce hit a key, and the view zoomed back out to the whole planet.

Imogene's stomach twisted. How many little girls hid down there in basements and fallout shelters, waiting for parents who were never coming back? She swallowed hard. "It's starting all over again, isn't it?"

"Maybe not. Australia's kind of a loophole. It might stay local." He didn't sound convinced. "But let's look at something pretty. You like nebulas? Or there's Saturn..."

Imogene nodded, trying to think of something hopeful. "Mars? Can we see the colonies from here?"

"Mars is on the far side of its orbit." He frowned for a moment. "Tell you what, though, we can look at Alpha Centauri. Of course you can't see the planets, much less any colonies, but the *Perseverance* should've gotten there something like sixty years ago, so maybe there is a colony."

"You really think they made it?" she asked as he leaned forward to adjust the controls. "I mean, nobody ever heard back from any of the deep space missions."

"Well, we weren't exactly listening." His ears folded. "They would have gotten there while we were still cleaning up from the Unification, and you know how much funding science programs have gotten since then."

Imogene shuddered. "Gods, that'd be awful. Calling and calling with no answer..."

"Yeah." Bruce's lips tightened. "Still, it's a nice thought there might be at least one continuation of human culture somewhere."

"Wait, what do you mean? We're continuing the culture right now, aren't we?"

"I don't know." He sighed, looking up at the pair of bright, golden stars centered in the screen. "Our ancestors were nothing but lab rats a hundred years ago, and kept tightly segregated even afterwards. How much human culture really made it into ours?"

"It had to come from somewhere," she countered. "You read history, and all the things we do have been done before."

"I suppose. What bothers me isn't so much what we kept, but what got lost. There were over thirteen billion people at the last world census. There's less than three today, even with us repopulating as enthusiastically as we can."

Imogene shook her head. "That's true, there's only so much a smaller group can keep alive. But it goes double for a deep space colony. They only had what? A few thousand?"

"But they prepared for it. We didn't. Everything we have was either picked up in the military, or force-fed by politicians after the human plague got going. Between that and what the Bureau of Standardization decided to sanitize, who knows what things were really like before the war?"

"I suppose we can't know." Which wasn't altogether bad, to her thinking. People who'd gene-splice a whole race of slaves couldn't be worth emulating too closely. "Maybe it doesn't matter. We're doing okay so far."

"Yeah, maybe." Bruce looked down at his hands and sighed. "I guess sometimes I think too much. And there's nothing we can do about it anyway."

"Heads down, face forward, eh?" She quoted the infantryman's maxim.

"Right," Bruce snorted. "Straight into a minefield." He glanced at his chronometer. "Anyway, we'd better wrap things up if we want to get any sleep." He leaned forward and set the telescope tracking back to its rest position.

Imogene rose to her hooves and pushed the chair back to its proper home. "Thanks for bringing me, though. It was fun."

"Certainly." He smiled, and a softness crept into his eyes. "We'll have to do it again sometime."

10

IN LOVE AND WAR

Things were starting to fall together, Imogene thought as she took her armor down from its pegs. A black heart outline around her initials now enlivened her breastplate, centered on the red and yellow field of the squad's new colors. She'd wanted just the bare initials required by regulations, but with a surname like Haartz, Victor and Alexei wouldn't let her get away without a heart involved somewhere.

Closer to the armory door, Victor sported the squad's most complex design, a clawed paw-print reminiscent of the great wild cats. Most of the others fell somewhere in between, with simple geometric patterns dominating. The point was identification, not fashion, so simple really was better.

Imogene slid on the helmet and wriggled her ears to settle them into their recesses, then snapped the helmet into her collar. They had two bouts scheduled in the Infantry Combat Simulation Center this morning, and she was looking forward to both the action, and the chance to boost her scores.

She kept doing better, but as training progressed the minimum standard rose too, keeping her straddling the line between safety and the Volga. Now, with the squad moving on to actual combat sims, she had a chance to prove her true competency.

That was the plan, anyway, but deep in a dark and semi-abandoned part of the base, their first match didn't start well.

She and Victor got separated from the rest of the squad, then forced into a dead-end corridor. After that, it was only a matter of time before they were overrun and dispatched.

"Well, that could have gone better," Victor said once the other team had departed.

"Yeah." Imogene sighed and pushed herself up from the floor. "Sorry if I held you back. I know I'm not as good as some of the others." Like Lauren. No matter how hard she tried, the lynx stayed that little bit ahead, and Victor always picked her if he had a choice.

"What? Not at all. You're a fine partner for this sort of thing." He clapped her on the shoulder, almost sending her to the floor again. "Whoops! There we are." He reached out to steady her.

They followed the overseer's directions back to the ready room, where most of the squad waited. The Sergeant was still missing, along with Lauren and Fiona.

Alexei glanced up expectantly. "How are things going inside?"

"Don't know," Victor said. "We got cut off and have been playing hide and seek ever since."

The rabbit grimaced and looked back down at his training rifle.

Moving past him, Imogene and Victor settled in to wait, him stoically, her doing her best not to fidget. She wasn't sure how much the squad's overall performance counted towards individual cull scores. If her squadmates still inside managed a win, it had to help at least a little. After her showing so far, she could use all the help she could get.

A good ten minutes passed before the door opened again to admit Fiona, who was followed shortly by Lauren and the Sergeant.

Sergeant Hendricks flipped up his visor, revealing his black and white spotted face. "It's a draw," the Dalmatian said. "We were taking too long, so they pulled the plug."

He waved down a chorus of groans and profanity. "They've got our next match waiting at one of the other entrances, so load up on ammo and power packs, then we're going in again." He followed his own order, then cast a steely blue gaze over his squad. "Everybody set?"

Imogene nodded along with the others, then snapped her faceplate into place and followed the Sergeant into the maze of ill-lit corridors.

Indoor navigation wasn't her forte, but they were obviously being taken into a different section of the complex than the first match. Nearly all the lights still worked, and the surroundings developed an industrial flavor with wide, high-ceilinged corridors which wove through a mess of interconnected chambers.

Plastic pellets crunched under Imogene's boots, evidence of past battles. Her guts clenched at every cross corridor, remembering the ambush that started off the first match.

They entered a large room set up as a field ration assembly line, and the Sergeant came to a halt.

"Okay, our job is to defend the kitchen here. Anyone from the opposing squad gets inside, it's over." His reflective visor swept back and forth as he sized up the situation. "Victor, take Fiona and scout back the way we came. See if there's anything easier to defend than this corridor. Ryan's with me doing the same over there." He waved towards a wide archway that connected their room with another. "Don't take long; I know the other sergeant, and she's not to be underestimated. The rest of you, secure the room."

Imogene pushed into the jungle of industrial-green food processing equipment, ducking under tangles of black power cables. She didn't waste time wondering why the guts of what looked like three different production lines had been crammed into this single chamber. Finding anything that might complicate their mission took priority.

She rounded a huge oven that towered over the room's far corner and confirmed there were only the two entrances. She was about to report as much, when Alexei broke the silence.

"Hey, there's a hole over here!"

"Trust a rabbit to find a hole," Lauren drawled from where she'd taken up position by the main door.

"What sort of hole?" Bruce trotted to where Alexei stood.

"I dunno." Alexei shrugged his armored shoulders. "It's a ladder shaft or something. Goes down maybe four metres into another room."

Imogene joined them and looked down at the rectangular opening near the door they'd entered though. The three of them stared into the darkness until Bruce looked up.

"Well, keep an eye on it until the Sergeant gets back. Then it can be his problem."

"We'd better check for more of them," Imogene said. "They'd be easy to miss."

"Yeah. You cover the archway, I'll take care of the hole patrol." Bruce waded into their field ration plant, pausing to check under every conveyor.

Imogene took up position beside the arch and frowned out at the adjoining chamber. The equipment on the other side of the arch was all metalworking tools: lathes, hydraulic presses, other things she couldn't identify. Several corridors entered the machine shop, and with so much heavy equipment to provide cover it would be hard to defend.

A flash of movement caught her eye. She swung her rifle up, tracking the target, then hesitated. Sergeant Hendricks' new red and yellow chest patch gleamed under her sights. Her shoulders eased, and she dropped her aim.

"Where's this hole I heard about?" he asked.

Imogene blinked twice before realizing the Sergeant had probably left his comm set to monitor the main channel even after switching his outgoing transmissions to a private one with Ryan.

"Over here." Alexei waved from where he stood above the opening.

The Sergeant bounded over to see for himself. "Choke points don't get much better than that." He turned on his headlamp to look down. "Keep watching. If anyone comes up, blow 'em away."

"Looks like that's the only one," Bruce said, his survey finished.

"Good enough." The Sergeant looked over to where Victor and Fiona had also returned. "Find anything useful?" he asked the big cat.

"No. The corridor here is the most defensible. It's a proper maze farther out."

"Right. Take Lauren and Imogene and cover it. Bruce, you've got the hole. Everyone else, with me. We're gonna set up out in that machine shop."

"Got it." Victor nodded sharply. "Want us to build a barricade?"

The Sergeant cast a glance around the chamber. "Only if there's loose stuff close. Tanya likes to move fast, and her bunch could get here any minute."

"All right." Victor waved Imogene away from the arch, and took up position with her at the kitchen's narrower entrance. Beside them, Bruce aimed his rifle down the hole, while across the doorway, Lauren crouched low.

Imogene watched the corridor, keeping her eyes and attention moving to stay focused. She had no intention of fouling up this chance to show her mettle.

A helmeted head popped into view, then jerked back.

"Contact!" she called out, tightening her grip on the rifle.

"Hold position," the Sergeant barked. "Make them come to you."

"I've got something too," Ryan broke in. "Center corridor. Ducked back out of sight."

Silence hung for a few tense heartbeats, and Imogene hunkered down to peer around the corner. Victor was tall enough to lean over her and poke his helmet—and rifle—out into the corridor. Opposite them, Lauren mirrored his pose.

Another movement caught Imogene's attention. This time she didn't wait to get a clear idea what she was shooting at. First she, then Victor and Lauren opened up with a hail of plastic pellets.

A long rectangular shape slid out across the passage, and Lauren broke off her fire. "Hey! What's going on?"

"Looks like an old desk," Victor said.

Imogene stole a better look. "But what are they doing with it?"

"*Mierda!* Get back!" Victor yelled as the muzzle of a heavy machine gun poked over the upended desk's middle.

Imogene jerked clear as the corridor filled with a spray of projectiles. It let up, and Victor swung out to return a quick burst. Over the comm, the Sergeant barked orders as his position was pressed hard as well. There was no help coming from that quarter.

She stuck her head out and yanked it back when another barrage of fire rattled past and into the equipment behind them.

"They're pushing it closer." She eased her crouch from one knee to the other.

"Great," Victor drew out the word. "I wish they let us have grenades in here." He stole another look, then shook his head. "We've gotta get around behind them. Fiona and I found another ladder shaft a few corridors over. Hopefully it connects with this one." He peeked out again to gauge the desk's approach. "Bruce, get over here and help Lauren slow them down. Imogene, you're with me."

Imogene blinked, certain she'd misheard. He wanted her rather than the more competent lynx?

"Wait, who did you say?" Lauren snapped around to face him, her tone echoing Imogene's confusion.

"You heard me. You and Bruce stay here. Imogene and I go kill them. Clear, Private?"

"Crystal." Lauren bit the word off like a piece of ice. Her gaze dropped from Victor to Imogene, and while the tinted visor hid her expression, anger radiated from the silver glass.

Imogene's heart fluttered. He was choosing her over Lauren. Granted, Lauren would have to cross the machine gun's field of fire to go with Victor, so there was some logic involved, but still! And he'd complimented her after the first match, hadn't he?

"Good. Come on." He pulled Imogene up behind him and moved to the hole Bruce had been guarding. Rifle slung over his shoulder, the big feline stepped out into the dark shaft and let himself fall.

Still flushed over what his choosing her implied, Imogene gave him a count of five to get clear, then stepped off after him. She landed lightly four metres below, knees and ankles bent. It was too dark to see, but a quick eye gesture to her suit's computer fixed that.

The blackness melted away into a gray/green image blending both light amplification and thermal infrared. Victor hadn't activated his suit's heat suppression, so she followed the white-hot glow of his backpack.

Skeletons of cable runways choked the passage, grabbing at her elbows and rifle strap. She twisted sideways and scooted deeper into the cramped and twisting labyrinth.

"Blast it!" Victor stopped and scanned rapidly left and right as their passage ended in a junction with two larger tunnels. "Wait, there it is." He turned left and jogged another dozen metres to stand in the pool of light cast from an opening above.

Coming up beside him, Imogene looked around. "Um, there isn't a ladder."

"I noticed." He turned and looked her up and down. "Climb on my shoulders and I'll boost you out. Then I can get high enough on the cable rack for you to grab me."

It wasn't pretty, and in full gravity wouldn't have been possible at all, but Imogene managed to hook her arms over the lip of the opening, and with a shove from Victor, scrambled clear. Then it was his turn. He scaled the cable runs until he could reach Imogene's outstretched hand.

Even at one-sixth gravity, her muscles strained to lift him into reach of the opening. Then he got his free hand on the lip, and all she had to do was hold firm as he pulled himself up and out of the hole.

He rose and unslung his rifle. "At least it was the right shaft. We'll be right on top of them."

Imogene followed him out the open doorway. He took several corners in rapid succession, then paused to glance cautiously around the next bend.

"Their corridor butts into this one," he said to Imogene before activating the squad's main channel. "Bruce, Lauren, we're in position. Give them a good burst while we move up, then leave it to us."

"Will do."

Victor rounded the corner and trotted to where a spray of pellets emerged from a doorway to strike the opposite wall. Imogene stayed close behind him, stopping when he did and waiting the tense seconds for their allies' covering fire to cease. Then Victor bolted across the doorway, firing as he moved to cover on the other side.

Before he reached it, Imogene slid up where he'd been and leaned out to shoot. She tracked her aim down over the three figures lying prone behind the desk. Taken by surprise, they didn't have a chance. She let her fire trail off a split second before Victor's also ceased.

"Got 'em," the big cat said in satisfaction. "Sarge, do you want us to hold here?"

"No. They're pushing into the machine shop. See if you can come around and flank them," the Sergeant's voice crackled over the comm.

"Right. Bruce, Lauren, over here."

At the other end of the corridor, a gray-suited figure stepped into view.

"Lauren's out of it," Bruce said. He climbed onto the desk and jumped easily over the fallen attackers.

Victor took point as they continued along the passage. He paused at the next doorway, which led into the machine shop. Once more he peeked cautiously around the corner.

"We're at the door behind the big red drill press," he reported. "Do we need to circle farther?"

"No," the Sergeant said. "They're in with the equipment now, and we've pulled back to the arch. Everyone in there is fair game."

"Okay, let's go." Victor waved Imogene and Bruce to follow him. They moved up into the cover of the drill press and stopped, Bruce watching ahead while Imogene and Victor turned to face the other directions.

"How many?" Victor asked.

"Three," the Sergeant said. "But I don't know where they are."

"We'll see if we can't flush them out. Stay sharp." Victor motioned Imogene to continue along the wall, while he and Bruce worked deeper into the machinery.

She crept forward, moving in spurts from cover to cover. Plastic pellets popped and rolled under her boots. Her eyes and aim scanned the way ahead. No sign of movement.

A confused burst of shouting from Bruce and Victor jerked her gaze towards the middle of the chamber. Her pulse spiked. She swept her rifle over the room, but couldn't see anything in the tangle of equipment. Should she rush in, or hold?

"That's two down," Victor said. "Still missing their sergeant."

"I saw someone moving near the middle," Bruce said. "Hold where you are, I'll try and move up on her flank."

"Got it. Imogene, status?"

Swallowing relief they were both okay, she glanced back the way she'd come. "About halfway along the wall. Haven't seen anyone."

"Good," Victor said. "Stay there, she might break your way. Bruce, talk to me."

The stag grunted. "Moving forward. I—" Bruce's comm icon disappeared. Dead, just like Lauren's and the other casualties.

"Damn it!" Victor growled. "Where is she? Imogene?"

Imogene risked a peek over her cover. "Don't know. You're closer."

"Wait, I see her." Victor surged from behind a giant lathe, paw-print emblazoned suit gleaming. He made it three steps before the enemy sergeant popped up from concealment and shot him in the chest.

Victor dropped to the floor.

The enemy sergeant ducked back, but too late to conceal her position.

Imogene sprinted forward. Teeth clenched, she dodged around a boxy plasma cutter and sprayed the aisle beyond with plastic pellets.

The enemy sergeant went down and stayed down.

"Exercise complete." The overseer's voice flooded Imogene's helmet. "Sergeant Hendricks' squad successful, with three members surviving. Kill tallies are..."

Imogene grinned as he listed out the kills. Not only had she bagged the sergeant, but she'd gotten credit for two of the three troopers behind the desk. And she'd survived. All that had to look good on her cull scores. Maybe even good enough to outshine her dismal performance in the first match.

As the overseer concluded, Sergeant Hendricks emerged from the archway's cover to offer his opposite number a hand up. "Not bad, Tanya, but it looks like I finally got the better of you. Even if it took defender's advantage and a new squad to do it."

The fallen sergeant let herself be helped upright before giving him a friendly punch. "You always were lucky," she said, looking around as the other casualties began rising. "Anyhow, we'd better clear out so they can let the next batch have their go."

Sergeant Hendricks nodded. He glanced around to be sure everyone was accounted for, then headed towards the exit. Imogene and the others fell into a double file and followed.

Watching the two sergeants in the lead, she decided they must be continuing their conversation on a private channel. Their helmets kept bobbing towards each other at odd intervals, and another round of unprovoked shoulder punching left little else she could think of.

The two squads parted ways after a time, returning to their respective ready rooms.

"Not bad in there," the Sergeant said, looking over his squad. "Keep it up, and you might even survive the cull."

Victor's hand fell on Imogene's shoulder. "We'll survive. Especially Imogene here. Three kills, that's almost half the squad all on your own."

Heat flashed from Victor's hand, flooding her chest and surging up into her face. She folded her ears to hide the flush. "Only because you set it up so I was in the right place at the right time."

"Right," the Sergeant said. "Not only did we win, but we did it as a unit, and I can tell you all are getting used to moving and fighting in the gravity. Like I said: keep it up and you might earn your moon-boots."

A silly grin tugged at Imogene's muzzle. She could do this. She *was* doing this.

Victor patted her shoulder again, then left her to strip off her training equipment.

Still smiling, Imogene hung her rifle on the rack, then glanced over to where Lauren stood unfastening her sensor-vest.

The lynx's lips were compressed into a tight line, and her whiskers lay slicked to her cheeks. She bared her teeth in a predatory snarl before Imogene could look away.

No one else seemed to notice Lauren's sour mood, and Imogene put it out of her mind. She laughed and joked with Victor and the others as they trooped back to the armory.

After a quick lunch came more unarmed combat practice. The first hour or so they spent with one of the instructors, once more going over the required techniques the squad had learned. Imogene had been working hard. She'd never have the natural grace of Victor or their instructor, but she was proud her skills had grown to the point she wasn't singled out for special remediation.

The more formal portion of the lesson concluded, and the instructor paired them off according to ability for some individual sparring. He named off pairs until only she and Lauren were left.

Imogene winced. They *were* close in skill, but the one time they'd been paired before, Lauren's enthusiasm—if not outright enjoyment—left Imogene feeling decidedly outmatched. But that was nearly a week ago, and she'd improved considerably. Now it was time to see if she'd improved enough.

On a blue mat in the far corner of the gym, Imogene and lynx faced off.

Imogene nodded to Lauren from her side of the mat. Lauren just grinned and began circling left. Imogene moved right, letting their distance close as Lauren's circle tightened.

Just before they came within grappling distance, Lauren flowed forward, right hand darting for Imogene's wrist. But Imogene was ready. She rebuffed Lauren, and both of them staggered backwards to circle once more.

The lynx's eyes narrowed, and her grin faltered.

Encouraged, Imogene waited until Lauren shifted her weight for another step, then made a move of her own. She darted in, dropping to one knee to grab Lauren's left leg just above the silver-fringed paw. She yanked, at the same time driving her shoulder forward into the feline's hip.

Lauren toppled backwards with an undignified yowl, and came to rest partially pinned under Imogene's upper body.

Pushing up to her hooves, Imogene offered a hand. Lauren ignored it, rising on her own to resume circling.

They were more evenly matched than Imogene had thought, and a number of indecisive scuffles followed, with hers still the only successful attack.

Lauren's smile was a thing of the past, her ears pinned back as she surged in once more. Frustrating Lauren's attempt to gain a hold, Imogene tried a clumsy counter-grab that also failed. As they separated, Lauren took an open handed swipe at Imogene's face.

She wasn't expecting that, and couldn't do anything more than let her head swing loosely under the slap. The blow came as more of a graze, but whether by accident or design Lauren's claws were out, and left a trail of parallel slashes across the tender flesh of Imogene's snout.

"Hey!" She dabbed her nose and came away with a smear of blood.

"You play with cats and you might get scratched." Lauren bared her formidable teeth in an ugly grin. "Maybe you should go back to the North Pole."

Imogene snorted, her brows lowering as she settled back into a ready stance. Her nose stung, but it wasn't more than a scratch. Let Lauren make her stupid jokes. Imogene was finally competing at the lynx's level, and she wouldn't allow trash talk or a little blood to upset her focus.

Lauren was angry, and angry people made mistakes. If Imogene stayed calm, she could show once and for all she was as good or better than the silver cat.

While not prohibited, striking attacks were discouraged in favor of grappling techniques that were more effective in armor. Since Lauren had started it, Imogene dusted off her memories from Basic. She wasn't particularly good with strikes, but maybe Lauren wouldn't be expecting an old-fashioned knuckle sandwich.

They closed again and grappled, this time salting their exchange with blows as well. Imogene twisted away from a grasping hand and managed to unload a punch into Lauren's lower ribcage. The lynx let out a grunt, but backpedaled when Imogene tried to follow up.

The increasing violence of their bout had drawn the instructor's attention, but before he could intervene, Imogene saw an opening and dove once more for Lauren's ankle. This time the lynx knew what was coming, and shifted her weight to bring a knee up solidly under Imogene's chin.

Something cracked as her jaw slammed shut, and an all-consuming pain was the last thing Imogene knew before falling backward into darkness.

11

PANDA PROBLEMS

"—the hell do you think you're doing?" The Sergeant's words floated into Imogene's mind. Foggily, she wondered what she'd done wrong this time. Her head hurt, and as she blinked her eyes to clear them, the bright light sent a stab of pain into her skull. The copper taste of blood filled her mouth, and when she coughed, something hard and sharp flew past her lips.

The blurry outline of a brown face blocked out the lights.

"Imogene?" Bruce's voice sounded almost as fuzzy as he looked.

She blinked, then managed to moan something close to a "Yeah". Moving her jaw set off another wave of pain, and the sound of blood rushing in her ears drowned everything.

Her vision cleared and she saw the Sergeant, fists on hips and tail thrashing. "Don't give me that 'accident' crap," he shouted at Lauren. "You've been spoiling for this. And you—" He rounded on Victor. "Don't think I haven't noticed you playing both sides. Make up your gods damned mind and settle things. One more problem, and all three of you go dirt-side so fast you'll burn up on reentry. You read me?"

Both Victor and Lauren straightened to attention, and gave sharp nods. "Yes, sir."

Imogene tried to nod too, but Bruce grabbed her head. "Hold still."

"How is she?" The Sergeant stared down at her, face impassive.

"Pupils look all right, but she spit out part of a tooth." Bruce didn't look away from her face. He had really nice eyes, Imogene thought fuzzily. Brown like his fur, but warmer and softer. "Did anyone call the infirmary?" he asked. "She needs to be checked over by someone better than me."

"Right." The Sergeant trotted away.

Victor approached and knelt beside her. He gave her hand a gentle squeeze. "Hang in there, *chiquita*."

She smiled, hoping she hadn't spit enough blood to look like a zombie. "Will do."

Pain pulsed through her head and jaw, but somehow being able to fix her gaze on the faint rosettes dotting his tawny gold cheeks made things seem better.

He stayed there, holding her hand between both of his until the medics slid her onto a stretcher and bore her towards the infirmary.

They couldn't fix her tooth. The thought throbbed in time with the pain in her jaw as she lounged in one of the infirmary's private rooms. Something about gravity and calcium chemistry and economics she'd been in too much pain to fully understand. They'd grow her a new one the next time she was dirt-side, but until then there was nothing to be done.

But Victor... He'd followed along until being turned away at the infirmary door. So had Bruce and Fiona, but the memory of Victor's warm hand and the concern glowing in his amber eyes pushed everything else into the background. Excitement fluttered in her chest every time she thought about what his actions meant. He could have stayed with Lauren in the gym, but he followed her instead. That was almost worth losing a tooth.

Almost.

She sighed and made a very conscious effort not to clench her jaw. At least it was a molar rather than an incisor. With Victor finally showing his interest, the last thing she wanted was to look like a gap-toothed six-year-old.

They'd kept her in the infirmary after extracting what was left of the tooth, which was probably just as well. Something in the drugs she'd been given sent her out like a light, then woke her up again in the small hours of the morning with no hope of getting back to sleep. At least here she could borrow a datapad and browse the grid without disturbing her barracks mates.

All the news focused on the war in Australia. It wasn't going well. No single story said as much, but it didn't take an intel officer to put the hopeful pieces together into a grim picture. Melbourne and Sydney were still in friendly hands, as was most of the interior, but how long the small Australian army and beleaguered UNA reinforcements could hold on was an open question. Not that the state-sponsored media would admit anything more than minor setbacks.

Disgusted, she canceled out of the news feeds to check her in-box. Nothing from her mother, but there was a message from Josh. She'd last heard from him right after the PAF started their offensive last week: safe, and steaming for San Diago.

She tapped the message, and his smiling face filled the screen.

"Hey Mom, and Imogene. Just wanted to let you know the convoy we're escorting is moving out. We're headed for Australia, but don't worry, the escort fleet is huge. No one's gonna mess with us, and even if they did there's a lot of more valuable ships to target than a punchy little destroyer. We might not even go all the way; some of the convoy is for New Zealand. I'll be fine."

The confidence in his tone warred with the unease in Imogene's belly. Why couldn't this all have waited six months? Then Josh would've been back in Helsinki and safe.

"They're running lots of extra damage control and evac drills, but I did get some shore leave in San Diago. A couple of the guys got plastered and went to see the LA Crater, and I sorta tagged along to make sure they didn't fall in."

Imogene snorted. Trust straight-laced Josh to end up the designated driver. He was grinning, though, and looked like he'd enjoyed himself.

"I'll keep you posted if anything changes," he said. "I love you both."

The message ended and a box popped up prompting her if she wanted to respond.

Her finger hovered over the reply button. This was the most free time and privacy she was likely to have. But there was no way she'd be able to hide she was in a hospital bed, or the slur from her missing tooth. Her mother was already upset about her joining Luna Corps. How much worse would it be if she found out Imogene had been injured?

She was searching for a positive way to spin the situation when someone stopped outside her room.

"Haartz?"

Imogene glanced up and nodded at the red vixen in the doorway. Her white smock rustled as she strode in. "Your scans came back okay; all your braincells where they belong. I'm gonna return you to active duty unless you've got any other problems?"

"Just an aching head and jaw."

The fox set a small vial on the bedside table. "Got some pills for that. One every six hours. Read the label, too." She glanced down at her datapad. "I see you're scheduled for an outside combat sim today. Try to avoid hard sucking. Ration tubes should be fine, but leave the last couple drops, eh? With things heating up, we need you soldiers out where you belong, not back here with complications."

Imogene rejoined her squad in time for breakfast, wincing every time her tongue brushed the empty socket where her tooth had been. She considered taking one of the fox's pills, but the vial listed light-headedness as a possible side effect. She needed to stay sharp for their exercise. With her scores skimming the red line, she couldn't miss any chance to improve them.

Besides, scrambled eggs were soft.

She'd only taken a small portion, but chewing on one side took forever. Everyone was waiting for her. Their expressions ranged from Fiona's open sympathy to veiled impatience from Alexei. At the far end of the table, Lauren toyed with her fork, occasionally glancing over at the others.

Finished with the eggs, Imogene downed the last swallow of stingingly acidic orange juice. That was good for another wince, but at least she was done.

On the way to drop off their trays, Sergeant Hendricks edged her off to one side. "I know the medics say you're fit for duty, but we'll be fine if you want to sit this one out."

And let her scores drop even lower? She straightened her shoulders and forced a smile. "I'm good. Just don't ask me to chew through a wall or anything."

The Dalmatian's lip quirked. "Right." He turned away and waved the rest of the squad to follow him towards the tactical block.

She wasn't really good. Her head throbbed, and the night's short, drugged sleep left her off-kilter. But she wasn't dying, and she'd be damned before missing out on today's exercise. Lauren wasn't going to stop her from showing Victor what she could do, or get her sent to the Rad Brigades.

They trooped down the kilometre-long corridor connecting the housing and tactical blocks, the click of claws and hooves echoing off the white-paneled walls. About halfway, a tech on a cart passed in the other direction, and their squad squeezed over to let him by.

As they spread back out, Lauren angled to come abreast of Imogene. The lynx stared at the paws of the people in front of them, and didn't look up as she spoke. "I'm sorry about your tooth. I didn't mean to do that."

Imogene's ears had flattened at the feline's approach, and were slow to twitch upwards again. "I can't say it'll grow back. I do appreciate your apology, though." She tried to keep her voice civil, but wasn't sure how well she did.

Lauren's yellow slitted eyes flicked up, and she gave a tight smile before drifting back in line.

From one of the tactical block's wide tunnels, a pair of double doors led into a mid-size briefing room. Thirty or so other soldiers milled about among the folding chairs, but only one stood out to Imogene.

"That's Jared over there, isn't it?" she half-asked Fiona.

"Yeah." The polar bear had turned her back to the room. "Don't look at him. Maybe he won't notice us."

But he was already striding towards them, the dark patches around his eyes giving him a skull-like visage. He stopped about a metre away and aimed his muzzle up at Fiona. "Just can't stay away from me, can you?"

She ignored him.

"Not even going to deny it? I knew you'd come around."

Fiona's jaw tightened, and she finally met the panda's gaze. "Get lost, Jared."

"Now that's more like it!" His black lips pulled back from his teeth. "I hear we're gonna be on different teams. Too bad, but don't think I'll take it easy on you just 'cause we're friends."

"We're not friends. And the day I need you to take it easy on me is the day after I'm dead."

A call from Jared's sergeant overrode the panda's reply. He glanced over his shoulder, then fixed Fiona with his dark eyes. "Just wait till we're outside. I'll shoot you full of plastic, then maybe let you see just how *easy* I can be." He ran a long, suggestive tongue over his muzzle before turning away.

After Jared left, Sergeant Hendricks came up beside them. "Panda problem?"

"Personal problem," Fiona said. "It's under control."

His pale blue eyes held her for a long moment. "Keep it that way. A level head doesn't get blown off." He turned to the rest of his squad. "Now everybody sit down."

They sat, and shortly a black and white border collie stepped up to the podium.

"Good morning, everyone." She leaned forward and swept her gaze over the assembled troops. "Today we're doing exercises in the hills a few klicks southwest of here. An abandoned base there will be defended by sergeants Angstrom and Campbell. Sergeants Hendricks and Martinez will attempt to capture the base's command center intact. The exact methods of attack and defense will be left to your discretion. The defenders will be equipped with simulated explosives, but let me stress that you are tasked to hold the base, not blow it up."

The collie frowned at a sergeant in the front row. "If the base is 'destroyed' you both lose, so consider it a last resort."

She looked across the audience. "As you should all have figured out yourselves, being outside makes this more dangerous. Don't jump off anything more than a few metres high, don't wander off alone, and most of all, do not engage in physical contact with the other team. You manage to puncture someone's armor, they'll be dead inside ninety seconds. And then *you'll* be dead ninety seconds after I find you. No fooling around."

After a pause to emphasize that, she activated the display screen on the wall behind her. "That's the big picture. Now, let's get down to the details..."

When the briefing concluded, their place at the back of the room made Imogene's squad the first out into the corridor.

But rather than leading them off to collect their equipment, Sergeant Hendricks lingered to one side. He waited while a double handful of people passed through the door, then stepped forward to accost one of the other sergeants.

"So, Tanya, looks like we're on the same side now." His whip-like tail wagged. "Just like old times, huh?"

The muscular hyena turned to face him, and her gray eyes twinkled amidst the mottled-brown fur of her face.

"Just like," she chuckled.

Sergeant Hendricks grinned and fell in beside her on the way to the armory.

Re-clad in their dull gray armor and bearing training weapons, the two squads arrived at the north garage. By far the largest chamber Imogene had yet seen, the titanic hall stretched away in both directions for hundreds of metres, while the walls rose at least four stories to a vaulted ceiling. Armored vehicles and mounds of crates littered the wide, lithcrete floor.

"All right, people," Sergeant Hendricks called over the distant rumble of idling vehicles. "We're supposed to give them half an hour's head start. Make yourselves comfortable." He waved towards a stack of metal crates beside the wall.

Sergeant Martinez nodded to her own troops and took a seat beside Sergeant Hendricks. Imogene climbed a little higher, settling behind the sergeants and next to Victor.

"Have you got any special plans, or do we just try and rush them?" Sergeant Martinez glanced over at Sergeant Hendricks.

He sighed, reaching up to scratch his nose through the open faceplate. "That base is a tricky one. Just the single entrance, and plenty of cover around it. Do you know the other sergeants? Are they likely to hole up inside or try for something fancy?"

"I don't know Campbell, but Angstrom's aggressive. Definitely not one to stay inside if he can help it."

"Hmm." Sergeant Hendricks gazed up at the arched ceiling. "Do you think we could lure him out? Away from the base?"

She nodded slowly. "Maybe. What's your plan?"

The Dalmatian took a moment to collect his thoughts before answering. "If we can get him chasing after four or five of us, the odds inside would be that much better."

"It's worth a try. But you'd need to make sure he thinks he's chasing all of us."

"So we send decoys from both squads and make sure they show off their chest patches. Better pick people who know how to move well, too. Make it look like there's more of them."

Imogene licked her lips. That probably counted her out of the decoy squad. Just as well. Decoys didn't have a high survival ratio.

Sergeant Martinez nodded faster as the plan took shape. "What about the main force? They'll have to be someplace out of sight, but close enough to move in fast."

"Yeah." He chewed his lower lip. "I don't know that valley very well. Is there enough cover for us to hide while they go by?"

The hyena shook her head. "There's plenty for fighting, but not to hide a whole squad. It's pretty narrow."

Higher up the stack of crates, Ryan cleared his throat. Everyone from both squads turned to look at him, and Imogene wondered what the ground squirrel sniper had in mind.

Looking suddenly nervous, Ryan spoke, "This is up in the mountains, past where we stopped the other day, right?"

Sergeant Hendricks nodded. "More or less. There's a little valley that comes in from the south. The abandoned base is in the foothills on the west side."

"So maybe we could send the decoys up the valley, like you said, but the rest come in over the ridge? The hills really didn't look too bad."

The Sergeant's quizzical look gave way to a thoughtful frown. "That just might work. I can't remember anyone ever hiking in over the mountain. They won't be expecting us to put in that much leg work on a training mission."

Sergeant Martinez tilted her head to the side. "That's gonna take a while, up and over whatever ridges and hills..."

A wicked smile spread over Sergeant Hendricks' muzzle. "Let 'em wait for us. Get bored, nervous." He rose to his paws. "Still, you're right. I'll see if I can't scare up some transport a little early." And with that, he was off, moving in graceful bounds between the parked surface crawlers.

He returned, followed by a boxy Paladin Infantry Fighting Vehicle. The squatty gray IFVs were as common up here as moon rocks, and carried a squad of infantry, along with three crew in a raised front cabin.

Sergeant Martinez joined him by the crawler and looked over their two squads. "I'll take the decoy party. Fast and light is my game."

"Right," Sergeant Hendricks said. "Take two more of yours, and I'll give you my two quickest. Ryan, Lauren, you're with her. The rest of you, mount up." He jerked a thumb towards the waiting crawler, then turned back to Sergeant Martinez. "We're gonna have a lot farther to go, so you can take your time. Give us till thirteen hundred hours, then go for it."

"I'll be there." She grinned, then made a quick pick for the rest of her team.

The remainder piled into the crawler with Imogene and her squadmates. It was a tight fit. Even with two of them up in the vacant gunner and navigator's seats, that left nine in a space barely large enough for eight.

Sergeant Hendricks climbed in last and pushed his way to the front of the cabin. He stuck his head up into the crew compartment to tell the driver exactly where to go, then hunkered down for the trip out.

The ride was short and smooth, until the increasingly rough last minute or so. With one final lurch, the vehicle came to a stop.

The thick lunar night greeted Imogene as she stepped out of the airlock. She engaged her suit's night vision and glanced around. They were parked in a steep ravine partway up a ridge, looking out and down over the floor of Santbech Crater.

Very down.

She shuddered and moved to join the others. The hillside wasn't unreasonable for walking, but she'd never have considered taking a vehicle up it.

Behind her, the Sergeant emerged from the crawler. "Straight up this ravine for now. And passive night vision only, unless we get into deep shadow."

The stars burned bright, and Earth's disc floated gracefully, casting enough light for the climbers' needs. They struggled perhaps half a kilometre upwards before the ravine brought them onto a subsidiary ridge. A loose rock shifted under Imogene's boot as she reached the crest, and she fell to hands and knees with a muffled yelp.

The Sergeant looked back, but didn't comment. Everyone from his squad had fallen at least once already. He and the people from Sergeant Martinez's unit fared better, but Imogene and her companions' scant two weeks of training hadn't prepared them for this.

Battling upright, Imogene trudged forward. The fall had jarred her head, setting her jaw throbbing again.

Even being careful to step in the boot prints of those ahead, her footing wasn't certain. The low gravity and lack of atmosphere played strange tricks with traction and balance. Luckily, the main spine of the mountains wasn't much farther, and she made it without falling again.

They'd aimed for a low notch in the otherwise craggy ridge line, and the Sergeant signaled a halt when they reached it. "We're making better time than I thought. Victor, come ahead with me. I want to see if we can get any closer without making targets of ourselves."

The big cat joined him, and they slipped over the summit and out of sight.

Imogene sagged to the ground with a sigh. Hopefully they'd get a chance to rest before assaulting the base.

The Sergeant was back within five minutes and waved everyone forwards. "Stay close to the outcrop here, and get down fast. Don't want to get sky-lined."

Mindful of his warning, Imogene pushed her weary legs to hurry through the exposed stretch. Reaching better cover, she paused and looked downslope.

The valley cut through the mountains, a few hundred metres wide and choked with rubble. Water had played no part in its formation, and the humpy, uneven floor looked wrong. Unnatural. The ghostly green light of her night vision made it hard to pick out details, but a thin ribbon of road snaked along the valley's western side. It came to an end about two klicks south of their position, where a large pile of rubble marked the entrance to an underground facility.

"Come on, no time for sightseeing," the Sergeant's deep voice filled her helmet.

With a guilty start, Imogene jerked her attention back to the task at hand.

The hillside grew shallower, and they made good time over the powdered dust. The Sergeant took them north, away from their target—and possible sentries—until they reached the cover of the valley floor. Then they worked south again through a field of massive boulders and countless small craters before stopping in the shadow of a house-size rock.

Victor, who'd been bringing up the rear, came into view and gave the Sergeant a nod.

Returning it, the Sergeant swept his reflective faceplate over his troops. "We're getting close. They're bound to have sentries out, so we'll hole up here and wait for Martinez to try her bit. Break out your rations if you want; we might have a busy afternoon."

Imogene settled down with her back to the boulder and pulled out a tube of EVA rations. The thick yellow fluid had an odd metallic flavor, but it was laced with stimulants as well as nutrients, and right now she needed both.

No one spoke as they made their liquid lunch, and the silence continued even after everyone finished.

They might be talking on private channels, Imogene supposed, but no one had the gumption to make a general comment until Alexei spoke up. "Why'd they abandon this base anyway? It's so close, you'd think someone would have a use for it."

"Radiation," one of Sergeant Martinez's troops answered. "It was a test station for some new kind of reactor that didn't work out. Now the whole place is too hot to handle."

"Oh."

How Alexei managed to cram so little enthusiasm into one syllable, Imogene didn't know. Not that she blamed him. Their suits were supposed to be shielded, but learning just how well didn't sound appealing.

"It's not much," Sergeant Hendricks cut in. "No worse than you get from the sunlight up here."

"True indeed," Martinez's trooper agreed. "But there's not much point in a base where you can't take off your suit, is there?"

Imogene chuckled along with the others at that, and settled back against the boulder.

Just then, Sergeant Martinez's voice came in over the comm. "Hendricks? Are you receiving? We're almost in position."

"Loud and clear." He hoisted himself upright. "We're about three-quarters of a klick north, and ready when you are. Let us know what's going on. We're out of visual."

"Okay," Sergeant Martinez said. "Moving up now."

12

TO THE VICTOR GO THE SPOILS

Imogene and the others stood in the shelter of their boulder, waiting for orders. Several minutes ticked slowly by before Sergeant Martinez spoke over the main channel.

"We've engaged and are pulling back. I think—yes, we've got most of Angstrom's squad and some of the others. Gimme a minute to pull them farther off."

"Got it." Sergeant Hendricks waved his unit forward.

In the middle of the pack, Imogene moved with all the skill she could summon, flitting from one shadow to the next. Anticipation of the coming action overrode weariness and the ache in her jaw, leaving her twitching to go.

The mound of excavated rubble loomed ahead, signaling they were close.

The Sergeant halted and peered around the dark gray rock that sheltered him. "I see two by the entrance, plus at least one just inside." He pulled back slowly and unslung his rifle. "Probably best to rush them. Once we're inside there's a stairwell on the left. Three floors. I want Victor, Imogene and Alexei on the bottom. Bruce, Fiona, you're with me on the main floor along with one of Martinez's squad. The rest of you, take the top. Clear the place room by room and make sure we're secure."

There were affirmatives from Victor and Martinez's corporal, who detailed one of his troopers to go with the Sergeant.

Sergeant Hendricks cast a quick look over his group. "How are we doing, Martinez?"

It took her a few moments to respond. "We've still got them. You better hurry."

"Right. Get set everybody." He turned to Victor, who had moved up beside him. "Take the one on the right. If you don't hit with the first volley, rush 'em anyway."

Victor nodded and leaned out from his side of the rock, waiting for the Sergeant's signal.

Crouched behind a boulder of her own, Imogene tensed, instinctively bracing for the crack of weapons fire that, in vacuum, never came. First the Sergeant, then Victor, jerked from the recoil of their rifles.

The Sergeant leapt forward. "Go! Go! Go!"

Imogene bounded after him into the cleared area outside the entrance. Two gray-suited figures lay unmoving in the dust, but more defenders opened fire from inside the tunnel.

First Alexei, then Martinez's Corporal and two of his troops fell, the gyros in their training backpacks sending them tumbling to the ground to simulate fatal hits. Victor and the Sergeant reached the entrance, and the remaining defenders collapsed under a storm of plastic pellets.

Imogene continued down the unlit tunnel with the rest of their assault force, and flipped on her headlamp when the Sergeant did. In close quarters against an enemy with night scopes and thermal camouflage of their own, clear vision outweighed stealth. They stormed through a vehicle-sized airlock, both its doors jammed open with metal girders, and into a small garage. Their headlamps reflected white where dead glow panels interrupted the dark lithcrete walls and ceiling.

The Sergeant pointed to the chamber's left side. "Stairwell. Move it, people! I want this place cleared ASAP."

Shadows from their headlamps danced crazily as the three teams split ways.

With Alexei shot, Victor's team was down to just him and Imogene. Her heart pounded from more than exertion as she glided down the stairs a pace behind him. She couldn't ask for a better chance to impress him.

At the bottom, a single corridor led deeper into the mountain. A few widely spaced doors pierced the thick, lithcrete walls.

No sign of hostiles.

When the stairwell door shut behind her, Imogene lost the already weak signal from Sergeant Hendricks' team. Like the lights and ventilation, the base's comm repeaters were long dead.

Victor muttered a curse she didn't catch, but waved her to follow.

At the first doorway, Victor jerked his head, and she bunched up behind him, both pressed against the wall beside the portal. He waited a scant moment to make sure she was ready, then rushed through the door.

Just as they'd practiced, Victor cleared the exposed doorway and dodged left. Right behind him, Imogene went right, making a U-turn around the doorjamb. She scanned her headlamp across the chamber, tracking her rifle with it.

A textbook hostile room entry, wasted on an empty chamber. A mass of cables hanging from the ceiling showed it might have been a computer lab at one point, but now the dingy room had been stripped to the bare walls.

They repeated their performance at the other doorways with similar results. One room held a number of built-in workbenches that warranted a brief search, but like the others, it proved unoccupied.

"Well, this is boring," Victor said after they cleared the last chamber.

Imogene glanced over at him. Moving in well-oiled concert with him had her feeling very proud and professional. It might be a little repetitive, but that was fine with her. "Yeah?" She chuckled. "I'll take boring over getting shot at any day."

"True." He clicked his tongue and headed back out to the corridor.

Continuing around a corner, two more doorways took off before the passage ended in a lithcrete wall. The left door led to an upwards stairwell, while the other opened into a large room with a double row of columns holding up its low ceiling.

It was deserted too, and they were about to leave when Victor pointed up at one of the support columns. "Say, what's that?"

A narrow black rod about twenty centimetres long clung to the column, just below the ceiling. Two short wires connected it with another rod on the column's other side, as well as a small gray box with an antenna.

Imogene let out a low whistle. "That would be a linear shaped charge with a remote detonator." She glanced at the other columns and chuckled. Several more were similarly equipped. "Looks like someone forgot to pick up their toys. We'll just have to return them, won't we?" She reached for the nearest rod.

"Wait!" Victor yelped. "You're sure they're safe?"

She pulled the self-adhesive bomb from its place and handed it to him. "Careful, but see the little red bits at the ends?"

He held the black stick like a poisonous snake. "Yeah?"

She let him squirm for a moment, knowing the faceplate would hide her grin. "Real ones don't have those."

"Tell me that first next time, huh?" He thrust it towards her.

She took the training mock-up with a chuckle, then started collecting the others. "Even real ones aren't bad, unless someone decides to set them off while you're unplugging them."

He gave an amused snort, then moved to assist. "In that case, I'll help you disable them. But just this once."

They stripped the room of explosives. Victor tossed her the last charge, then turned towards the door. "Upstairs and report." He was all business again.

As they entered the second stairwell, bits of garbled transmissions echoed through Imogene's helmet. Near the top, it resolved back into understandable speech.

"—are we supposed to do then?" Bruce asked.

"I don't know," Fiona growled.

New comm icons lit for both of them, along with a third showing they'd switched from the squad frequency to an open channel.

Victor increased his pace, and Imogene followed him out into the main level.

A dozen metres from the stairwell, Bruce and Fiona stood in the corridor, weapons raised.

At the end of the hall, a lone defender faced them from beside the command center's doorway. He was unarmed, but clenched something small in his outstretched right hand. Beside him a heavy machine gun and an assault rifle lay entangled with a second, fallen, defender.

Victor stopped beside Fiona and surveyed the situation. "What's going on?" he asked.

"They shot up the rest of our team, then ran out of ammunition." Her aim didn't waver as she answered.

"So why don't you shoot him?"

"Just try it," the gloating voice of Jared Chey broke in. "You shoot me, and I'll blow the whole place to bits."

Victor's helmet turned towards Fiona. "What's he talking about?"

Before she could answer, the panda continued. "See this here?" He gestured broadly with the device he held. "It's a dead man's switch. I rigged up the charges under the command center myself. My thumb leaves this button, they go off, and we both lose."

"I see," Victor said. "So we have something of a stalemate."

Jared laughed. "For you, maybe. But my squad is gonna be back any minute now, and then you're toast."

"That's a good point," Victor said. "But luckily, we have one too. Imogene, show our friend here what we found."

Grinning widely, she produced a handful of the shaped charges and waggled them back and forth. She'd have liked to see Jared's expression, but listening to his string of unoriginal profanity was almost as good.

The panda edged towards the command center's door, but a burst of pellets bounced off the wall beside him, and he froze.

Shifting his aim back onto the panda, Bruce glanced at Victor. "So now what do we do with him?"

"If this was for real, we'd keep him for intelligence—not that he has any—but I say we just let Fiona shoot him."

"Is that an order, sir?" Fiona asked.

Victor snorted. "Does it need to be?"

Without further comment, the polar bear fired, sending a burst of plastic pellets bouncing off her ex-corporal's armor.

His training backpack responded to the hits and threw him to the floor, spurring another wave of profanity.

Victor shook his head and turned away. "You'd think he could learn more than those three words."

The others turned their backs as well, and Fiona gave a derisive grunt. "Words never were his strong suit. Too bad he's not much good with actions either."

An inarticulate snarl burst over the comm, and Imogene looked on in shock as Jared took Fiona in a flying tackle. The force of his attack sent them sailing a half-dozen metres down the corridor. Jared came to rest on top, grappling wildly with his larger opponent.

Fiona uttered a wordless cry, then, "Shit! I'm losing pressure!"

Victor cursed and bounded after them. "Get him off of her!"

Right behind him, Imogene and Bruce raced forward. Heart in her throat, Imogene clenched her teeth, oblivious to the pain from her molar. Faceplates weren't *that* fragile! Had Fiona's combat locks failed, letting him open one of her suit seals?

Victor leapt at Jared, knocking him off and rolling them both farther along the corridor.

Unsure whether to help him, or try to aid Fiona, Imogene skidded to a stop beside the fallen polar bear. While Bruce scrabbled to unseal his med-kit, she stared down at the spiderweb of cracks fanning out over Fiona's supposedly bullet-proof silver faceplate.

"Is she okay?" Victor called.

Imogene tore her gaze away from Fiona to see him pinning Jared face down against the floor.

"I don't know." Bruce didn't look up from his kit. "Her faceplate's cracked."

"How the hell'd he manage that?"

"Defective glass? Who knows?" Bruce pulled a canister of emergency sealant from his pack and sprayed it at Fiona's helmet. The greenish liquid foamed violently for a split second before solidifying into a thick, lumpy coating.

"Talk to me, Fi," said Bruce. "How's your pressure?"

"That did it." Her voice shook. "It's stable at seventy percent."

"Good." Bruce layered on another coat for good measure. "Are you okay, otherwise?"

"I think so."

With a sigh of relief, Imogene glanced around. Behind them, Jared's teammate had risen and looked on uncertainly, while from the other direction Sergeant Hendricks bounded towards the altercation.

"What in blazes is going on here?" the Sergeant barked.

Relinquishing his hold on the now unresisting panda, Victor rose. "He jumped Fiona and was wrestling with her. I pulled him off and held him down."

Sergeant Hendricks turned to Fiona. "You okay, Fiona?"

"Yeah. I can't see through this green stuff, though."

"And what about him?" The Sergeant jerked his head at Jared.

"I'm all right," the panda said sullenly.

"For now, anyway." The Sergeant's growl echoed the anger rising in Imogene's chest. He gestured for Jared to get up, and looked around at the others. "Everyone else is good, I take it? Then we're done here. Victor, go find the upstairs team and meet us outside. The rest of you, come on."

Bruce pulled Fiona upright, and with Imogene's help, guided her along the passage. Imogene split her attention between that and keeping a wary eye on Jared as they headed back to the surface. She wasn't surprised to see the glare of headlamps coming down the entrance tunnel towards them. Jared's teammates had doubtless returned from their wild goose chase, and were coming now to recapture the base.

In the lead, Sergeant Hendricks waved to the oncoming lights. "We've had an incident inside, and I'm calling off the exercise."

Imogene braced herself, expecting anything from annoyance to outright hostility from the incoming troops. But that wasn't what they got.

"It's a bit late for that, Rob," Sergeant Martinez said. "You're all that's left of it."

Sergeant Hendricks stopped dead. "Tanya? What are you doing here?"

She stepped into the light from his headlamp. "I thought we might give you a hand, since we ran out of targets outside. Your kid Ryan here is a real natural." She nodded to the ground squirrel standing beside her.

MoonDust | 133

The Sergeant resumed walking. "You mean you took out a whole squad-and-a-half with just five of you?"

She laughed, falling into step beside him. "I'll admit, there was some luck involved." Then her tone turned serious. "What about your 'incident'? I'm assuming everyone's okay?"

"Yeah. Cracked faceplate." The cold anger in his voice made Imogene shiver.

Out on the surface, Sergeant Hendricks called in their situation, then waved everyone to make themselves comfortable while they waited for return transportation.

Other armored figures trickled in from the boulder field, and before long all thirty-two soldiers assembled around the tunnel's mouth. The members of the different squads formed into distinct clumps, and Imogene wasn't sorry at all to watch Jared lope to the far side of the clearing and sit with his squadmates.

Fiona heaved a sigh as they sat her down on a rock. "Well, that was fun. Maybe they'll finally kick him out this time."

Beside her, the Sergeant growled. "More than that, if I have anything to say about it. With his record, he's going straight to the Volga."

"What exactly happened?" Ryan asked.

Fiona sighed again. "Oh, he was the last one left inside and had run out of ammunition, so I shot him. Then he jumped on me..."

The stubby ground squirrel mulled this over before replying. "If he was the last inside, and we got all of them outside, that means we won, right?" He turned to the Sergeant.

Sergeant Hendricks shrugged. "They might call it a draw because of the fight. But yeah, I'd say so."

Imogene's spirits perked up, and Victor chuckled. "I hadn't thought of that," he said "We'll have to celebrate tonight!"

"Not only that," the Sergeant added when the agreement to Victor's suggestion died down. "I got your final cull results this morning."

Imogene's ears twitched against her helmet's padding, trying to lay flat. She'd been doing better, but what about the fight with Lauren? Did disciplinary problems figure into the scoring? Her jaw started throbbing and her middle twisted as the Sergeant continued.

"I didn't want to tell you before the exercise and let you get cocky," he said. "But you all passed. We get to stay a unit, and stay on Luna."

The tension drained from Imogene. She glanced around at her squadmates, then at Victor, and allowed herself a proud smile. Acceptable. She was acceptable.

Fiona's green smeared helmet bobbed. "Isn't that kinda fast? When I was new, we took a full month to pass."

"It is," the Sergeant said. "I haven't heard anything official, but I figure with things going sour dirt-side they want as many troops in the field as they can get, and aren't being picky. Which leads to the next item: Not only did you all pass, we're being activated. We ship out tomorrow."

Imogene blinked, then added her own voice to the confused tumble of overlapping cheers and questions.

"Hey, hey," the Sergeant waved them down. "One at a time. I'll tell you what I know, and then you can all speculate to your hearts' content. We've been assigned to the security detail at Pons missile base. That's about six hundred klicks west of here, in the highlands. There's a supply convoy leaving at oh-dark-thirty tomorrow, and we're part of the cargo, so don't celebrate too hard if you want to get any sleep."

Everyone digested this, then Lauren spoke up. "That's way behind the lines, so I'm guessing these would be planetary bombardment missiles?"

"Right," the Sergeant confirmed. "Pons is a PBM installation."

Fiona groaned. "That means it's a tin-can out in the middle of nowhere, doesn't it?"

"Probably." The Sergeant nodded. "Which brings us to one last point: if you need anything from the PX, you'd better get it tonight. I don't know what the setup at Pons is, but it's bound to be a lot worse than here."

Now it was Ryan's turn to groan. "A shopping spree, a celebration, *and* a good night's sleep? All in the next twelve hours?"

"Ten, actually." The Sergeant's tongue-lolling grin carried through into his voice. "I'm sure you'll manage to fit everything in somehow."

Out of her armor and back in their barracks, Imogene managed to snag one of the first showers. She hurried through a sketchy wash, intent on making enough time to send a quick message home without missing too much of the revelry that was sure to mark their last night at Santbech.

Her datapad wouldn't connect to the base computer, and she had to waste time finding a public terminal. Without bothering to check her in-boxes, she recorded a brief message for Josh about her new assignment. When she was done, she hesitated, then tagged on her mother's address as well. Shutting her out wouldn't solve anything, and while pretending nothing had happened wasn't likely to bring her mother around, it was all Imogene could think to try.

She hit send, then put her mother out of her thoughts. Tonight was her chance to solidify things with Victor, and maybe even mend fences a little with Lauren.

Where she'd come from was important, but so was where she was going.

Trotting smartly through the brick-walled passages of the recreation deck, she popped out into the courtyard almost on top of a group of her squadmates.

Victor led the group, padding hip-to-hip with Lauren. Ryan and Alexei trailed behind, but Imogene hardly registered their presence. Her eyes were locked on Lauren—and on the lynx's arm, encircling Victor's waist. He leaned into Lauren's hold, golden arm draped comfortably around her shoulders.

Deep in Imogene's stomach, something twisted. She blinked and fought to keep her ears from flattening. Her mind ran in tiny circles. He and Lauren—but he'd said—and now...

She couldn't think, only stare at the two felines.

Time crawled before Victor spoke. "Hey, Imogene." He tried to give her one of his toothy grins, but didn't quite manage it. "We were all just heading over to the dance club." He tilted his head towards the colorful and noisy establishment across the courtyard from their usual haunt.

Her head was spinning too much to form a coherent reply, so she didn't say anything, just kept staring up at him.

Pressed against his side, Lauren looked on with a self-satisfied smirk.

Victor cleared his throat and plowed onward. "Say, we left Bruce and Fiona back at the bar. Maybe you could go and convince them to join us?"

Dropping her gaze, Imogene nodded. "Right. Maybe."

He shifted uncomfortably, watching her for another moment before yielding to Lauren's pull.

Imogene's vision blurred as the they walked away, and the whole weight of the mountain above squeezed down on her chest.

She might have survived the cull, but apparently she was far from acceptable.

13

ROAD TRIP

Once again, Imogene had all her personal belongings in a duffel bag slung across her shoulder. But this time, she also wore ninety kilos of armor and toted an assault rifle. The rifle's power pack and magazines rested in her armored backpack, tucked between the emergency rations and freshly issued demolition supplies.

Her squadmates stood beside her. Some looked decidedly worse for wear, victims of a late night followed by an all-too-early awakening. Around them, the garage buzzed with activity as the convoy prepared for departure. Mountains of crates arrived, then waited to be loaded by hand and forklift into the thirty or so cargo vehicles.

Imogene glanced to her right, where Victor and Lauren stood together. She clenched her teeth, sending pain out from the gap where her molar should be. Slow, dull pain. She'd taken enough meds to ensure that. Yesterday she needed a clear head for their exercise. Today, a little fuzziness was good.

And not just for her jaw.

She looked away from Victor, out over the crowd of infantry and support people. A trio of large personnel carriers nibbled away at them, taking forever since the infantry needed to remove and store their armor before boarding.

Normally she found vehicles cute, but the bus-like, many-wheeled carriers did nothing for her. She made a hasty business of disarmoring when their turn came. Her demolitions pack went in a blast-safe red cubby, and the rest wherever it would fit.

She swung up into the airlock and continued past a refresher into the passenger cabin. She recognized Sergeant Martinez and her squad already seated, and gave a thin smile. She didn't want company, but somehow having slightly familiar people nearby felt good.

With the back row completely unoccupied, Imogene slid into the farthest right corner. There were plenty of seats, so she left her duffel on the one beside her to discourage potential seatmates. The prospect of making smalltalk was more than she could bear.

It was still night outside as they emerged onto the surface, and would remain so for another five days. The cabin lights dimmed, and pressing her face to the window, she could make out the general shape of the land.

The uneven terrain slid past at a brisk clip, and in the distance, starlight glinted off countless solar panels that covered the crater's wall.

The cabin grew quiet, most of the others catching up on their interrupted sleep. In the row ahead of her, sergeants Martinez and Hendricks' heads both nodded. The Dalmatian's floppy left ear had somehow turned itself inside out, and Imogene suppressed a chuckle.

Her amusement faded as her gaze fell on Victor and Lauren. The felines slept, leaning comfortably against each other's shoulders.

Imogene frowned and turned back to the darkness outside. She thought she'd at least been in the running, but now she wondered. Had he ever even considered her? His toothy smile floated in her mind's eye and grew impersonal. He smiled at everyone. Why had she thought she was something special?

The darkness outside held no answers, only an increasingly lofty view of the crater as they climbed. A huddle of prefabricated buildings guarded the narrow pass in the rim mountains, but the line of crawlers didn't slow. They trundled through the puddles of light cast from the guard station, then descended into the wide valley beyond.

More than an hour had passed since they left, and Imogene wasn't surprised to hear someone moving down the aisle, followed by the click of the refresher's door closing. It opened again after a few minutes, and someone slid her duffel aside and sat beside her.

"You don't mind if I sit here for a bit, do you?" Bruce asked quietly, his soft brown eyes seeking hers. "Everyone else is asleep, and Alexei was starting to snore."

Imogene glanced forward to where the rabbit lay sprawled into what had been Bruce's seat. She gave a rueful shake of her head. "At least he's not travel sick like on the shuttle."

Bruce grimaced. "That can't have been fun."

"No."

There was silence for a time before the stag spoke again. "I didn't see you around last night. Did you meet up with Victor's bunch?"

"Yeah." Her mind skittered away from the memory, and she forced a tight smile. "Decided to turn in early."

An emotion she couldn't place crept into his eyes. He held her gaze for a long moment before he flicked his ears and snorted. "Wish I'd been as smart. Now I'm dead tired, but if I sleep, that'll just screw my schedule up even worse."

Imogene sighed. "I guess sometimes you're better off accepting things, even if you feel like shit for a while."

He gave her another long look, then a small smile. "Still, it's not all bad. They get to sleep, and I get a lovely view."

His gaze shifted to the starlit landscape out her window, but had it stayed locked with hers just a moment longer than it should? Something tingled in Imogene's chest, but she shoved it away. Victor had looked at her and smiled too. And

Ryan, and Fiona, and that wolf from Sergeant Martinez's squad she'd never even spoken too. Just being friendly, all of them.

She turned back to the window, wishing her own problems were something a good night's sleep would cure.

A wave of thick air hit Imogene's nose when she stepped out of the carrier into a dimly lit garage. Ozone vied with the rancid odor of low temperature nano-lubricants, while from somewhere nearby came the tearing scream of a power grinder attacking some unfortunate piece of metal.

She rubbed sleep from her eyes, then glanced down at her chronometer and winced. Just after oh-two-hundred of the next day.

The rest of the squad piled out behind her, and Sergeant Hendricks barked for their attention.

"Welcome to the working man's side of Luna." He waved towards the garage's low, soot-smeared ceiling and the dozen crawlers packed in where six would be more comfortable. "Now you'll understand why anyone with any pull stays at the big bases."

"Tell me again how long we're stuck in this sardine can?" Alexei asked.

The Sergeant chuckled. "Not long. This is the Piccolomini N guard station. We're going somewhere even smaller." A huge yawn split his muzzle and he blinked. "Anyway, this is where we get off. Make sure you get your armor and weapons."

Imogene rummaged in the storage compartments, rubbing shoulders with Sergeant Martinez's troopers, who were also unloading. The hyena sergeant padded up beside Sergeant Hendricks and thumped him on the shoulder. "Have fun out there in the boonies, Rob."

He shook his head and grinned. "Don't get too smug. This place isn't much better."

"Maybe, maybe not. At least we'll get some traffic going by to liven things up."

"True. And you get to sleep in a real bed tonight."

"That's the spirit, make me feel guilty." The hyena yawned, then stuck out her hand. "It's been good to see you again, Rob. Take care."

He took her hand and shook it, his tail wagging slowly. "You too, Tanya."

She gave him one last smile before leading her squad off into the base.

"Right, people." The Sergeant turned and cast an eye over his subordinates' weapons and armor. "Double check it's really all yours and you didn't forget anything. I'll go see about our ride out to Pons."

He returned a few minutes later and jerked his muzzle towards a stack of crates being unloaded from one of the transports. "Haul your gear over there. The pick-up team's running late, so they're dumping everything headed for Pons in that pile. Including us."

Shifting their gear took several trips, and Imogene wondered if it wouldn't have been easier to just put the armor on, walk to where they wanted it, and take it off again. On the final trip, Victor angled into Imogene's line of travel, edging them off towards the far side of the pile.

Her chest tightened, but she kept her gaze on the armored leggings she was carrying.

"Imogene." He tried one of his toothy smiles, with a bit more success than he'd had the other night. "I just wanted to say I'm sorry if I gave you the wrong idea. You're a great person, and a fine soldier. But like needs to stay with like, you know?"

Imogene's lips tightened as he mouthed that old saw. Sure, she couldn't bear him children the way a feline like

Lauren could, but did that matter so much? He must think so, unless it was just an excuse to choose the lynx. She fought the urge to frown. If it was an excuse, would that make things better or worse? Either way, she was still inadequate.

When she didn't answer, Victor shifted uncomfortably. "I hope we can still be friends?"

She met his eyes and screwed her muzzle into a smile. "Yeah."

He'd never promised her anything; what right did she have to blame him? That's what her head reasoned, but her heart just wished he'd leave her alone to try and forget. A whiff of his warm sandstone scent reached her, and the knife in her guts twisted. Leave her alone, or wrap her in his arms and tell her he'd changed his mind. That he loved her, and Lauren could go hang herself.

She looked down again before he could see the moisture welling in her eyes. "You'd better get back," she whispered. "Don't want to give Lauren the wrong idea, too."

Victor hesitated, then padded around their pile of crates to join the rest of the squad.

Imogene dropped the armored leggings and let herself slide down beside them. She wrapped her arms around the hollow ache in her middle, closed her eyes, and tried her best to make the world go away.

Several hours passed before a growing clamor brought her back to full wakefulness. An older style four-wheeled freight hauler backed towards them, the strident beeping of its backup alarm rousing everyone and sending them scurrying out of the way. The truck stopped a metre from the stacked crates, power plant idling before the driver shut it down.

A hatch popped open at the front of the vehicle, and a tall brown wolf stepped out. He didn't bother with the short ladder, just floated to the stained lithcrete. Light gray fatigues hung loosely on his slender frame, and he bore a captain's rank tabs, along with the crossed yellow arrows of the Strategic Missile Corps.

Right behind him came a female jaguar in a quartermaster's green jumpsuit. Black markings liberally sprinkled her golden fur, and she moved with a sinuous grace.

Sergeant Hendricks stepped forward and sketched a salute. "Sergeant Robert Hendricks. You must be our ride?" He extended his hand.

The wolf shook it without bothering to return the salute. "Jack Schuld. I'm the XO out at Pons. This is Gwen Flores." He nodded to the jaguar who had come up beside him. "She's our quartermaster, and also a pretty decent cook."

She gave a wide smile at this, and shook the Sergeant's hand in turn.

Sergeant Hendricks took a step back and glanced around. "Well, it looks like the locals have made themselves scarce, so why don't we give you a hand with the loading, and then we can get under way?"

Jack snorted. "Assuming we can get the truck started again. That's why we're late." He cast the vehicle a dirty look before opening the double doors to the cargo compartment.

With the whole squad, it didn't take long to shift the pile of supplies. Some of the larger crates looked daunting, but in the light gravity they all proved manageable with two or three people.

"You might want to stack the last of this so you can sit on it," Gwen said when they were almost done. "There's only one free seat up front."

Imogene grimaced. There wasn't a connecting door between the cargo and crew compartments, and without an airlock, that meant they'd be stuck in the windowless space until they reached their destination.

"How far is it out to Pons?" she asked.

Gwen shrugged. "About five hours. Why?"

"I'm thinking of putting my armor back on. If we're going to be bouncing around with the cargo, I want some protection."

The jaguar nodded. "Probably a good idea. It gets a little rough in places."

The rest of the squad armored up too, including the Sergeant, who surprised them by passing up the front seat to ride in back with his squad. The rear door closed with an ominous thunk, then the truck lurched forward, carrying them out into the lunar night.

14

PONS

It was well past lunchtime when Jack called over the comm to announce they had finally arrived. They spent a few more minutes navigating through the base's access tunnel and airlock, then the truck ground to a halt and someone outside swung open the cargo compartment's doors.

Following the others out, Imogene paused to look around.

This chamber reminded her of the garage at Santbech, only in miniature. The vaulted ceiling rose a modest two stories, and the available floorspace was almost completely filled by the truck and two Paladin Infantry Fighting Vehicles. A handful of utility buggies nestled by their charging stations along one wall, while a wide doorway led into another chamber, choked with crates and pieces of disassembled machinery.

Standing by the tailgate, Gwen cleared her throat. "I'm afraid our logistics detail consists of me, plus anyone off-duty who doesn't manage to hide fast enough." She gave a wry smile. "The squads you're replacing are gonna be busy packing up, so if you could give me a hand unloading it would be great."

"Certainly." The Sergeant waved his troops to get started, and climbed back into the truck himself. He hefted a box of canned pears and handed it down to Gwen. "You said *squads* we're replacing? As in plural?"

"Yeah." She passed the crate on to Imogene. "They're getting shifted up to the front, along with one of the Paladins. At least that's what the colonel said."

"Huh. Should keep us busy if they want to run full patrols."

"I suppose so." Gwen took another box and frowned. "I'd only thought as far as having eleven fewer people to cook for."

He gave her a quick grin. "We'll manage. Infantry's always good at that."

Handing boxes along the line, Imogene wasn't so sure. If they were stripping seasoned troops from rear positions and replacing them with green recruits, there had to be a reason. And probably not one that would help her sleep at night.

They had most of the supplies unloaded when a wave of new people flooded into the garage. Most of them were armor-clad infantry, with a few drivers and techs mixed in.

The two sergeants pulled Sergeant Hendricks away for a few quick words, while their troops shuffled about noisily. Some of them started climbing into one Paladin, only to be called back out and directed to the other.

It was chaos, and after a very disjointed night's sleep, Imogene felt the strong urge to crawl behind their neatly stacked crates and wait for it all to go away.

In the confusion, Jack reappeared from wherever he had gotten to. After a quick look in the back of the truck, he yelled for attention and waved the rest of the departing infantry inside.

The sergeants concluded their conference and split up to rejoin their squads.

Jack swung the truck's cargo doors shut, then motioned Sergeant Hendricks' group to follow him. He led them from the garage into a white-walled corridor, then stopped beside the first pair of doorways.

"These are our armory and pressure suit storage," he said. "If you want, you can change out of your armor before I show you the base."

Sergeant Hendricks unsnapped his helmet. "Sounds good to me."

In the armory, Imogene shed her armor and hung it in a locker near the door. Two lockers down, Bruce did likewise, while on the room's other side Victor and Lauren laid claim to adjoining cubbies.

Imogene looked away and sighed. Some detached, logical part of her was starting to think they might make a good match. But that didn't mean she had to like it.

Gear safely stowed, they followed Jack to a cross corridor.

"Sleeping quarters." He nodded along the short side passages. "You infantry get the left branch pretty much to yourselves. Us missile minders are on the right."

Alexei pushed forward so he could see along the corridors and whistled. "Boy, they weren't kidding when they said this place was a tin-can! If this is all of the housing, anyways..."

The corner of Jack's muzzle quirked upwards. "Yep. In fact, if you stand right here where the corridors meet, you can see just about everything. Let me run you along the main corridor, then you can get settled in."

Following, they passed a communal refresher, a combined lounge/mess hall, and some utility areas. A security door blocked the corridor's far end, and Jack stopped in front of it.

"The command center's through here. Just a couple computer terminals, but it's why the rest of this exists." He waved to include the base and its surroundings. "Colonel Hasara's on shift inside, but I imagine you'll see her at dinner." He trailed off, then gave a swish with his tail. "Anyhow, that's about everything. I'll let you all get unpacked."

Back in the housing corridor, Fiona pushed open the first door and stepped inside. "Cozy little place, isn't it?" she asked, tossing her duffel onto one of the beds.

Imogene looked over Ryan's head into the small chamber. It was cozy, all right. Two double bunks, four lockers, and about two square metres of floorspace. She set her duffel on the other bunk. As the only two unattached females, it made sense for them to share a room.

Later, they chatted in the lounge with Jack and some of the other base personnel waiting for dinner. An arch connected the lounge and mess hall, and from the pleasant smells wafting through, Imogene guessed they didn't have much longer to wait.

Just then, an elegant-looking ring tailed lemur stepped in from the corridor. Patches of dark fur surrounded her large orange eyes, making them seem sunken into her mostly white face, while behind her a long black and white tail arched gracefully. She paused in the doorway, looking over the new faces before speaking. "Good to see you arrived intact. I'm Colonel Zella Hasara, commanding officer here."

Sergeant Hendricks rose, and they exchanged salutes before he moved forward to shake her hand. "Sergeant Robert Hendricks."

She nodded and smiled. "They sent me your file." Her smile widened as she turned it on the remaining newcomers. "But the rest of you I'll have to get to know the old fashioned way."

She and the Sergeant moved off to one side, and the interrupted conversations resumed.

Imogene hadn't been paying much attention to the group nearest her. Alexei had cornered two crewmen from the remaining Paladin, and was grilling them about some detail of the vehicle's drive system, while she and Ryan listened with increasing boredom. She finally gave up on the conversation entirely and leaned back against the wall to watch the gathered people.

Colonel Hasara had concluded her discussion with the Sergeant, and now worked her way through the new infantry. She moved smoothly from person to person, never seeming to intrude, picking up names and a few personal details, then gliding on to her next target.

The colonel made it through five of the eight new arrivals before a metallic clang drew everyone's attention.

Behind the counter that separated the mess from the kitchen, Gwen lowered the two pans she'd used as an impromptu dinner bell. "Everything's ready when you are." She gave them a wide, and toothy, grin.

With a few good-natured complaints, Jack and the other missile techs formed a line and filed past the serving counter.

In line a few places ahead of Imogene, Victor paused to sniff and look down curiously at the steaming pot of reddish-orange stew that was the main offering. "I'm not sure I've ever had this before. It certainly smells interesting." He looked up at Gwen inquiringly.

The jaguar smiled. "It's a fish curry. Or as close as you can get with the supplies up here."

Smiling back, Victor scooped out a good-size helping. "Curry, huh? It's supposed to be rather spicy, isn't it?"

Gwen rested her hands on the counter and leaned forward. "It can be, but this is pretty mild. The colonel has me keep things from getting too...heated." Her voice fell to a throaty purr and she flicked her whiskers at him. "Give it a try, and if you're still feeling adventuresome, come see me. I'll spice things up for you."

Next in line, Lauren snorted. She bumped her hip into Victor's, nudging him away from the jaguar and her bubbling stew.

Gwen watched them, and her shoulders slumped just a little. She took a breath then, and smiled, helping Lauren to a ladle-full of curry.

Besides the curry, there was steamed rice, wholewheat rolls, and a fruit salad that tasted almost as good as if it hadn't been made with canned and frozen ingredients. Imogene had never tried curry either, and found this "mild" version more than hot enough for her tastes. It irritated the still-healing gap where her tooth had been, but not enough to be more than an annoyance.

Some of the others moved into the lounge when they finished, but Imogene headed for her quarters. She felt less dejected now that they were settled in and moving forward, but tomorrow was going to come early. And if she knew anything about the Sergeant, it wasn't likely to be restful.

A vigorous pounding on the door signaled the start of a new day. Blinking in the dim light, Imogene slid down from her top bunk. Across the tiny sliver of floor, Fiona rose as well, and the two of them pulled on their fatigues and headed for the corridor.

Breakfast was already well under way when they reached the mess hall. Imogene made her selections from the array of baked goods, eggs, and cold cereals, then took a seat beside Fiona and opposite Bruce.

The stag nodded them a good morning, and sent Imogene one of his understated smiles. She smiled back before slathering jam over a muffin. Her misreading of Victor's intentions had left her questioning everything, but at least friends like Bruce and Fiona proved she wasn't a total waste of oxygen.

A little later, Ryan and Alexei trailed in and sat across the table from Imogene.

Alexei took a huge bite of muffin and looked around as he chewed. "Where's the Sergeant?"

"I'm not sure." Bruce set down his coffee and wrinkled his wide, black nose. "He was here earlier, but then he and Colonel Hasara went off somewhere."

Alexei flopped one ear. "Probably finding more crates for us to shift. I thought we were supposed to be security guards, not cargo haulers."

"I heard the sarge and Gwen talking about patrols yesterday," Imogene offered. "Maybe he and the colonel are working all that out."

"That'd be my guess," Bruce said. "Not much else we're good for, except standing at attention outside doorways or something."

Alexei shuddered. "That makes tromping around outside look good all right. Or even moving boxes."

Ryan glanced up from his cornflakes and poked the rabbit. "What's that, 'Lexei? You'd rather work than loaf against a wall somewhere? And I thought I knew you!"

Imogene and Bruce chuckled while Alexei just rolled his eyes.

Sergeant Hendricks arrived later, and stood in the doorway. "Good. You're all here, and finished eating." His gaze slid over Alexei, who hurriedly stuffed the last of a fourth muffin into his mouth. "As you've probably guessed, our job is mostly to be on hand in case anything goes wrong. We're also gonna be doing regular patrols around the silos so you cubs don't get too fat and lazy."

Ryan elbowed Alexei again and whispered, "See? No loafing allowed."

Ignoring the byplay, the Sergeant continued. "We'll work out a rotating schedule, but I want to take everyone around the perimeter this morning so you know the routine. Now, let's get suited up!" He turned with a sharp wag of his black and white tail, leaving his subordinates scrambling to clear their dishes and follow.

Lauren and a few of the others ducked into the refresher as they passed, catching up with the rest in the armory.

"Full kit and weapons, people." The Sergeant watched the late arrivals struggle into their armor. "Trouble only comes when you aren't ready for it."

Armored up, they tromped into the garage, then over to the line of parked surface buggies. The short-range vehicles had an open cockpit just large enough for two people, with a small cargo space behind, then a boxy housing around the flywheel power supply.

"We've got a lot of ground to cover," the Sergeant said, "so we'll be using these. Just like a car or go-cart back home, but take it easy till you get a feel for the gravity." He strode up to the nearest buggy and snapped his rifle into a clamp in the cargo area.

The rest of the squad moved to claim their own buggies, except Lauren.

"I've...gotta head back inside," the lynx said, her eyes darting uncomfortably. "I'll be right back."

"What for?" Ryan asked. "Do you need any help?"

Already edging towards the corridor, Lauren glowered. "That jaguar's cooking isn't sitting well, okay? It won't take a minute." With that, she bounded away, leaving her comrades looking after her.

A few seconds passed, then the Sergeant shrugged. "Better than in her suit." He turned back to his buggy and disconnected it from the charging station before climbing into the driver's seat.

Imogene headed for another of the buggies and followed his example. While she unplugged it, Bruce slipped into the passenger seat. She'd been expecting Fiona, but he wasn't a bad option. Better than Lauren, anyhow. She tucked the cord into its compartment, then looked down at him. "You're sure you don't want to drive?"

"Nope." The stag gave her a wink. "I trust you."

"That makes one of us." She flicked her ears, which didn't work out so well inside a helmet. She settled in beside him.

True to her word, Lauren returned before anyone could grow impatient, and climbed in beside Victor.

Night still shrouded the surface, and a dusty gray slope stretched to the limit of their headlamps. The small buggy skittered under Imogene's guidance, and she was glad the

Sergeant set a sedate pace. Going much faster over the deep ruts and loose dust would definitely leave Bruce wishing he'd driven.

A klick or so south, the ground dropped away to their right, and they followed the rim of a mid-size crater. A small, hand-lettered sign marked a suicidally steep trail leading to one of the missile silos, somewhere in the murky depths below. Eventually they came to a loop trail that encircled the whole installation, and followed it around. The patrol took all morning, and Imogene's stomach started growling long before they returned to the base.

The squad trooped into the mess hall, and Gwen looked up from tidying behind the counter. "Finally found your way back, I see." She tilted her head to one side. "I was just about to start putting things away."

Sergeant Hendricks picked up a tray and glanced over at the sparsely populated dining area. "We must be more than half your customers. Wouldn't do to lose all that business."

Her black-spotted muzzle split in a wide grin. "No, I suppose it wouldn't. Well then, help yourselves." She waved broadly to the waiting food, then leaned on the counter to watch them file past.

They shuffled forward, and Imogene looked hungrily at the platter of diagonally cut sandwiches.

Then Lauren reached the counter, and the line ground to a halt. "It's not more of that spicy crap, is it?" She stared down at the serving platter suspiciously.

Gwen arched one dark eyebrow. "It's a sandwich. Ham, cheese, bread. The worst thing on them is army-issue mayonnaise, which isn't spicy, but still might count as crap."

That got calls of agreement all around, and Alexei nearly dropped his tray laughing.

Lauren didn't look convinced, but reluctantly took a sandwich. She added a handful of corn chips, but avoided the steamed vegetables and potato salad.

Behind her, Victor had no such compunction. He took a hearty helping of everything, and gave Gwen an apologetic smile before padding off with Lauren.

Gwen rolled her eyes, then turned to help Imogene load up her tray.

It might have been hunger adding spice, but the sandwich tasted good to Imogene, the much maligned mayo included. The mayo was better than the processed ham, actually. She rolled a bite around in her mouth, separating the flavors. After two weeks eating whatever was served, she didn't really notice meat anymore. She'd have to be careful next time she was home; that carelessness would probably annoy her mother and Josh more than purposefully ordering steak.

Imogene sighed. It would have been nice to seek some maternal commiseration over Victor, but every day she and her mother stayed at odds, the less chance she saw of things improving. By the time they could see each other again in person, vegetarianism would be the least of her worries.

15

CALM

Armor Corps sergeant Mike Sommer had always dreamed of serving his country as a professional seat restraint tester. At least that's what Imogene suspected after five minutes riding behind him in the Paladin's crew compartment. There was a perfectly good road, but at the first opportunity, the stocky, russet-furred wolverine took off cross-country. The tank-like personnel carrier could take the abuse, but his passengers were another question.

Strapped into the navigator's seat, Imogene looked out the tiny slit windows at the desolate gray landscape. The sun had risen the day before and cast a raking, low-angle light over the craters and boulder fields.

Beside her, Alexei took the gunner's position, while between and in front of them, Mike sat in the sunken driver's seat.

Learning to drive Luna-style vehicles was supposed to be part of their initial training, but with the rush to leave Sant-bech, instructing them had been shuffled off onto the local Armor Corps contingent. Which at Pons, meant Mike.

A smoother area came into view, and Imogene wondered if he would detour to avoid it. He didn't, taking them out into the middle of the dusty plain before killing the engine.

"All right." He glanced back at Imogene. "Move on up behind me so you can see the controls better, and I'll give you the rundown."

There wasn't much space on the floor between her seat and Alexei's, but Imogene slid into it anyway. The driver's seat

156 | Ton Inktail

was sunk halfway into the floor, so kneeling behind let her look over Mike's shoulder and see everything.

He perked his round ears at her. "Do you play any of the 'Tank Commander' games?"

"Only once or twice."

"Excellent! You'll have some idea how things work, without being cocky. The basic controls are the same, but take it slow; there's no reset button out here." He went over the details then, along with a warning or three against common mistakes, before letting Imogene take his place.

Pressing the ignition button, she brought the crawler to life and gripped the T-shaped steering yoke. The controls were less responsive than the simulators she'd used, but still fairly simple. After twenty minutes crawling around the flats and over a few small craters, she was confident she could handle the vehicle alone.

She surrendered the hot seat to Alexei, and strapped in for what proved to be a bumpy ride.

If Mike's driving had been rough, Alexei's was horrible. Both of them took delight in hitting every available obstacle, but at least the wolverine had experience. Imogene's nails dug deeper and deeper into the seat cushion as Alexei raced from one end of the training field to the other, then spun into a tight corner before lurching forward again.

"Watch it!" Mike yelped. "Not so fast on the side hill. It'll roll."

"Right, sorry." Alexei slowed and cast a grin back at them. "I've always wanted to do this."

"I can tell." Mike's ears lay flat, but he managed a weak smile. "How about this: you slow down, and I'll let you drive us back to the garage. Deal?"

"Sure. The base is...left, right?"

"Right," Mike said. "Left."

Closing her eyes, Imogene shook her head. They really were two of a kind.

With their earlier tracks to follow, Alexei brought them home without mishap. The painstaking crawl through the narrow entry tunnel and airlock set Imogene's teeth on edge, but when he cut the engine, everything seemed to have gone off without a hitch.

They climbed down into the passenger compartment, then out onto the lithcrete.

The first indication everything wasn't right came with the smell of canned pears. Imogene's mouth watered. Hopefully it was something Gwen was cooking up rather than spilled coolant. But given the strength of the smell and the fact they were in the garage, the latter seemed more likely.

Then she noticed the puddle spreading from behind the Paladin. Mike saw it too, and stifled a curse. With an ugly look at Alexei, he hurried around to the vehicle's far side.

She and Alexei trotted after and arrived in time for the tail end of a sigh.

"You"—Mike jabbed a finger at the white rabbit—"are a lucky son of a gun."

Peering past him, Imogene saw her nose had been right. A case of preserved fruit lay crushed under the Paladin's treads. Alexei had come in just a hare's breadth too close to the pile of new supplies.

Alexei padded over and knelt beside the ruined cans. "Yeah?" He looked up at the others. "Now I just have to hope Gwen doesn't kill me instead."

Before Imogene could see what Gwen's wrath would amount to, Sergeant Hendricks entered the garage and pulled her aside. "We've got a call holding for you."

"A call?" Imogene's throat tightened. Real-time comm channels to Earth were reserved for official business. Or family emergencies.

The Sergeant nodded, muzzle set in a tight line. "Come on. You can take it in the colonel's office."

Colonel Hasara wasn't in her office near the end of the main corridor, but the Sergeant entered confidently and pointed Imogene to the computer terminal. He stepped back out and closed the door as Imogene slid into the lemur-scented chair. Without its owner's biometrics, the terminal wouldn't let her do anything important, but the communications program was already running.

Her mother's face filled the screen, red-rimmed eyes staring somewhere above the camera, jaw working in tiny nervous biting motions.

"Hi, Mom," Imogene said. "I'm here."

The three-second time lag between Earth and moon passed before her mother responded. The older caribou's face softened, ears folding back in relief.

"Imogene, I'm glad you're okay. Josh...Josh got hurt."

Forgetting the delay, Imogene blurted a question even as her mother continued. "They won't tell me what happened, just that he's in a hospital in New Zealand with burns and a broken leg."

Imogene frowned. The leg might be an accident, but burns? "Is he going to be okay?"

"I don't know. They said he's not in danger, but they won't let me talk to him." Her mother wiped away a fresh spate of tears, then folded her ears even tighter and looked right into the screen. "Imogene, honey, I'm sorry about before. I love you, and while I wish you'd found some other job, nothing will ever change that."

"I love you too." Tears of her own clouded Imogene's eyes and she blinked them away. "I shouldn't have let them ship me out so fast. They offered a later flight, but I didn't think it would matter. I should have stayed and worked things out with you first."

"It's okay, honey. I'm just glad you're happy. At least you sounded happy, in your letters."

"I am." She fought back thoughts of Victor. Now was definitely not the time. She pricked her ears up. "It's not quite how the posters make it look, but I'm doing good. This is what I want to do."

"That's good. I miss you."

"I'll be dirt-side again in about three months. Josh should be home by then too, and we can all go down to Kaivopuisto and watch the leaves change."

After the comm delay, her mother smiled. "I'll look forward to it."

"Me too." Imogene watched her mother, wishing she could lean forward and give her a hug. "Tell Josh to get better for me, when they let you call him. I love you both."

"I love you too, honey. Take care of yourself up there."

Imogene stared at the blank screen after the call ended. Tears welled up, and she dabbed at them, uncertain if they were from the thought of Josh in a hospital bed somewhere or the relief of clearing the air with her mother. She wanted nothing more right now than to hop on the next shuttle to be with them. But the only way that would happen was if she qualified for a sole survivor discharge, and she definitely didn't want that.

She scrubbed her eyes again, then got up and left the office.

The moment the door opened, the scent of spiced and simmering pears filled her nose. With the aroma came a flood of warm memories—pies her mother baked; the fancier but not as tasty ones they'd sometimes buy at the park; fighting with Josh over the last piece.

Gwen's voice floated out of the kitchen, scolding Alexei not to burn the filling or she'd stick him in the oven instead of the pies. Ryan snickered, and the Sergeant's low voice rumbled something she didn't catch.

Imogene paused, unable to keep her lips from quirking up at one corner. Three months was a long time away from her mother and brother. But at the rate things were going, she'd have a second family here before her tour was over.

🐾 🐾 🐾

With her arms full of dirty clothes, Imogene paused outside the lounge door. An irregular staccato tapping made her ears twitch, and she poked her head in through the door just in time for a small white ball to hit her on the nose. She jerked back with a reflexive yelp.

"Sorry about that." Jack stepped into her field of view with a guilty grin.

She freed one hand to rub her nose. "No harm done, I guess. What are you up to in there, anyway?" She stuck her head cautiously back inside.

The wolf's ears perked up, and he gestured to a folding table that occupied the center of the lounge. "Ping-pong. Someone pulled the table out of storage this morning."

Across the table, Gwen gave her a sheepish wave.

Imogene smiled, then turned back to Jack. "How does that work with the gravity and all?"

He raised one bushy eyebrow. "Don't tell me the folks at Santbech let you loose without learning lunar ping-pong?"

"I'm afraid so."

"That will never do." A serious expression fell over his features and he shook his head. "Take care of your laundry, then report back here so we can rectify their terrible over-sight."

Imogene forced her eyes wide and nodded. "I didn't realize it was so important. I'll hurry." She gave the wolf a wink and trotted off towards the laundry. They'd started another game before she returned, so she leaned against the doorway to watch.

Gwen seemed to be the better player, and before long, she sent the ball skimming over the net to strike Jack's court, then sail away past his frantic counter-swipe.

He caught his balance on the edge of the table and sighed.

The ball floated across the room, moving at an impossible angle and dropping only slightly before it disappeared behind a sofa in the far corner.

Gwen chuckled and set her racket down on the table. "Looks like you still need some practice, Captain. I think I'll take a break and let you two go at it for a bit." She flopped onto the lounge's other sofa and spread her arms along its back.

Jack cocked his head at Imogene. "Well, care to help me find the ball? We've only got the one left since the techs discovered they were just the right size for cleaning the waste reprocessor's tubes."

They reclaimed the ball and began batting it back and forth. As Imogene was coming to accept as normal, the ball fell towards the table quite slowly. But you could still hit it sideways at normal speeds, which made things tricky. Between that and the fact she'd never been very good to begin with, they spent more time hunting for the ball than actually playing.

It was during one of these pauses that Sergeant Hendricks stepped in from the corridor. "Where's the rest of the squad?"

The Dalmatian's expressionless face set off tiny warning bells in Imogene's brain. She straightened, fingers tightening on her racket. "Um, the last patrol are asleep. Alexei and Ryan were with the Paladin crew in the garage. I don't know where Lauren is."

From the sofa, Gwen snorted. "Did you check the refresher?"

Imogene flicked her ears at the jaguar's remark. Lauren's ongoing intestinal distress—along with her insistence that Gwen was not only the cause, but was somehow doing it on purpose—had made her a staple of the base's more crass humor. At first Imogene had been secretly pleased, but now she just felt sorry for her.

Jack chuckled, but the Sergeant's whiskers didn't so much as twitch. "Get Ryan and Alexei and get suited up, then meet me in the garage," he said. "One of our shuttles just got shot down on approach to Tycho. We're bumping up our patrols."

The bottom dropped out of Imogene's stomach. Tycho was only a few hundred klicks away, and unlike Australia, the moon offered little political ambiguity to hide behind. She'd seen incidents like this worked out before, but never when tensions were already so high.

"Shit," Jack said.

"Yeah." The Sergeant's blank expression darkened into a frown. "PAF are saying it was in their airspace, but that's a load of crap." He turned to Imogene. "Get moving. This is no drill."

🐾 🐾 🐾

Cold, and so very wet. The air heavy with the musk of sodden fur and concrete. Beams from hand-lights flashed and skittered across the water, while Josh and the other littles cried. Another rumble shook the shelter, and Mother's arm crushed her close. It was getting deeper, the water. Hooves, ankles, armpits—frozen and forgotten below the surface.

She wanted to leave. Wanted to find Father and go home, but they wouldn't let her.

The floor sank away, and she clung to Mother as the crowd surged forward. Angry words at the door, a scream. Colder then, freezing wind. Snow and fire and darkness. Smoke flowing like water. Turgid. Burning. The distant thunder sharp now, and close. Men shouting and running. Mother's hand, painful and tight, dragging. Less fire, more darkness. Still the cold and smoke.

Thick, oily smoke, fluid and drowning, filling her lungs and stealing her breath—

Imogene sat up gasping. Darkness filled their room, and for a moment she could have sworn the air held a trace of smoke. The scent faded before it could properly register, leaving her to pant at the flat, recycled atmosphere before rolling out of bed.

The refresher lights flickered on when she entered. She leaned on the nearest sink and stared into the basin. That particular nightmare hadn't troubled her for some time now. She'd forgotten the raw fear and confusion it left in its wake.

At least it hadn't been the other dream. No one should have to dig their father's corpse out of a fallen building, much less a terrified six-year-old. She couldn't remember his ruined face, just the blood-red medic's diamond on his helmet. That same age-worn symbol that should have protected him and the hospital where he'd died. But modern war respected no noncombatants.

Behind her, the door opened again, and the click of claws on tile made her look up.

"Are you okay?" Fiona asked quietly.

Imogene took a deep breath. "Yeah. A bad dream. Sorry I woke you."

"It's all right." The white bear rested a hand on Imogene's shoulder. "Do you want to talk about it?"

Did she even want to think about it? "Not really. I just need a minute to clear my head."

Fiona's round ears twitched, and she gave a small smile. "Okay. If you change your mind, you know where to find me." She patted Imogene's shoulder, then clicked her way back towards their quarters.

The new patrol schedule was hell, especially with their one squad doing the work of two. Still damp from the shower after a late evening patrol, all Imogene wanted was to eat something and fall into her bunk. Not that sleep provided much of an escape lately. Maybe Gwen had some sedative teas hidden away that would stop the dreams?

She barely made it into the mess hall before Alexei popped up beside her.

"Have you heard?" he demanded, his whiskers twitching.

Recoiling from his sudden appearance, Imogene flattened her ears and snorted. "Heard what?"

Alexei backed off, his nose and whiskers still aflutter. "They carpet bombed Sydney. All our guys inland are cut off now. The High Chancellor's about to make a live statement." He retreated back into the lounge, gaze darting to the wall-mounted display screen.

Imogene followed more slowly and came up behind the sofa where Bruce, Jack, and now Alexei sat. The screen showed only an empty podium with a backdrop of the UNA's red and blue circle crest. She looked down at Alexei.

"Any idea what's so important he's telling everyone in person?"

"I don't know." He glanced up at her. "It's got to be about Sydney, though. Right?"

Bruce rolled his eyes. "Right. High Chancellor Braxton is getting off his tail just to tell everyone what the news grids have been blaring for the last three hours?"

"So what do you think it is?" Alexei thrust out his chin.

"I'll admit, the timing with Sydney is suggestive, but it has to be bigger. I'm wondering if we're pulling out altogether. Now *that* would be worthy of a live address."

"Pulling out?" Alexei asked. "You think we'll just roll over and let the pandas win?"

Bruce shrugged, while beside him, Jack's muzzle bobbed in a nod.

"It makes sense," the wolf said. "We can't keep going with resupply through contested airspace, so unless we retake a port somewhere, the game's pretty much up. It's either going to be pulling out, or some sort of treaty settlement."

Imogene pursed her lips. It was the same shabby game that had played out across Scandinavia when she was little. Invade some technically neutral nation, grab as much territory as possible, then rewrite the treaties afterward to suit whoever won. If the locals were lucky they might even keep titular independence.

On the screen, a figure moved up to the podium, and Imogene's companions fell quiet.

A powerfully built tiger with just enough silver around his muzzle to look distinguished, High Chancellor Braxton had been head of the UNA's governing council for as long as Imogene could remember. Today, he'd passed up the dark suit he usually wore in favor of the general's khakis and beret he'd earned before entering politics.

"Greetings, my fellow citizens. As most of you already know, the military situation in Australia has deteriorated. I won't repeat the details, but suffice to say that despite our troops' gallant efforts, our position there is no longer viable." He paused, looking gravely into the camera.

Imogene's lip twisted. So they were pulling out, after all. Probably good for the civilians and soldiers in the short term—especially since a truce would make sure Josh got back to Helsinki—but giving up still rankled. Never mind the longer term implications.

The Chancellor raised his muzzle, and a steely resolve entered his voice. "However, we will not allow temporary setbacks to dictate our actions, or turn us from the course we know to be just."

Her ears twitched at this, and Bruce sat forward on the couch.

"Earlier today, the Commonwealth of Australia petitioned for admittance into the Unified Nations of America, and was accepted by a unanimous vote of the governing council. The mainland of Australia, and all its outlying possessions, are now sovereign UNA territory and will be defended as such. The Pan-Asian Federation has been given twenty-four hours to break off hostilities, and a further forty-eight to begin withdrawing troops. If by that time we are not satisfied of their full cooperation, we will consider them in violation of the Armistice of 2143 and proceed by any and all means necessary."

The tiger nodded, and some of the hardness left his features. "These are trying times, but rest assured that our cause is just, and in the end, we will prevail. Thank you, and good night."

The picture cut to an image of the UNA crest, and silence filled the lounge.

"Well, that was unexpected," Jack finally said.

"By any means necessary," Alexei repeated. "What does that mean, exactly?"

Bruce sagged back into the sofa. "Just what it says. The Armistice is the cornerstone of all the other territorial and arms control agreements. Antimatter weapons, orbital bombardment, the Heartland Immunity Treaty...he's threatening to put it all back on the menu."

16

THE FALL

The deep-throated blare of an alarm jolted Imogene from slumber. Instinctively, she slapped at her chronometer to silence it, but the howling continued, coming from a speaker above the door.

In the other bunk, Fiona mumbled and pushed her pillow down against her ears.

Imogene staggered over to her locker and threw on her fatigues. A base-wide alert meant one thing: trouble. She crouched to shake her sleeping roommate.

Fiona swatted at her with a massive, white-furred arm.

Imogene dodged and redoubled her efforts. "Come on, we've gotta get up."

The polar bear growled and rolled out of her bottom bunk. "Why?" Her voice was thick with sleep.

"I don't know." Imogene stepped around her towards the door. "Just get dressed."

The bright lights of the corridor stabbed her retinas. She blinked, trying to focus on the disheveled crowd filling the passage. Sergeant Hendricks' shirtless, black-spotted form pushed through the mass of furred bodies.

"Weapons and armor, people! Move!" He waved them towards the armory, then dashed for the command center.

Pulling off her recently donned clothing as she ran, Imogene's thoughts spun. The alarm had stopped. They'd keep it going if the base were under attack, wouldn't they? But to wake everyone up, something had to be very, very wrong.

Before anyone finished sealing their armor, Sergeant Hendricks appeared in the doorway. His face was grim. "All right, there's some serious shit going down. We're sitting okay here for now, but I want everybody armored and with weapons nearby at all times." He pushed his way through to his own locker. "I didn't get the details, but there's been some giant explosion in Asia, and now everyone's scrambling."

Victor glanced up from his armor. "What do you mean a giant explosion? We didn't bomb them, did we?"

"I hope not." The Sergeant's muzzle tightened. "Some of the missile crew might know more. They were awake when it happened."

Even with his late start, the Sergeant had his suit on before the last of his squad finished. Taking his rifle down from its rack, he checked the safety before slapping in a power pack and full magazine. "Weapons hot and ready, people, but for gods' sakes keep the safeties on. Imogene, Bruce, you've got guard duty in the command center—don't ask me what you're supposed to be guarding it against. The rest of you are with me; there're some old entrenchments outside we need to check out and fix up."

Imogene and Bruce met Colonel Hasara coming out of her office and followed her through the security door into the command center.

The door clicked shut behind Imogene, sealing them into the small and unimposing room. The only furnishings were four computer terminals, two set into the far wall and the other two freestanding.

Captain Jack Schuld and the red-furred squirrel lieutenant who was his usual shift-partner sat at the built-in terminals.

"Nothing new." The wolf glanced over his shoulder. "We're down to three comm sats, but the fiber line's still working."

Colonel Hasara dropped into one of the vacant swivel chairs. "Okay. Sing out if anything changes." Her long, ringed tail flicked nervously against the floor, then she looked up at Imogene and Bruce. "You can relax. Regs say you have to be here, but they don't say you can't be comfortable."

Imogene took up position beside the room's only doorway, her rifle propped against the wall by her knee.

Across from her, Bruce did the same. After a moment he cleared his throat. "What exactly is going on, if I may ask? The Sergeant said something about an explosion?"

The colonel sighed and rubbed the gray fur of her forehead. "I really wish we knew. Jack, tell them what you told me."

The wolf spun his chair to face them. "We were watching the news feeds, like we usually do. A little after midnight, they cut right out of the middle of an interview and started talking about some huge explosion in central Asia. It was all very confused. They got a satellite image up, with a big black cloud spreading out over China. Farther west it was still night, and the clouds were all lit up red and orange from inside..." His voice trailed off, a haunted look behind his brown eyes.

No one spoke, and after a pause he continued. "Then the civilian grid went dead, and we got put on Alert One. I'd already sent Lothar here to wake the colonel, and I guess you know the rest."

The impact of what he'd said took a moment to register. Then it did, and a shudder ran down Imogene's spine.

"Do we know what it was?" Bruce's voice sounded tight, his brow knitted with worry. "An accident? A preemptive strike?"

"Whatever it was, it was big," said Jack. "You could watch the black cloud spreading, pushing all the little white ones along before it... I just don't know."

A horrible thought crept into Imogene's mind. "What about Europe?"

Jack shrugged and shook his head.

"I'm sure we'll know more soon," the colonel said. "Command won't leave us hanging."

Imogene grimaced. Eurasia was a big place, and there was a long way between Helsinki and China. New Zealand was even farther. She could only hope they were both far enough to keep her family safe.

After a time, the energy granted by adrenaline began to fade, and the colonel sent Imogene in search of coffee. She found the mess hall deserted, but someone had the forethought to set the coffee maker into full production, which helped. Returning with a tray of steaming mugs, she set them down at the unoccupied computer terminal.

"I didn't know how you take it, so they're all black, I'm afraid." She took one herself and retreated to her corner again.

Colonel Hasara took a mug and smiled. "Black is fine."

The two at the console rose, and Jack stretched his lanky arms, scraping claws against the low ceiling before he lifted a mug to drink. A tone sounded from the console, and he jerked to face it with a curse.

"We just lost the last sat-link," he said. "All we have now is the secure fiber line to Santbech."

The colonel's ears flattened. "Are the sats jammed, or shot down?"

Jack typed rapidly at the console before replying. "I can't tell. We're getting increased radio noise, but it doesn't look like enough for jamming."

The screens flared and died, and all but the red emergency light went dark. Imogene's heart rate spiked and she grabbed her rifle.

"Damn it!" The colonel jumped out of her chair. "EMP? Power failure?"

The screens flickered back to life, and Jack's claws clicked over the keys. "High altitude EMP," he confirmed. "We're right under one of the launch paths for replacement comm sats.

Someone's gotta be shooting them down as fast as they can launch."

The colonel nodded. "What's our status?"

"Missile systems are okay, and some comms. The rest is a mess. Looks like we burned out a board somewhere in the main computer."

"Get the techs after it. We need to be one hundred percent, ASAP."

Another, more strident tone sounded, and a red light on the console began to flash. The three missile techs froze, eyes riveted on the blinking light.

"Oh no, gods, no," the colonel breathed.

Imogene's gaze darted from the light to the colonel and back again. "What? What is it?"

"It's a launch order." The colonel closed her eyes briefly before she snapped into action. "Jack, decode and confirm. Lothar, get the infantry back inside."

Imogene couldn't think. She just stood there, eyes wide and ears straining against her helmet to flatten. This couldn't be real. It was some terrible mistake, or a sick, sick joke. But one look at the colonel's grim expression showed she was deadly earnest.

The lemur paced behind her subordinates. "How are we doing with that message, Jack?"

The wolf shook his head. "It's—corrupt. The header and the first seven target-sets are there, but the last three and the confirmation codes are missing."

Her tail twitched. "Then get them to send it again."

"Right." He typed frantically for a few seconds, then looked up. "The line's dead. It's showing a break somewhere past the third repeater."

This time her tail did more than twitch. "And the sat-link is still down? Do we have any outside comms at all?"

Jack glanced down at the screen, then back up, shaking his head helplessly.

The colonel turned and paced over to the wall, then drove a fist against the white paneling. "Blast it! Enter the seven we have and pull the rest from standing orders."

Jack looked over at her in disbelief. "You're not seriously going make a launch based on some fragmented transmission?"

Her tail thrashed as she turned to face him. "I don't know. It came over the secure line; there's no way it could be a hack or computer error. Someone with clearance at Santbech keyed in each and every character. I have to assume it's a valid order, and I'll be damned if I let some cable-cutting PAF bastard keep me from carrying it out!"

The wolf's jaw tightened, but he spun back to the console to resume his rapid typing.

Colonel Hasara stood by the wall, visibly regaining her control, then moved up behind the other tech. "Are Sergeant Hendricks and his people inside?"

The squirrel looked up nervously. "Yes, sir. I've got them standing by in the garage."

She patted him on the shoulder. "Good, that's fine. Let's close the blast door then."

A long minute crawled by, then Jack stopped typing. "I've entered the coordinates, Colonel."

She stepped over to his side. "Bring up the targeting plot."

The screen changed, and the colonel let out a low whistle. Imogene shifted to get a better view. Dozens of red pinpricks covered Asia and eastern Africa. It hadn't seemed possible to feel more sick, but now her stomach knotted itself into a solid mass. If just a fraction of the colonel's warheads got through, they'd erase half the planet.

"A full spread. Figures." The colonel's lips twisted down at the corners. "All right, lock it in. Lothar, I'm gonna need your seat since we didn't get the codes for an automatic launch."

Jack turned to the colonel, a heavy look in his eyes, ears flat. "You're really going through with this?"

Her gaze didn't waver as it met his. "I am. And if you won't help, I'll get Captain Mercier in here, and she will."

"At least wait till we get the seismic monitors back online. We can wait, and only commit if we pick up other launches."

The colonel snorted. "And hope the next EMP doesn't take us out completely? Or that we don't miss the other launches while we're blind? I'm not willing to take that chance. Are you?"

Jack looked down at his hands, and Imogene was sure he was going to refuse. A tense handful of seconds passed, then he nodded. "I'll do it." He reached up and pulled a chain with a key on it from around his neck.

Beside him, Colonel Hasara produced a key as well.

Inserting them on opposite sides of the console, the two missile technicians entered a long string of characters into their terminals, then sat still while the biometric scanners re-confirmed their identities. A small green light above the console flicked on, and the colonel looked over at Jack.

"On my mark. Three, two, one, mark."

They turned their keys in unison, and the green light went out.

Nothing happened.

Imogene released the breath she hadn't realized she was holding and glanced around. Maybe the whole horrid mess was just a joke, after all?

She was about to ask if something had gone wrong when a gentle tremor shook the floor beneath her hooves. It built into a growling, shaking roar, then slowly died as the distant missiles escaped their launch tubes and clawed frantically upwards into the silent blackness of space.

17

EVAC

Half an hour later, everyone gathered in the mess hall. Those who had somehow managed to sleep through the alert and subsequent launch had been roused and filled in. Gwen even laid out an early breakfast, but no one had much appetite.

Once everyone was seated, Colonel Hasara stood to address them. "As I'm sure you're all aware, we received a launch order, and have carried it out successfully." This met with a glum silence, and she hurried on. "We've since lost communications with Command. Under those circumstances, our orders are to seal the base and withdraw to regional headquarters at Santbech, assuming contact cannot be reestablished en route."

She paused, her orange eyes sweeping across the twenty-some-odd people of her command. "I want us out of here ASAP, so everyone needs to get their effects in order. Jack, give the techs a hand shutting down the power and life-support. Gwen, see about loading some rations and other critical supplies. Everyone else, get packed, find a pressure suit, and assemble in the garage." She nodded sharply and left them to carry out her orders.

Emptying her locker, Imogene stuffed her fatigues into a duffel. She began to cram the smaller bag holding her other effects in on top, then hesitated. The small bag's zipper resisted briefly, but she yanked it open. Her gauntleted fingers slipped into the jumbled grooming supplies and other oddments, and came up with a pair of photos, laminated together in hard plastic.

The first was old, and she spared only a fleeting glance at her father, fishing with her five-year-old self. The photo on the other side was current, showing her and Josh with their mother beneath a maple tree. They were all smiling, and she bit her lip remembering the day it had been taken. It was just before she'd left for Basic, and her mother had skipped work so the three of them could spend the afternoon together.

Where were they now? Were they okay? With communications severed, there was no way to find out.

The tromp of armored boots thudded in the corridor, and Fiona's locker clanked shut.

War wouldn't wait.

Clenching her jaw to keep her emotions in check, Imogene tucked the photo away and slung her duffel over her shoulder. She took up her rifle and followed Fiona to the garage.

Gwen and a handful of others loaded boxes from a hand cart up into the truck. They seemed to have things under control, so Imogene moved to stand with her squadmates beside the Paladin.

After several minutes, Ryan shifted. "It just doesn't seem real, somehow," he said in a small voice.

No one spoke, then the Sergeant slowly shook his head. "No. No, it doesn't."

"W-what are we gonna do now?" Ryan stammered.

Alexei put an arm around the ground squirrel's armored shoulders. "Don't worry, everything will be okay."

Ryan looked up imploringly at the rabbit. "But how could it be? It can't have been just us that got the order. And the PAF must have launched too! How can anything ever be okay again?" His voice grew shrill by the last, and he sounded close to tears.

Before Alexei could answer, Lauren snarled. "You think we don't all know that? Get a grip for gods' sake!"

"Leave him alone!" Alexei turned on the lynx. "He's just scared, like the rest of us."

Lauren scoffed, and was about to reply when the Sergeant wheeled to face them. "Shut up! The lot of you." He glared back and forth between them. "Now is not the time for school-yard antics. We've got a job to do, and I expect you to do it with at least the semblance of professionalism. Is that under-stood?"

Lauren swallowed whatever she'd been about to say and gave a crisp nod. Alexei followed her example, then turned his attention back to Ryan.

Imogene kept her eyes fixed on the cracked lithcrete floor and shivered. Ryan was right. Nothing could be "okay" ever again.

Before her mood could darken further, Colonel Hasara and Jack stepped out of the corridor and into the garage. They each carried a duffel, and wore the same bone-white, one-size-fits-all emergency suits as the other non-combat personnel.

The colonel tossed her bag into the truck, then turned to survey the waiting troops. "Jack, call the roll."

The wolf pulled a datapad from beneath his arm and began reading off names. Reaching the end with no absences, he looked up and nodded.

With a flick of her tail as acknowledgment, the colonel raised her voice. "Everybody, mount up, and move out."

Jack stayed where he was, waiting while the white-suited support troops climbed into the truck's rear compartment. He sealed the door behind them and trotted quickly towards the cab.

Imogene's group loaded up too, letting Mike and his two subordinates climb in ahead of them. The infantry followed, settling in with more shifting around than usual. Most of their duffel bags fit under the seats, but between those that didn't and everyone's weapons, things were tight.

Imogene claimed her customary seat at the farthest end of the left bench and strapped in. Then came the familiar start and stop, start and stop as they passed out through the base's airlock for the last time.

The squad's mood had been dour to begin with, and the Sergeant's outburst made everyone think twice before breaking the heavy silence. With the less rugged truck dictating their route, the ride was smooth, and after a time Imogene began to nod in and out of a light doze.

She wasn't sure how much time had passed when the crawler came to an abrupt stop. Reaching up to rub the sleep from her eyes, her gauntlets clanked against the lip of her helmet and she thought better of it.

"Yeah," Mike's deep voice floated down from the crew cabin. "Looks like you're high-centered. The rim of that little crater's got you good."

"Great. Could you give us a push over it?" Jack asked.

"I'm not sure that's a good idea; that old truck doesn't have any skid plates, and we could mess up the drive train."

"Right." The wolf sounded annoyed he hadn't thought of that. "What do we do then?"

"The ground here's pretty loose, I'd say we dig it out from under you."

"That'll take a while, won't it?"

The wolverine snorted. "Better than shredding your undercarriage."

Jack was silent for a minute, then, "Okay. The colonel says get some of the infantry to do it. We don't want anyone poking holes in these flimsy emergency suits."

"Will do." Mike leaned to peer down into the main compartment. "Hendricks? You get that?"

Across from Imogene, Sergeant Hendricks nodded. "We'll take care of it."

"Shovel is in the outside utility locker. There should be one on the truck, too," Mike offered before settling back into his seat.

The Sergeant glanced around the compartment. "Right, everybody out. We'll see how many shovels there are, and the rest of you can stretch your legs."

Imogene's seat at the front of the crawler left her with the last group to cycle through the airlock. Gray hills loomed to either side of their small valley, while ahead, higher outcrops rose to what might warrant the label of mountains. Countless craters pocked the nearer hills and valley floor, ranging in size from tiny divots up to a few truck-eating monsters.

Several dozen metres ahead, the truck rested nose-down in a crater. One rear wheel was lifted clear off the ground, and the other sunk hub-deep in the fine gray dust. Bruce and Victor had found a pair of short-handled shovels, and set to work undermining the high-centered vehicle.

Sergeant Hendricks had exited with Imogene and bounded over to them. "Careful it doesn't come down on top of you," he said, kneeling down to peer under the truck.

Victor kept working, his answer punctuated with grunts. "Don't worry, it's just stuck on one high spot. There's good clearance everywhere else."

The Sergeant gave Victor a nod he probably couldn't see, then settled back to watch.

The rest of the squad stood off to one side, and Imogene moved up to join them.

As boring as the inside of the Paladin had been, watching two sets of legs sticking out from under a truck was hardly an improvement. She shifted restlessly, then looked upwards, but couldn't find Earth. Only a slender crescent should be visible at this point in its cycle. Maybe that coupled with the unfamiliar surroundings had confused her?

But finally spotting it, she saw the normally blue and white arc had turned an ugly gray-black, blending with the darkness beyond. She raised one hand to shield the sun's glare, and her mouth twisted into a grim line. It was hard to make out, but a scattering of faint, reddish glows marched across the planet's night side.

With a violent shake of her head, she forced her eyes down to the powdered dust between her boots. They didn't know for sure what was happening on Earth. Couldn't know. And dwelling on that helplessness would only make it worse.

In the crater, Bruce and Victor made steady progress. All four wheels were on the ground now, and the stag crawled out to begin clearing the wheels that had spun themselves into the dust.

Something flickered across the sky.

Before Imogene could look up, there was another flash and the truck jerked under a heavy impact. A spray of dust shot out from beneath the vehicle and spread in a strangely perfect arc without air to make it billow. Shrapnel and small rocks pinged off Imogene's armor a moment before the dust reached her.

By reflex, she threw herself flat. Much too late to avoid the blast of dust and gravel, her dive brought her into the cover of the crater's rim. Confused shouts flooded the comm, voices yelling, demanding to know what was going on.

Imogene cursed, clutching her rifle, but unsure where to aim. Her heart pounded as she scrambled over the rim and into the crater proper. She looked up, scanning the hills for any sign of their attackers.

The squad scattered, and the Paladin lurched into reverse, Mike taking it backside-first into one of the larger craters.

Imogene's guts twisted as the seconds crawled by, but nothing more happened.

The Sergeant shouted down the other comm chatter. "Does anyone see anything? Mike, anything on the scopes?"

All his replies came back negative, and Mike ventured a further guess. "Meteoroid?"

Beside the truck's front wheels, the Sergeant nodded. "Probably. If anyone was out there, why stop with one shot?"

The quavering voice of a missile tech broke in. "If we're safe, we could use some help back here. Captain Mercier's suit is leaking, and Gwen—Gwen's gone."

A spike of ice stabbed Imogene's chest. Just like that, Gwen was dead?

"Gods blast it!" the Sergeant snarled. He scrambled upright and bounded towards the back of the truck. "Is everyone else okay?"

This time the only negative was Victor. "I'm all right, but I can't move. The truck's got me pinned."

"Okay, someone get him dug out." The Sergeant reached the truck's rear door, but paused with his hand on the latch. "Is there any atmosphere still in the truck?"

The same tech answered. "No. There's...nothing."

Bruce joined the Sergeant, and together they pried the double doors open and climbed inside.

Imogene and the others rose shakily to their paws and hooves. Down in the crater, Lauren and Fiona kicked up a fountain of dust as they worked to free Victor.

Nearer to the cargo compartment, Imogene moved towards the open door to see if she could help. She looked inside—and instantly regretted it.

An ugly gash ripped through the truck's left wall, and a twisted, fist-size hole marked where the meteoroid had exited through the floor. But that wasn't what made her turn away and begin to retch. Her glimpse may have been fleeting, but it was more than enough to show Gwen had been sitting *directly* in the object's path.

Head down and leaning with her hands propped against the side of the truck, Imogene coughed and sputtered. She tried to use the suit's sick-tube, but nothing came up, only more bile-laced saliva like the spatters already smearing her faceplate. She was still breathing heavily when the shadow of someone approaching made her look up.

Bruce stood there. The silver faceplate hid his expression, and he spoke no words, just nodded once and laid a comforting hand on her shoulder.

She gave a weak smile, then remembered he couldn't see it. Not trusting her voice, she reached up and clasped his gauntlet instead.

18

HARD RAIN

Once more inside the Paladin and following the damaged truck south, Bruce turned to the Sergeant. "Do meteoroid strikes like that happen often?"

The Dalmatian shook his head. "Not normally. But if there's heavy fighting, we can expect a lot more. Between the low gravity and no air to slow it down, shrapnel here can go thousands of klicks or even get into orbit."

Still feeling queasy, Imogene looked up from cleaning her faceplate. "You mean if someone blows up a tank on the other side of the moon, the turret might land on us?"

"Probably not the whole turret. Bigger things take more energy to get moving. But shell fragments, or even gravel thrown up by explosions, yeah. The last big fracas was a little before my time, but I've heard some ugly things."

Ugly things indeed. Imogene's mouth went dry as she imagined fighting on a battlefield where every near miss sent dozens of smaller projectiles zipping off in random directions.

"So what happens if more start falling?" she asked. "Just hope we don't get hit?"

"That's about the size of it." The Sergeant's lips compressed to a tight line. "But remember, the Paladin has better armor than the truck. If something that size hits us, it might knock us around a little, but we'll be okay."

Imogene nodded grimly and turned back to her helmet. She didn't have any proper cleaning supplies, but did the best she could with more spit and a corner of her spare fatigues.

It took another two hours to work their way south through the hills. Something was wrong with the truck's rear steering, making the vehicle hard to manage. The front steering still worked, and the colonel decided to press on rather than attempt repairs.

Occasionally, Imogene heard the unmusical clank of small objects striking the Paladin, and she shivered to think how their unarmored companions might be faring.

Without satellite comms, they had to enter visual range of the Piccolomini N guard station to open communications. After explaining their situation, the colonel obtained permission for them to enter the base's garage and investigate the truck's steering problem.

Imogene had never felt quite so glad to have a few dozen metres of solid rock hanging over her head. The garage still stank, but now an eerily quiet replaced the bustle of two weeks ago. Only a lone supply truck remained of the many vehicles she remembered, leaving the space echoingly empty.

A pair of armored infantry moved to meet them. As they drew closer, the blue and purple unit patches of Sergeant Tanya Martinez's squad came into view.

The colonel and Sergeant Hendricks stepped forward.

Sergeant Martinez nodded politely to them both. "Colonel, the CO would like a word with you in the command center, if it's not inconvenient."

Colonel Hasara looked back to where Gwen's remains were being carefully unloaded. The Paladin crew and a maintenance tech from the truck poked around and under the damaged vehicle.

Turning back, she nodded. "Very well. I'm not familiar with the layout here."

Sergeant Martinez waved her trooper forward. "Dez, take the colonel down to the command center."

The two of them headed off, and the remaining troops relaxed. Imogene hovered near the sergeants, hoping

Martinez had some news from Earth. The guard station was on a main route between Zagut and Santbech. They had to know more than an isolated missile crew.

"Glad to see you're okay, Rob." Sergeant Martinez clapped him on the shoulder.

Sergeant Hendricks gave her a tight smile. "You too, Tanya." His smile faded. "How are things holding up here?"

"Not good," she said bluntly. "Satellites and relay towers are all dead, and we lost the land lines about an hour ago. They had us out doing patrols before the meteoroids picked up. Now we're just hunkering down until we get further orders from Command."

Sergeant Hendricks cursed. "I was hoping the lines here would still be working. Was there any news about Earth?"

The hyena shook her head. "Not after the first half-hour. Traffic through here has picked up, though. There was an armor column from Zagut bigger than you would believe. We had to shut down the pass while they went through, and they had orders to take all our IFVs and all but two squads of infantry."

"I wondered why it was so quiet." Sergeant Hendricks glanced around the empty garage. "If they're stripping the guard stations, it must be bad."

The corners of her lips twisted down. "Rumor is the PAF are pushing south into Mare Nectaris. The Zagut column were headed north to shore things up."

Imogene frowned. They'd crossed the dark plains of Mare Nectaris three weeks ago on the trip out to Pons. Had their road to Santbech turned into a combat zone?

One of the techs who'd been working on the truck approached. "Excuse me, but where's the tool-crib? We're gonna need some hydraulic line and splicing tools."

Sergeant Martinez gave him directions, but before he could leave, Sergeant Hendricks caught his eyes. "What sort of time frame are we looking at?"

The tech shrugged. "An hour, maybe."

"Good enough." He let the tech go and turned to Sergeant Martinez. "Mind if I run my people through your mess hall?"

"Heh. Cook's been making sandwiches like he thinks he's gonna win the war all by himself. If you can put a dent in 'em, you'd be doing us a favor."

The steering was indeed repaired in the promised sixty minutes, but then the aging truck's power plant refused to start. With no one qualified for the needed repairs, the delay stretched from hours into days as they probed deeper into the vehicle's mechanical heart.

A few other units crossed through the pass, including several message couriers and an emergency comm repair crew. From their cussing, Imogene gathered the meteoroids were shredding the fiber lines faster than they could repair them.

She didn't want to think about that. What would a meteoroid which could damage an armored conduit under a metre of moon dust do if it hit a person? One fox on the repair crew swore the damage had to be sabotage, but to Imogene, that was an equally grim, if less terrifyingly random, prospect.

All the couriers were bound for the large bases farther east or west, and the only orders they had for the guard station were a generic "hold position", and for Imogene's unit, nothing at all.

After close to three days, the truck reluctantly shuddered into life. Imogene wished it had stayed broken. The quarters they'd borrowed here were spartan, but they were safe. Outside, rocks and bits of metal continued to rain from the cloudless, ink-black sky—sometimes more, sometimes less, but never stopping.

Colonel Hasara made them shut the truck down and restart it a dozen times before deciding it was reliable enough to resume their transit east to Santbech.

Imogene almost suggested waiting at the guard station. With all the courier traffic they could request new orders without risking the trip to Santbech, and in the meantime they'd be shoring up the ruinously shorthanded guard detail on an important pass.

But orders were orders, and Luna Corps wasn't a democracy, so she bit her tongue and climbed into the Paladin beside her squadmates.

The pass at Piccolomini N wasn't a normal mountain pass, but rather a low spot in the long line of cliffs encircling the Nectaris Impact Basin—a crater so large no one was quite willing to call it one. From the guard station at the top, they could look out over the rugged hills below, and just glimpse the ancient lava plain, or mare, at the basin's heart. The much smaller crater of Santbech lay near the basin's other side, far out of sight and more than five hundred kilometres away.

Even with the gentler slope of the pass, the road had been blasted into the mountain side, and descended in a precarious series of hairpin corners. From the bottom, the track took off northeast, headed for the plains of Mare Nectaris.

They'd been traveling a good six hours, about a third of the way, according to Mike, when they met a large convoy limping towards the pass. A pair of lumbering mobile-hospital crawlers led the way, and behind them trailed a motley string of vehicles. Tanks, personnel carriers, other things mauled beyond identification, all bearing the scars of combat, but all still crawling doggedly forward.

Imogene's group pulled over to let them pass, and the colonel hailed them. "Hello, the convoy. This is Colonel Hasara, lately of Pons PBM base. Might I ask where you're headed?"

The voice that answered her was deep and gravelly. "Captain Collins out of Zagut. The medics are evacing back there, and we broken toys are tagging along."

"I see," said the colonel. "We're heading for Santbech. Can you tell me anything about the road ahead?"

"It's ugly. There's fighting out on the mare."

"This far south?" she asked sharply.

"Yeah." The captain sounded discouraged. "They broke through the line at Mädler two days ago. If you're for Sant-bech, I'd strongly recommend cutting south around Fracastorius."

Mike broke in. "That's some rough country, especially for the truck."

"It is. But things weren't looking good when we left, so I'd say it's your best bet."

Colonel Hasara took over the conversation again. "All right. Thank you for the information."

"Not a problem. Best of luck to us both!" the captain signed off.

The convoy moved past, but the colonel's truck stayed where it was. After a pause, her voice came across the comm once more. "Mike, how bad is the track south? Can the truck make it?"

He sighed heavily. "Well, I've only been over it in a crawler, and it sure wasn't built with wheels in mind. But if you're careful, and take it slow...maybe."

There was another, longer, pause. "It's probably the better part of valor. We'll give it a try."

Despite Mike's trepidation, the first hour or so was no worse than what had gone before. Then they came to the end of the narrow valley the cutoff had followed, and as the road climbed into the hills, their progress fell to a crawl.

Imogene held her breath each time they slowed to a stop, sure the truck had become stuck again. The hail of meteoroids had grown worse, and she had no desire to test their effect on infantry armor. Especially not while laboring to free a stranded vehicle.

But somehow the truck persevered, and they came down into another valley.

Mike and his crew had begun swapping seats so the driver could try and catch some sleep, and those in the truck presumably did likewise. Imogene's chronometer showed it was now evening of their fifth day out from Pons, but time had little meaning in the cramped belly of the Paladin.

Early the next morning, Imogene and her squadmates stood in the shadow of their personnel carrier, waiting impatiently while the missile techs ate and used the Paladin's tiny refresher. Both functions could have been accomplished in their suits, but it wasn't pleasant. She glanced at the truck and grimaced. Mike's crew had patched up the cargo compartment before leaving Piccolomini N, but dozens of new—and thankfully smaller—holes left the techs relying on their emergency suits again.

Rest stop completed, they started exiting the Paladin, and Imogene cast a last look around.

The sun shed a harsh light over the barren valley, illuminating kilometres of pale dust. Farther off, a heat shimmer danced, obscuring the dark jumble of a long-dead lava flow.

The shimmer moved closer, and Imogene gnawed her lip. "Do we get heat shimmers up here? Without air?"

"No." Annoyance underlaid the Sergeant's tone as he turned to her. "Why?"

She raised her arm, pointing to the disturbance. In the short time she'd looked away, it covered nearly half the distance towards them. The shimmering resolved into countless puffs of dust, exploding up from the surface.

"Shit," the Sergeant spit. "Everybody inside! Get that truck moving!"

Imogene scrambled to comply, and the colonel's voice cut across the comm. "What is it?"

"Meteoroids. Our shower's turning into a monsoon."

Imogene's guts clenched as she climbed into the Paladin. She held on tight as the two vehicles abandoned caution and sprinted for the distant hills. They pulled away from the approaching hail of meteoroids, and Imogene felt a flicker of hope. If they reached the hills, they might find a gully or clump of boulders. Anything to shelter the truck.

Then the truck spun out.

"Gods blast it all to hell!" Mike shouted. "Hold on, Jack. I'm gonna push you."

A sickening crunch shuddered through the Paladin.

"Stop," Jack's voice exploded over the comm. "You're scraping us over a bunch of rocks. I just lost the rear drive line."

The Sergeant's gaze snapped to Imogene. "Get out there and get it cleared!"

In their mad rush to reenter the Paladin, she'd ended up by the airlock, and she, Bruce, and Fiona were the first ones out. A single glance at the roiling wall of dust sweeping in on them stopped her heart. Something struck her thigh, and she stumbled backwards. She caught her balance against the Paladin and stared down at a shiny silver dimple in her armor. Whatever it was hadn't punctured the titanium, but still left its mark.

Shaking herself, she pushed upright and bounded after Bruce and Fiona. Dust flew out from where they dug, and Imogene dove in beside them. She clawed at the loose material. Her gauntlets scraped against larger rocks which she heaved aside. Then the truck was clear, and Bruce yanked her upright.

"Come on!" He shoved her towards the Paladin's waiting airlock.

The hatch closed behind them and the Paladin surged forward, grinding into the truck's bumper. Braced against the airlock's ceiling and Fiona's broad back, Imogene fought to stay upright.

The inner door opened, and she threw herself into the nearest seat. She pulled the restraints as tight as they would go. The truck must have gotten free, because they continued jostling forward at a faster pace.

The pinging of debris against the Paladin's armor rose to a constant clamor, and Mike cursed again.

"We're not gonna make it," he shouted to Jack. "Stop down in that crater. I'll pull up beside and give you some cover."

That was the last thing Imogene heard. She'd been in a tin-roofed building during a hailstorm once. This was a thousand times worse. A machine gun roar of impacts, interspersed with brutal thuds that set the Paladin rocking on its treads. What felt like minutes crawled past before the deluge slackened.

"I can't raise the truck," Mike said into the relative quiet.

Sergeant Hendricks growled. "They can't have held up under that beating. Everybody out; they're gonna need help."

The first thing Imogene saw was a white-gloved hand. It lay in the dust outside the airlock, with no sign of its owner. Swallowing against a wave of nausea, she yanked her gaze away.

Beside the Paladin, the truck looked like it had been attacked by a flock of metal-eating birds. The cargo compartment was stripped down to the frame, and the cab pounded into a misshapen lump. Twisted scraps of metal littered the ground, covering white-suited bodies.

"Victor, Alexei, check the cab," the Sergeant called. "The rest of you, fan out. Someone might have crawled underneath or gotten thrown clear. Check it all." He waved to the broken crates and crumpled sheets of what had been the truck's walls and roof.

Imogene circled to the right, along with Fiona and Ryan. Most of the remains were beyond the help she, or anyone else, could give. Grim silence filled the comm channel, punctuated only by an occasional exclamation or sharp intake of breath.

They'd covered about half the debris field when Victor gave an excited yell.

"We've got a live one!" he crowed from where he and Alexei had pried open the ruined cab. "Bruce, Lauren, get him inside pronto. One of these little rocks might pop his suit."

They passed Jack's weakly moving form down to their waiting squadmates, then Alexei wormed his way deeper into the shattered vehicle.

Returning her attention to the search, Imogene took a single step before a meteoroid struck her from behind. The impact sent her face first to the ground. She cursed and scrambled back up to her hooves. The meteoroid shower intensified, dozens of tiny dust-explosions blooming around her.

Alexei crawled backwards out of the wreckage. "The colonel and the other one in here are dead."

The comm let out a burst of static, and a few metres to Imogene's left, Ryan flew over backwards. He didn't move to get up, so she called out to him. "Ryan? You okay?"

He didn't answer.

Atop the ruined truck, Alexei launched into a mighty leap, beating Imogene to the ground squirrel's side by heartbeats.

"Ryan? Ryan!" Alexei shook his shoulder.

Imogene looked down, and an icicle broke itself off in her chest.

What lay behind Ryan's shattered faceplate was no longer recognizable. Her stomach lurched, and she backed half a step away. This wasn't real. Couldn't be.

"Status?" the Sergeant barked.

"He's—dead." Her voice broke.

The Sergeant cursed. "Everybody back inside! We can't do any more good out here."

Alexei stayed crouched beside the fallen squirrel. He'd given up on shaking, and now just held Ryan's gauntleted hand.

Imogene stumbled towards the Paladin but paused, looking back at him.

Victor had followed Alexei at a less reckless pace. He laid a hand on his shoulder. "Come on, Alexei. We gotta go."

The rabbit looked up at him. "But, we can't just leave him here!"

Victor patted him again. "I know, but we don't have time or space. We'll come back for him. I promise."

Alexei gave Ryan one final look, then surrendered to Victor's urging. He rose, and with the big cat's arm still clasped around his shoulder, stumbled towards the Paladin.

The three of them were the last back inside the crowded personnel carrier, and fell heavily into their seats.

At the front of the compartment, Jack sat across from Sergeant Hendricks. The wolf stared at the floor, his helmet held loose in one hand.

Mike stood at the foot of the crew compartment ladder. He looked from Jack to Sergeant Hendricks, then back. "So, what's the plan?"

Jack didn't look up, just shook his head wearily.

When it became clear he wasn't going to say anything, Sergeant Hendricks took charge. "On to Santbech. Those were our orders."

"Okay," Mike said. "Without the truck, we should make the outer guard station in three or four hours."

An especially loud clank made everyone wince. The Sergeant locked eyes with Mike. "Try and make it three."

They had been under way again for some time when Alexei finally spoke.

"I told him it would be okay," he said in a flat voice.

Victor put a hand on the rabbit's knee. "You couldn't have known."

Alexei fixed dull eyes on the feline's gauntlet. "We'd barely gotten to know each other, and now...now he's gone."

Victor opened his mouth, but nothing came out. A pained look crossed his face and his mouth closed.

Alexei started quietly sobbing, and Imogene looked away. She closed her eyes, seeing Ryan beside her at the rifle range. His shy smile as he helped her. The buck-toothed grin when he teased Alexei. Her throat tightened. Of everyone here, why did it have to be him?

A minute passed, then Lauren slammed a fist against her armored thigh. "It's those bloody pandas' fault, that's what it is! Ryan, the truck, everything else! It feels like an accident or the will of the gods, but it's not. If they hadn't started this, everything *would* still be okay!" The lynx's eyes narrowed to angry slits, and she pounded her fist again.

Everyone looked up at her outburst. Across from Imogene, the Sergeant nodded faintly, while Bruce's brow knotted in a worried frown.

Alexei pulled himself together and watched the silver feline with wide, red-rimmed eyes.

Seeing she had everyone's attention, Lauren bared her teeth. "It's all their fault, and once we get to Santbech, and then out to the fighting, we'll make them pay!"

19

CONTAINMENT

A third of the way along the wide valley which ramped up to Santbech Crater's southern rim, their lone Paladin pulled to a stop. Ahead, the double line of hills flanking the valley closed in and the rim mountains rose, with only a narrow notch to mark the pass.

Mike's reddish-brown head appeared at the top of the ladder. "I need a command decision here."

Sergeant Hendricks glanced over at Jack.

Imogene looked too, and bit her lip. The wolf had put his helmet back on and seemed to be asleep. He'd been having trouble concentrating, and after checking him over, Bruce said he might have a mild concussion. There wasn't much they could do about it, other than let him rest.

Grimacing, Sergeant Hendricks unfastened his restraints and climbed partway up the ladder. "What's the problem?"

"It looks like there's a battle going on up ahead," said Mike. "See those flashes just below the pass? Could be EMP rounds, or maybe HEAT. Somebody's got a radio jammer running, too. We'll need to be right on top of them before we can ask what's going on."

"Hm." There was quiet while the Sergeant thought. "This is out of my field. What do you think?"

"Well, we can get over on the east side of the valley, then crawl north along the foothills and hope we get an idea of the situation before someone with a better scope decides to shoot us."

Imogene shifted uncomfortably in her seat. Sneaking unannounced into a combat zone was a good way to get shot by your own troops, especially since they were behind PAF lines.

"Could we retreat and circle around to one of the other passes?" the Sergeant asked.

Mike's face twisted. "Yeah, thing is though, the south entrance is the most sheltered. If they're here, they're probably everywhere."

The Sergeant shrugged. "Do what you think is best. Falling back and waiting is an option, too."

"And hope the big rocks keep missing us? No thanks." Mike settled back into his seat. "You all better strap in, things might get bumpy."

Things did indeed get bumpy. Mike and his crew were good at what they did, and took the crawler lurching and bouncing northward, utilizing every scrap of the barren landscape's scant cover.

Imogene cinched her restraints tight and concentrated on not getting sick.

They crept to the top of a low ridge the better part of an hour later, close enough now for the Paladin's sensors to give them a clear view.

"It's a battle all right," Mike drawled. "Looks like our guys have pulled back into the pass. PAF bastards will have a hell of a time rooting them out of there."

Sergeant Hendricks was once more partway up the connecting ladder. "Assuming they want to capture the base. If not, all they need to do is get some laser artillery up there long enough to bring down the defense screen. Then they can lob enough antimatter into the crater to make sure no one's coming out alive."

"You think they'll use tactical annihilation weapons? They're about as dangerous to the user as the target."

"I don't know," the Sergeant said. "See that group hanging back on the left flank? You can't quite tell, but they sure look like Cobra launchers to me."

Imogene shuddered. The long-bodied PAF missile carriers had only one purpose: to neutralize deeply buried installations. If the attacking force included them, they had no intention of capturing Santbech intact.

Mike peered at the scope. "Could be. Either way, we're cut off from the base." He turned to the Sergeant. "What do you want to do?"

Sergeant Hendricks slowly shook his head. "Let's see if—"

Something struck the Paladin's flank, shredding metal and knocking the crawler flying.

Imogene's helmet slammed against the wall and she saw stars. The vehicle spun through a sickening barrel-roll, then struck the ground and started to tumble down the hillside.

Ripped from their restraints, several of the squad joined the Sergeant in a tangle of limbs. Gray-armored bodies crashed against each other, as well as the walls, floor, and their still seated comrades.

The butt of a rifle grazed Imogene's nose, then spun away. Faintly through her blast-deafened ears, she heard someone yelling. Louder was the menacing hiss of escaping atmosphere. Her suit sensed the pressure drop and her visor snapped shut.

She wasn't sure how long they tumbled. The lights had failed and the spinning seemed to go on and on, until at last the crawler came to rest upside down and tilted forward at a shallow angle.

Hanging from her restraints in the dark, it took a moment to remember how to turn on her headlamp. It clicked on, throwing cold light over a mass of twisted metal filling the aft end of the compartment. Her suit's ambient pressure gauge read zero. She glanced at Jack, making sure his primitive fishbowl helmet was sealed tight. Mike and his crew had the same type. Hopefully they'd sealed up in time, too.

The yelling stopped, and the silence pressed in against her. "Is everyone okay?" It was a lame question, but something drove her to speak.

Her words broke the spell, letting forth a flood of overlapping babble.

Across the compartment, Alexei fumbled with his seat restraints. They parted suddenly and he floated free, drifting down to join the jumble of weapons and equipment covering the compartment's ceiling.

"All right! All right!" Bruce shouted. "Everybody quiet down. Sarge? Are you reading?"

The chatter died away, but no answer came.

Bruce cursed. "Everybody sound off. Bruce here, and okay."

Imogene struggled with her own seat restraints, but paused to report. "Imogene, all right."

"Victor here," the big cat's voice rasped through gritted teeth. "My leg's messed up. Bleeding."

Imogene's gaze jerked to Victor's seat and found it empty. He must have been thrown loose.

Lauren, Alexei and Jack all checked in, while in the crew cabin, Mike said the other two were dead. Everyone had freed themselves from their restraints now, and did their best to stay out of Bruce's way as he examined Victor.

"Fiona, okay." The polar bear was the last to report. "The Sergeant's over here. Dead. One of the duffel straps got twisted around his helmet and kept the faceplate open."

Imogene's chest tightened. She hadn't known Mike's crew, but the Sergeant was her friend. Just as much as poor Ryan, if in a gruffer way.

If the Sergeant were dead, that left Jack and Mike as the only ones with more than a month or two experience up here. A leaden brick settled in her guts. The wolf and wolverine were good enough at what they did, but neither one gave her the confidence Sergeant Hendricks had. He always knew what to do. How to do it.

After a heavy silence, Fiona cleared her throat. "How's Victor?"

"He hurts like hell," Victor grunted before Bruce could answer.

Kneeling by Victor's side, Lauren whimpered and squeezed his hand tighter.

Bruce shook his head. "It's not good. A shard of what looks like the airlock door is broken off in his armor's knee joint, and continued bleeding means it went deep. If it doesn't stop, we can cinch his femoral tourniquet tight, but then he might lose the whole leg." He glanced up from Victor. "Mike, the survival tent is in the *outside* locker, right?"

Mike's dark eyes flicked to the ruined mess where the airlock had been. "Yeah. Assuming it's not mangled in with the rest of our tail end."

"And good luck getting to it anyway," Bruce shook his head again. "I gave him some painkillers, but without atmosphere there's not much more I can do."

Imogene's heart twisted. They couldn't just let him die. Not Victor.

Lauren jerked her head up. "What do you mean you can't do anything? You're supposed to be trained for this!"

Bruce sighed. "Look, in the back of his knee like that there's a good chance it nicked an artery. I can't fix that with him in a suit, and he'll asphyxiate if we take it off. Frankly, he's lucky the suit membrane managed to reseal around something that big."

"It didn't," Victor's voice had grown weaker. "I'm showing a slow leak."

"Shit!" Bruce rummaged in his kit after a canister of emergency sealant. "Why didn't you say anything?"

Victor chuckled. "I don't think it's gonna matter. There's an awful lot of blood in here."

Lauren looked down at him, tightening her grip on his hand. "Damn it, Bruce, do something!"

"What?" he shouted back. "You want to pull him out of his suit and try to fix him, be my guest!"

She snarled, gathering for a lunge at the stag. But Victor still held her hand, and wouldn't let go. She let out a frustrated yowl and collapsed beside him, folding herself into a ball around the wounded feline's hand.

Imogene's gaze darted around the compartment. There had to be something they could do. There was always something you could do. She had to believe that. Neither the engine compartment nor the tiny refresher would hold pressure. What they really needed was to summon help and get Victor into an undamaged vehicle.

She turned to Mike. "Did we get into comm range? Can we call for help?"

"No. Even if we were, the whole power system's offline. We're dead in the water."

She licked her lips. "Then we need to get out. Try and find the tent, or walk until we can raise someone on our suit comms." She glanced at the compartment's rear again. "The airlock's a write off. Is there another way out?"

"There's an escape hatch on top of the crew cabin. Probably jammed, though, with us upside down." He turned and clambered down into the inverted cockpit.

Imogene followed. The helmetless bodies of the other two crewmen hung strapped into their seats, and after one stomach twisting glimpse of their grossly swollen features, she kept her gaze locked on Mike.

He undogged a small hatch in what was now the compartment's floor. It fell open a centimetre or so, then stuck. He stomped down on the hatch with one boot, but it resisted his efforts.

Imogene stopped him when he moved to kick it a third time. "Can it open in?"

The wolverine's ears flattened in disgust. "No, blast it. And the cutting torch is in the outside locker, right next to the tent."

"Can we take apart the hinge?"

"Not from in here."

The two of them stared down at the hatch. The others chattered over the comm, but Imogene tuned them out. She had an idea, but needed to think it through.

Before she could finish, Bruce stuck his head into the ladder way. "Any luck in here? Alexei and I have been prying at the mess where the airlock was, but it's solid."

"Maybe." Imogene looked up at him. "You're sure the other way's hopeless?"

"More or less. What do you have in mind?"

"We can blow up the hatch."

There was silence, then, "Is that safe? With us in here?" Bruce asked.

"I'll admit it's not great, but with all the air gone we should be okay. And it sure beats waiting on the off chance someone comes to rescue us."

"Yeah," he drew the word out slowly. "If you think it's safe, I guess it's the best thing going."

Imogene nodded and unfastened her armored backpack.

Where most of her squadmates' packs carried only ammunition and EVA rations, fully half of hers was devoted to a selection of explosives, detonating devices, and other demolitions paraphernalia.

She studied the problem with a critical eye. Probably best to cut the hatch free from its hinges; no point blowing a new hole when you already had one. The hinge was on the outside, which made things a little harder, but five minutes, two linear shaped charges, and a remote detonator later, she was ready.

Imogene climbed into the main compartment and waved everyone to the back. "All set? They're small charges, shouldn't be more than a flash of light." At least she hoped so.

She'd done some live-fire training on Earth, but this was the first real test of her skills. She glanced down at Victor. Now wasn't the time to fail.

"Here we go." She flipped off the remote's safety cover, then hit the button. A tremor ran through the vehicle—just enough to tickle her hooves. In the silent vacuum, that was her only indication anything had happened.

Flicking the safety back on, she smiled tightly. "Not even a flash. No problem."

Down in the crew cabin, a charred crack marked where the charges had done their job, neatly shearing the hatch from its hinge. A spark of pride rose in Imogene's chest as she pulled the now unsecured hatch out of its frame. Paint burned off her suit's fingers as she grasped the freshly cut edge, but she paid it no mind.

The others crowded around the top of the ladder and stared down with her at the open hatch. Or rather, at the gray dust and gravel clogging the space just outside.

Imogene's shoulders sagged. "Great. Now what?"

Alexei snorted. "Now we dig. It can't be that far to the edge of the crawler." He climbed down beside her and set to work.

She watched for a moment, then joined him.

The loose, dry dust caved back in almost as fast as they could remove it. After a frustrating start, Alexei grabbed a helmet from one of the dead crewmen. Using it as a shovel, he bailed dirt into the cab where Imogene shoved it out of the way.

The hole grew quickly at first, but slowed as they tunneled away from the hatch. All the spoils had to be hauled back, passed up into the crawler and dumped, scoop by laborious scoop.

Imogene's arms grew tired, then began to ache. She was about to call some of the others to take a turn, when Alexei broke through.

"Go check the tent," Imogene said. "We can dig the rest out later."

The rabbit's muffled cursing came across the comm, then, "Found it! And it looks okay. No damage."

A bright orange bag appeared at the bottom of the hole, and Imogene hauled it up and passed it to the others in the main compartment. Bruce and Lauren unpacked the tent and got Victor and themselves inside, then inflated it. The rip-proof material puffed up like an ugly gray mushroom, filling half the crawler. The zippered airlock had a clear plastic door, and after a minute Bruce looked out and gave a thumbs up.

"We're all set in here," he said. "We'll call if we need anything."

He twisted off his helmet and his comm icon disappeared from Imogene's heads-up display. Just as well—she'd dreaded hearing to the play-by-play anyhow. She glanced around the narrow confines of the Paladin, then down at Alexei, lying in the tunnel below the hatch.

"Well, I suppose we should keep digging," she said. "Victor's not gonna be up to any wriggling, and Fiona just plain wouldn't fit."

Alexei squirmed back into the hole. "Okay. You keep at it from this end. I'll start outside with the shovel."

By the time they cleared a large enough passage and climbed back up into the Paladin's main compartment, Bruce had finished treating Victor.

Imogene's stomach turned at the amount of blood pooled on the tent's floor and spattering everything inside, but Victor's pale gold chest still rose and fell. Lauren sat holding his hand, while Bruce crouched near the clear plastic airlock.

Swallowing both her nausea and concern, Imogene turned to Jack. "The tunnel's as good as it's going to get, Captain. What do we do from here?"

The wolf sat with his back against the wall. He looked around at the others and shook his head listlessly. "I...I'm sorry. I'm Missile Corps. Just a glorified tech. Maybe do some admin work now and then. This..." He gestured around the ruined Paladin. "I don't know what to do about any of this."

Imogene raised a hand to rub her forehead. It struck her helmet, and she lowered it again. "Well, we've got to get Victor help. Bruce, can he make it to the base?"

"No." The stag was blunt. "He's gone into hypovolemic shock. I managed to stop the bleeding, but I don't want him moved unless it's into an evac crawler."

Imogene looked around the group. "So we need to go find help. Any volunteers?"

Alexei cleared his throat. "I think we should all go. Crap's still falling from the sky, and in case you've forgotten, there's a war going on outside."

Lauren hadn't moved from Victor's side. "I'm staying with him." Her tone dared anyone to disagree.

Bruce nodded. "Good enough. Keep him warm, and if he wakes up, don't let him move."

"Wait, you can't go too." Lauren's eyes widened. "What if he starts bleeding again?"

"Apply pressure." Bruce put his gauntlets back on as he spoke. "Tighten the tourniquet again if that doesn't work. You took the basic aid courses, and to be honest, that's all I can do for him now either. He should be okay for five or six hours, but he needs to get to a hospital."

Bruce crawled into the tent's airlock and zipped it shut behind him. "Besides, if the rescue team has to fight their way to the base, they're gonna need me a hell of a lot more than Victor does."

20

ANNIHILATION

Imogene studied the map on her heads-up display as they hiked north, but with the LPS satellites shot down it was more trouble to scroll to their current location than the low resolution map was worth. She could see the hills around them, and knew where they had to go.

On foot it was even easier to remain hidden in the cover of the hills. Ten kilometres and three hours of gray dust and airless rocks passed before they came into sight of the battle ahead.

Bruce approached a boulder-strewn skyline with caution, then waved Imogene and the others up beside him. "No doubt about it; they're pushing right up into the pass."

Peeking from behind a dark outcrop, Imogene surveyed the plain separating them from the jagged hills of Santbech Crater's rim. Hulks of armored vehicles littered the flats, left behind as the tides of battle swept higher up the valley's other side. Yellow flashes and short-lived clouds of dust marked where the fighting now raged in the pass between their valley and the deep crater sheltering Santbech Base.

Even using her rifle scope, Imogene couldn't tell the difference between PAF and UNA tanks at this distance. But there was no question the unit of laser artillery nearing the summit was PAF. Santbech's laser-based defense screens could only block physical projectiles, so the PAF's first step in attacking the base was to knock out the screen emitters with lasers of their own. What happened after that would depend on if they wanted to capture, destroy, or simply bury the base.

She scanned the hills for the missile carriers Sergeant Hendricks thought he'd seen earlier, but if they were there, she couldn't spot them. Maybe the PAF were planning to take the base intact. A prize like the factory-fortress of Santbech wasn't something to destroy lightly.

A few metres above her on the ridge, Mike stared through his rifle's scope. "No way we're getting through that. They're packed practically tread to tread."

"What if we circle around?" Bruce asked. "On foot, we don't really need the pass."

The wolverine nodded. "That'll get us in, provided the perimeter turrets aren't set to shoot anything that moves. And I don't think we're gonna find anyone willing to help until the battle at the pass is settled, so getting out should be okay too."

Imogene frowned. "We're talking at least a day then? You really think Victor can wait?"

Mike looked down the slope at her and shrugged. "I'm open to suggestions."

"Wait a minute," Bruce cut in. "Something's happening. It looks like they're disengaging."

Imogene swung her own rifle up and trained its scope on the pass. Sure enough, the PAF had broken off, retreating in a disorganized rout. But why fall back when they were winning? She looked up from her scope and caught movement across the sky.

A burning star twinkled in the blackness, arching up from deep inside the crater, then falling towards the pass.

As if in response, dozens of other rocket flames shot from a fold in the hills before them, skimming the crater rim and stabbing down at Santbech, even as the first rocket plummeted towards the PAF formations. Missile carriers that had been hidden from view scattered, the ugly elongate vehicles joining the chaotic retreat.

"They're giving up!" Alexei laughed. "Look at them run!"

The words barely left his mouth before a flare of pure white light erupted from the base beyond the pass. A burst of electromagnetic radiation accompanied the visible light, and an ear splitting shriek ripped through Imogene's helmet. Her heads-up display went dead, along with all her suit's other systems.

The rim of the crater shielded them from the blast's full force, keeping them from being instantly cooked. The light lasted only a fraction of a second, replaced as the crater rim disintegrated into an expanding wall of dust and debris. Some of the pieces were the size of small mountains, and the whole mass hurtled outwards at terrifying speed.

With an inarticulate yell, Imogene dropped behind her boulder. Jack was there too, and she crawled on top of him with some vague notion her armor might protect them both.

Then the wave hit.

There was no sound, but the ground jumped and trembled. Flying dust choked the vacuum around her, blocking out the sun. There might have been a second and third flash, but it was impossible to be sure. The rain of rubble increased, and small stones pummeled Imogene's back. Most of them felt slow moving, probably kicked up by secondary impacts.

Under her, Jack writhed, clawing deeper into the dust. With her comms and life-support offline, all she could do was try to stay atop the struggling wolf. It was good he was struggling. It meant he wasn't dead.

Hours seemed to pass, although it couldn't have been more than a minute or two. Then the storm abated.

Imogene didn't notice exactly when, but the comforting hum of her rebreather resumed. Thank the gods most military systems were hardened against electromagnetic pulse weapons. That hardening cost dearly in terms of performance, but right now she'd definitely take her primitive suit that worked over a modern one that didn't.

Using the boulder to push herself upright, she dislodged a thick coating of dust that had settled over her. Then she looked up and gasped.

A dozen metres to her left, a new crater yawned, easily deep enough to swallow a tank. Many of the smaller craters looked fresh too, while farther along their ridge a large bite of rock was now missing.

Turning her gaze towards the pass, Imogene shuddered. The whole area was unrecognizable. The pass was still there, but cut deeper by a misshapen, ovoid crater. A glassy sheen gleamed on its walls, and what looked like molten rock pooled at the bottom, glowing an evil reddish-black.

The feeling drained from her body as she stared at the devastation. All she could think was to wonder distantly how the single incoming warhead had left so large a hole. The tech manuals said at most two hundred metres. This had to be more than a kilometre. Were the manuals wrong? Or had the PAF held back some of their missiles, accidentally adding power to the doomed base's counter-strike?

That made more sense. The manual couldn't be wrong.

She was barely aware of Jack rising beside her until his muttered "Gods!" broke the silence.

She jerked, staring first at him, then at two more figures staggering upright. One was Alexei, but the other's chest patch had been scared beyond recognition.

"Imogene, Jack. Good." Bruce's voice identified him. "What about Fiona?"

Imogene shook off her shock. "I...don't know. She was farther down the ridge." She pointed to where she'd last seen the polar bear.

Still leaning against the boulder, Jack caught Bruce's arm as he passed. "Mike?"

The stag shook his head. "His suit didn't restart."

Jack let him go and sagged back. Bruce and Alexei continued on, and after a moment, the wolf shuffled after them.

Imogene followed, and a few minutes later, found Fiona half-buried in a small crater. She lay face down, a softball-size chunk of twisted metal embedded deep inside her life-support backpack.

Imogene's throat closed up, and she turned quickly away.

Losing control wasn't an option. If grief took over now, it wouldn't let her go. She had to turn that ever expanding sorrow into something else. Anger. Anger came easiest, but who to blame? The PAF? The politicians who set everything in motion? The all too absent gods? It hardly mattered, so long as it burnt her emotions down to sullen embers.

She could deal with embers.

Trudging back to the boulder that had protected her, Imogene probed in the dust for her rifle. She found it, and sat down heavily to inspect the weapon. Not a scratch on it, and the tiny info screen flickered cheerfully to life with no sign of damage.

"Great." She ground the word between her teeth. "All our friends may be dead, and we've got nowhere to go, but when we get there, we can still bloody well kill something. Just great."

The other three reclaimed their weapons. Bruce and Alexei stood while Jack slumped down beside her, helmet resting against his knees.

Alexei tilted his head to one side. "Nowhere left to go? We're going on to the base, right?"

Bruce gave an exasperated sigh. "You see that shiny new crater over there? That's what the base will look like. Everything left is gonna be buried or fused solid, and we can't wait for them to dig themselves out."

"There's gotta be someone who isn't buried," Alexei insisted. "We're still here."

"Probably, but remember whose troops were farthest from the blast?" Bruce looked out over the battlefield. "If anyone is still operational, they're gonna be PAF. The jamming's gone, but I'm not picking up any UNA signals except ours."

Imogene took a deep breath and pushed her growing despair to the back of her mind. No matter how hopeless things seemed, Alexei was right. They couldn't give up. Not with Victor counting on them. She looked up at Bruce. "So they're PAF. Does it matter *who* we get to help?"

"Victor needs a hospital," Bruce said. "Assuming any PAF medical units even survived the blast, do you really think they'd waste space on prisoners?"

Imogene's muzzle tightened. Of course the PAF would have wounded of their own. More than any mobile hospital could hope to handle.

Alexei hefted his rifle. "I'll be damned if I surrender to a bunch of pandas anyway."

No one spoke, then Bruce sighed. "It won't help Victor, but surrendering might not be a bad idea. Our air won't last forever, and I'd rather be a POW than a corpse."

Jack hadn't said anything so far, but suddenly perked up. "Borda. We can go to Borda."

"And what is Borda?" asked Alexei.

"It's a fuel depot. Maybe a hundred klicks south. We can make it before our rebreathers' power runs out."

Bruce turned to face him. "You can get us there cross-country?"

"I can try," Jack said. "I was only there once, but it's better than nothing."

There was a long silence, then Bruce nodded. "Better than nothing. Alexei, Imogene, what do you say?"

Alexei agreed quickly.

Imogene closed her eyes. A hundred kilometre hike meant giving up any hope of helping Victor. But was there any real hope here? She glanced out at the tortured battlefield. Even if any UNA troops had survived, they'd be in even worse shape than she and her friends.

Nodding slowly, she rose to her hooves. "I guess we're running out of options."

The hike back to their stranded Paladin grew longer with each step. Imogene couldn't remember the last time she'd stolen more than scattered moments of sleep. The others flagged too, rising slower each time a missed step or small meteoroid sent them sprawling.

Jack continued to be lucky. He was hit only once, and that failed to puncture his suit. He picked up a limp, though, and said he could feel a nasty bruise forming.

At last they reached their overturned vehicle, and Bruce broke the weary silence. "Lauren? We're back. Don't shoot us as we come inside."

"Bruce?" Lauren sounded anxious. "Thank the gods you're back. He...hasn't woken up."

"What's his monitor say?"

She paused a moment, then, "Vitals are mostly the same, but the heart irregularity's gotten worse."

Bruce cursed.

Frustration roughened his voice, and a helpless, hopeless despair rolled over Imogene as well. At least everyone else had died quickly. Victor was alive, but there was nothing they could do to keep him that way.

"But it's okay, right?" Lauren asked. "You brought help."

Bruce sighed heavily. "I'm afraid not. They nuked the base before we could reach it."

"What do you mean?" Lauren's voice took on a shrill note. "There must have been someone left to help. Didn't you even try?"

"No," Bruce said. "We're lucky to be alive, and we were twenty klicks out. Anyone closer is gonna be too busy with their own problems to give a tail flick for us."

Following Jack and Alexei, Imogene slithered through the dusty tunnel, then forced her weary muscles to haul her up into the main compartment. She didn't bother standing, just pulled herself off to one side and collapsed.

In the tent at the rear of the cabin, Lauren sat beside a barely breathing Victor, his left hand clutched in her lap.

"So what are you going to do?" Lauren asked.

Last in, Bruce stopped with his head and shoulders sticking up out of the crew cabin. "There's another base south of here. Jack's gonna show us the way."

"Okay," Lauren said. "You'd better get going."

The stag scoffed, his carefully neutral tone turning acidic. "Look, we've been walking for eight hours, and awake for more than I can count. We're exhausted. Mike and Fiona are dead. The Sergeant's dead. Victor's as good as dead. I can't help him, and I hate that more than I know how to say, but it's the way things are. Now, I don't care about the rest of you, but I'm going to rest for at least six hours and then head south. You all can do what you want." He withdrew down into the crew compartment.

The silence hung thick, and Imogene looked over to Lauren. "I sorry, but he's right. I don't think I could make it more than another klick."

Across the cabin, Alexei and Jack both looked away and nodded.

"I see." Lauren drew a long breath. "And I'm not stupid enough to go off on my own. So now we wait."

Imogene jolted awake. The tail fragments of a dark dream pounded through her head, and for a terrible moment smoke filled her nostrils and she felt the crushing weight of water. Then it was only her suit's padding, pressing sweat-damp fur against her skin.

She forced her breathing to slow. Against the far wall, Jack and Alexei slept, while Lauren seemed not to have moved at all. Her chronometer showed almost eight hours had passed since they returned to the Paladin. She'd more than half expected Lauren to wake them after Bruce's six hours were up.

Lauren turned, her open visor exposing her face. Damp fur matted her cheeks, real tears darkening the silver coat to match her tear-line markings.

With a few blinks and eye gestures, Imogene opened a private comm channel. "How is he?"

"He's dead." Lauren's voice came rough, but the words held no intonation. Not even the veiled scorn she directed at everyone but Victor and the Sergeant.

Imogene's gaze flicked down to Victor's golden fur. Another friend gone. That warm smile of his darted through her mind. The energy with which he attacked life, the fire in his eyes when he spoke of his family's warrior tradition. Now he was dead without even seeing combat, all because a two-credit seat restraint had failed.

Her chest ached, swollen with more death and loss than it could hold.

And how much worse must Lauren feel?

She raised her eyes from Victor's still form, wishing Lauren could see through the tinted visor to the pain and sympathy Imogene knew was written across her face. They might have been rivals, but no one should have to go through something like this alone.

"I'm sorry."

"Are you?" A hint of inflection crept into Lauren's voice. "You really are." She looked back down at Victor, and her shoulders slumped. "I guess that makes you better than me, somehow."

Imogene shook her head. "No. He was a squadmate, and so are you. You must feel sorry for Ryan and Alexei, right?"

"I suppose."

"Same thing, then."

Lauren didn't say anything.

Imogene wished she knew what more to say or do. Fiona would have known. Or the Sergeant.

After a time, she fished out a tube of EVA nutrient. Sucking in a mouthful of the metallic tasting fluid, she wrinkled her nose and swallowed. The field rations they'd been living on might be unappetizing, but she had a feeling they would be remembered fondly after a few days of this thick, yellowish slop. She finished nearly half the tube before Lauren spoke again.

"Did Jack say how far this base of his was?"

Imogene hastily cleared her mouth. "He wasn't sure. Something like a hundred klicks."

"So at least thirty hours march, plus rests...two and a half, three days?"

"The terrain is pretty broken. I'd say three or four." She took another swallow of her rations.

Lauren looked out of the tent at their sleeping companions. "Do you think we should wake them? Four days is going to cut things close with the rebreathers."

Imogene hadn't thought of that, and frowned. "Yeah. First let's see about going through the...casualties' supplies. If we have their power packs, we can push things out to a week or better."

The lynx nodded, and together they collapsed the tent, folding it around Victor as a sort of shroud. Then they turned the Sergeant over and sorted through his equipment. Imogene didn't bother with ammunition or the rifle power packs. Rations, water, and the main life support power pack were all that mattered now.

"That's one," Imogene said when they'd finished. "And the drivers make three. Why don't I take care of their supplies?"

"All right." Lauren stared down at Victor and his discarded armor. "I'll...finish up here."

Bruce sprawled asleep under the ladder way, and Imogene stepped carefully around him to reach the dead crewmen.

Still terribly swollen, their exposed features had grown hard. The blood and other fluids would have boiled until the elastic force of the skin and tissues made up for the lost air pressure. What didn't boil off froze as the bodies cooled. It was definitely not a flattering way to be preserved for eternity, and Imogene tried not to look too closely as she worked.

She was climbing back into the main compartment with the two power packs when Bruce woke. She wasn't sure if she'd bumped him, or if he roused on his own. Either way, his sudden comments over the main comm channel woke Jack and Alexei, and the five survivors divvied up the scavenged supplies.

It didn't take long, and then Bruce looked over to the pile of their personal effects. "What about our duffels?"

Imogene shrugged. "I'm just gonna take a set of fatigues and whatever else I can fit in my pockets."

Lauren had moved Victor to lie with the Sergeant, so there was space to unstack the duffels and find their own.

Naturally, Imogene's was at the bottom, and by the time she freed it, the others were already sorting out the possessions they wanted to keep. She opened the drawstring and grimaced. Her toothpaste hadn't taken kindly to the change of pressure, and sticky green goo covered everything.

She picked out her datapad and a few health and grooming items, then discarded the rest. Toothpaste smeared her family photo as well, but rather than try to clean it now, she wrapped the small rectangle of plastic in a spare shirt and tucked it into her backpack.

It was a week now since both sides had launched their planetary bombardment missiles. Had Josh and their mother survived? She gnawed her lip, thinking of the dozens of red markers carpeting the target map back at Pons. And that was only a single missile cluster. How many thousands of other warheads must have been launched?

She shied away from that question. All she could do now was hope. Hope, and keep moving forward.

Outside, lunar dusk drew near. Shadows lay strong over the rumpled gray landscape, and while there was plenty of light for now, only a few days remained before the sun would sink below the horizon. They were on their own, and somehow the desolate hills and craters seemed even more forbidding than usual.

Last to emerge from the tunnel, Jack rose to his paws. "Borda is south and east. The road goes north around these hills, but we can cut through them. Then there was a big valley, and some more hills."

Bruce nodded. "I looked the route over on the map. Even with the satellite positioning system down, I think we can manage. Heads down, face forward."

21

HOOFING IT

Imogene picked herself up out of the dust for what felt like the thousandth time. They'd been traveling steadily for the better part of ten hours and were nearing the crest of a tall ridge. Above, Jack and Alexei stood on the skyline. They weren't that much farther ahead, and she drove her weary legs on to join them. Just as she came to a stop beside the white-suited wolf, another meteoroid threw her flat.

"That's it," she said. "I've been knocked down three times in as many minutes. And I know we've all seen the bigger ones starting up again. I say we find someplace sheltered and rest until they slow down."

Jack offered her a hand up. "No argument from me. This maggot skin suit may have turned out to be tougher than it looks, but I'm still getting beat up where you guys just get knocked over."

Imogene's mouth tightened at the reminder. "Yeah. Sorry about that."

"Not your fault." He shrugged.

Bruce reached the ridge and moved up on Jack's other side. "They seem to be coming from the north. Someone's still fighting up there, I guess. Let's drop down the ridge a bit. That should block some of them."

The far side of the ridge was steeper than the one they'd climbed. Scree slopes filled the spaces between cliff-like outcrops, and a fine layer of fresh dust covered everything. Imogene slipped and fell more than once, but the meteoroids did reduce noticeably.

Then Lauren spotted a deep cleft between a boulder and a cliff face. Everyone fit inside, and its entrance offered a view of the way ahead.

"So, is this your big valley?" Lauren waved at the uneven plain below.

Jack wriggled up beside her. "I don't think so. It should be pretty wide. This can't be more than a few klicks to the next ridge."

"Figures," Lauren grumbled, then crawled back into the crevice.

They rested for several hours, eating, sleeping, occasionally creeping towards the entrance to gauge the severity of the meteoroids. Eventually they set forth again, down the ridge and then eastwards across the rugged valley.

Imogene watched her power readout drop past twenty percent with a worried eye. She had the Sergeant's power pack to replace hers when it failed, but the hills ahead seemed endless.

Three ridges and eleven hours later, she topped a final rise and looked out over a wide, flat-bottomed valley. Thirty klicks of pock-marked dust spread themselves out before a line of forbidding mountains stabbed into the star-specked sky.

"*That* would be the big valley." Jack waved forwards. "Coming from this side, I'd guess those mountains are the outer rim of Borda."

Beside him, Imogene suppressed a groan. "It's big enough, all right. Those mountains look mean, too."

"Yeah." The wolf sighed. "The base is pretty high up on the north rim. If we angle that way, maybe we can hit the road."

Lauren stared at the empty landscape. "There isn't gonna be any cover worth mentioning out there. We should find someplace to rest before leaving the hills, then try and make it across to the mountains in one push."

Imogene glanced over at her. The lynx's arrogant self-assurance had returned, but how was she really coping behind that brusque front? Probably the same as the rest of them: one thing at a time, without thinking about what it all added up to.

She was right about finding shelter, though, and Imogene kept her eyes peeled as they descended.

Behind them, the sun hung low in the black sky. Every rock and hummock promised shelter in its long, dark shadow, but none gave true protection. At last they settled on a pair of tank-size boulders. One leaned in towards the other, but the narrow space between them still left Imogene feeling exposed.

They rested as long as their dwindling power supplies let them dare, then struck out across the flats.

Smooth, dusty terrain fled past under Imogene's loping bounds. The valley floor was easy, and even the rolling foothills hardly slowed their march. Scattered pea-size bits of rock and metal continued to drizzle, but she ignored them as much as she could. The best course of action was to hurry on to Borda.

As they climbed, the drizzle turned to a ballistic hail, pelting in from the north. She kept her visor pointed down and her legs pushing her forward. Then a wave of larger impacts broke over the landscape, and Imogene's blood turned cold.

Her gaze darted over the bleak surroundings. No cover. All they could do was sprint for the still distant mountains.

Towers of dust shot up from the larger strikes, leaving craters the size of manholes. She dodged around the holes, praying she and her friends wouldn't be hit.

With the others close behind, she bounded up a gentle ridge, then stopped dead, teetering on the lip of a previously hidden crater. The bowl before her was large enough to hold a score of personnel carriers, but too shallow to provide cover from the meteoroids.

She turned and took three steps before something slammed into her chest. Knocked breathless, she cartwheeled into the crater. Rock, dust, and starry sky spun past as she rolled. Her suit took most of the punishment, but the final collision that stopped her tumble left her stunned.

Lying in the darkness, she struggled to get her lungs working. Up on the rim, her squadmates stood outlined against the stars.

"Imogene? Are you okay?" Worry tinged Bruce's voice.

"I think so," she said by reflex.

A cough sent a jab of pain through her lower ribs. Broken? Fear crushed down on her. She forced in a slow, careful breath. The pain came again, but less, and not sharp. Probably just a bruise. She pulled herself upright and looked for the best way out of the crater.

A deeper blackness within the gloom caught her eye.

Toggling on her night vision, she studied the crater wall. "You guys better get down here! There's a tunnel or some-thing."

She scrambled for the dark hole even her suit's sensors couldn't penetrate. It was a tunnel all right, wide enough for a truck and rising to an arch well above her head. She turned on her headlamp and moved deeper into the rough-hewn passage. It ended in a solid rock wall a dozen metres from the entrance, with a narrow shaft bored straight up to the surface.

Jack staggered a few paces inside, then slumped against the wall. He heaved a sigh and let himself slide down until he was sitting on the rubble-strewn floor. "Ah, that's better."

Bruce nodded. "Much longer out there and we'd all be in trouble." He glanced at Imogene. "You're sure you're okay? That's quite a dent you've got there."

She couldn't see her own chest from inside the helmet, but her hands found a fist-size indentation left of her solar plexus. "Just a fierce bruise, I hope." She licked her lips. "Not a bad trade for finding this place."

"And exactly what is this place?" Alexei returned from his own exploration of the short passage.

"Who knows?" Bruce tipped his helmet at Jack. "From what Jack said, we're getting pretty close. Maybe they thought about putting in a defense turret or comm relay. I'm just glad it's here at all."

"Yeah," Alexei said. "Good job finding it, Imogene."

"Luck." She waved away his praise. Settling down beside Jack, she pulled out a tube of rations. The storm outside grew worse, and she watched with a numb detachment. The floor of the crater looked like it was boiling: short-lived fountains of dust erupting everywhere, punctuated with larger blasts that cleared to reveal new, metre-wide craters.

They watched in silence for some time before Alexei sprang upright. "Hey! There's someone out there!" He bounded towards the entrance.

Imogene rose and ran after him. "Where?"

He stopped just inside the tunnel and pointed. "There, coming over the rim. Another one's with him."

Sure enough, two gray camo-clad figures were sliding recklessly down into the crater.

"Quick, turn on your lights so they can see us!" Bruce's headlamp flared, and he switched to a general comm channel. "Hello! Over here!" He waved.

The one in the lead turned towards the tunnel. He gave a frantic wave of his own, but didn't respond to Bruce's hail.

"Hello?" Bruce tried again. "Lauren, can you tell what channel they're using?"

"I don't know. Gimme a minute."

Outside, the two newcomers struggled closer. Only a few dozen metres of crater floor were left, but any progress against the hail of debris came hard won. Imogene rocked on her hooves, muscles tensed, as if she could help them run faster by sheer force of will.

Painful seconds ticked by, then the leader broke into range of the waiting headlamps, revealing the odd camo-patterning of his suit—

And the Pan-Asian Federation crest emblazoned on his shoulder.

Imogene's eyes went wide.

Lauren hissed and clawed after her rifle. "They're PAF!"

Without thinking, Imogene fumbled to unsling her own weapon. Her concern for the newcomers twisted into dismayed confusion. Of all the combat scenarios she'd imagined in idle moments, this was not one of them.

The two PAF soldiers came to an uncertain stop. The leader made a placating gesture, while his shorter companion froze. Neither bore a weapon.

Alexei's aim shifted back and forth in agitation. "What do we do? We can't just shoot them, can we?"

"Why not?" Lauren growled. "They're fucking pandas."

Anger twisted in Imogene's nerve-wracked guts. Here, weak and unarmed, were two of the people responsible. Responsible for Victor. For her mother, and Josh, and Ryan. For the whole bloody mess.

And it would be so easy to pull the trigger.

One of the larger meteoroids struck between the two PAF soldiers, sending up a spray of debris. Falling to his knees, the leader wrapped his arms around his head, cowering against the onslaught. How many times on this hellish march had she fallen just like that? Helpless. Terrified.

Imogene shook her head sharply. "Damn it, they're people!"

She dropped her rifle and lunged to grab hold of Lauren's. The lynx yanked back, and the two of them tumbled to the ground. Imogene pulled the weapon free and tossed it farther along the passage. She shoved away from the cursing and flailing feline, scuttling clear before rising to her hooves.

By the entrance, Alexei lowered his weapon and Bruce waved the bedraggled PAF soldiers forward again. They skidded inside and collapsed. One happened to fall beside Imogene's abandoned rifle, and Bruce hastily reclaimed it.

Before he could pass it back to Imogene, Lauren shoved between them. She backed Imogene up against the wall and leaned in until their mirror-finish faceplates touched.

"Don't you do that again. Ever. You fuck with me, Rudolph, and you *will* regret it." She pulled back and glared at the others. "That goes for the rest of you, too."

Silence filled the tunnel, then Lauren spun and headed in search of her weapon.

Imogene sagged against the rough stone. Whatever understanding she might have rebuilt with the lynx seemed to have collapsed. But she didn't regret her action. She was certain of that.

Bruce watched Lauren go, then returned Imogene's rifle. "Anybody know how to do a comm hook-up with PAF equipment? What frequencies are they going to be using?"

"Doesn't matter," Jack said. "It'll all be encrypted. Just use the wide-band emergency channel. They should pick that up."

"All right." The stag turned to where the PAF soldiers sat recovering. "Hello? Can you guys hear me?"

The one who had been in the lead bobbed his blocky helmet. "Yes. We are receiving." He gave the words an odd intonation, flat, yet strangely musical at the same time.

"Good. Are you both uninjured?"

"My companion's wrist may be broken."

Imogene cast a searching look at the second soldier, who sat with one arm cradled close. She wasn't familiar enough with the angular, crustacean-like PAF armor to judge if the wrist joint was damaged, but given the onslaught outside, it was a miracle both soldiers hadn't been pounded flat.

"Who cares if they're okay?" Alexei spoke over the squad's private channel. "Are there more of them out there? That's what I wanna know."

Bruce glanced over at him, then back to their new prisoners. "Do you need painkillers? Or sealant? That's about all I can offer right now." The wounded soldier's helmet shook side to side, so Bruce continued with Alexei's questions. "What are you doing here? Are you alone?"

The leader didn't answer right away, but turned to look at his partner. There was a pause long enough for a brief exchange, and the second soldier shrugged. The leader looked at Bruce. "Yes, we are alone. We became separated from our unit, and our armored car was then damaged."

"So you were trying to rejoin your unit. Where are they?"

"I...do not know." The soldier sounded uncomfortable.

"They withdrew to the north." The clear, female voice of the second soldier broke in. "We were rearguard scouts."

"Shut up, Ming-Xue! They do not need to know that!" The first soldier rounded on her.

"You think it matters? They are long gone by now. You upset him, and he might let the angry one shoot us. You know they wanted to."

"No one's shooting anyone." Bruce overrode an angry retort from the first soldier. "At least not if you both behave. Now, you said they went north. How long ago?"

Ming-Xue looked up at him. "Six or seven hours. I do not know exactly."

"So as far as you know, there are no more PAF forces in the area?"

She nodded.

Bruce toggled to the squad's channel. "It sounds like we're okay for the moment, then."

"If you trust her," Alexei put in.

Bruce sighed. "Right. If we trust her. I don't see it makes much difference one way or the other, though. We still need to reach Borda. Jack, do you think we can make it in one more push?"

Inside his clear helmet, the wolf frowned. "Probably. I'd feel better if we'd found the road."

Alexei gave a cynical snort. "I'd feel better if we knew our friends here didn't blow up the base before they left."

Bruce turned back to the prisoners. "Were you attacking the base at Borda?"

"No," Ming-Xue said. "We are scouts."

"What about the rest of your unit? Did they attack it?"

Reluctantly, she nodded.

"And did they win?" Bruce kept his tone level.

"I do not know. The colonel was very angry to be ordered to withdraw."

"That's something, anyway." He let the words trail off, then switched channels once more. "I guess we'll just have to take our chances with the base. Anything else you guys can think of?"

"What about their names?" Imogene asked. "If we're stuck with them, we may as well know what to call them."

Bruce relayed the question.

"I am Private Guan Ming-Xue, ID number—" She rattled off a long string of letters and numbers, then looked over at her companion.

He just sat with his arms crossed over his chest.

When he remained silent, Ming-Xue spoke up. "He is Private Omar Arain. I do not know his numbers."

"We don't need them." Bruce waved dismissively. "Now, we're going to wait for the meteoroids to die down, and then continue on to the base. Don't make any trouble and we'll get along. Okay?"

Ming-Xue quickly agreed, and Omar gave a grudging nod.

Bruce looked around at his companions and sighed. "We'd better post a proper guard this time; I don't trust them not to try running off." He took a few steps back from the PAF soldiers, then settled down by the passage wall. "Alexei, why don't you and I take the first watch and let the others get some sleep?"

Imogene hadn't realized just how tired she was until he mentioned sleep. She'd been running on little more than nerves and adrenaline. Now the dull pain from the meteoroid returned to her ribs, and every muscle ached. She stretched out beside Bruce, glad her drooping eyelids wouldn't give her time to brood on what might or might not await them at Borda.

22

BORDA

The last rays of the setting sun illuminated the installation below them. Set into a small, cirque-like valley about halfway up Borda Crater's north rim, it consisted of a central dome, joined with a boxy, above-ground garage that looked to have been added later. There were a few other outbuildings, and on the valley's far edge, a tall comm tower poked up from the gray ridgeline. All in all, it was a lovely example of a pre-Unification era base.

Or at least it had been.

Imogene's heart sank as she took in the destroyed vehicles littering the valley floor. On the ridge, a pair of railgun turrets lay in ruins. Two walls of the garage had collapsed, leaving the roof crumpled in on whatever might remain inside. Once sleek and silver, the dome's walls gaped with countless holes, some smooth and circular left by kinetic energy rounds, others bearing the jagged edges and charring of high explosives.

The silence lay heavy as they stared down at the ruined base. Finally, Lauren gave a dismissive snort. "So this is our last, best hope, huh Jack? Not much to look at."

Alexei turned to the white-suited wolf. "There must be other bases nearby, right?"

"No." Jack sagged visibly, his voice wooden. "There's nothing."

Pulling her eyes away from the scene below, Imogene looked over at them. "It might not be as bad as it looks. There's bound to be tunnels under the dome. They might be okay. We should hurry while there's still some light." She began picking her way down the steep slope into the valley.

Their way took them past one of the abandoned vehicles, and Imogene spared it a lingering glance. It was a Fire Ant IFV —the PAF answer to the Paladin—and seemed largely intact. One tread had been torn free, and its protective skirt was nowhere to be seen, but that looked to be the extent of the damage.

But right now she was more concerned with the base. Up close, the destruction looked even worse. Some of the gashes cut clear through all four floors, letting her see into the shattered interior. No light came from the surviving windows, and her comm hails continued to go unanswered.

An airlock pierced the side of the dome nearest them, but as they drew closer a deep dent in the door came into view. First Bruce, then Bruce and Alexei together struggled to force it open.

"Bloody thing's jammed," Bruce growled after a third attempt. "We're gonna have to get a lever."

Imogene looked up from a jagged gap she'd been studying. "You know, we could just crawl in through one of these holes. It's not like there's any atmosphere left for the lock to protect."

Bruce turned to face the nearest ground-level opening. "Yeah? Some of that stuff looks pretty sharp. We'd have to leave Jack outside or risk cutting his suit."

She shrugged. "Someone needs to keep an eye on the PAF anyway. They've played it straight so far, but I don't like the idea of them crawling around in there with us."

"Are you okay with that, Jack?" Bruce asked.

The wolf snorted. "Do I have a choice? You go explore. We can figure out how to get me inside later."

"Okay. We'll try to keep it quick." Bruce took two bounding steps over to the hole and bent to peer inside. "I guess this one's as good as any. Hold my rifle till I'm through the worst of it." He unslung the weapon and passed it to Imogene.

She watched the stag ease his way into the cavity, then handed both his rifle and hers through to him. She ducked to follow him. The low opening forced her to hands and knees, and metal scraped against her backpack. Then she was through and into a dark space filled with broken furniture and twisted beams from a collapsed wall. She turned on her headlamp before accepting her rifle back from Bruce.

Lauren and Alexei followed, and the four set off into the ravaged base.

The rooms deeper inside had suffered less damage, but none showed any sign of survivors. Both power and atmosphere were gone, leaving the dome a broken shell. Bodies lay mixed in with the debris, though mercifully fewer than Imogene had dreaded. Either the base had been thinly staffed, or the bulk of its personnel were elsewhere when the attack came.

At the center of the dome they found a stairwell beside an inactive freight lift. The emergency door that should have protected the stairway had jammed halfway down, giving easy access.

Alexei cast his headlamp between the two sets of lithcrete stairs. "Up or down?"

"Down, I think." Bruce ducked under the door to join them. "The upper levels are probably even worse."

After three flights, the stairs ended, letting out into a small lobby. The freight lift's open door faced a heavy armored portal, which was closed. Alexei moved to the emergency airlock beside the sealed blast door.

"Hey, this one's got power!" He thumbed the green-glowing open button. The door slid aside, and he stepped into the tiny compartment beyond.

"Wait!" Bruce stopped him before he could close the door. "Let someone in with you so we only have to cycle it twice. No point wasting whatever power is left."

Imogene tensed at the thought of getting stuck in a powerless airlock, and made sure there were manual valves and latches before crowding in next to Alexei.

The airlock closed, and she smiled at the welcoming hiss of air flooding in around them. They stepped out on the other side of the blast door, into a dim corridor. The glow panels pulsed at their lowest setting, and shadows brooded at the corridor's far end.

Imogene didn't care. For the first time in nearly a week, her suit's sensors showed a full atmosphere outside. She cracked open her visor, letting in a puff of cool air. It reeked of burnt electronics and felt oddly moist and heavy, but she breathed deep regardless.

Beside her, Alexei opened his faceplate, and his pink nose twitched. "It stinks in here."

"Maybe." Imogene filled her lungs again. "I see you're not closing your visor again, though."

"No. It's okay, I guess."

Behind them, Bruce and Lauren stepped out of the airlock. The stag flipped up his visor and took a deep breath of his own.

"Gods, that feels good!" He reached up to rub his wide nose with one hand, then glanced at the glow panels. "And power, too. Good."

Lauren shook her head. "Life support's down. Listen."

Everyone fell quiet, and Imogene strained her ears. Only the soft *plink* of dripping water broke the silence. Without the distant whirring growl of a ventilation system, this place might be little more than a tomb.

An echoing metallic clank made her jump. She spun around, unable to tell where it came from.

"What was that?" Alexei's whiskers twitched, and he unslung his rifle.

"Someone else must be down here." Bruce cupped his hands around his mouth and called out. "Hello? Is someone there?"

Another clank answered, followed by the hastily retreating click of claws against the cement floor.

Lauren hissed. "Great. Now they know we're coming."

Bruce shot her a dirty look. "They're probably on our side." He raised his hands again. "Hello! You can come out. We're UNA; we won't hurt you."

They waited tensely, but the only reply was the slow drip of water.

Finally, Bruce sighed. "Well, that didn't work. We better go find whoever it is before they get the bright idea to attack us." He took point, edging cautiously down the shadowed corridor.

The one unlocked door they passed opened onto a second stairwell, this one leading only down. The dripping sound came from the darkness below, along with a stronger waft of burnt wiring and the musty smell of wet lithcrete.

Imogene's headlamp sparked rainbows off the turbid water filling the stairwell, and she backed quickly away. The scent of charred electronics changed to the black reek of burning fuel oil, and old memories of cold and darkness and fear crawled across her skin.

"Flooded," Bruce said. "Save it for later."

Or for never. Imogene forced herself to take another look. The oily surface glowered back at her, but remained smooth and still. Not rising. Not a threat.

"Yeah." She swallowed hard and backed out into the corridor.

A few dozen metres and a handful of locked doors later, the corridor ended in a junction. Two branches curved away to the left and right, following the outline of the dome above.

Standing in the junction, Bruce repeated his hail. "Hello? We don't want to hurt anyone. We're UNA."

"How do we know you're telling the truth?" An angry voice came from somewhere down the left-hand corridor.

"I guess you don't," Bruce said. "Why don't you come on out, and you can see for yourselves?"

A whispered conference echoed down the passage, then the voice called again. "All right, but you come to us. And no weapons or funny business!"

Alexei nudged Bruce forward. "They're your friends. You go first."

"I was going to anyway." He handed his rifle to Imogene. "You all stay here. Don't want to crowd them." He turned back to the left branch and walked slowly, hands held out from his sides and palms forward.

He passed two open doorways before the angry voice stopped him. "That's close enough. Now turn around so we can see your rank tabs and backpack."

Bruce did as he was told, spinning slowly in place and finally coming back around to face the doorway.

"That's a UNA suit all right. He must be okay," a new, deeper voice spoke.

"Yeah, I s'pose so," the first voice admitted. Its owner, a short, plump raccoon, stepped into the corridor's dim light. Gray camo fatigues marked him as infantry, and he held an assault rifle.

Another figure followed, this one a massive brown bear. He stood at least two metres tall, and his bulky frame pulled the material of his blue coveralls tight whenever he moved.

The raccoon stepped up to Bruce and offered his right hand. "Sorry about that. We had to shoot some leftover PAF buggers who got inside earlier. Can't be too careful."

Imogene grimaced. Had those "leftover" soldiers been trying to attack, or surrender? Either way, she hoped the

Borda survivors would be more tolerant of PAF who were already prisoners.

Bruce took the raccoon's hand and shook it. "No, I don't suppose you can. What's the situation here?"

"Looking up, now that you're here." The raccoon released his hand and stepped back. "We were starting to think nobody was coming. You are the relief party, aren't you?" He looked hopefully up at Bruce, then over to where Imogene and the rest had joined them.

Silence filled the corridor.

"Ah, no," Bruce said. "We just spent the last four days walking here from Santbech. We were hoping you hadn't been hit, too."

The raccoon's bushy tail went limp. "You mean you aren't here to help?"

Bruce spread his hands. "We'll do what we can."

"Right." The raccoon's lips twisted. "Can't ask more than that. I'm Private Scott Kyles, by the way, and this is Aaron Donne." He gestured to the brown bear. "There are a few others, but you can meet them later."

Bruce introduced himself and his companions. "And we've got three more waiting outside. One's in an emergency suit, and we didn't want him to cut it coming in though the wreckage. Do you have a cutting torch or something we can borrow?"

The bear nodded, massive head rising and falling like the tide. "We have tools, yeah. Let me get my suit and a cutter, and I'll give you a hand." He turned without waiting for a reply and lumbered off.

They watched him go, then Scott looked back around at the others. "Aaron's the only mechanic we have left. He'll take good care of you."

After a moment, Imogene cleared her throat. "We noticed your air supply isn't working. Do you know if it's repairable?"

"The equipment's fine," Scott said. "Aaron just turned it off to save power."

"Then the power plant's in trouble?" She glanced up at the dim glow panels with new concern.

He sighed heavily. "You could say that. It's chin-deep in what's left of our fresh water supply. Most of the reserve power cells were down there too, so we're turning off everything we can."

"How much is left?"

"Maybe twenty percent. Aaron said it should hold for a week at the rate we're going." He licked his lips nervously. "That should be long enough for help to get here."

"I hope so." Imogene's frown deepened. "At least we have time to come up with a plan. That's something."

Scott's small round ears folded, and he blinked. "You think they might not come?"

She shook her head reflexively. "Someone will come." That was a given. The UNA Armed Forces didn't leave their people to die. "It's how soon they come I'm worried about. Everything's gone to hell, and it might be a while before anyone thinks to pick up the pieces."

Beside her, Bruce nodded. "Hope for the best, but plan for the worst."

Scott's brown eyes flicked up at him, then back to Imogene. "I guess you guys have a better idea of the big picture. We've been out of touch for a while now. You said they hit Santbech too? How bad was it?"

"Bad." Bruce didn't mince words. "They got enough annihilation bombs into the crater to seal the base. I'm not sure who held the field, but I wouldn't be surprised if the PAF are moving in sappers to blow up whatever's left underground."

An uncomfortable silence fell and lasted until Aaron returned. The grizzly now wore a tech's lightly armored and sky-blue pressure suit. He had a compressed gas cylinder tucked under one arm, and the bulky power supply of a portable plasma cutter dangled from his other hand.

Imogene and Bruce accompanied him up into the airless dome.

"All right then, where did you come in?" Aaron peered along the corridors radiating out from the stairwell.

"Couldn't we just cut the latches off the outer airlock?" Imogene suggested. "That would be a lot faster than clearing out the mess we came though."

"No," he said. "I don't want to mess up the doors any worse than they are. Airlocks are fiddly and expensive. Just pick whatever hole you think is best and I'll clean it up for you."

Imogene shook her head in bemusement. She might not have been an engineer, but the dome was clearly a write off. Worrying about a few door latches seemed like trying not to scratch a vehicle's paint while dragging it to the scrap yard.

He was the one with the cutter, though, so they led him back to where they'd entered. The final chamber looked even worse after visiting the intact lower level. Part of the ceiling had collapsed, tearing a goodly amount of one wall in with it. Beams and wall panels filled the room, jumbled with crushed and twisted office furniture.

Aaron surveyed the damage. "Not bad, considering. How 'bout you two clear out as much of the loose stuff as you can, and I'll start cutting."

"Anything we can help with from outside?" Jack's voice came over the comm.

"I don't think so." Aaron set down the plasma cutter and began attaching the gas cylinder. "It's pretty cramped in here, 'specially if you're in a thin suit. Just sit tight."

He made short work of sectioning the collapsed roof and wall debris, then moved on to smoothing and enlarging the hole in the dome itself. When he'd finished, the jagged rent they'd crawled through was replaced by a low, lopsided arch.

Bruce tossed the last piece of scrap aside with a satisfied grunt. "Okay, Jack. Send the other two ahead so we can all get back inside."

There was a short delay, then Ming-Xue ducked in through the opening. Omar followed close behind, while Jack trailed at a careful distance.

Aaron glanced up from disassembling the cutter, then did a double take. "What the—? You didn't say they were PAF!" He scrambled away from them and cast an accusing glare at Imogene and Bruce.

"It's okay," Imogene raised her hands in a calming gesture. "They're our prisoners. We picked them up in the hills a few dozen klicks west of here."

Looking back at the newcomers, Aaron growled. "Why in blazes didn't you just shoot them? What good are they to us here?"

Imogene blinked. They weren't much good, really. Not if sentient lives were counted like machine parts, to be kept or discarded by sheer practicality.

But people weren't machines.

Before she could figure out how to explain that, Bruce sighed. "I don't know, but they *are* here. There must be a storeroom or something down below, right? Lock them up and we'll worry about it later."

"You realize they're the ones who did this?" Aaron waved to indicate the ruined dome. "The others are *not* going to like this. Hell, I don't know if I like it!"

"What are we supposed to do then?" Bruce asked. "Let them go? Start killing unarmed prisoners? I'm open to suggestions."

"That's not a bad idea," Aaron said darkly. "No one's gonna notice a few more dead pandas."

23

BREATHING ROOM

Imogene and Bruce herded their prisoners down the stairs. Imogene went through the airlock first and stepped out to find Lauren and Alexei waiting. Both still wore their much abused armor, although Alexei had discarded his helmet somewhere.

"Took you long enough." Lauren's whiskers twitched. "I had Scott find some accommodations for our...guests. It's all ready."

The tone she put on *guests* made Imogene's ears want to lay back, but she flipped up her visor and gave a tight smile. "Good thinking. Thanks."

Ming-Xue and Omar were next through the airlock. The shorter Ming-Xue snapped her faceplate open as soon as they emerged, taking a deep, appreciative breath of the open air. Imogene couldn't tell if her delicate white-furred features were those of a mouse or a rat. Ming-Xue saw everyone watching her and looked down self-consciously.

Omar stepped up beside her, but kept his visor down.

The airlock cycled again, letting in Bruce and Jack. Lauren glanced at them, then strode off down the dusky corridor. "Come on. The sooner you get them settled, the sooner we can have some real food and some sleep."

Alexei trotted along beside her, and Bruce waved the two prisoners to precede Imogene and himself.

At the end of the passage they turned right, following the curving outer corridor. Most of the doors they passed were on the inner side of the passage, but a few pitch-black tunnels radiated out through the dome's foundations. Probably access passages to the fuel depot's storage bunkers.

After completing close to a quarter circuit, Lauren took them into a cluttered storeroom. "There's a smaller room at the back we cleared all the stuff out of." She thrust her muzzle at a door nearly hidden behind a shelving unit. "I figure we can keep their suits and stuff out here, and them inside."

"Sounds good." Bruce turned to the prisoners. "You heard her. Leave your armor on the shelf over there. You have some fatigues with you?"

Ming-Xue nodded. "In our packs, yes. But I will need help removing my armor." She shifted her broken wrist.

"Right." Bruce yanked off his gauntlets and threw them onto a shelf. Imogene could tell the anger in his voice was directed at himself for forgetting the rat's injury, but Ming-Xue shrank back against the piled crates.

Bruce looked at Omar. "You first then, so you can help her. I don't know how PAF suits fit together."

Reluctantly, Omar removed his helmet, revealing himself to be a rabbit with dusty brown fur and dark eyes. His ears were long and sparsely furred, reminding Imogene of the wild desert hares that had descended each night to feast on the watered lawns at the base in Ankara.

He shed the remainder of his armor and dug into his pack in search of clothing.

"Here now, let me see that!" Lauren snatched the mass of fabric he pulled forth. "Don't want you sneaking anything else in there with you." She shook out the garments to reveal an emerald green fatigue jacket and trousers, both trimmed with yellow stripes along the seams and cuffs. No incriminating weapons clattered to the floor, and Lauren thrust the clothing back at its owner.

The brown hare clothed himself, then started unfastening Ming-Xue's armor. They saved her injured arm for last. A piercing squeak split Ming-Xue's tight-clenched lips, and

Imogene's stomach lurched in sympathy. She jerked her gaze away before the metal gauntlet came free.

A few more muffled exclamations came from the white rat while Bruce examined her wrist.

Screwing up her courage, Imogene glanced back in time to see him release Ming-Xue and nod.

"It's definitely broken. I'm not good enough to say for sure, but I'd guess not badly. I'm gonna immobilize it." He swathed her hand and arm in pale yellow thermoset bandages, then ran a UV light over his work to fuse and harden the plastic.

When he was done, Ming-Xue cradled the cast against her middle. She looked up at him, lips pricking into a pained smile. "Thank you. I am glad you are willing to help us."

Bruce hunched his shoulders. "Yeah. Try not to use the arm much, okay?"

She nodded and shuffled to join Omar in the inner store-room.

Once the makeshift prison's door was locked behind them, Bruce heaved a long sigh. "Well, that's one less thing to worry about." His tired brown eyes drifted closed for a moment, then popped open. "But our mousey friend isn't the only one who took a hard knock." He cast the dent in Imogene's armor a significant glance. "You've been favoring that side. I want to feel your chest."

Before Imogene could raise her hand to the dent and the dull ache behind it, Lauren snorted. The silver feline's whiskers slicked back and her muzzle twisted in disgust. "Much as I'd love to stay and watch, I'm going for some chow. Happy groping."

She spun and paced out with Alexei at her heels.

Imogene's cheeks grew hot. That's not what he'd meant. She shot the stag a quick look.

He rolled his eyes, then made a point of turning his back, which was more than anyone usually bothered to do in their close living conditions. His courtesy only made her blush harder, and she cursed Lauren for complicating what should have been a simple affair.

Under the suit, her brown and cream fur stuck up in a matted mess. Fully half of it lay against the nap, stiff and wiry with dried sweat. She brushed at it with her hands, but made little progress. A whiff of trapped body odor reached her, and she winced before pulling on her last—and now only—set of fatigues.

"All right." She settled down on a crate and pulled up her gray camo patterned jacket, holding the hem just below her breasts.

Bruce knelt beside her, smoothing back her fur to expose the bruised flesh beneath. His firm fingers sliding over her midriff sent an electric tingle up her spine. The feather-light caress crept upward, spreading delicious warmth towards—

She clamped down hard on her feelings.

That wasn't why he was touching her. He was a medic, and she was his patient. That was all. It was bad enough she'd forced her misinterpretations onto Victor's friendliness; she wasn't going to do the same thing with Bruce.

"How is it?" She kept her tone as casual as her writhing emotions would allow.

He slid his hands over her again, feeling her ribs. "Hard to say. There's some swelling, but that could go either way. Can you describe the pain? Anything sharp or grating, especially when you breathe?"

She filled her lungs, concentrating on the stretchy ache above and left of her belly. "Not really. It's just sore."

"Good." He rocked back and stood. "Probably just a deep bruise, but let me know if anything changes."

Still fighting down her mixed feelings about his closeness, Imogene straightened her shirt and followed him out of the room.

A quarter turn around the dome's ring, another storeroom had been converted into a sort of common area, with the crates restacked to serve as tables and chairs. A double handful of dispirited looking people gathered here, including Lauren and Alexei, Jack, and the two survivors they'd met earlier. A few talked quietly amongst themselves, but most were quiet, glancing up only briefly before returning their dull stares to the gray walls and ceiling.

Jack had changed out of his suit into a blue coverall, its too-large folds hanging almost comically from his slender frame. He set aside a half-eaten tray of field rations to greet them.

"Everything settled?"

"More or less." Bruce took a pair of field rations from an open carton beside the wolf. He passed one to Imogene before letting himself collapse onto a crate.

Imogene sat next to him and pulled the self-heating tab on her rations. Setting the food aside to cook, she took a closer look at the gathered survivors. Their support-branch uniforms made a sort of shabby rainbow: olive green quartermasters, dull red cooks, muddy yellow clerks—all with ears and tails drooping listlessly. Scott the raccoon wore the only combat fatigues, and was the only one who would meet her eyes.

"So," Scott broke the silence. "What are your plans now? We've just been handling things as they come up." He addressed the question to Bruce.

The stag peeled open his now steaming rations before answering. "Right now I'd like to eat, then get out of this suit and sleep. You guys wouldn't have a shower down here, would you?"

Scott shook his head. "The water system's busted anyway."

"Right." Bruce sighed. "After that, I don't know." He looked sideways at Jack. "But you're supposed to be in charge, Captain. Any ideas?"

"Not really. My head's getting better, but concentration's still flaky. I suppose we ought to see about fixing the power plant."

Lauren frowned, nodding agreement as she cut in. "What about comms? If we can call to let them know we're still here, they'll send a recovery team faster."

Scott looked over to Aaron.

The bear cleared his throat. "Radio antennas got pulverized—local and satellite. The fiber line was okay before the attack, but all the equipment is up in the dome. Dunno what shape it's in now."

Lauren's lips pulled back from pointed teeth. "The line is the important part. If it and the transceiver are okay, I can work around whatever else may be broken."

"Hmm," Aaron said. "I know more about nuts and bolts than bits and bytes, but I can at least go check whether or not the comm center is still there."

"Good. You do that," Lauren said. "I'm gonna need some rest before messing with anything technical, so no hurry."

Aaron rose with a wry chuckle. "Not much else to do around here. I'll see what I can find."

Imogene watched him go, then turned her attention back to her meal. She wasn't entirely sure what it was supposed to be. Some sort of thick stew or a runny casserole. Two smaller compartments held white stuff that might be mashed potatoes and a cake-like object she assumed was dessert. The plastic tray had a detachable spork cast into one edge, which she broke free and put to good use. The rations were a far cry from the meals she'd enjoyed at Santbech or Pons, but after days of nothing but liquids, her stomach greeted it eagerly.

Bruce finished after she did, and used his long tongue to clean out the remaining drops of whatever the runny brown stuff had been. He set the tray down and looked up. "That's phase one of my plan done. I'm guessing if there's no showers, there's no beds either?"

Scott shrugged. "There's plenty of storerooms. Take your pick."

"Okay." Bruce pushed himself up from the crate. "We should be back at it in six, seven hours. If any of you come up with something we can help with, hit us up then."

The rest of the Pons contingent rose and followed Bruce into the darkened corridor. After they moved out of earshot, Alexei gave a dismissive flick with one ear. "They won't, you know."

Imogene arched her brows. "They won't what?"

"Come up with anything. Did you see the looks on their faces? I'll lay you odds it was either Scott or Aaron who've done everything important since the attack."

"Hmm," Imogene hedged. Even if what he said was true, it was hard to blame them. Having your base destroyed and then being trapped in the dark with nothing to do but wait couldn't be conducive to a positive outlook.

Ahead of them, Bruce peered into a darkened doorway. "This one looks about right." He flicked on the glow panels, dialing them down to the lowest setting.

Inside, silver crates a metre or more in each dimension formed a cubist's haphazard dreamscape. Not what she'd normally think of as a good sleeping place, but with the low gravity a padded bunk was more for psychological comfort than physical.

While she looked around, Bruce found a likely pair of crates and started shucking his armor.

Imogene claimed her own section a bit farther from the door. Already in her fatigues, she gave the others a chance to change, then glanced around. "I didn't think of it, but we should probably bring the PAF some food. Anyone want to give me a hand with that?"

"Why don't you just get the locals to do it?" Lauren stretched lazily, her claws scraping the crate she lounged on. "They seem pretty eager to please."

Imogene shook her head. "The less they have to do with each other, the better. I think that tech Aaron was serious about shooting them."

"Suit yourself." The lynx flopped down to lay at full length, showing off her fangs in an impressive yawn.

Neither Jack nor Alexei seemed eager to assist, either.

Bruce hefted his rifle with a sigh. "Why not? Let's get it over with." He followed her into the corridor, and the two of them retraced their steps, stopping to collect an armful of field rations.

Imogene dumped the rations on a shelf beside the PAF's discarded armor. She picked two from the pile, then unlocked the inner door and pushed it open.

Bruce hung back, rifle ready in case the prisoners decided to try anything.

Ming-Xue and Omar sat a few metres apart, backs to the far wall. They both looked up, and Omar glowered.

"Brought you some food." Imogene took two steps, depositing the rations in the middle of the room before retreating again.

Omar only watched her, but Ming-Xue gave a slight smile. "Thank you." She looked past Imogene, trying to tell who else was with her, then met her gaze once more. "Would you tell us what is going on? Why is the ventilation system dead?"

"We turned it off to save power." Imogene couldn't see any harm in telling her that much. "It still works, and we'll turn it on again when we need to."

"I see." The white rat nodded. "It is good the base systems are intact."

Omar made a rude noise. "If they are saving power, something is broken. I told you: this base is dying." His gaze darted to Imogene, as if expecting some confirmation or denial.

She didn't offer either. "Is there anything else you need?"

"Not that you will give us, I think," Ming-Xue said.

Imogene snorted. "Fair enough." She backed out through the door, sliding it shut and locking it behind her. She leaned against the door and sighed before turning to face Bruce. "I'm not sure I'm cut out for this."

The stag re-slung his weapon and gave a low chuckle. "I don't think I'd like you half as much if you were. Things will work out. We just have to muddle through until they do."

"And right now, that means rest." Imogene's lips quirked into a lopsided smile. "Muddled heads make for poor muddling, or something like that."

"That they do." He gave her a friendly pat on her shoulder as they walked back to their quarters. "That they do indeed."

24

POWER PLAY

Smoke coiled through empty streets, black snakes flowing on an icy wind. Cold. So very cold. Water dripped from her fur, freezing where it hit the cobblestones, soaking the dead otter's jacket wrapped around her shoulders. Otter musk and blood and oily choking smoke.

Shadows advanced through the smoke and flames, shouting, shooting, storming closer. Mother's hand closed like a vise on her own, yanking her back. Back the way they'd come. Metal boots crushed concrete, closer, closer. Faster than her hooves could carry her away. Her heart pounded. The you-nah men—they were coming. Coming to kill her.

Snow turned to gray dust. Thunder split the air and she fell—so much slower than she should. She couldn't move. Everything floated. She had to run, but fell again and again. The you-nah men were coming. Or the pandas? She couldn't tell, but knew she had to run. Gray cliffs were burning buildings, and a crater gaped black—stairs falling into darkness.

Mother's hand again, pulling her down, forcing her into the dark. She fought, sobbing, gasping sooty air. The water was waiting. It would come again, freezing, choking, smothering like smoke. The water would come again. And this time there would be no escape.

Eyes snapping open, Imogene panted stale air. She started at the shadowy outlines of the storeroom, not quite believing it was real.

But Alexei was snoring. Who'd dream about that?

She ran her fingers over the UNA crest on her fatigues' shoulder. She was a you-nah man now. And who hunted the hunters? In her sleep-addled state she wasn't sure. It seemed like things would be better if no one hunted anyone. That was a nice thought. Better than wondering if she had become one of those half-remembered monsters from her childhood.

Pan-Asian, Unified Nations, did it really matter? The UNA had killed Father, and now Mom and Josh were probably dead too—vaporized in a PAF attack if they were lucky, poisoned from both sides' radiation if they weren't.

And over what? She had more quarrel with Lauren and Jared than she did with the supposed enemies locked in the storeroom.

Why couldn't everyone just leave well enough alone?

She held on to that idea of a world where people got along, even as her eyes closed and she drifted back to sleep.

When Imogene and her comrades arrived for breakfast in the common room, they found Scott already hard at work, rummaging amid the heaped cartons, pulling out ration trays and sorting them by flavor. Imogene grabbed one that claimed to contain scrambled eggs and sat down between Jack and Bruce. Before she could decide what the spongy stuff inside actually tasted like, Aaron arrived.

Lauren set down her half-finished tray and fixed him with yellow, slitted eyes. "What did you find out about the comm center?"

Aaron blinked, but took her directness in stride. "Hard to say. It's still there, but the upper levels are a mess. Some shrapnel went through the comm room, and gods know what all it hit."

Lauren pursed her lips. "Did you try turning any of the equipment on?"

"No. We cut power to the dome; there's a mess of melted wiring up there and it kept tripping the breakers. I can try turning just the comm center back on."

"Do that." Lauren glanced at her remaining food. "I'll be done in a minute, and then you can show me the comms."

Aaron accepted her command with a firm nod and turned to leave.

Swallowing hastily, Bruce called after him. "Hold up. Why don't we figure out what everyone should be doing before we run off every which-way?"

The bear turned and stood in the doorway. "Okay. Shoot."

Bruce frowned, organizing his thoughts. "Well, getting the comms working is a good idea. But failing that, we need to try and help ourselves. There's plenty of food and water down here, and the depth should keep us safe from meteoroids. If we can get power back for the heating and air recirc, we should be good for at least a couple months—"

Alexei choked. "Months?"

"I'm sure it won't come to that," Bruce said. "Still, power is the important thing right now."

Shifting to lean against the doorjamb, Aaron nodded slowly. "That's right, as far as it goes. But the power plant was running when it flooded. The generators are fried, and I can't fix 'em."

Imogene looked up at Aaron. "You must have backups? Or some portable generators?"

"Backup's downstairs too, and tried to kick in right after the mains failed. They're all toasted. I don't know about portables—" He turned to where Scott was still reorganizing boxes. "Hey, Scott! Do you know if there are any portable generators tucked away where I wouldn't have seen them?"

The raccoon pulled his nose out of a crate long enough to give Aaron a disgusted glare. "You think if there were I'd be keeping it to myself?"

"Just asking." He made a placating gesture, then looked back at Imogene. "That's a 'no' then, I guess."

She wrinkled her leathery nose in thought. "What about a vehicle's power plant? Could you tap into one of those and feed it into the base?"

"Probably." Aaron's fur rippled as he frowned. "It would depend on the vehicle, assuming any of them are even still working."

"Should be easy enough to check." She glanced at Bruce, then Alexei. "You guys up for a little more hiking?"

Alexei shrugged, and Bruce nodded. "That sounds good. Jack, what do you think? Any ideas?"

"Hm?" The wolf looked up from listlessly stirring his food. "No, you go ahead. I'll...I'll be here."

Imogene took in his motionless tail and sagging shoulders. Despite having slept, a weariness filled his brown eyes. The worry she'd felt before flared stronger. The last week had been hell for everyone, but especially him. Now they had some respite, she hoped he could recuperate.

Aaron didn't notice, or maybe didn't care. "All right. You might check the railgun turrets, too. I know they pull main power from the base, but I'm not cleared for tactical stuff. They might have backup systems." He turned to Lauren. "I'll go get power to the comms back on for you. Won't be a minute."

The bear lumbered off, leaving them to finish their breakfast. Then, after re-donning their armor, Bruce, Imogene and Alexei headed outside.

The sun had finally slipped below the horizon, shrouding the small valley in darkness. Amid the stars, Earth hung low in the western sky.

Imogene hadn't seen it during their eastward trek, hidden as it was behind them. But if she were honest with herself, she knew she'd been avoiding the sight. Now it had caught up with her, and she couldn't turn away.

Perhaps a third of the way through its month-long cycle, a fat crescent of daylight shone on the lower left side. But this wasn't the natural mosaic of blue and shining white—rather, a flat gray blanket covering everything. Beyond the day/night terminator, the planet's disc formed a dark circle against the stars.

Imogene continued to stare, and her eyes adjusted to pick out darker, sooty streaks across the cloud cover. The night side revealed more detail too: a sinister patchwork of red, glowing malignantly in the darkness. She shied away from thinking what might cause whole continents to burn. Simple forest fires couldn't be so widespread and bright, could they?

Her mother and Josh were down there somewhere, assuming they'd survived. Assuming *anyone* survived—

Imogene wrenched her gaze away and fixed it on the ground. She needed to concentrate. Worrying about things beyond her control wouldn't keep her and her friends alive. She had a job to do, and if they wanted to keep breathing, she'd better do it well.

"So, where to first?" Bruce's voice crackled into her helmet.

Imogene shook her head to clear it.

"The crawler we passed yesterday seemed in pretty good shape." She looked across the valley to the where the Fire Ant made a fuzzy green block in her night vision. "There were a couple more vehicles by the access road, but I think we should check the garage first. Everything out here was damaged badly enough to abandon; whatever's in the garage only had a roof fall on it."

"Makes sense. Let's get on with it, then."

On the dome's southeast side, the garage had been partially hidden during their arrival. Closer now, Imogene decided it was indeed newer than the other buildings. Blocky and painted a uniform dull gray, it contrasted with the almost reflective silver skinned dome. The dozen-metre-long walkway connecting the two was useless now, knocked over and crushed under a Paladin IFV.

Walking up to the abandoned vehicle, Alexei scoffed. "Someone didn't watch where they were going." He bent to peer in through a rough opening where the engine maintenance hatch had been. "I'm guessing this one won't be much use."

"Yeah," Imogene said shortly. At least two gray-suited bodies lay jumbled in with the debris, and Alexei's flippancy bothered her. Shaking her head, she turned to the garage. "How do we get inside? I'm sure the airlock isn't working."

Alexei left the Paladin to investigate the ruined walkway. "There're some gaps in this big enough to crawl through." He knelt, then slithered headfirst into the rubble.

Imogene stepped forward in time to see the rabbit's boots disappear down one of the larger rents.

His helmet popped back into view, blinding her with his headlamps. "No problem. It's pretty open once you're inside. I'll go see if I can get into the garage."

He returned a bit later and crawled out of the rubble. "Nothing. There's two little buggies, but their flywheels are running down. Hardly worth the trouble to dig 'em out."

Climbing over the walkway, they completed a loop around the dome and headed north along the access road. The nearest vehicle was another PAF Fire Ant, though in nowhere near as good a condition as the first.

The treads looked okay, but the airlock refused to open, so Alexei climbed in through a gaping hole where the weapons and command turret had been. He reported the engine compartment seemed to be intact, but none of them knew how to test it when the cockpit controls were nothing but melted plastic.

Leaving it as a "maybe", they continued onwards. A few more crawlers littered the way out of the valley, none warranting more than a brief glance. Holed, twisted, or flat-out blown to bits, they were all useless.

As Aaron suggested, they also checked one of the railgun turrets perched on the valley's rim. The above-ground portion was in sorry shape, armor deeply scored and access panels blown open. It was also above the sheltering rim of Borda's crater, and tiny meteoroids peppered Imogene as Bruce and Alexei wriggled inside to confirm there'd never been a backup generator anyhow.

On their return, they circled to inspect the first Fire Ant. As Imogene had noted earlier, one tread was missing and some of the running gear had been damaged. But the vehicle still had power, and whoever left it hadn't set any security measures. The airlock admitted them without trouble.

That should have been hopeful, but the cramped compartment inside reminded her uncomfortably of the one where Victor and the Sergeant had died. At least there were no bodies. The crew and passengers of this crawler had escaped. Probably just far enough to join the dozens of casualties littering the valley outside.

"Dinky little thing." Alexei looked around in disgust, then crawled up into the command turret that occupied the vehicle's rear. There was theoretically room for two, but neither Imogene nor Bruce moved to join him.

Alexei examined the controls, muttering to himself. He switched to the turret's other seat and gave a satisfied grunt. "I think I've got it. You guys ready?" He threw a switch without waiting for an answer.

The engine rumbled to life, sending a gentle thrum through the floor plates and up into Imogene's boots.

"Hey, it worked!" Alexei laughed. "Want me to drive us back to the base?"

Bruce snorted good naturedly. "With only one tread? You're welcome to try."

"Oh. Right." He shut off the engine and slid down from the turret. "But it does work. That's more than you can say for anything else in this dump."

"Indeed." The stag's smile faded. "Let's just hope we can find a really long extension cord."

"No," Aaron said bluntly. "We don't have a kilometre of electrical cable, and even if we did, the loss at that low of a voltage would be awful."

Bruce frowned and took another bite of his field rations before answering. "How much cable do we have?"

"That'll take that kind of load? Maybe sixty metres."

"Then you're saying we need to get the crawler right up to the front door?"

Aaron hitched his massive shoulders. "Pretty much. Or we can just wait. Your friend said the comms looked repairable. If she can fix them, there's no reason to mess with the crawler."

"I hope so." Bruce didn't sound convinced. "But it won't hurt to try something else in the meantime. Would you come out and look at it? None of us are mechanic enough to assess the damage."

The bear's black nose wrinkled. "If you want. I'll suit up while you finish eating."

After he left, Imogene glanced over at Bruce. "You didn't sound very hopeful Lauren can fix the comms."

"Oh, I don't doubt she can manage." He gave a moody flick of his ears. "I'm just not sure there will be anyone on the other end to talk to. You saw what happened to Santbech, and it was a regional headquarters."

"Yeah." She poked at her food, then glanced up again. "What if it is that way? Everywhere? What do we do?"

"That's why I want the Fire Ant operational. I really hope the relief party gets here sooner rather than later, but if it is later, I want to be alive to complain about it."

Imogene blew out her breath in a snort. Somehow their situation didn't seem so bleak with Bruce and his dry humor nearby.

They finished eating, then suited up and accompanied Aaron to inspect the Fire Ant.

Most of what Imogene knew about PAF vehicles was how to blow them up, but on the surface at least, the damage didn't look bad. The protective skirt that should cover the right-hand tread was gone, along with the tread itself. Twisted bits of both littered the area, fanning out in all directions. The many small wheels that ran inside the tread had plowed themselves hub-deep into the dust, and two near the middle were missing.

After several minutes poking around, Aaron straightened. "The tread's a write off. Shredded. Two running wheels gone, and a third's been warped. Have to take it off too. The chassis looks kinda crumpled and there are some stress cracks, but it's hard to tell how bad with everything half-buried like this."

"Is that stuff we can fix?" Bruce knelt to take a closer look.

"Probably, since we have that other one for parts." Aaron waved towards the second Fire Ant a klick or so north. "First thing is getting it dug out. We've got some shovels back at the base..."

They spent the rest of the "evening" toiling to clear the running gear. Unfortunately, the crawler's wheels tended to settle deeper into whatever hole they dug. Finally they ran girders scavenged from the garage under the crawler to support it while they continued to dig. That seemed to work, and they cleared the last of the dust before returning to the dome for food and rest.

Lauren had the guts of three different computer modules spread out in the storeroom-cum-dining area, and was poking at them with a data-probe when Imogene and the rest arrived. She set the probe down and stretched before turning to face them.

"Nice of you to join us." The lynx's whiskers twitched sardonically. "Did you get your crawler fixed up?"

Bruce shook his head. "It's dug out now. Aaron said we might get it working tomorrow or the day after." The stag collected a package of rations and let himself fall onto one of the ubiquitous crates. "What about the comms? Any luck?"

"Sort of. The transceiver took some shrapnel. The emitter and receiver arrays are okay, but the controllers and decoding boards are messed up." A frown crept across her face, then she gave a decisive jerk of her chin. "Nothing I can't fix."

"Glad to hear that," Bruce said. "I'll let you get back to it."

About half a meal later, Scott appeared in the doorway. He carried some unidentifiable piece of equipment that trailed a rainbow of wires. "Is this the bit you wanted?" His white eyebrows arched hopefully.

Lauren took the device from him and peered at it before nodding. "It is. Go see if you can find any more. I need at least three."

"Right." The raccoon turned smartly and trotted off.

Imogene watched him leave. "He certainly seems more...enthusiastic."

"He's been helping me the last couple hours," Lauren said. "To tell the truth, I think he's kind of glad to have someone tell him what to do." She cast Imogene a sidelong glance. "I even had him take your PAF buddies some lunch since you forgot."

Imogene winced. She wasn't used to having other people to look after, and with the PAF safely tucked away they were easy to forget. "Sorry about that. And thanks for taking care of it."

The lynx flicked her tufted ears and left it at that.

After finishing their meal, Imogene and Bruce made a point of checking on the prisoners. While they were at it, she also changed out the twenty-liter bucket that served the PAF as a latrine. She would have felt worse about the primitive setup, but with the water system broken, the rest of them were making do with the same.

Thinking about it more, Imogene grew miffed that Lauren sent Scott to check the prisoners alone. Nothing had happened, she supposed, so it wasn't worth making an issue over. Still, it seemed almost as if Lauren were trying to provoke an incident.

25

HELL OR HIGH WATER

Imogene's dream of flooded fallout shelters and choking smoke seemed to have taken a night off, and while she wasn't exactly chipper, the next day found her ready to get started repairing the crawler.

That positive outlook didn't last long; her lack of mechanical skills left her feeling rather useless. Mostly she just held spare tools or pointed a hand light and tried to stay out of the others' way.

After a good deal of hammering and cursing, the warped running wheel came free. Then they moved on to stripping the other Fire Ant for parts. Alexei's pestering of Mike and his crew was the only experience any of them had working on treaded vehicles, and even with the illustrated field manual it took considerable trial and error—and yet more cursing—to first release the tension-keeping sprocket, then unlink the tread.

A new wave of meteoroids falling at steep enough angles to enter the crater drove them back inside, and they ate lunch while waiting for the storm to pass.

In what Imogene took as a hopeful sign, Jack tagged along when they went back out. He helped haul parts between the crawlers, then joined Imogene on "Here, hold this" duty. The job didn't really need five people, and after a time he left them to carry on.

They'd almost replaced the first running wheel before hitting a snag. Imogene didn't fully understand the problem, but there was apparently some spring-loaded fastener Aaron couldn't force with the tools at hand. He sent her inside after more tools while he moved on to the next wheel.

Circling around the dome to their rough entrance, she caught sight of Jack's off-white suit beside the silver wall. He'd leaned back against the dome, gazing at the dark sky, and didn't seem to notice her coming up beside him.

"I thought you went back inside," she half-asked.

The wolf startled and glanced down. "No, just looking at the stars." He spoke slowly, as if lost in thought. "They're so bright and perfect. Whatever happens, they just keep on shining. It's...comforting, somehow."

Imogene looked up. "They are very pretty."

"Hmm." He turned his gaze back to the dark sky.

He fell silent then, and Imogene was about to go inside when he spoke once more. "Are there really any gods out there, do you think?"

"I don't know." Her gaze slipped from the sky down to the dead gray mountains. His question struck too near the dark thoughts she'd been burying with hard work and pragmatism. "Sometimes it's nice to think so, but with everything that's happened...I don't know."

Jack didn't answer right away, and when he did, his voice took on a bitter note. "We never can, can we? Just blunder from mistake to mistake, hoping it all means something and will fall out right in the end. That's all any of us ever do."

"Good things happen too." Imogene wasn't sure she believed that right now, but said it anyway. "Good things happen, and there's always a chance things *will* work out."

"Maybe." He sounded about as convinced as she felt. "And the stars will keep burning either way. Like I said, comforting."

They gazed upwards in silence, then Jack spoke again. "I've been watching Earth, too. Do you think the clouds might be clearing, just a little?"

Imogene let her eyes center on the charcoal gray disc she'd been avoiding. If anything, it looked worse to her, the dark bands thicker and more pronounced across the leaden clouds.

Slowly, she shook her head. "No. Not really."

"Yeah." Jack sighed. "Neither do I."

He didn't speak again, and she left a few minutes later. With two more wheels to fix, Aaron didn't need the tools in any hurry, but there was no sense keeping him waiting. She passed Jack again on her way out. He didn't say anything, and she left him to continue his star gazing.

"That should do it." Aaron gave the last lock-nut a final twist several hours later. "Let go of the tension-keeper and see if anything falls apart."

At the other end of the vehicle, Imogene and Bruce eased up on the pry bar wedged between the tension-keeper and the chassis. The large sprocket they'd been holding back slid upwards, taking the slack out of the new tread and pulling it taut.

Nodding to himself, Aaron surveyed their work. "Looks good." He turned to Alexei. "Why don't you get inside and give it some power. If it's still good, then you can give us a ride back."

"Will do." The rabbit sounded eager, and wasted no time climbing into the small airlock.

Both Imogene and Bruce backed hastily away from the crawler.

"Uh, Aaron, you might want to move back a little. Finesse isn't one of his strong points," Bruce cautioned him.

"I *can* still hear you," Alexei's disembodied voice cut in. "And I'll be careful. Is everybody clear out there?"

Aaron moved back several metres, then gave the okay.

There was no sound to indicate Alexei had started the engine. The crawler rocked slightly, then the repaired tread began to creep around its serpentine track. At Aaron's request, he ramped up the speed, and the individual cleats became a blur.

"Okay!" Aaron called out. "Slow down and give it some juice on the other side."

The Fire Ant lurched, the motion from its other tread causing the vehicle to pivot until the repaired tread caught hold on the sides of their trench. The whole crawler pitched forward, leaving behind the tangle of struts they'd stuffed under it for support. Alexei brought the vehicle to a stop and waited while the others climbed inside.

"Where to, fellas?" He poked his head down from the control turret and gave a playful flick of his whiskers.

Bruce chuckled. "Just back to the dome please, driver. We've got dinner reservations it'd be a shame to miss."

"Right then, I'll step on it. Hold on to your tails!" Alexei vanished back into the turret and set them into motion. All kidding aside, he took things slow and careful, never going much faster than a brisk walk.

"Huh. Looks like Jack's outside waiting for us," Alexei said as they neared their destination. "Anyone know how to turn on the comms so we can say hello?"

Imogene frowned. She hadn't expected the wolf to still be outside. "Try your suit comm?" she suggested. "This thing would only talk PAF anyway."

"Good idea." He paused for a moment, then raised his voice. "Hey, Jack. You reading? We've got the crawler up and purring. Just stay where you are, and I'll try not to run you over."

Jack didn't respond.

Alexei snorted. "Probably turned off his comm and fell asleep. Let me get us parked and we'll go wake him up." He pulled the crawler within a half-dozen metres of the entrance, then killed the engine.

Imogene stepped down from the airlock and looked over at Jack. He was right where she'd left him, leaned back against the smooth silver dome. Drawing closer, something about him seemed different, but she couldn't tell what.

Then it clicked.

His normally clear fishbowl helmet was opaque. Not only that, she realized with a sickening jolt, it sat loose on his shoulders. The collar seal had been disengaged.

Imogene's stomach knotted, and she stumbled to an uncertain stop. "No," she whispered. "Not like this."

"What? What is it?" The others were out of the airlock now, crowding around her.

"He, he's..." She couldn't make herself say it.

Bruce inhaled sharply. "Oh gods." He stepped forward and locked the helmet back into place.

It was far too late. They all knew that. Ten seconds to lose consciousness, maybe another ninety before heart failure. He might even have been dead when Imogene passed him on her way back out to the crawler. She didn't think his helmet had been frosted over then, but how long would that take? It was solid white now, a thick layer of ice crystals hiding whatever his last expression might have been.

"Give me a hand, would you?" Bruce looked back at the others. "The least we can do is take him inside."

Aaron and Alexei silently helped carry Jack's body into the dome. There was an office a few doors down the corridor, and they laid him gently atop its desk.

"Why would he do that?" Alexei glanced back and forth between his companions.

"I don't know," Bruce said. "He was a little down, we all are, but this..."

Imogene watched from the corridor. Her conversation with the wolf played over again in her mind. She'd never known anyone who killed themselves, much less been the last person they talked to. She didn't know what to think or feel, apart from horrible. A mass of knots twisted in her stomach, growing ever tighter. It took everything she had to stay on her hooves and follow along behind the others.

No one spoke as they tromped through the airless dome, then down the bleak lithcrete stairs to the airlock. Aaron and Alexei went through first, leaving Imogene and Bruce to wait at the foot of the stairs.

The stag reached over to squeeze her gauntleted hand. "Are you okay?"

Were any of them okay? Really? She wasn't sure anymore, but that wasn't what he wanted to hear.

"Yeah." She looked into his reflective faceplate and gave a return squeeze. "I'll be all right."

She kept quiet as they changed out of their armor and headed to the defacto dining room. Scott and a few others were there, along with Lauren.

The lynx sat hunched over her electronics, and glanced up briefly. "So, how are things outside?"

"Jack's dead," Bruce said flatly. "Suicide."

Lauren looked up again and blinked, then her muzzle twisted and she flicked her ears. "Unfortunate. Can't say I'm surprised, though. What about the crawler?"

"Gods' sake! The man's dead, and all you can do is ask about the crawler?" Bruce's long ears laid back against his skull.

"What do you want?" Her tone remained calm. "He's dead. There's nothing I can do about that. If we all want to stay alive, we need to keep focused on repairing the base."

Bruce's jaw tightened, and his expression darkened further.

Imogene stepped up beside him and put a hand on his elbow. Whether she meant it in restraint or support she wasn't sure.

He gave Lauren a hard stare, then turned away.

Alexei spoke up into the silence. "We did get the crawler running. It's parked outside."

Lauren took a deep breath. "That's good. Thank you, Alexei." She looked over to Aaron. "You can start recharging the power reserves then, right?"

"It's not quite that simple." The bear ran a hand over his brown headfur. "Crawlers run mostly on low voltage three-phase, and that's not what we need. We had a converter that will handle it, but it's down in the power plant."

"Can you find it and bring it up here?" Lauren asked.

"Yeah. It's built into the other equipment, though, and underwater now. It'll take some work."

Imogene suppressed a shudder. She didn't envy Aaron having to wade down into that watery darkness. Not one little bit.

"Tomorrow then." Lauren glanced down at her comm boards. "I should be ready to put all this back together by then too, and hopefully we can get an idea of how long before help arrives."

Bruce snorted. He still looked angry, but took it out on a carton of field rations, roughly tearing through the cardboard and pulling loose one of the plastic trays.

Selecting her own meal less aggressively, Imogene sat beside him. Her stomach had settled somewhat, but her appetite was gone. She only toyed with the food. After Bruce finished, the two of them checked on the prisoners, then retired to their shabby quarters.

The others were gone when Imogene awoke. Tugging absently at her sleep-rumpled uniform, she trotted towards the dining room. She hadn't missed them by much. Bruce,

Alexei and Lauren were still peeling the wrappers from their field rations.

Bruce gave her a tight smile and passed her an unopened tray.

From his seat farther back, Aaron watched them eat, then cleared his throat. "Well, I guess we're all here." He paused, then seeing he had their attention, went on. "I was thinking more about it, and I'm gonna need some help. All the power is out downstairs—obviously—so I need someone to hold a hand light, and probably one more to help get everything untangled."

Lauren nodded. "I could use a hand hauling all this equipment back upstairs too." She turned to Alexei. "You wouldn't mind, right?"

"Sure." He flicked an ear in agreement. "Better than getting wet."

Aaron looked over at Imogene and Bruce. "Looks like the three of us then."

Imogene swallowed hard. Just the thought of descending into the flooded power plant filled her veins with ice water. She could refuse, but what would Bruce and the others think of her? Afraid of a little water. She forced her ears up from their fold, and tried to steady her nerves. She'd done okay on the sewer course in Basic. It wasn't fun, but she'd kept it together.

She could do this.

"All right." She projected confidence into her tone. "We can use our suits, though, right? Then we'll have lights built-in and we can stay dry."

Lauren snorted. "Air-tight's not the same as waterproof. I'm sure it'd keep you dry, but what about the electronics? Are they all rated for submersion?"

Imogene frowned. "I don't know."

"Neither do I. But if they fry, what are you going to do next time we have to go outside? Hold your breath?"

"Okay, so it's not a good idea." Imogene crossed her arms over her chest.

Lauren just smirked and went back to eating.

Forcing herself to do likewise, Imogene methodically cleared her tray. Even eating slowly, it didn't take nearly long enough, and then there was no more excuse to delay. With a growing sense of dread, she followed Bruce and Aaron out into the corridor.

Aaron already had his tools gathered in the stairwell, along with a hand light for each of them. While the grizzly futzed over his equipment, Imogene took a light and pointed it down the stairs. She counted seven steps before the stairway disappeared beneath the dark, oily-looking water. Her pulse quickened, but she forced herself down to the last dry step, then knelt to peer along the surface. Maybe an arm's length of open space separated the water and the lower level's ceiling. Grimacing to herself, she climbed back up to the landing.

"How does it look?" Bruce gave her an encouraging smile.

"Wet."

He chuckled. "I imagined that." He looked down at Aaron. "Any risk with all that water and electricity?"

"Nah." Aaron hitched his shoulders. "I disconnected the main lines, and everything else has either already shorted or is self-contained enough to ignore." He straightened from his tools and began unfastening his blue coveralls. "Might want to leave your fatigues here. No point getting everything wet."

Imogene shed her outer garments along with Bruce, then followed Aaron down into the water.

With each step, the cold liquid soaked into Imogene's fur. Her lungs tightened. By the time they reached the bottom it was up to her armpits. A shudder rippled from her ears all the way to her tail. The cold, the flickering light cast by hand lamps, the smell of wet fur and lithcrete—

She concentrated on breathing regularly and fought to remain calm. There was no danger. It was just water, and if it became too much, all she had to do was turn around and walk back up the stairs. Still focused on her breathing, she trailed behind the others.

This level was smaller that the one above, and despite the water they soon arrived at their destination. Dials and readouts, both digital and analog, covered the small equipment room's walls, and a double row of electrical cabinets took up most of the floor. Everything was painted a pale, industrial green, except the mess of multicolored conduits suspended from the ceiling.

Aaron looked back over his shoulder. "The bit we need is in the last enclosure on the left, and unfortunately it's on the bottom rack."

Bruce waded over to the indicated cabinet. "We'll deal with it, I guess. How well is it attached?"

"Better than I'd like." Aaron's ears flattened. "Ten or twenty set screws and a bunch of cables and conduit." He caught up with Bruce, then unlatched the cabinet. A palpable wave of burnt electronics stench wafted out.

"Phew!" Bruce backed away.

"Yeah." Aaron shook his head glumly. "Hopefully the converter wasn't running when it flooded." He set his tools down atop the cabinet. "Anyhow, I was thinking one of you could take the lights while the other helps me down below."

Bruce glanced at Imogene. "I can do the underwater bit, unless you'd rather?"

Thank the gods he was here to spare her from *that*. She managed a shaky smile. "No, that's okay. Holding lights is a specialty of mine."

He smiled back and passed her his light, then turned to Aaron. "Looks like I'm your stag. Any special plan?"

"Take a good long breath and grab a screwdriver. If you get started on the set screws, I'll see about the electrical connections. I'll probably need help with some of the conduits."

Nodding, Bruce did as the bear suggested.

Aaron followed a moment later, leaving Imogene to try and position her lights to best effect while giving the others room to work.

After about thirty seconds, Bruce resurfaced and shook the water from his eyes. "Gods, that's cold!" He took several deep breaths, then ducked back under the surface.

They settled into a rhythm, thirty or forty seconds working, then about twice that recovering for the next attempt.

Despite her bravado, holding a hand light did little to distract Imogene from her growing unease. Her fur wasn't thick or oily enough to provide much insulation, and the water sucked out her warmth. With it went her last shreds of positive outlook. There was a very real possibility they'd die here. Frozen, asphyxiated, starved to death—the possibilities tumbled through her mind. And what chance of rescue? The Earth was burning. Who would care about a handful of lost soldiers?

Sunken within herself, she barely noticed Bruce or Aaron. If they asked her to move the lights she would comply mechanically, but it hardly seemed to matter. She managed to hold herself together until they finished the job.

Then she fled.

Sometime later Bruce found her, still damp and shivering, huddled behind a desk in one of the main level's unused offices. Quietly, he approached and set her fatigues down on the desk. "You forgot these. And now would be a really bad time to catch a cold."

Wiping her nose with the back of one hand, she looked up. "You think it would matter?"

"Of course it matters." His brows knitted and he knelt beside her. "Why wouldn't it?"

She sniffled again and shook her head. "We're all gonna die. Everything's dying. Victor, the Sergeant, Jack—" Her voice caught roughly. "I, I didn't know he was gonna kill himself!"

Sliding an arm around her shoulders, he pulled her close. "Nobody did. It's not your fault."

"But I talked to him. I told him the clouds weren't getting any better, and, and they're not," she sobbed. "They're not, and my mother and brother were down there, and, and now—" Her voice failed her. Crying in earnest now, she buried her face in his shoulder and wept.

He just held her, rocking back and forth until the storm of her emotion had run its course.

Finally she pushed away, scrubbing at her sore eyes and nose. The last time she'd shed more than a few bitter tears had been before her father died. He'd held her like this when her little tabby cat had to be put down. Back then his arms had seemed much bigger and stronger than Bruce's could ever be, but that feeling of safety and protection was the same. Bruce was a medic, just like he'd been. Maybe it came with the profession.

Bruce shifted slightly, and Imogene suddenly felt very awkward. "Sorry about your shirt." It sounded lame, even to her, but she had to say something.

"Don't worry about it." He gave a slightly crooked smile. "It was already filthy."

Imogene snorted, then caught his warm brown eyes with her own. "Still, thank you."

"That's what friends are for. We've all got to pull together now, or everything will fall apart." He raised his eyebrows. "Are you going to be all right?"

"I think so." Imogene was surprised to realize she actually meant it this time. "Yes, I think I'm gonna be okay."

26

CONVERSION

Imogene woke to find the light from the corridor even dimmer than usual. Every second glow panel had been disconnected to save power. Noticeably cooler, the air tasted thick and hung heavy in her lungs. There wasn't much time before the dying base pulled them down with it.

Her muzzle set in a grim line, she set out in search of the others.

In the common room, Bruce and Aaron groped elbow deep in the disemboweled power converter, testing for water damage. Alexei watched, and Lauren sat to one side, her slim fingers fluttering over a datapad.

Imogene took a field ration and sat. "Any luck with the comms?"

"Some," Lauren's yellow eyes flicked up, then back to her screen. "We're getting through to a routing node near Santbech, but the control software's been erased. I'm trying to patch something together."

Encouraged, Imogene nodded and took a bite of her unsavory-looking steak and eggs. She hadn't expected the comms to yield anything at all. Munching away, she divided her attention between the two prongs of their repair efforts.

Lauren sprang to her silver paws. "I'm in! Buffering the transmission..."

Breakfast forgotten, Imogene and the others crowded around. Maybe things *weren't* as bad as she'd feared.

"This is Acting Section Commander Drayman." The voice came tinny over the datapad's speaker.

Alexei whistled, and Imogene sucked in a fervent breath. There *was* someone there. Someone in charge. Everything was going to be okay.

"Yes, sir!" Lauren said. "This is—"

That wonderful, tinny voice cut her off. "All units are ordered to hold position until communications can be reestablished. Scan sat channels red 15 through 25 and hold position until relieved."

The message began to repeat, and Imogene's hope crumbled into dust.

"It's just a recording." Alexei's ears drooped. He nudged Lauren's shoulder. "Try some other line."

Lauren's whiskers slicked back. "I can't. That's the only good connection. The rest are showing hardware faults."

A leaden silence fell over the room.

Bruce twisted his lips into a wry grimace. "Well, it was worth a try, but I guess that's that."

"No it isn't." Lauren's eyes sparked at him. "We're gonna set up an antenna and scan like we were ordered to."

"Why?" Bruce arched one dark eyebrow. "If there was a working satellite, wouldn't our suit comms have picked it up?"

"That depends on how many satellites and their orbital arrangement. If there's just one and it's in a low polar orbit, we might only get signal here for a couple hours a month. That's why we need to get an antenna set up and tied in with the base computers; it can alert us when one comes overhead, without somebody having to sit outside scanning for it."

Aaron nodded. "Makes sense. Do you need help, or should I keep on with the power converter?"

"I think Alexei and I can manage." She glanced over at the rabbit, who shrugged.

They left, and Imogene settled down to finish eating. Bruce and Aaron dug back into the converter's guts. The bear's multimeter beeped on and off, cutting through their low murmurs and sounding like some lonely coded signal from a bygone era.

Imogene sighed. What were the chances Lauren could actually raise anyone? Comm sats might be above the hail of second-hand bullets and meteoroids plaguing the surface, but they made tempting and easy targets. She swallowed a mouthful of tasteless scrambled eggs and tried to look on the bright side. Anything that kept Lauren out of everyone's fur while they concentrated on more important matters couldn't be all bad.

"That about covers it." Aaron disentangled himself from the mess of wires. "Nothing left but to plug it all together and pray."

Imogene bolted the last of her food and stood. "Anything I can help with?"

"Not really," Aaron said. "We ran all the cables yesterday. Just have to hook it up and turn on the crawler."

It didn't take long. They set up the converter on the floor just inside the airlock, then Bruce suited up and went out to start the Fire Ant's engine. The converter gave a loud click as the power began to flow, then settled into a whining hum that hovered on the edge of audibility and made Imogene fold her ears.

"It's taking it." Aaron licked his lips. "It's taking it." He pulled out a datapad and brought up a status screen. "Slow, slow but steady. We should have the reserve cells up to full inside ninety minutes."

Imogene peered over his shoulder at the readout. "And that's enough power to keep things running here for a week or better, right?"

"If we scrimp, yeah. But we've got bunkers and bunkers full of fuel for the crawler. We may as well turn the lights and life support back up to normal and just recharge every couple days."

That sounded awfully good. The dark and dank ate away at morale—her own in particular. Getting things at least a little closer to normality would help everyone start thinking clearly again.

The power continued to flow, and after a time Bruce came back inside. He tucked his helmet under one arm and stood beside Imogene. "Everything working?"

Aaron gave a satisfied nod. "Seems to be."

"Is it supposed to be making that whining noise?" Bruce looked down at the converter. "It's bloody irritating."

Aaron frowned. "What noise?"

"You can't hear it? High pitched humming, cuts right through you?"

"It's been getting worse," Imogene said. "I thought it was just warming up or something."

Aaron's frown deepened. "No, I can't hear anything." He knelt down and leaned his head close to the converter. "Still nothing. It's smelling pretty hot...maybe we better—"

A crack like a gunshot rang through the corridor, and Aaron screamed. He fell backwards, clutching his face. The lights flickered and died. The converter crackled and hissed, and Aaron screamed again.

Blinded in the dark, Imogene stumbled forward to help, but tripped and landed in a tangle. Bruce cursed over the sounds of Aaron's anguish and the dying sputters of the converter. Then the stag's headlamp came on, throwing a harsh light over the scene.

A thin wisp of smoke rose from the converter, and beyond it, Aaron cowered against the wall. He'd stopped screaming, but still clutched his face, letting out a continuous low moan.

Imogene scrambled over to him. He didn't seem injured, apart from whatever had happened to his face, and with Bruce's help she eased him into a sitting position.

"Oh gods—it burns." The bear's deep voice shook.

Gently, Imogene pulled his hands away from his face.

He resisted briefly, then gave in. A thick reddish fluid matted the fur of his face and hands. It didn't look like blood; the color was wrong. Tiny bits of metal glinted in the red stuff, and his eyes were squeezed tightly shut. The skin around them was starting to swell.

"What is that stuff?" Imogene asked.

"I don't know." Bruce's headlamp swung from Aaron's face to the still smoking converter. "Some kind of coolant. Help me get him up and over to the stairwell. Whatever it is, we better get it washed off." He glanced at the injured tech. "You understand, Aaron?"

"Yeah," Aaron spoke through gritted teeth. "I can't see. My eyes are on fire."

Imogene and Bruce hoisted him upright and steadied him to the flooded stairwell. He stumbled on the narrow steps and fell headfirst into the water.

Biting her lip against the wet and cold, Imogene waded in and helped him up.

Aaron resurfaced, took a few breaths, then plunged his head into the water again. He scrubbed frantically, and the water took on a reddish tinge.

"Can you stay with him?" Bruce asked. "I saw a full-size med kit in one of the storerooms."

Imogene nodded, and he hurried off. The light from his headlamp went with him, and the water seemed to rise into the darkness. Imogene's guts twisted, but she forced away the fear, locking her attention on keeping Aaron steady. She didn't know how long they stood there, partway down the stairs, but it felt like a long time.

Finally the clank of boots and a faint light from the corridor marked Bruce's return. "How's he doing?"

"Better," Aaron answered for himself. "But still very painful, and I can't see."

"Okay. I took a quick look at the converter, and one of the big capacitors ruptured. Do you know what they fill them with?"

Aaron shook his head. "I think I've got most of it out, though. It just hurts, not burning anymore."

"There's some saline in the kit," Bruce offered. "If you think you've got it all out, we can rinse your eyes with that and then bandage them."

Imogene guided the bear up to the landing and helped him lay down on the floor. The skin around his lips and nose was inflamed too, although not as badly as his eyes. Both were swollen nearly shut, and when carefully pried open to irrigate, were blood-shot.

While Bruce worked, Scott appeared in the doorway. His tail twitched uncontrollably, and he gripped a hand light almost hard enough to crack the plastic. Bruce and Aaron filled him in on what had happened, then sent him off to reset the breaker that was probably responsible for the power outage.

A few minutes after he left, the glow panels flicked back to their gloomy half-life. The ventilation system coughed, sending out a puff of slightly less fetid air.

"That about does it." Bruce leaned back from putting the finishing touches on Aaron's dressing. "Looks like both thermal and chemical burns, but I'm not sure. I wish we had a real doctor."

Aaron pushed into a sitting position and winced. "I'm just glad you're here. Our medic was upstairs when the dome went." He reached up and felt gingerly around the bandages. "Any pain pills in that kit? I could really use some about now."

Bruce found him some pills, and they took him back to the common room. Everyone else was accounted for and unhurt, although understandably shaken. After making Aaron as comfortable as possible, Imogene and Bruce went to check the prisoners. She didn't really expect them to have hurt themselves in the dark, but it was best to check, and almost time to feed them again anyway.

"Why did the lights go out?" Omar demanded as soon as the door slid open. The hare was up on his paws, brown fur rippling as his muscles tensed.

Imogene stepped into the small room, but kept her distance. "We had a problem with the power supply."

"And the air? It is getting very thick. Why do you not turn on the life support? Another *problem?*" He thrust his chin forward aggressively.

Her jaw tightened. "You should know, you're the ones who shot up the base."

"It was not us," Ming-Xue put in quietly. "We are scouts."

The white rat sat cross-legged in the room's far corner, broken wrist held close. Her wide blue eyes sought Imogene's and held them earnestly.

Imogene sighed, struggling to build a wall around her misplaced anger. "I know."

Ming-Xue dipped her muzzle and gave a tight smile.

"But there is a problem? With the power?" Omar persisted.

Turning back to him, Imogene snorted. "I think that's obvious. Your friends did a good job."

His ears twitched, but he let her barb pass. "Exactly what is broken? I have done some electrical work. Perhaps I could assist."

Imogene's eyes narrowed. "I'm not sure. And why this sudden urge to be helpful?"

"Ha! I want to die here no more than you. If you let the air degrade so far, that must be close."

Logical, but could they trust him? No matter how nice it would be if everyone worked together, Imogene wasn't stupid. She offered a noncommittal flick of her ears.

"We'll keep that in mind." She set down the field rations she'd been holding, then backed out of the cell. Closing the door, she turned to face Bruce. "What do you think? With Aaron out of action we could use any help going."

"Maybe." The stag nodded. "But I want another look at the converter first. It might be something I can fix myself."

Imogene followed him back to the site of the accident, then waited while he went out to shut down the Fire Ant, which was still doing its best to push power into the ruined converter.

It didn't take a technician to tell the converter was a mess. One component the size of a tuna-can had torn itself apart, and the rest showed charring. More of the red goo spattered everything, and they both avoided touching it.

Bruce made a helpless gesture and stood up. "Out of my league. Obviously that capacitor needs to be replaced, but I don't even know where to start with the rest."

"Then should we let Omar take a look?" Imogene pushed up to her hooves as well.

"Might as well. I don't think he could make it much worse."

They picked up the suitcase-sized converter between them and carried it back to Ming-Xue and Omar's cell.

Their prisoners hadn't finished eating, and looked up in surprise. Omar quickly set down his rations and came over.

"This is our main problem at the moment." Bruce nudged the converter with one hoof. "It burned out, and we aren't sure how to fix it."

Omar knelt beside the singed electronics. "It is a normalizing high-step converter, yes? I do not know if I can fix it, but if you give me tools I will try."

"What do you need?"

The brown hare glanced up. "To start? A multimeter, needle-nose pliers, and both flat and cross-head screwdrivers. Maybe a soldering set and spare parts once I know what is wrong."

"All right." Bruce turned to Imogene. "Keep an eye on them." He trotted off, leaving her alone with the two PAF prisoners.

Omar watched him go, then returned his attention to the converter.

Sitting in her corner, Ming-Xue finished her meal and leaned back against the wall. "If this is repaired, we will have power and air again? We will be okay?" She looked inquiringly up at Imogene.

"As long as the food and water hold out." She flicked her ears. "Hopefully we can call someone for help before that."

Ming-Xue frowned. "Surely you have sent someone out for help?"

"Not yet. We need to stabilize things here first."

"I see." Ming-Xue fell silent, wrapping her furless tail around her paws.

Her honest disbelief struck a chord with Imogene. She had no great hope of Lauren contacting anyone, and while she refused to let herself sink into despair again, she knew the odds of a timely rescue went down with each passing minute. When they came to Borda a week ago, it seemed like a relief. Now the base felt more and more like a trap.

Bruce returned with a pair of gloves and some rags in addition to the requested tools.

"Careful of the red goo," he handed over the caution along with the tools. "We're not sure what it is."

Omar swabbed some up with his finger, sniffed, then wiped it off on a rag. "Melted forium gel. Tastes very bad." Not bothering with gloves, he mopped up most of the goo and started to probe around with the multimeter.

He hadn't been working long when the cell door slid open and Alexei entered. "There you are," he huffed at Bruce. "The power's still out in the comm center, and Lauren's getting pissed off. I tried asking Aaron for help, but I can't make heads or tails out of his instructions. Then he said I should ask you."

Bruce sighed. "Right. I'll see what I can do." Shaking his head, he turned and left.

When Alexei made no move to follow, Imogene arched her brows at him. "Aren't you going to go tell Lauren or something?"

"Nah, I don't think so." His whiskers twitched. "She lost a lot of work when the power cut out. She may know computers, but she's got a hell of a temper to go with it."

"She does at that." Imogene's tongue slid over the mostly healed space where her missing molar had been. She didn't blame Alexei for wanting to steer clear of the lynx until she'd had a chance to cool down.

Omar cleared his throat and they both looked down at him. "Could I have a flat-head screwdriver? The only one your friend brought is a cross."

"I can get you one." Alexei nodded, then looked over at Imogene and frowned. He tugged her away from Omar and lowered his voice. "Why are you letting him mess with this anyway?"

"He knows some electrical stuff. Bruce and I figured with Aaron blinded it was the best thing to do."

"I s'pose." He nodded again. "You might keep it quiet, though. Lauren wouldn't like you giving them tools and stuff. Especially without asking her first."

He left then, and Imogene narrowed her eyes at Omar. She believed he and Ming-Xue understood the situation and were willing to work towards mutual survival, but Lauren would never trust them, or any help that came from them. Scott and the other survivors mostly fell in that same hostile category. Best to avoid mentioning Omar's cooperation for now.

Alexei returned and handed a screwdriver to Omar.

The brown hare thanked him, then resumed his work. He was slow and methodical, which Imogene took as a good sign. On the other hand, the pile of rejected components he was amassing didn't bode well for an easy repair. Finally he made a clicking noise with his tongue and sat back.

"It is not good," he said in his oddly flat intonation. "There is much damage. Most I could repair if I had parts, but the mid-step regulator has fused. I do not know if a small base like this would have a suitable replacement."

"What about the rest?" She pointed her muzzle at the collection of circuit boards and larger components he'd removed.

"Useless, but common." He gave a dismissive wave. "There should be no trouble finding substitutes."

"We'll see what we can find, then. Thanks for looking at it." Imogene knelt and shoveled the rejected bits into an empty carton.

Omar slid his borrowed tools in alongside them and stood up. "Perhaps...I could help you search?"

"Later, maybe." Imogene eyed his expressionless ears and down-sloping lagomorph muzzle, then turned to Alexei. "Could you give me a hand with the converter?"

He grunted an affirmative and helped her carry it to the outer chamber. They slid the converter onto a shelf beside the prisoners' armor. Imogene checked the cell door was shut and locked, then the two of them headed out into the corridor.

Bruce was coming the other way and nodded a greeting. "You finished up inside? What's the word?"

"He says it needs more parts," Imogene said. "Some special bit in particular. I thought we'd go ask Aaron if there are any spares."

"Okay. We can go do that now. Lauren's getting everyone together for a meeting or something."

Alexei grimaced. "Great. Could you tell if she was still angry?"

"No more than usual." Bruce flicked his ears, then glanced at the door to their makeshift prison. "You checked that you got all the tools and stuff back, right?"

"Yep," Alexei reassured him. "One pair of pliers, two screwdrivers, one voltmeter, and a pile of burnt electronics."

"Good enough," Bruce said. "Let's go see what Lauren wants."

27

OUT OF TIME

With all twenty-three survivors together, the common room felt crowded. The shelving units had long since been pushed aside, and crates set up for seating, but elbows and tails still bumped and jostled to make room for everyone. The warmth from so many bodies made a pleasant contrast to the chill seeping through the base, but by the same token, the air inside grew even thicker and more distasteful to breathe.

Last to arrive, Imogene's group settled near the door.

Aaron was recounting the accident for the others' benefit. Whatever had been in his pain meds was working a bit too well; he'd picked up a drunken slur, and seemed to almost be enjoying himself.

Lauren waited a moment after he finished, then spoke, "Thank you, Aaron. I think that's more detail of what went wrong than any of us could ask for." Sarcasm dripped from each word, but the bear just smiled and nodded. She rolled her eyes, then turned them on Imogene and Bruce. "What's the status of the power system? If I'm busting my tail to fix the comms, I damn well want there to be power to run them when I'm done."

Bruce hitched one shoulder. "It's not good. The converter's damaged, and we only got the reserves up to about fifteen percent before it blew."

Farther back, Scott frowned. "How long will that last us?"

"Maybe three, four days."

"And then what? Can we fix the converter? Try again?" The raccoon's eyes darted from face to face with each question.

Bruce sighed. "I don't know. Some of us looked at it, but we're gonna need more parts." He turned to Imogene. "What did you say it was?"

"The mid-step regulator. It's fused, and we didn't know if there's a spare...?"

"Nah." Aaron shook his head. "Nothing like that."

"I don't suppose you could jury-rig something similar?" Imogene asked.

"Without my eyes? Hell no." He chopped the air emphatically. "And just how soon they might get better, I can't say. Never been blind before, y'know?" He ended with a snorting chuckle.

"Right." Her ears twitched uncomfortably and she looked away.

"What about you?" Scott's gaze latched on to Lauren. "You did a good job fixing the fiber line. Maybe you could figure something out?"

The lynx wrinkled her nose. "I doubt it. There's a big difference between computers and power systems."

"Oh." Scott's tail went limp.

"Speaking of them, what about the sat-comms?" Imogene asked. "Any time estimate?"

Lauren's ears flicked back and her eyes narrowed. "It'll take as long as it takes. Longer when people decide to kill the power without warning."

"That was hardly intentional," Bruce cut in. "Right now we need to figure out what to do about life support and power." He paused to let his words sink in, then turned to Aaron. "I know you can't help with any of the physical work, Aaron, but you're still the best electrician we have. Are there any other power reserves we can tap? Weapons systems maybe? Or the buggies in the garage?"

The bear frowned, pulling the bandage over his eyes tight. "Weapons stuff was all downstairs. You might get a little from the buggies, if we can figure how to drain 'em. They're probably pretty run down by now anyway."

"All right, suits then. A base this size should have a decent amount of EVA equipment. It won't be comfortable, but at least we won't suffocate."

Aaron gave an amused snort. "Not as soon, you mean. We got no way to recharge the power packs."

His drug-induced bluntness settled over the gathering like a layer of thick, gray dust. At the back of the room a young ferret began to cry softly and was comforted by her seatmate.

Imogene watched them dully. She hadn't spoken more than three words to either of them. Didn't even know their names.

Finally, Lauren broke the silence. "There is still the Fire Ant. Even if we can't take power from it, there's nothing wrong with the life support, and we have plenty of fuel."

Her words sent a flutter of hope through Imogene. Then she looked around the crowded chamber, and her heart sank again. "It won't work. You'd be lucky to get half of us in that little crawler."

"Well, the rest could wait outside," Lauren snapped. "Who knows? Maybe we can scrape together enough PAF suits and power packs for everyone. The Fire Ant's bound to have a charger for them."

An image of the dismembered bodies littering the valley flashed through Imogene's mind. There couldn't be more than a handful of PAF suits that could be repaired. Certainly not enough for everyone.

Alexei frowned, evidently thinking along similar lines. "But what if we can't? What happens when the people in UNA suits run out of power?"

"Then we find out who's who, of course." Aaron bared his teeth in another snorting laugh. "On the other hand, I wouldn't be surprised some bunch don't decide to just drive off before it came to that."

"Nobody here would do that!" The rabbit's ears jerked upright and he looked around for support.

Aaron just chuckled.

"Well, they wouldn't," Alexei said sullenly.

Scott's white eyebrows drew together during this exchange, and he spoke slowly into the quiet that followed. "What about those PAF you have locked up? If we're all going to suffocate, shouldn't we get rid of them now and save the air for us?"

The corner of Lauren's mouth quirked upwards at this. "That's a good question." She looked over at Imogene and Bruce. "We let you keep them earlier. What do you say now?"

All eyes turned on them.

Imogene shrank under their gaze. Then something inside her dug in its hooves, and she shook her head.

"None of this matters." She stood up and cast her eyes over the suddenly quiet gathering. "It's more than two weeks since the attack here. If any help was coming, it would've been here by now. Scraping out a few more days or hours—it doesn't matter. No one is coming."

"Someone will come," Lauren spat. "You think they'd just leave us? The section commander said to hold position. Any day now a relief column will get here, and we need to hold on until they do."

A rumble of agreement swept the Borda survivors.

"Normally, yes," Imogene conceded. "But this isn't some little border skirmish. If we want help we're gonna have to go out and look for it. They probably don't even know we're still here."

"And how do you know it's not just a skirmish?" Lauren asked.

Imogene's jaw dropped. "We should've been more than seven-hundred klicks behind friendly lines here! And you don't think it's an all-out war? Damn it, just go outside and look up! You honestly think anyone cares about us now?"

"So then what? Disobey orders and abandon the base?" Lauren's lips twisted in scorn. "You said yourself we can't all fit in the Fire Ant. Who gets to walk? And where would you even go?" Her ears flicked forward. "We have to wait here. It's our duty to hold the base, and someone *will* come."

Alexei's whiskers twitched nervously, but he nodded as she spoke.

Imogene looked around at the other survivors. Most of the base personnel clearly agreed with Lauren.

Bruce wore his usual worried frown. He glanced over at the others, then back to Imogene and gave a slight shake of his head. She could tell he agreed with her, but he was right; no one was ready to accept just how bad things really were.

Imogene gritted her teeth. "All right. If you all want to stay here and hope, that's what we'll do. Bruce, Alexei, let's get suited up and start looking. We've got our armor, so that means we need seventeen more suits—of one sort or another—and as many power packs as we can find."

Lauren looked like she wanted to object, but Imogene spun on her hooves and left before the lynx could do more than glower.

Searching through the rubble for EVA suits and power packs was grim work. UNA suits weren't a problem, plenty hung in the airlock ready rooms. There were power packs there too, but more would be needed. That meant looking for bodies.

Most of the dead inside the dome had been suitless, but outside, the remains of several infantry squads littered the landscape. Each ruined vehicle had held suits for its crew, and needed to be investigated as well.

In the solitude of her armor, Imogene brooded. Once, she looked up to where the Earth hung as an ash-gray disc, then quickly looked away.

She knew she was right. Everything they had ever known was being swept away. If any of them were going to survive, they needed to realize that soon. Lauren's promise of a simple comm call and a swift rescue echoed empty. Did the lynx even believe it herself, or was she just clinging to the last fragments of order and control? Either way, arguing with her couldn't have helped matters.

Five hours combing through the battlefield yielded only three PAF suits in good enough shape to repair. Assuming they crammed into the Fire Ant like sardines in an armored can, that still left four or five people reliant on the UNA suits they had no way to recharge.

They gathered the suits and all the power packs they could find, piling them in the stairwell outside the basement airlock.

Returning with the last of their spoils, Alexei added them to the bulky heap. "You think they'll all fit in the airlock?"

Bruce punched the airlock's open button and shrugged. "No reason we can't make two trips." The airlock didn't open, and he thumbed the button again. "Assuming we can get in at all—"

The door opened and a gray blur launched out.

Bruce yelled as the attacker hit him. The tackle carried him backward into the wall, where he and his assailant slid to the floor in a tangle of limbs.

A second figure emerged from the airlock and moved purposefully towards Imogene and Alexei.

Imogene backpedaled, belatedly recognizing Omar and Ming-Xue's angular gray armor.

Ming-Xue closed on them, her motions showing a graceful familiarity with the low gravity. Neither she nor Omar spoke, leaving Bruce and Alexei's profane exclamations the only comm traffic.

With a yell, Alexei surged forward. He grabbed at the rat, trying to catch the injured arm she kept close to her middle.

She twisted aside, evading his clumsy grab and making a clean one of her own. With a flick of her good wrist, she redirected the rabbit's attack and sent him sprawling into the airlock.

Imogene took another step backwards and felt her boot brush the bottom stair. Bruce and Omar still writhed together. She didn't dare take her attention from Ming-Xue long enough to see who was winning.

The rat started forward again, silver-tinted visor hiding any expression.

Dread pooled in Imogene's belly. Her unarmed bouts with Victor had taught her enough to know that even with a broken wrist Ming-Xue outclassed her in every way. She dredged her memory for any tricks the big cat might have taught her. But all she found was his warm scent and the feel of his hard muscles when her bungled attacks left them both fallen and hopelessly entangled—

She narrowed her eyes. There was no way she could win, but she might be able to make sure Ming-Xue lost.

With a feigned grab at Ming-Xue's leading wrist, she threw herself at the rat.

Ming-Xue batted the grab away, but Imogene's artless tackle plowed into her. The rat managed to pivot, coming down atop Imogene, but both ended up on the floor. Ming-Xue was definitely the better fighter, but Imogene held on stubbornly, twisting as hard as she could at Ming-Xue's broken wrist. Alexei returned to even the odds, and between them, they subdued the rodent.

By the wall, Bruce had Omar face-down, arms pinned firmly behind his back.

"Everyone okay?" Bruce asked.

"I think so." Alexei was still breathing hard. He glanced at Imogene, who nodded.

"Good." Bruce hoisted Omar up, keeping his arms behind him. "Let's get them back inside."

Bruce and Omar went through the airlock first, then Alexei and Ming-Xue, leaving Imogene to bring up the rear.

She stepped out almost on top of the prisoners, backed into the corner with Alexei guarding. The Borda survivors crowded the rest of the passage, ears flat and teeth bared. Imogene tensed. Not good.

Between the two groups stood Bruce and Scott.

Blood matted the fur above the raccoon's left eye, and his ears lay back against his skull. He held a rifle—fortunately pointed upwards—and his ringed tail thrashed against the legs of those nearby.

"I don't care." Bruce crossed his arms. "I'm not letting you kill them out of hand."

Scott snarled. "Why the hell not? They've proven they're dangerous!"

"Yeah," the stag grunted. "But that's not something you get to decide alone. Remember, they could have killed you, but they didn't."

Imogene's pulse throbbed in her ears, but she forced her breathing back under control. The part of her reeling from the fight agreed with Scott, but the rest of her knew Bruce was right. She couldn't blame Ming-Xue and Omar for wanting to get away from people who planned to murder them. Actually, she wished they'd gotten away. It would have made every-thing easier.

She slid up beside Bruce, further blocking Scott's aim.

At the corridor's far end, Lauren came into view. She wore her armor, and in her hands was another rifle. Pushing through the crowd, she surveyed the situation. "You caught them? Good." She nodded approvingly. "Alexei, get out of the way so we can shoot them."

"Here now." Bruce sidled between Lauren and the prisoners. "Are you sure that's what we really ought to do?"

Behind her open visor, Lauren frowned. "Of course. They're using up air, anyway."

"That's true," said Bruce. "But don't you think we should at least talk about it first?"

"I don't see what's to talk about." She peered around him to where Alexei still stood by the prisoners. "Alexei, I told you: you're in the way."

He looked from Bruce to Lauren uncertainly, then slowly moved aside.

Imogene edged closer to Bruce. She'd believed they could curb Scott's aggression, but adding Lauren into the mix...

Bruce locked his eyes with Lauren's. "First off, who put you in charge? And don't try to argue a few months' seniority between privates. Obviously you and Scott want them dead, but what about everyone else?"

The lynx snorted. "Fine. Let's ask." She turned to face the rest of the corridor. "Everyone who thinks we should let them keep breathing our air, raise your hands."

"A vote?" Imogene couldn't contain herself. "You're talking about murdering two prisoners of war! How can this even be an option?" She searched the angry faces around her, hoping for some glimmer of compassion. A few eyes fell guiltily when her gaze met them, but few—precious few.

"She does have a point," Bruce said into the silence following her outburst. "Apart from any moral issues, killing them could be a very bad idea if anyone ever found out. Do you all trust each other not to blab to some war-crimes committee? I sure don't."

That wasn't what Imogene meant at all, and she cast him a sideways glance.

But his words had an effect where hers hadn't. The beginnings of doubt crept through the crowded corridor.

Seeing this, Imogene swallowed her own feelings to shore up their new position. "At least give it some time. This isn't something to decide lightly, and we'll all have clearer heads tomorrow."

That got a few reluctant nods from the Borda personnel, and on the sidelines, Alexei looked relieved. "I think that's a good idea," he said. "I'm not sure we should keep them, but this is all going too fast."

Lauren's eyes narrowed and she shot Alexei a sharp look. Most of the locals still seemed willing to back her, but she lowered her rifle. "All right. A few hours won't make much difference if it'll keep you happy." Her glare returned to Imogene and Bruce. "But I want them back in their cell with a guard on the door until they're dealt with."

Bruce gave a curt nod. "That's only prudent."

They took the captives back to their storeroom prison and stripped them of their armor.

Ming-Xue whimpered as her injured arm came free, and Imogene struggled to suppress a surge of sympathy. The rat had brought it on herself. Bruce inspected the cast and added another layer of thermoset where the first had been cut to fit in her armor.

While Bruce finished, Alexei turned to Scott. "How did they get out, anyway?"

"I don't know." The raccoon glowered at the two prisoners. "By the time they attacked me out in the corridor, they were already suited up and headed for the airlock."

Bruce stepped into the cell and glanced around. "They've got the door's service panel off—somehow—and there's a screwdriver wedged in behind the locking actuator." He looked up at Alexei. "I thought you said you got them both back?"

Omar snorted, the first sound he'd made since being recaptured. "Stupid rabbit brought me another, and lazy caribou didn't notice."

Alexei rounded on him, shoving the now unarmored hare into a shelving unit. "You tricked me!"

Omar just smirked, and Alexei shoved him again, harder this time.

"Why in blazes were you giving them tools in the first place?" Lauren demanded.

No one spoke for a moment, then Bruce cleared his throat. "We had him look at the power converter, after the accident."

Scott turned his glower on Bruce. "So all this is your fault?"

Rather than answer, Bruce hefted the access panel. "We should be good after I put this back on. You didn't bring them any other tools, did you, Alexei?"

"Just the bloody screwdriver." He scowled at Omar, who had the sense not to bait him further.

It only took a few minutes to replace the service panel and prod Ming-Xue and Omar back into the cell.

"Right," Bruce said when the prisoners were secure. "I don't think they can get loose again, but we'll post a guard to be safe. I can take the first shift."

"No," Alexei said. "I'll do it. I'm too angry to sleep anyway."

Bruce cast him a measuring look, then nodded. "Come wake me when you get tired."

"I will." He took Scott's rifle and checked it was in order before settling down on an empty crate.

They left him to it.

The common room buzzed with conversation that died the moment Imogene stepped through the door. It didn't take a great deal of imagination to guess what had been under discussion.

Imogene's jaw tightened. All they'd managed was to buy a little time. Afraid anything she might say in the prisoners' defense would only make matters worse, she ate quickly and then retired.

Despite the weary aches in every joint, sleep didn't come easy. The whole situation was circling the drain. They needed help, but the others would never accept that in time. Setting off alone in search of rescue was tantamount to suicide, though, especially on foot.

She couldn't leave Ming-Xue and Omar here to die, either. By accepting their surrender she'd made it her responsibility to see them treated fairly. There'd been far too much blood-shed already, and living only mattered as long as she could live with herself.

She had to take care of them. Somehow.

Those thoughts and others like them rolled around her head, occasionally crashing together and giving off sparks of short-lived hope. Then one spark refused to die. It grew brighter, and slowly reshaped itself into the beginnings of a plan. She wasn't sure she liked it, but it was better than nothing, and so she teased after its details until sleep finally found her.

28

SEEDS OF BETRAYAL

Imogene didn't know how long she slept. She hadn't meant to sleep at all, and berated herself for missing her chance to act. But glancing over to where Bruce made his sleeping place, she saw there was still time.

The stag was there, and speaking softly with Alexei. In fact, the rabbit's arrival was probably what had woken her. Their conversation concluded, and Bruce left quietly while Alexei moved to his own resting place.

Imogene lay still. Alexei probably wouldn't like what she'd planned, so she waited.

After a time, he began to snore.

Lying closer to him, Lauren mumbled something and rolled over to face the wall.

Imogene gave them a few minutes more, then rose carefully and made her way into the corridor.

With everyone asleep, the distant *plick* of water dripping in the dead power plant filled her ears. She tread as softly as she could, but each click of hoof against lithcrete seemed like a gauss round hitting stone. At last, she reached their makeshift prison and slid the outer door closed behind her.

Seated on a crate near the inner door, Bruce watched her. "I like nocturnal games as well as the next person, but this hardly seems the time." He kept his voice low, tone serious.

Imogene sat down beside him. "That's not why I'm here."

"I didn't think so. Why then?"

Her green eyes caught his brown ones. "Tell me, honestly, do you believe we have any chance of getting rescued?"

He grimaced and looked away. "It's possible."

"But not likely."

Wearily, he shook his head.

"So the logical thing to do is go look for help, right?"

"It'd be pointless," he said. "We couldn't get more than a hundred klicks, and it would take days."

Imogene looked down at her hands. "Not if we took the Fire Ant."

"Lauren and the others would never go for that."

This was the part that worried her. But she'd made up her mind to see this through, and after a deep breath, she took the plunge.

"That's why we don't ask them."

Bruce let out a low whistle.

"They won't be much worse off," she added hastily. "I did the math. With the power packs we have already, they should be okay for a good two weeks. If we can't find help by then, there isn't any coming anyway. At least this way everyone will have a chance."

"It's an idea." He frowned thoughtfully. "I don't much like it, though."

"Neither do I," she said. "But if we wait for the others to agree, it'll be too late."

Bruce's frown deepened, and he didn't reply right away. He finally nodded towards the cell door. "What about them? I don't fancy their chances without us here."

"That's the other reason we need to do it now. Scott and Lauren are gonna kill them. I know you're not dumb enough to think we can keep protecting them. We've got to get away as soon as possible, and take them with us."

"Of course." Bruce heaved a long sigh. "I need to think about this."

"Fair enough, but think fast. I'd really like your help, but one way or the other, I'm leaving tonight." She rose and trotted to the door. There were preparations to be made.

She'd worked out this part of her plan in detail. Quickly but quietly, she moved through the base. In less than fifteen minutes she returned, now armed, armored, and with a satchel full of supplies.

Bruce sat where she'd left him. He rose to face her, still wearing a worried frown.

"I'll do it." He didn't look happy, but gave a decisive nod. "If you're set on doing this, I'll go with you."

A hard knot of tension melted from Imogene's chest. Their gazes met, and she laid a gauntleted hand on his arm. "Thank you."

His muzzle tightened and he squared his shoulders. "Well, it's your plan. What do you need me to do?"

Imogene let her hand drift back to her side. "We're about set. If you'd wait while I make sure our friends are...agreeable, then you can go get your armor and personal stuff. Meet us back here, and we'll head out."

"All right." He hefted his rifle and moved aside to let her open the cell door.

As expected, Ming-Xue and Omar were inside, both fast asleep.

Imogene tapped the barrel of her rifle against the door-jamb.

The two PAF scouts woke faster than she would have believed, and Omar sprang upright. His eyes darted to the weapon in her hands, then narrowed. "So, you have come for us?"

"Not exactly. Bruce and I are leaving. You can stay if you want, or you can come with us. Your choice."

The hare's eyes narrowed even further. "And what is the trick?"

"No trick," she said. "The base is fucked. No one will admit it, so we're going for help. You're coming along so we don't find you full of holes when we get back. Simple."

Ming-Xue rose more slowly and cocked her head at Imogene. "The others do not know of this?"

"No."

The white rat glanced over at Omar. "I doubt we will get a better offer."

His lips compressed to a thin line, but he nodded.

"Get suited up, then." Imogene waved them out of the cell. "The sooner we're out of here, the better."

Behind her, Bruce was already headed for the dim corridor.

Imogene's preparations included a set of shears to trim Ming-Xue's cast. The rat's jaw clenched as they forced her plastic-wrapped forearm into the armor, but she managed to remain silent. Then Imogene backed off and watched impatiently while they donned the rest of their suits.

A crackle from her comm made Imogene jump.

"I've got my stuff, but Lauren and Alexei are gone." Bruce's voice filled her helmet. "Don't wait for me. We can meet up at the crawler."

"Damn it!" Imogene spun to face the corridor. The doorway was empty. No sign of lynx or rabbit.

Snapping the last piece of his suit into place, Omar looked up. "What is it?"

"Trouble." Imogene glanced back to make sure both her charges were ready. "Come on."

She moved up to the doorway and stuck her head out into the ring corridor. Still no one in sight, so she turned left, taking the shortest route possible. At the junction of the ring and spoke corridors she repeated her careful reconnaissance. The airlock door waited at the end of forty metres of shadowy corridor. Waving the PAF to follow, Imogene entered the passage.

They'd reached the midway point when a gray figure stepped out from the flooded stairwell.

Lauren.

Imogene skidded to a stop. Her eyes jerked to the rifle Lauren held ready, then to Alexei as he moved up beside Lauren. Omar cursed, and farther back, rapid boot falls signaled Bruce's arrival.

"Going somewhere?" A smirk slithered across Lauren's muzzle. "And in such poor company."

Imogene's chest tightened, but she forced determination into her voice. "We're leaving. We're going to go find help—"

Lauren scoffed. "And oh-so conveniently running off with our only working life support system. All for you and your boyfriend and your filthy PAF buddies."

"We're going to find help, and for that we need the crawler, yes." She turned to Alexei. "We are coming back. I promise you that. But if no one goes for help, none is ever going to come."

His aim began to waver.

"Don't listen to her! She's lying!" Lauren's smirk disappeared in an angry snarl. "She doesn't care about her duty, or about any of us. All she cares about is herself and those bloody PAF!"

"That's not true." Imogene fixed her eyes on Alexei's. If she could persuade him, Lauren might back down. "I want us all to get out of here alive, and this is the only way that's going to happen."

Alexei's whiskers twitched frantically, but his aim drifted farther and farther.

Imogene spread her hands, palms outward, and kept her tone calm. "You helped us gather the power packs. You know there's enough for at least two weeks. We'll be back with help before then, and none of this will matter. You won't have to shoot me, or Bruce, or anyone else."

"Shut up!" Lauren's claws tightened around her rifle. "Don't try and make this about us. You're the ones disobeying orders!"

Alexei's gaze darted between Imogene to the lynx. "Damn it, Lauren, I can't do this!" He let his rifle fall out of line.

Lauren snarled. "Then I will!" In one fluid motion, she shouldered her rifle, aimed, and pulled the trigger.

Time seemed to slow. Bruce and Alexei yelled, but their words didn't hold any meaning. A tooth-jarring impact slammed into Imogene's chest. Her breath left in an agonizing whoosh. She fell backwards, another bullet striking her shoulder and making her spin as she sailed into Ming-Xue. She and the rat went down in a tangle of limbs.

More shots split the air. Or were they echos? It was too hard to think or breathe to be sure. She lay on her back, hands seeking her chest as she coughed and gasped. People were yelling, but she couldn't piece together what they said.

Bruce's brown-furred face pushed into view, blocking out the lithcrete ceiling. His lips moved, terrified eyes flicking from her face to her chest. He pulled her hands away, and relief flooded his soft chocolate eyes.

"—you okay?" His words started to make sense again.

She managed to suck in a proper lungful of air. "I don't know. Yes?"

She reached up again, feeling the divots in her chest and shoulder armor. The one above her heart went clean through to the ballistic fabric under the titanium, but now that she was thinking again she could feel the bullet hadn't gotten inside. It felt like she'd been hit with a bat. Or a meteoroid.

She pushed herself up on her elbows, looking for Lauren. The lynx lay a dozen metres away, hissing and kicking. Alexei knelt in the middle of her back, a thin trail of blood running down the white fur of his cheek.

"Hurry up," Alexei called. "Scott and the rest will be here any minute. If I'm gonna get shredded for letting you go, you blasted well better get away."

Ming-Xue and Omar edged past the snarling lynx and bounded for the airlock. Bruce pulled Imogene to her hooves and helped her down the corridor.

"We are coming back," she said as they passed Alexei. "We're not leaving you."

He glanced up, dark eyes holding hers. "Yeah. I sure hope so."

Night's deep shadow lay heavy over the gray hills. The Fire Ant and the narrow road crawling past its headlamps were the only signs anyone had ever been here. Imogene never thought the stark, lonely vista could feel so welcoming.

A few kilometres out from Borda the road forked, and Bruce pulled the crawler to a halt. "I guess the next question is where we're going." The red glow of the instrument panel glinted off his eyes as he looked at Imogene. "We know there were PAF in Mare Nectaris, so I'm thinking east, into Fecunditatis?"

Imogene rubbed the bruise forming across her chest. She hadn't considered where to go, only getting away from Borda. "What about back to the guard station at Piccolomini N?"

Bruce shook his head. "That's skirting awfully close to where the PAF might be. Besides, we need someplace with enough resources to mount a rescue mission. The garrison at Piccolomini was stripped to the bone already."

"South, then? The farther we are from the front lines, the better our chances of finding someone who isn't in even worse shape than us."

"True." Bruce flexed his fingers on the control yoke. "But the map has more and closer bases east." He craned his neck to peer down at Ming-Xue and Omar, sitting in the main compartment. "What about you? Any ideas?"

Ming-Xue edged closer along the bench seat and aimed her pink nose up at them. "There are no roads south from Borda. We would need to circle some distance, or attempt cross country. I would suggest north to Bellot. The tracking station there has little military value and might have been bypassed."

"How far north?"

"Perhaps four hundred klicks. Past Santbech, then east."

Bruce raised one eyebrow at Imogene. She shrugged. Anywhere was better than the corpse of a base at Borda.

Several hours later they entered the battlefield surrounding Santbech. The broken shells of tanks and personnel carriers loomed up from the shadows. Deep craters broke the roadway, and the gray suits of fallen infantry littered the dust.

Bruce sent out a hail on the emergency channel, but there was no response.

Imogene clenched her jaw against the parade of destruction, but didn't look away. If worse came to worse, and their search for help failed, there were enough power packs here to last a long time. Maybe even another vehicle in close to working order.

Despite that grim hope, she felt better when the last mangled body fell behind them, and only the clean lunar plains and sharp, cold stars remained.

"Do you have things under control?" she asked Bruce. "I might grab some food and a nap."

"All right. Leave your rifle up here. I'll keep an eye on Ming and Omar until you wake up."

Imogene propped her rifle beside his, then slid down into the main compartment. Omar dozed in the far corner, but Ming-Xue looked up and offered a small smile.

Returning the smile, Imogene selected some of the PAF rations that had been left in the crawler. She turned the foil pouch over in her hands, searching for the self-heating unit.

There wasn't one, so she tore off one corner and raised the pouch to her muzzle.

"You should warm it first." Ming-Xue took the packet from her and put it in a small cubby. A timer started counting down. "Still not quite food, but better than cold."

Imogene chuckled. A soldier's opinion of field rations transcended nationality, it would seem. How many other things did that kinship extend to? She looked from the cooking food over to Ming-Xue's friendly blue eyes. Maybe she'd have a chance to find out.

The timer hit zero with a low beep, and Ming-Xue handed her the now warm packet. Steam billowed out when Imogene peeled it open, along with a whiff of spicy beef stew. Not wanting to burn herself, she examined the packet for some sort of eating utensil.

"No silverware either, huh?"

"No. Let it cool slightly, then eat it from the pouch. Built-in forks and heating tabs are wasteful."

"But very convenient." Imogene let her ears flop in exaggerated dejection.

Ming-Xue laughed. "And when have you known convenience to sway a leader's mind? Unless it is their own." She flicked her whiskers and returned to her seat. "Perhaps you should have taken some UNA rations with us."

"Hmm." Imogene squeezed the stew into her mouth, savoring the strong, if greasy, flavor. "I think yours taste a little better, though."

The white rat's eyes twinkled as she curled her tail across her lap. "Maybe we can have our people give yours the recipe."

A series of thumps pierced the soft darkness wrapping Imogene. Groaning a protest, she squeezed her eyes tighter and flattened her ears.

The yell which followed jolted them erect again. Her sleep-clogged eyes snapped open and she groped for her absent rifle.

"Do not move."

The voice was Omar's, and she blinked until the brown hare came into focus. The hare, and the rifle he held leveled at her head.

Imogene's heart skipped, then pounded double time. The crawler had stopped, and across the compartment, Bruce sprawled near the open door to the refresher. Ming-Xue covered him with their remaining rifle.

Omar nudged Imogene's helmet forward with one paw. "Put this on. You are going for a walk."

Fumbling to form some plan, her mind spun as she reluctantly donned the helmet and stood. She and Bruce were herded over to the airlock. Omar covered them while Ming-Xue dug into the supplies Imogene had brought. She took out all the PAF power packs and several fistfuls of EVA rations, then handed the reduced satchel to Imogene.

Taking it, she caught and held Ming-Xue's gaze. "Why are you doing this?"

The rat's whiskers twitched. "We appreciate what you have done, but if you find another UNA base, we will become prisoners again. That is not acceptable."

"So instead you just leave us here?" Imogene asked.

Ming-Xue looked away. "It is...necessary. I am sorry."

Imogene's lips tightened. "So am I." She snapped her visor shut and stepped into the airlock.

Bruce crowded in beside her, and the inner door slid shut. A few seconds later the outer door opened.

"Move out where we can see you." Omar's voice came over the emergency channel.

Teeth clenched, Imogene complied. She and Bruce moved well clear of the Fire Ant, then turned to see it already trundling off to the north. Angry heat rose in Imogene's chest, and she fought the urge to grab a rock and throw it after the departing crawler.

Bruce slammed one fist into his other hand. "Damn the both of them! And me, too." His visor turned towards Imogene. "I should have been more careful. I should have woken you up."

The anger and recrimination in his voice tempered Imogene's own feelings. "What happened, anyway?"

"I stopped to use the refresher. You were asleep, and I *thought* they were, too. I took the rifles, of course, but they jumped me when I came out. I should have been more careful!" He drove his gauntleted fist into his hand again.

"It's not your fault," Imogene said. "We should have tied them up or something. I trusted them too much."

Bruce just shook his head and turned to watch the Fire Ant disappear over a low rise. He sighed and looked over at Imogene. "Well, at least this solves one problem. I wasn't looking forward to explaining why we were in a PAF crawler."

"Except now we're out here on foot, with no real idea where we are, and no weapons." Imogene couldn't keep the bitterness from her voice.

"All valid points." The stag nodded. "Still, we're alive. And as long as we are, I don't intend to give up trying."

No, they couldn't give up. Not with everyone left at Borda counting on them to bring back help. Pulling her gaze away from the departing crawler, she took stock of their surroundings.

It was still dark. Sunrise wasn't for another few days, but enough starlight shone for her suit's night vision. They were in a wide, flat-bottomed valley, bounded by rolling hills to the east and steeper mountains to the west. The usual scattering of craters marked the gray dust, but none large enough to hamper navigation. The trackway they'd been following snaked away to the north. The Fire Ant reappeared from the dip it had passed through, forming a bead of light along the rutted gray thread.

"Do we follow them?" she asked. "Or head off on our own somewhere?"

Bruce shrugged. "No chance we'll catch up, but staying on the road is a good idea. It still goes to Bellot."

"Logical." Imogene took one last look around the empty valley, then started the long walk north.

29

LOST AND FOUND

Time didn't matter on the dusty abandoned road. Imogene's chronometer ticked off the hours, but in the weeks-long lunar night, they were nothing but numbers. When she and Bruce grew tired, they stopped. When they were rested, they moved on.

The meteoroid showers had died away to almost nothing, for which she was extremely grateful. But no sign of habitation appeared either, and as the days and kilometres shuffled past, fear festered in her belly.

All the gray valleys and craters looked the same, and without satellite positioning, she couldn't tell where on the map they were. They had to be in the mountains northeast of Santbech, but there was no telling if Bellot lay just over the next ridge, or hundreds of kilometres distant.

If it was hundreds, they were dead. They could never cover that kind of distance. All she could do was hope her hasty actions hadn't doomed them both.

Late on the third day, her bounding low-gravity strides brought her to the summit of a gentle saddle. They'd been climbing for hours, but she hadn't guessed just how high they were until the next valley spread itself out before them.

Imogene stopped, weary body refusing to follow as her eyes traced the way ahead. Far in the distance, craggy mountains rose on the valley's other side, and the road stretched cruelly towards them, barren and lonely for as far as she could see.

Falling to her knees, she hugged herself tightly and closed her eyes.

Bruce took another few loping bounds before he realized she was no longer by his side. He turned, mirror finished visor seeking her out. "Imogene? What's wrong?"

She squeezed her eyes shut tighter. "I'm sorry."

"Nothing to be sorry about. If you're tired, we'll rest."

"Tired? Gods yes, I'm tired." Her muzzle split in an anguished grin. "Tired of walking, tired of watching my friends die, tired of everything I do falling apart. Yes, I'm tired. And I'm sorry."

Bruce knelt beside her, put one hand on her armored shoulder. "You're not the one who was awake when Ming-Xue and Omar pulled their stunt. It wasn't your fault."

Imogene opened her eyes again and snorted. "No? That's just the latest, anyway. Did I ever tell you how I ended up in the infantry?"

Bruce mutely shook his head.

"The Navy dumped me there after I was too seasick to walk straight. My boyfriend had even pulled strings so we'd be on the same ship, and I spent our last two weeks together throwing up all over him."

"That's not your fault either, you know."

Imogene looked back down at the dust between her knees. "Yeah? How about waiting for him like a fool while he screwed some rabbit? And then running away to the moon when I found out? Does that prove I'm useless, or should I add throwing myself at Victor, too?"

"Damn it, Imogene, you're not useless." Bruce's grip on her shoulder tightened. "You're special in more ways than I can count, and Victor was a fool not to see it."

Imogene blinked.

After an uncomfortable pause, he spoke again. "I like you. A lot. I didn't want to push you, after Victor, and since we left

Pons it's hardly been the right time. Now's not much better, but I have to say it: I think I love you."

Lost for words, Imogene stared up at him. A warmth began melting its way through her, but she clamped it down before it could carry her away. "Really? You're not just saying that to get me moving again?"

"If I was, would I admit it?" She could hear his familiar, wry smile. "But no, I'm not. You're beautiful, and getting to know you as a person only compounded the issue."

"Oh, Bruce..." She reached up, taking his hand from her shoulder between both of her own.

That pleasant warmth trickled back into her chest, and she probed after its source. She hadn't realized how much she'd come to trust and rely on the rust-colored stag. They were already partners in a way she'd never felt with anyone before. And if the fluttering feeling that came along with the warmth was any indication, there was more at work than simple camaraderie.

She gave his gauntlet a squeeze. "I like you too, and I'm so sorry I dragged us both out here to die—"

"No." He used their linked hands to pull her upright. "I won't let that happen. We're going to go north, and we're going to find help, and no one is allowed to die until I say so!"

A smile tugged at the corner of her lips, and Imogene shook her head. "And who could argue with that? All right then, north it is."

🐾 🐾 🐾

The mountains ahead were painted a searing white by the rising sun. The valley still lay in deep shadow, and the contrast hampered visibility. They were well out into the flats now, and the distance to the mountains shrank steadily. As did their supplies. Water and food they could ration, but there was nothing to be done about power. Only one spare power pack remained, and while Imogene's read-out showed green for now, it wouldn't be long before both of them needed it.

A flicker of light sparked ahead. Probably just a stray bit of glare from the sunlit peaks. But then it came again, longer this time. Hope she'd thought dead blossomed in Imogene's chest.

Bruce's graceful bounds came to a ragged stop. "Did you see that?"

"Headlights." Her excitement bled into the word. "And coming this way."

They stood still, watching, but the light didn't reappear.

"Could you tell how far...?" Bruce asked tentatively.

She didn't take her eyes off the horizon. "It couldn't be too far. If they're headed south, they should be here in a couple minutes."

"Hmm." Bruce agreed. "Do you suppose we should get off the road? At least until we have some idea who they are?"

His caution brought Imogene back to the reality of their situation. "I don't know. This could be the only chance we get. When that vehicle leaves, we need to be on it. One way or another."

"Surrender? But what if it's a tank or something? No room for prisoners." Another flare of light erupted, and he paused. "We better decide fast, whatever we do."

Imogene glanced up at the approaching lights, then down at the road. "I've still got my demo stuff. Not enough to kill a tank, but I could shake them up. Make them stop."

She pulled off her pack and dug out her two 300-gram blocks of putty explosive. Detonators pushed easily into the blue putty, and she synced them to a remote trigger, then covered them with a paper-thin layer of dust. No harm done if the oncoming vehicle was friendly, or large enough to accept prisoners, but if it was a PAF tank she could set off the explosives and immobilize it.

Hopefully.

She turned to Bruce. "We need someplace to hide until they're on top of it."

"How about that?" He pointed to a mid-size crater a dozen metres to their left. Without waiting for an answer, he took a running leap. He cleared several metres before leaving a single pair of boot prints. He pushed off again, making another three metres before losing momentum and returning to normal length bounds.

Imogene didn't have his raw power, but she copied his technique, leaving only scattered prints to mark their passage. With luck, whoever was coming wouldn't notice until it was too late.

Deeper and fresher than it had looked, irregular crags studded the crater's rim. Only a sprinkling of pale dust covered the dark bedrock. Imogene crouched behind an outcrop that offered a good view of the road, but shielded her from the approaching lights.

A dim glow crept over the road, then brightened as its source drew close. She flipped off the safety and rested her thumb on the firing switch. A flash of yellow headlamps burst into view. She tensed, squinting against the glare, then relaxed with a sigh.

This was no PAF tank. The antiquated silver crawler trundled along on six large wheels, and bore a UNA crest. Emblazoned below the crest were the full moon and crossed core drill and rock-pick of the UNA Selenographical Institute.

Bruce sat back and laughed. "Geologists! We're hiding from geologists!"

Imogene flipped the safety back on and snorted. "Better safe than sorry, I guess. We'd better call them before they get out of comm range."

Past her explosives now, the crawler rolled away at a good clip.

"Right." Bruce toggled to a general frequency. "Hello, selenographical crawler. Are you reading?"

There was a pause, and the crawler slowed to a stop.

"We read you." The voice that answered was strong and male. "Who is this?"

"Private Bruce Andersen, UNA infantry. My friend and I have been stranded out here, and could really use a lift."

The geologist chuckled. "I think we can arrange something. What's your location?"

"Just off the road, about two hundred metres behind you."

"Got it. Good thing you called, we'd have driven right on by."

"Yeah. It's not too healthy for infantry to be seen first these days."

"I can imagine." The geologist's tone turned grim.

Relief oozed through Imogene as she retrieved her explosives, then watched the crawler turn around and came back. Climbing into the airlock, she barely waited for the pressure to rise before pulling off her helmet. Six days trapped in a suit was about five and a half too long.

Beside her, Bruce seemed to share her sentiments. He removed his helmet too, and gave her a quick smile.

The airlock let out directly into the crew compartment. Only the front two of six seats were in use, and their occupants peered back curiously.

"Just the two of you?" The golden retriever on the right was the one they'd spoken to. He looked to be approaching the far side of middle-age, and his fur was more yellow-blond than gold. He wore a jumpsuit patterned with bold blue and yellow checkers.

The other geologist was a brown rodent of some sort. Imogene thought pack-rat, but couldn't be sure without seeing his tail. He too wore a one-piece suit, his a solid yellow.

"Just the two of us," Bruce confirmed. "I'm Bruce, and this is Imogene Haartz."

"William Palmer," The retriever said. "And Louie Hesler. He doesn't talk much, so don't let it bother you."

Louie bobbed his head, then turned back to the controls. He hadn't bothered to shut down the power plant, and wasted no time getting under way again.

The crawler lurched, encouraging Imogene to sit down.

William shot an apologetic smile. "So what are you two doing out here? We haven't seen hide nor hair of anyone for two hundred klicks."

"It's kind of a long story," Imogene said. "Suffice to say some people thought they needed our crawler more than we did."

"That's cold." The retriever frowned. "Our station's been cut off for a couple weeks now, but I didn't think things had gotten *that* bad." He licked his lips, still frowning. "You wouldn't have any news, would you? We're headed for Santbech to try and find out what's happening."

"You don't know...?" Imogene met his earnest brown eyes and trailed off. "Santbech is gone. Two, three weeks ago now. I don't have details, but the PAF were all through this area. They seem to have pulled back for now..."

William sighed and covered his eyes. "It really is war then? We weren't sure." He sat silent for a moment, then, "What about Earth?"

"We haven't heard anything since the first day."

"I see." He pursed his lips. "Louie? Get this thing turned around. We can head back to base and then try for Messier or Lindbergh."

"Actually," Bruce cut in before the rat could comply, "we've got some friends stranded farther south. If this rig could take fifteen or twenty, it might mean life or death for them."

Louie had started to slow the crawler, but now looked over at William.

The retriever narrowed his eyes. "Where, exactly?"

"Borda. It's a little south of Santbech."

"I know where it is." His ears flopped as he gave an irritable shake of his head. "But if there are PAF loose, we don't have any kind of weapons or armor."

"We didn't see anyone coming north, but there's no guarantees." Bruce locked gazes with the geologist. "Borda's in bad shape. Before we lost the crawler, we were out looking for help."

"And you found us." William stared down at the floor, then sighed. "We can make Borda in maybe seven hours. Looks like you've got yourself a rescue party."

🐾 🐾 🐾

"Unidentified vehicle, halt and state your business."

The challenge crackled through the crew compartment, startling Imogene awake. She didn't recognize the voice, and wondered if their saviors had gotten lost. But the crater ahead was definitely Borda. The sun had finally risen, and in its glare the two ruined railgun emplacements were unmistakable.

"Halt, or you will be fired upon. This is your last warning."

Imogene's stomach churned. That clipped military tone didn't belong to anyone they'd left at Borda.

Already slowing, Louie stopped dead, throwing everyone against their restraints.

William leaned forward and hit a button. "This is UNA Selenographical Institute transport 517-A. We were told there were survivors at Borda in need of assistance."

"Acknowledged. Standby." There was a long pause, then their unseen interrogator spoke again. "You're cleared to enter the crater. Stay on the road and follow all instructions."

"Wilco. Thank you." William flicked off the comm and waved Louie to take them forward. With one ear cocked inquiringly, he looked back at Imogene. "Friend of yours?"

Imogene just shook her head. They crested the rim of the crater and got their first look inside.

Imogene's jaw dropped. Gray camo-painted crawlers packed the flats around the silver dome. Close to fifty UNA vehicles, mostly tanks with some Paladin IFVs and a lone mobile command unit. Although a few bore combat damage, all looked fully functional. Rescue had come to Borda all right, but it hadn't needed Imogene's help.

"Well, somebody's still organized," William said dryly. "Maybe they'll have some news."

"I hope so," Imogene said. Rejoining an organized force should have been a relief, but somehow the sight of so many undamaged vehicles made her uneasy. After focusing so long on simple survival, this reminder of the larger conflict seemed surreal.

One of the tanks turned to track them with its turret as they descended into the crater. It let them draw to within half a kilometre, then a new voice came over the comm. "That's close enough. Stop and exit the vehicle. General Slate wants to see all of you inside the base."

"Will do," William acknowledged. He waited while Louie brought them to a halt, then stood up. "Looks like we're in for a bit of a hike."

A Paladin passed them about halfway to the dome, headed out towards their parked crawler. Looking back over her shoulder, Imogene saw a group of soldiers dismount and begin inspecting the geologist's vehicle. Trust was apparently in short supply here—not that she blamed them.

The hole Aaron had cut in the dome's wall had been enlarged, and they had no trouble entering. A pair of guards stationed just inside directed them to the lower levels.

Imogene stepped out of the airlock and flipped open her visor. Clean, fresh air filled her nostrils, and somewhere nearby a portable generator purred. The corridors teamed with dozens of ivory-suited vehicle crewmen poking around. A few carried supplies, but most seemed to just be enjoying the chance to get out of their crawlers.

An officious badger with a sergeant's rank tabs waited for them. She took Imogene and the others to a storeroom where a clump of officers stood around a makeshift table. Maps littered the surface, along with datapads and empty beverage containers.

A handsome mottled-brown wolf looked up. His dark gray Armor Corps uniform bore a general's gold stars on the collar, and the hard lines of his face demanded obedience.

"You're the geologists?" His gaze slid over William and Louie, then stopped on Imogene with a frown. "And infantry? Why aren't you with your unit?"

Imogene straightened her already stiff posture. "We're all that's left of it, sir. Us and two others who stayed here."

His tail swished. "You're the two that cut off on your own, then? Interesting." He turned back to William. "I'm commandeering your crawler. We need it to move wounded and supplies. We're short on manpower too, so I want you in an ad-hoc infantry squad, unless you have expertise to make yourselves useful elsewhere?"

Both geologists shook their heads.

"Dismissed then, but stay in the base. Someone will find you when we need you."

Imogene shifted uncomfortably. The general's last comment was clearly directed only at the geologists.

After William and Louie left, the general addressed the badger who had brought them here. "Find Porter and that rabbit. I want to see them in my office."

Imogene reached up to finger the bullet hole in her armor's chest. With a chain of command reestablished, Lauren wasn't likely to try that again, was she? A hopeful thought, but the ache in her ribs made it hard to believe.

The general's gaze fell on her and Bruce. "You two, come with me."

He led them to one of the abandoned offices and made himself comfortable behind the desk. He looked up at them with a neutral expression. "So, tell me why the two of you took it upon yourselves to leave."

Imogene tried to find enough saliva to swallow the lump in her throat. She wished she knew what Lauren might have told him. It would make doing damage control easier.

Before she could screw up the courage to begin, Bruce took charge. "We went to find help. Life support here was compromised, and there wasn't enough air for everyone."

"And you took two PAF prisoners?"

Imogene bit down on her tongue. How badly had Lauren twisted things? And what direction? To justify shooting her, or cover it up?

"Yes, sir," Bruce said.

"But you didn't bring them back. Or the Fire Ant."

"No, sir." Bruce drew a deep breath. "There was an accident in the mountains. We lost control of the crawler. Imogene and I managed to get out, but the PAF didn't."

All true. Sort of. But would he believe it? Imogene kept her gaze locked above the general's head. The less she offered, the better.

One of the general's ears flicked. "Tragic. And the crawler? I need more armor."

Bruce shook his head. "It's unrecoverable."

As he went on to describe meeting William and Louie, the badger sergeant returned with Lauren and Alexei in tow.

Imogene snuck a look at Lauren. The lynx's eyes narrowed, but she kept her expression neutral and faced the general. Beside her, Alexei gave Imogene a tight smile. He had a healing cut across his nose, and what might have been a bruise darkening the ring of pink flesh around one eye.

Imogene's lips tightened. Things couldn't have gone well for him after she and Bruce left on her boondoggle.

When Bruce finished, the general fixed Lauren with his sharp, golden eyes. "Are they trustworthy?"

"I don't know." She glanced sideways at Imogene, tone professional and face still unreadable. "If you asked me an hour ago, I'd have said no. Honestly, I never expected to see them again."

Alexei's ears pricked. "But they did come back! With help, like they promised."

Ignoring his outburst, the general continued. "Are you willing to work with them? We're desperately short on infantry, and you four have experience together."

Imogene cringed inwardly at that, but fought to keep her face vacant. Lauren must *not* have told him everything.

Lauren's slit-pupiled eyes locked with Imogene's for a long moment. Finally she nodded. "Yes, sir. If that's what needs to happen."

"Good answer, Porter. You've done well holding things together here. Now you've got yourself a field promotion and a squad. I'll give you the two geologists, and you can take your pick from the other survivors. Talk to Lieutenant Duren about supplies and transport. That will be all."

Leaving the general's office, Imogene's nerves relaxed just a little. Surrounded by the bright lights and bustle, things that had seemed logical in the darkness of a dying base now sounded dangerously close to treason. Thankfully the general didn't seem interested in pursuing that angle. With a little luck, it might even be forgotten in this whole hellish mess.

Alexei clapped Imogene on the shoulder. "It's good to have you back. If these Armor Corps fellows hadn't shown up, you really would have saved our tails."

"I'm glad you all made out okay too." She smiled back. "What about Aaron? How is he?"

"Better. General Slate has some real doctors, and they think he'll be okay."

On Imogene's other side, Bruce let out a relieved breath. "That's good to hear. I guess everything here is getting better. I hardly recognize this place with the lights on."

"Quite an improvement, huh?" Alexei twitched his pink nose. "Since the general got here yesterday, things seem a hundred times better."

"Why *are* they here?" Bruce asked. "Did the sat-comms start working?"

Alexei glanced at Lauren. She didn't answer, so he went on, "No. Lauren got the antenna fixed up, but General Slate was looking for fuel. I hear they're what's left of four or five companies that got pushed south out of Mare Nectaris. The general was regrouping to try and reclaim Santbech, but the PAF had already gotten their burrow busters in."

A queasy feeling rose in Imogene's gut. Deep bases like Santbech took a lot of killing. With the entrances crushed and surface defenses destroyed by the missile strike she and her squadmates had witnessed, it would have been a race between the defenders tunneling out and the PAF sappers with their drilling rigs and high-yield annihilation bombs.

"Everyone was gone by the time General Slate's column arrived," Alexei said. "Just drill holes and craters."

A dark silence fell, then Bruce shook himself. "Well, at least he managed to save you guys. What's the plan going forward?"

Alexei's ears perked up. "That's the good news. The PAF aren't pressing any deeper. The general figures their command and control is just as screwed up as ours, and that they're running out of supplies. Now that he's got more fuel and a chance to regroup, we're gonna head north and hit them back."

"What about the bigger picture?" Imogene asked. "Any word from Command? Or Earth?"

"Nope. Near as I can figure, we're still cut off. They said they'd been past three or four other bases and we were the first one with survivors."

Bruce frowned. "Damn. Have they seen *anyone* since they came out of Nectaris?"

"I don't think so," Alexei said. "Why?"

"I just wish we had some idea how bad things are," Bruce said. "If we're some of the only people left, it would be bloody stupid to keep on fighting."

Ahead of them, Lauren's ears twitched. She stopped and turned to glower at the stag. "Shut up. I heard more than enough of your pessimistic drivel before, and I'm not going to put up with any more. We're still in the service, in case you didn't notice. If someone higher up says fight, you bloody well fight, and let them worry about if it's a good idea."

Bruce blinked rapidly. "I didn't say I wouldn't fight. I was just thinking what it would mean if we did."

"Well keep it to yourself. Nobody needs to hear that defeatist crap." She flicked her dark tufted ears and turned away.

Bruce shook his head, but fell in behind her without further comment.

Imogene swallowed hard. General Slate might have taken Lauren in hand, but how far did his control extend? All that stopped her from demanding some sort of transfer was the fear of drawing more attention to her botched departure. Seen in the wrong light, that sort of thing ended more than just your career.

She cast another glance at Lauren and wondered if getting away from her might be worth the risk.

30

SHADES OF GRAY

The new members of Sergeant Lauren Porter's squad received a motley assortment of scavenged armor and equipment. Imogene was glad she only needed a new rifle. Poorly fitted armor was better than none at all, but in a firefight, an awkward movement could cost a life.

She and the other original members—just Lauren, Alexei and Bruce now—sat around the room they'd been given, helping William, Louie, and a ferret named Jessica get up to speed on their new equipment. Scott the raccoon filled out the eighth spot in the new squad, but as an infantryman he already had his own gear.

The door to the corridor opened, and Imogene looked up.

"Fuck," said the panda standing in the doorway. "They didn't tell me it was you."

"Jared?" A sour taste twisted Imogene's mouth. "What are you doing here?"

Jared shrugged. "My job. War kinda trumps disciplinary action."

Lauren's lip curled. "It's a war all right, but aren't you on the wrong side?"

He blew air out under his tongue in a rude noise. "What, you thought I'd defect the first chance I got? I hate those PAF assholes more than you ever will."

"I doubt that, bamboo-boy," the lynx spat.

Jared's muzzle bunched, but he kept his temper. "That's right; I'm a panda. You have any idea what it's like going through life with everyone convinced you're out to get them?

Wasn't for the PAF, we pandas would get as much respect as everyone else. So fuck them, and fuck you. The only difference I see is I'm allowed to kill *them*."

He turned to Imogene. "Come on. The general's got a bunch of bombs he wants set up."

"Not so fast." Lauren stood up and thrust an open hand towards the panda. "Let's see some orders."

Jared barked a cynical laugh. "You think they're cutting formal orders for anything anymore? Give him or the lieutenant a call if you don't believe me."

Lauren's eyes narrowed. She pulled out a datapad and slid her claws over the screen. A moment later a muffled voice buzzed from the directional speaker and Lauren answered. "Yes, sir. We've got a panda down here claiming he's got orders to set demolition charges. Is that true?"

Whoever was on the other end buzzed again, and Lauren nodded. "Yes, sir!" She folded the datapad and jerked her muzzle at Imogene. "It's legit. Make sure he doesn't screw anything up."

Jared glowered and stomped out into the corridor, forcing Imogene to hurry after him. After Lauren was out of earshot, he slowed and turned his round, black and white head to look at Imogene. "So, you four are here. Fiona make it, too?"

She shook her head.

"Damn. Waste of a great piece of ass." He shoved open the door to a storeroom and waved at a pile of crates that hadn't been there a week ago. "Grab a box. I'll get the detonators."

The red labels on the crates marked them as bulk putty explosives. In the low gravity she had no trouble hefting the hundred-kilo box and following Jared into one of the fuel bunker passages radiating out from the main part of the base.

"What exactly are we doing?" she asked when they reached the first blast-proof door.

"What d'you think? We're setting the base up to blow. Can't risk the PAF getting all this fuel." He set down his box of detonators and swiped a key-card over the fuel bunker's lock. The wide lithcrete and metal door hissed, then swung open. Lights came on inside, revealing long shelving units stacked with the small off-white cubes of stabilized antimatter fuel.

Imogene set down her own crate and pulled off the lid. A five-year-old's jackpot of sky-blue modeling clay filled the metal case, neatly cut into 500-gram blocks.

Jared passed her a Type-3 Kinetic Shock Sensitive detonator. Good for improvised demolitions, they didn't need wires, and weren't bothered by radio jamming or poor reception. The shock from any nearby blast served as the triggering mechanism. Of course that was their main drawback, too: close kin to landmines, they were bloody dangerous and hard to locate and remove.

"Set up thirty kilos in five or six charges and hide them in with the fuel or behind the glow panels," Jared instructed. "I'll work on the next bunker."

She frowned. "Shouldn't we just rig it to collapse the access passage rather than trying to demolish the whole place?"

"Nah, nowhere to hide 'em out here. Besides, this way we might get the fuel to blow, too."

Imogene suppressed the urge to roll her eyes. "Stabilized antimatter is non-reactive. You need special equipment to break it down."

Jared laughed. "That's what the instruction manuals say. Normally they're even right, but it's not the whole story. Enclosed like this, we might be able to hit it hard enough to get a chain reaction going. Even if we can't, it should bring down the roof and contaminate everything." He gave the blue block he was working on an affectionate pat. "I hope it does work. It'd be one hell of a bang."

She cast a wary look down the long shelves of white cubes. There was a lot of trapped energy here, and this was only one of the bunkers... Could he be right? She struggled to remember how fuel cubes worked. Something about magnetic bubbles and nano-polymers, but the details eluded her.

The first five crates of explosive took care of the fuel bunkers. The sixth and last went in the dome itself, broken into small charges and well hidden.

That last part rankled with Imogene. Kinetic sensitive detonators were dangerous enough without concealing their location. But the general's orders were clear: rigged to blow and well concealed. Imogene had to clench her teeth and remind herself just how thin the ice between her and a court-martial already was. Now was definitely not the time to question or disobey any more orders.

"That's all of them," she said to Jared when the last soft blue bomb had been tucked behind a utility access panel. "What's your plan for the primary detonator? Some kind of booby-trap?"

"The general's leaving the worst wounded behind to keep an eye on things. I'll set them up a little manual-triggered device. General's telling them the charges will just mess up the fuel bunkers." Jared chuckled. "Poor fucks; no clue they're a living fuse."

The unease in Imogene's chest clenched into an icy knot.

"Just so." A calm voice from behind them made her jump. General Slate stood in the doorway, arms crossed over his chest. "And if you don't want to join them, you'd better keep your maw shut. What's our status?"

"Almost done, sir." Jared's spine stiffened and he clasped his hands behind his back, looking more like a soldier than Imogene had ever seen him.

She straightened too, twisting her face and thoughts into the careful neutrality she'd learned in Basic: don't think about anything, especially how much you despise the officer standing in front of you.

The general's hard gold eyes held Jared for a moment. "Good. Get suited up and meet me outside. I've got another project for you two."

🐾 🐾 🐾

People in ash-white suits swarmed among the parked tanks, hauling supplies out of the base and redistributing ammunition. Amid the chaos, General Slate's dark medium-duty armor stood out. He waved Imogene and Jared to follow him around the dome.

"Shake a leg," the wolf said. "We're moving out in ninety minutes."

Even more vehicles filled the flats on the dome's other side, including a bedraggled tactical missile carrier.

Like its PAF cousins she'd seen destroy Santbech, this carrier was a long, boxy creature, and had probably been ugly even before war made it into a monster. The cowl protecting the missile rack had been ripped away, leaving maybe a metre of jagged metal near the hinge. Holes the size of her fist pocked the armored driver's compartment, as well as the lone remaining missile.

General Slate slapped the missile's nose cone. "I need you to take out the warhead and set it up with a remote trigger."

Imogene choked. "You want us to dismantle it?" She cast another look at the shredded missile casing. "You're lucky it hasn't blown up already!"

The general's cold silver faceplate turned to regard her. "The warhead is undamaged. Now get to work."

Imogene had never worked on anything like this. The theory was simple—a magnetic shell holding a single gram of anti-hydrogen atoms like an overgrown metallic walnut. It didn't take anything special to break the shell and release the demon within.

Working together carefully, she and Jared removed the dull metal sphere from its shock-isolators. Then it took only minutes to mold a block of the blue putty explosive around it and add a radio detonator.

"Fuck," Jared said when they were done. "I like to blow shit up, but this is a little too much."

"Yeah." She heard a quiver in her voice that had thankfully been absent from her hands.

The panda chuckled. "At least you know it's gonna really ruin some PAF's day."

Imogene closed her eyes and wished the helmet would let her rub her forehead. She'd gotten into demolitions to breach doors, and knock down communications towers. Not to destroy bases staffed by friendly wounded, or cobble together IEDs with enough firepower to level a small city. She didn't want to guess how General Slate planned to use it.

They loaded the weapon into a cardboard field ration box —mercifully assigned to a different crawler than Imogene— and joined the rest of the company for the trek north.

The relief she'd felt the last time they left Borda didn't return. A cold lump of dread took its place, settling deep in the pit of her stomach. They might be traveling with a large, well supplied column this time, but that did nothing to ease her discomfort.

Last time they'd been looking for help. Now they were looking for a fight.

Bruce sat beside her amid the boxes in the cargo truck carrying their squad. His strong, quiet presence anchored her, giving her the strength to hold on.

She didn't know how to act towards him since he'd admitted his love. In some ways nothing had changed, but at the same time everything was different. She felt like she was back in high school, second guessing everything she said or did. It was annoying and exhilarating, and she wished they had more privacy to explore her feelings properly.

Still, it felt good to have him close.

Two days out from Borda, General Slate's scouts spotted a company-size group of PAF vehicles. His larger force surged forward to engage, and in the back of their truck, Imogene's heart pounded. But fortunately—or not, she wasn't sure—the smaller PAF unit fled. Undeterred, General Slate gave chase, following them into a twisting maze of interconnected craters and tight, cleft-like valleys.

As the minutes ticked into hours, Imogene's pulse returned to normal. The column's faster pace jostled her and the others around the windowless cargo compartment, which in the low gravity took on an unsettling resemblance to a ship in high seas. With each rolling bump she'd float up from her crate and take several seconds to come back down. She locked her jaw against the rising nausea and held on.

Finally the truck lurched to a stop. Imogene sighed. She'd managed not to puke, and—

"Ambush!" Lauren's voice filled the squad channel. "They're shooting up our tanks. Out and cover!"

Imogene had no clear memory of leaving the truck. Just a jumbled impression of panicked movement, then blinding sunlight flooding down into a narrow defile between two hills.

Sparks crawled over the ravaged hulk of their rearguard tank. Static spiked across the comm with each blue-white flash as the tank's capacitors discharged in a mechanical death rattle.

Shrapnel pinged Imogene's flank, and she bounded for cover. A heap of boulders welcomed her into their shadows.

Trapped in the narrow valley, General Slate's tanks churned the gray dust.

A rocket flashed down from the ridge across from Imogene, lancing into the convoy. The truck ahead of theirs disintegrated in a storm of razor-edged metal.

Adrenaline screamed along Imogene's veins. She dropped flat, fighting back panic. If they hit the truck carrying the annihilation bomb, the whole valley would be scorched into radioactive slag.

Static cracked as the general's tanks opened fire. Round after round of fragmentation shells pounded into the ridge where the rocket had come from. Short-lived clouds of debris shot up as each blast shredded everything it touched.

No more rockets came, but Imogene kept her head down anyway. No way she was risking herself without a bloody good reason. Eventually, the crackles and flashes from the shelling stopped, and she peeked out to see their convoy still mostly intact, scattered across the valley's floor.

"Everybody up," Lauren said. "They think they got 'em, but we're moving up to do a sweep."

Imogene slithered from her sheltered pocket and joined her squadmates in a loose double line. With a few dozen low-gravity bounds, they loped past General Slate's command crawler.

Bits of metal littered the ground, radiating from the carcass of their lead tank, now charred and blocking the road ahead. Tension started building in Imogene's guts again. The PAF had bottled them up, trapped between the two ruined tanks and the steep hillsides. But why hadn't they followed through on the attack?

Bruce cleared his throat. "What are we looking for?"

"Whatever shot those missiles," Lauren said. "Probably shoulder-fired coming from the rocks like that." She waved to the ridge the tankers had been pounding. "When we get up there, we'll find out."

"But what if they didn't get all of them?" Jessica squeaked.

Lauren made a throwing away motion with her non-rifle hand. "Then we'll clear 'em out. That's what infantry do."

Imogene's fingers tightened on her weapon. Playing bait to protect more valuable armored vehicles was her least favorite part of the foot soldier's mandate. PAF tactics called for at least a squad's worth of infantry on a skirmishing attack like this.

They fanned out, Bruce to Imogene's left and William on her right. The hike to the ridge left her itching to bolt for the nearest cover and hide. Thousands of inky shadows leered at her, with no way to tell when a new attack would turn the valley into a killing field.

Teeth gritted, she plowed onward.

Near the middle of where the tankers had been shooting, Alexei found part of a gray-armored leg. A few less identifiable bits turned up too, along with a single unfired rocket. Lauren called in their find while the others widened the search.

"Nothing," Bruce reported from farther along the ridge. "Looks like just the guy with the rockets. Strange they'd leave him unsupported like that, though."

Lauren's helmet bobbed in a slow nod. "They're probably low on troops, or just trying to slow us down rather than cause real damage."

"That last part worked, anyway," said Bruce. "If we have to check for skirmishers we'll be lucky to make more than a few klicks an hour."

Imogene and her squadmates searched a kilometre or so along the valley while the destroyed tank was shoved out of the road. A little later, another infantry squad moved up to relieve them.

Relieve was definitely the right word as far as Imogene was concerned. Adrenaline had given way to a cold sweat and fluttering stomach that refused to settle. Some of the others ate when they returned to the truck, but all she could manage was a little water.

Overall, the column made better time than Bruce's gloomy estimate. Long sections of the narrow mountain canyons were clear of good hiding places, and it was possible to move forward with minimal delay. But inevitably they would round another corner and find the road ahead bracketed with mounds of loose rock and boulders. Then the infantry would dismount and move ahead on foot, clearing the way metre by airless gray metre.

It was nerve-wracking at first, walking methodically forward, never knowing if the next pool of shadow hid an enemy, or only more rocks. But no one could maintain that level of tension indefinitely. After a time Imogene's anxiety settled into the background—always there, but no longer dominating her every thought.

"No, it's true," Jessica protested. "All the cute guys up here are either spoken for, or total jerks."

Imogene couldn't suppress a smile. From the way the ferret said "jerks" she'd had ample experience with this latter type. Shaking her head, Imogene picked her way forward. She was about halfway up the boulder studded rock-slide they were searching, with the squad spread out at regular intervals above and below her.

"Now, take you." Jessica waved at Alexei. "I'm sure someone like you already has a special someone...?"

"I—no. Not any more." Alexei looked downslope towards Louie and Imogene. "What about you, Louie? You got something warm waiting for you?"

The geologist just shrugged.

Jessica snickered. "I bet he does. 'He with most says least.' Am I right, boy-oh?"

"Oh, leave him alone." Imogene glanced over at the rat. "He's shy."

Louie hunched his shoulders. "Not shy. Just don't talk when I got nothin' to say." He continued forwards, moving up into the gap between two boulders. He stumbled then, and fell back the way he had come.

"Clumsy, too." Jessica giggled. "Come on, no sleeping on the job." She made a graceful bound, coming to rest beside the fallen rodent. No sooner had she landed than she tumbled backwards too.

It was almost comical, and Imogene started to laugh. Then she noticed the bullet hole in Jessica's helmet.

Cursing, she threw herself flat. "Contact! Mid-slope, west side. Louie and Jessica are both down."

"Everybody, cover!" Lauren's voice overrode the scattered exclamations. "Where's it coming from?"

"I don't know." Imogene slithered into the shade of a large boulder. "They were ahead of me and uphill. I didn't see the shooter."

"Anyone else?" No one spoke, and Lauren growled. "Right. Forward carefully guys, and stay low."

Imogene checked her rifle's safety catch was off, then crawled on knees and elbows towards Louie. Jessica was clearly dead, but she had to make sure of the quiet rat. She rolled him over, and grimaced at what she saw.

A hole the size of her thumb punched clean through his breastplate. The titanium composite and ballistic fabrics should have stopped a single round from an assault rifle. Whoever was up ahead must have something more powerful. Not surprising for a rearguard skirmisher, but she called it in anyway before resuming her advance.

Avoiding the gap where Louie had been shot, she circled to the right and down. The rocks that way were larger, and if she stayed in their shadows she might remain unseen. A dozen metres later the cover ended, and she stopped to survey what lay ahead. The rock slide seemed more active here. Steeper, with nothing larger than a football for thirty or forty metres.

"I think I have them." William's voice held no emotion. "Hundred and fifty metres ahead, clump of jagged boulders three-quarters of the way up. There was movement, but it's stopped."

Imogene spotted the formation in question. One house-size rock in the middle had split in two, and a heap of smaller fragments masked its base. Someone dug in amongst them would have plenty of cover, along with a commanding view of the canyon.

"I see it," Lauren said several seconds later. "Any indication of other positions?"

"No. If they had a proper setup we'd be dead by now."

"Can you move up on them without being seen? It doesn't look good here along the bottom."

"I think so," William said, tone still flat. "There's some larger rocks at the top of this clear area."

"Okay. Bruce, get up to William's position, then both of you head over the top. The rest of us will see what we can do down here. Imogene, what's your position?"

"On the edge of the clear spot. I've got a good line of fire up into the jagged rocks."

"Stay there, then. You're cover fire and support."

"Got it." Imogene repositioned herself, backing up slightly into deeper cover. She sighted in on the rock formation and waited, trying not to worry about Bruce. At least he was with the upper half of the pincher movement. That should help some.

The seconds crawled as the others moved forward. At one point a helmeted head bobbed into view. It disappeared before she could react, but confirmed the PAF position.

"We're ready," Bruce said at last. "What's the plan?"

"Nothing fancy, just rush the bastards," Lauren replied. "Imogene, light 'em up and try to keep their attention off us. Everyone got it?"

A chorus of affirmatives answered.

"Right. Go!"

Imogene lined her crosshairs on where the helmet had disappeared, took a steadying breath, and squeezed the trigger.

Suppressive fire didn't work as well in the silence of vacuum, but hopefully the spray of stone chips and dust would get his attention. She let off another long burst, then squirmed backwards to relocate. No point making herself *too* good of a target.

Over the comm came the confused shouting of her squadmates moving in for the kill. Then she saw them among the rocks and hastily took her finger off the trigger. At this range one gray suit looked much like another, and she wanted to be damn sure who she was shooting at.

It didn't matter in the end. There was only one PAF soldier, and they made short work of him. He managed to kill Scott before the end, but that was the last thing he would ever do.

They scouted a bit farther to make sure the area was secure, then returned to deal with the bodies.

The nervous energy from the fight faded rapidly, leaving Imogene with a weary numbness. She felt grateful she hadn't known Louie or the others well, and hated herself for feeling that way. They all had friends, families. Just because she didn't know the details shouldn't cheapen their loss. Should it?

She didn't know. But when first their relief squad, then the remainder of the column arrived, all she wanted to do was crawl back inside their truck and forget.

Lauren was the last to enter the vehicle and snap up her visor. "We did a good job out there today." She cast an approving gaze over her four remaining subordinates. "We protected the column, and gave those bloody pandas something to think about."

Her praise fell flat in the cargo compartment's dejected atmosphere.

Shaking his head, Alexei spoke quietly. "He wasn't a panda. He had hoof-boots."

"Whatever." She shrugged. "The point is we did our job, and did it well."

William growled, the emotionless facade he'd worn since the attack falling away. "Well? You call losing three people doing well?"

Lauren took off her helmet and frowned. "Yes. If he'd used those rockets, we could have lost three or even four tanks before they nailed him. It's hard, but that's our job."

"Gods!" William said. "You don't feel anything for them, do you? They're dead! And for what?"

"Of course I feel for them." The lynx flattened her ears. "But it's our job to protect our territory. It's everyone's job— and there's no more honorable way to die than defending our people. I'm sure your friend knew that, and would feel the same way."

William snarled. "You think he gave a shit what color they paint these mountains on a map? You think anyone does? No. He's dead, and it's fucking pointless."

"Pointless? So you'd rather let the PAF have their way then?"

"Frankly, yes. Odds are we're all gonna die up here, and your general's making sure it happens sooner rather than later. I wish I'd never gotten involved."

Lauren's fur bristled. "Well you are involved, gods damn it. So you'd bloody well better follow orders."

"Or what? You'll lock me up?" He gave a bitter laugh. "No, kitten, I'll play along. But don't ever tell me this is anything but a waste."

He turned away, leaving Lauren quivering.

She stood there, jaw working silently before she wheeled on the others. "You all, check your equipment. I don't want any surprise failures." Not waiting to see if they complied, she stalked over to her seat and began dismantling her rifle.

Hastily, Imogene and the others followed suit. William might have been willing to risk the feline's wrath, but Imogene didn't see any point in antagonizing her further. They were at war, and even if the yellow dog was right, there was nothing any of them could do to stop things now.

31

ROADSIDE ATTRACTION

The Armor Corps sergeant knelt, studying the dusty ruts left by a group of vehicles. Two sets of track diverged here, one heading into a steep-walled canyon on the left, and another following a less rugged path to the right. The tracks going left were the subject of the sergeant's study.

Both sets looked the same to Imogene. She shifted from hoof to hoof, scanning the gray landscape. They'd secured the area before General Slate and his sergeant came to see the tracks, but yesterday's sniper hunt had driven home the need for vigilance.

The sergeant stood up. "These *are* definitely newer. I can't say how much with all the shit that's been falling out of the sky lately, but the ones going right show a lot more scarring."

"That's what I said," William agreed. "And if they went in there, there's a good chance we can swing east and cut them off."

General Slate looked from the tracks up to the geologist. "How do you figure that? The map's got at least four other ways out of that canyon."

"I've been all through these mountains. It looks passable on the maps, but the only places you're getting vehicles in or out is here and an even narrower gap about forty klicks north-east."

"You're sure?" The general's tone dared him to hedge.

William gave a firm nod. "Much as I'm enjoying your show, I'd rather cut to the finale."

General Slate gazed up at the canyon mouth, then around at his massed tanks. Finally he turned to Lauren.

"Porter, your people and what's left of Gamma Squad are gonna watch this entrance. Set up on that ridge." He waved to a high knob two or three klicks south of the canyon mouth. "Make sure you take enough supplies for an extended EVA. I can't spare any vehicles to stay here."

His silver faceplate swung to Imogene. "Haartz, find Chey and get your special package planted out there where the canyon opens up. If they come out this way, you know what to do."

Imogene's stomach twisted. She knew what to do all right. The question was if it was a good idea. She glanced from the canyon to the ridge, trying to juggle the distance versus the antimatter bomb's yield.

The general shifted, and she snapped her gaze back to him. "Yes, sir." She nodded sharply and bounded off towards the supply truck carrying their bomb.

"We'll take care of them, sir." Not even the comm's tinny speakers could scrub the blind certainty from Lauren's voice. "What do you want us to do if they don't come out?"

"I'm hoping we can drive them back into the trap here, but either way someone will return to pick you up. Hold position until relieved."

Another knot curled itself into Imogene's guts. Once again, the decaying chain of command offered that promise: "Someone will come for you." How many more times would it hold true?

Gamma Squad turned out to be Jared Chey, plus an otter and a fox. Merging them in brought Lauren's command back up to a full eight person squad.

As General Slate's column crawled off into the east, Imogene and Jared deployed their jury-rigged antimatter bomb. A small hole and a thin layer of dust with the detonator's antenna just clearing the surface took care of things.

Another few minutes tromping around left enough tracks to disguise what they'd done, then they rejoined the others on the ridge.

"Everything set?" Lauren asked.

Imogene stepped into the shallow pit that had been dug behind a boulder on the ridgeline. "Yeah. It's tied into this remote trigger." She pulled the transmitter from her suit's thigh pocket. "Wait till they're centered over the bomb, then just flip off the safeties—"

"And blow those PAF fucks sky high," Jared added with throaty chuckle. "This is gonna be good."

Imogene's lip curled. She could justify annihilating the PAF without warning like this since it would help keep her friends safe, but Jared's twisted animosity sickened her. At least protocol kept the trigger in her control. Jared might be qualified too, but Lauren hated him even more than she did Imogene.

"Are we gonna be safe here?" Doubt filled Alexei's voice. "Those antimatter missile carriers back at Santbech left awfully big craters."

Imogene nodded. "We're a good three klicks out, and the ridge here should stop debris and radiation. Plus, that's only a single warhead. Gods only know how many were at Santbech. Keep your head down, and we should be good."

Bruce lay in the shadow of another outcrop, and she settled in next to him.

"Is what you told him true?" Bruce's soft voice came over a private channel. "That may only be one warhead, but we're a hell of a lot closer than last time."

"I don't know." She licked her lips and cast a long glance towards the canyon. "Radiation's no problem; it goes straight. But debris is a crapshoot. When the time comes, make sure you're behind something solid and cover your faceplate."

He reached over and squeezed her hand. "Don't worry. Wherever you are, I'll be right beside you."

A tingle of warmth flowed up from his hand, and she squeezed back. It was good to have someone to watch her back. And she knew she'd be watching his, whatever happened.

Below their position and several kilometres away, the canyon mouth gaped dark amid the pale gray stones and dust. Nothing moved save the slowly creeping shadows as the lunar day stretched on and on. Noon passed, and the sun slid lower as Imogene and the others took shifts watching and sleeping.

On what would have been the third Earth day, Imogene watched a small vehicle zip out of the canyon. After hours staring at the same unchanging landscape, the reality of what was happening didn't quite register. Then it did, and she scrabbled in her pocket after the detonation trigger.

"Scout car," Lauren said, tracking it with her rifle scope. "Let it go. We want his friends."

With the trigger clenched in her left hand, Imogene raised her own scope to watch.

The PAF scout car slowed where the deep tracks of General Slate's tanks turned east, but it didn't stop. It fled south, passing a klick or so west of them without giving any sign they'd been spotted. Peripherally, Imogene noted her squadmates rousing and checking their equipment, but she kept her gaze fixed on the canyon.

Minutes limped by on broken hooves before another vehicle emerged. Dark and low-slung, a Komodo tank hunter rolled forward. A Fire Ant with missing skirts followed close behind.

Imogene watched, estimating the kill radius. If there were any survivors, she didn't want them on her side of the resulting crater.

A mobile hospital crawler trailed the Fire Ant, then a supply truck, and another hospital crawler. And another... She scanned her scope back along the line of PAF vehicles. A dozen more medical and support units, with a lone, pockmarked tank bringing up the rear. About twenty vehicles, all told. The full force General Slate had been pursuing.

Traveling close together like that, the whole column fit easily inside the vaporization zone, never mind the full kilometre-wide kill radius. Probably best to detonate just before the first hospital crawler reached the bomb.

She licked her lips, eying the blood-red diamonds which marked the medical vehicles as noncombatants.

"There's hardly any combat units," she said.

Lauren shrugged one shoulder. "If they had troops, they wouldn't have been using sneak attacks. Get ready, they're coming up on where you buried it."

Imogene looked back down at the hospital crawlers. Did this really need to happen? The question lay thick and oily at the back of her mouth. With only three armed vehicles, it'd be a waste of the bomb, wouldn't it? Or of whatever supplies could be seized from those trucks? There were a thousand reasons she could give besides the real one eating away at her gut.

But she already knew the answer. Knew there wasn't even a question. She had her orders, and so did Lauren, direct from the muzzle of a two-star general.

The crimson medic diamonds stared back at her, and for a moment the dark lines of her father's bloodied face wavered below them. How many wounded soldiers lay in those crawlers, thinking they were done? How many frightened little girls were waiting for their father to return home?

If there was any home left.

Her eyes darted to the soot-black sky where Earth smoldered like a sullen coal. The world was dying. Was already

338 | Ton Inktail

dead. Now it was her turn to throw another log onto their collective pyre.

Her thumb trembled over the firing switch.

This was her duty. To make sure she and hers were the last to go down into that final darkness. Just a few more seconds...two, one—

Something in her chest crumpled. Her thumb snapped down, flipping the safety cover back into place.

"No."

She mashed down the trigger's reset button. Ten seconds to erase the code.

"What?" Jared's bellow overrode a shout from Lauren.

Nine seconds.

Lauren grabbed her arm, prying at the trigger. The safety cover flicked open again as Imogene shoved at Lauren's helmet. She slapped it down, shifting her grip to keep both it and the reset depressed.

Jared was on his paws, barreling towards her.

Eight seconds.

Too long.

She pulled back her arm and threw the trigger as far as she could.

"The fuck?" Jared yelled, staring at the puff of dust where the trigger landed. "You bitch! You fucking PAF loving slut!"

"Get the fuck down!" Lauren snarled at him. "They're gonna see you. We're putting up too much comm traffic already. Get the fuck down and give me another trigger. I might be able to hack the detonation code."

Giddy and shaking from what she'd done, Imogene shook her head. "That's a kilobit key. They'll be gone before you try the first billion codes."

Jared roared something unintelligible and vaulted over their boulder. He bounded after the trigger.

"I said stay down!" Lauren's rifle tracked after him. Imogene shouldered the lynx aside, but hers wasn't the only weapon zeroing in on the panda.

A blinding flash exploded fifty metres downslope, followed by a rain of shrapnel. The PAF tank adjusted its aim and fired again. Another flash and spray of dust erupted as the fragmentation round chewed into the hillside.

The hospital crawlers scattered, and the Fire Ant added a burst from its twin 50-mm gauss cannons to the mix.

A pair of strong hands grabbed Imogene's ankles and yanked her back from the boulder. Bruce. He pulled her deep into their foxhole and flopped down beside her, one arm over her shoulders, holding her down.

The comm crackled static with each new explosion, and the ground tremored. Someone screamed, cut suddenly short.

"Stay down! Everybody stay down!" Lauren sounded frantic.

"You've got to surrender," William yelped. "They don't know we haven't got anything that can hurt them. They're gonna pound this whole ridge flat!" Another crack and a rain of gravel punctuated his words.

"No! We've got orders—Imogene, give me another trigger."

Static cut in on her words and something metallic pinged off Imogene's armor. She burrowed deeper, pressing her face-plate into the dust.

"I told you, it won't work," Imogene said. "You're gonna get us all killed!"

Lauren pushed Bruce aside and clawed at Imogene's demolitions pack. "Me? This is your fault. Now shut up and do as you're told!"

William snarled. "Damn both of you." A red icon lit on Imogene's display as he opened an emergency channel. "Stop! We surrender! Stop shooting!"

One last shell exploded, followed by a deathly silence.

Lauren ripped Imogene's pack free and began rifling it. "I didn't authorize that," she spat at William. "I'll see you hang for this." Her vizor snapped towards Imogene. "Both of you."

"At least you'll be alive to try." Disgust dripped from the geologist's tone. "Or maybe not. They haven't answered yet."

Imogene swallowed. What *was* taking so long? She pushed up just enough to glance over at Bruce. His faceplate turned to meet hers.

Still alive.

Some of the tension eased from her spine. She reached out to take his hand.

The red icon flashed again, and a crisp PAF voice spoke, "Come down off the hill. Leave your weapons."

"Acknowledged." William's rifle already lay in dust, and he rose without giving it so much as a glance.

Imogene reclaimed her pack from where it lay beside Lauren and emptied it of explosives before snapping it back into place.

Alexei and Bruce stood too, along with Rocco, the fox from Jared's squad. Alexei propped his rifle against a boulder while Rocco fished grenades out of his pack.

Lauren crouched in the foxhole, bent close over her datapad and a trigger from Imogene's pack.

William nudged her shoulder. "You really want to stay up here alone? They'll probably send someone to check our gear."

The gray metal of her gauntlets clenched into fists, but she rose.

They could only find parts of Jared and his otter squadmate. Imogene wished she could remember the otter's name other than "rudder-tail" as Jared had called him. Seeing him lying there and knowing the role she'd played in his death tore a hole in her heart and filled it with something more hollow than vacuum. He deserved to be remembered properly.

She couldn't bring herself to feel the same about Jared. She wanted to, but all that came for the dead panda was contempt. If he hadn't exposed their position, the PAF would have rolled on by, oblivious how close they'd come to annihilation.

No one had needed to get hurt here.

Looking up from his dead squadmates, Rocco growled. "Why in blazes did you sell us out?"

She wasn't sure if he meant her or William, but Imogene answered. "It's a medical unit. What good would it have done to blow them up?"

"What good?" the fox said. "How about keeping your squadmates alive? Y'think?"

Imogene's eyes fell to where most of the otter's upper body lay in the dust. Eugene. That had been his name. "Yeah. It was a bad call. I'm sorry."

"*I'm sorry*," Rocco mocked. "Fat lot of good that does any of us now." He spun on his heel and started descending the ridge.

Imogene clenched her teeth and followed. This wasn't what should have happened, but it *was* her fault.

The Fire Ant's turret tracked their progress down from the ridge, while the tank and the Komodo repositioned to cover the canyon mouth. Imogene followed the line of their weapons towards the dark cleft. How close behind was General Slate? Not close enough if the PAF were willing to stop and take on prisoners.

A squad of armored infantry emerged from the Fire Ant, half of them heading for Imogene's group while the rest bounded up the ridge. The PAF sergeant stepped forward when they met.

"You are in charge here, Lieutenant?" He looked at William.

"Not exactly." The geologist rubbed a hand over his borrowed armor's rank tabs. He half-turned to Lauren, but the lynx remained silent.

342 | Ton Inktail

The sergeant shrugged. "We are to search your effects. Have your people cooperate."

Imogene stood stiff as a PAF trooper pulled everything from her pack and pockets.

Useful things like rations and power packs went into his own pockets, while most of the rest were tossed aside. A few of the most benign items, he returned. The grimy set of fatigues she'd been wearing since Pons, a plastic hairbrush, her hoof shears—but not the matching pick—and a dust encrusted toothbrush.

Then they were herded into the back of a supply truck. Once all six of them were inside, the PAF sergeant's voice crackled over the comm.

"Take off your armor and cycle it out through the airlock."

Imogene grimaced. They wouldn't even need to lock the door to turn the truck into a prison. The airless void outside offered perfect security.

She shucked out of the armor that had become a second skin. Without that hard shell, she felt exposed in a way her fatigues did nothing to remedy. As she pulled on her gray camo jacket, something fell and clattered to the compartment's dull metal floor.

Her family photo.

Green toothpaste still covered the laminated rectangle. It was dry now, and she scratched away just enough to reveal her mother's smiling face. That was all she could bear. Blinking away tears, she tucked the photo back into her pocket.

Gaze fixed on the floor, she avoided her companions' eyes. She'd betrayed them all, sacrificing any small chance they had of seeing their loved ones again to indulge her moral delusions. She sank onto one of the metal crates lining the dim compartment.

Bruce sat beside her and wrapped a comforting arm around her shoulders. "This isn't your fault. Jared shouldn't have drawn their attention."

Hearing her own thought echoed from his lips only made it sound even more unworthy. She wanted to tell him how wrong he was, but before she could do more than glance up, the airlock hissed open.

Four armored figures stepped out, including a tall woman with a colonel's crescent moon and twin yellow stars on her shoulder. Her visor snapped open, revealing a tiger's black stripes and icy blue eyes.

"I need information," she said. "Give it to me, and I will not become annoyed." Her gaze slid over the prisoners before settling on William. "You had no proper weapons. What was your plan? And why did your trooper break cover?"

"Don't look at me," William said, running a hand over his blue checkered jumpsuit. "I'm supposed to be a civilian."

Her eyes narrowed and the long barbs of her whiskers twitched. She reached into her suit pocket, and what she withdrew made Imogene's stomach lurch. The small remote detonation trigger fit easily in the tiger's gauntlet.

"We found this below your position." She held it out for all to see. "What is it linked to?"

Lauren snarled and sprang, claws grasping towards the trigger.

The colonel snatched it away, and the butt of a guard's rifle slammed into Lauren's side. She fell, hissing and spitting.

A grin split the tiger's muzzle, the first real emotion she'd shown. "So, it is important. What does it do?" She toyed with the trigger, her eyes drifting over the prisoners.

Imogene shuddered as the cold blue gaze lingered on her. A cruel amusement sparked in those cyan pits. Amusement paired with something else—something not quite right that sent Imogene's ears flat against her skull.

"Tell me, caribou. I see how you quiver. I am pressed for time, and you have little value to me beyond information. I will have your friends depressurized one by one." She turned to her troopers. "Put the lynx in the airlock. She makes too much trouble."

Lauren yowled and fought as two of the soldiers grabbed her, claws skidding useless over their metal armor.

Imogene wrenched her gaze back to the colonel. A smile lurked on her striped muzzle, growing wider as Lauren yowled again. Any thought the tiger might be bluffing drained from Imogene's mind. She swallowed hard. Her inaction had already forced her squadmates into captivity. She couldn't stand by and let that failure compound into their deaths. General Slate's trap was miss-sprung and useless now anyway.

"Wait," she said as they forced Lauren into the airlock. "There's an annihilation bomb."

The colonel's eyes returned to Imogene, disappointment flashing through them before the cold blue erased all emotion. "What yield and where?"

"One gram. It's a little left of the road. The Fire Ant is parked right on top of it."

Lauren growled, but the colonel ignored her, speaking instead to one of her troops. "Find the bomb and relocate it deeper into the canyon. I will follow shortly with the Fire Ant and Komodo. The bastards chasing us will find their trap not quite where they expect it."

Imogene clenched her fists, suddenly wishing she'd kept quiet.

The colonel's icy gaze sliced into her, a row of fangs baring themselves in something far, far removed from a friendly smile. "Thank you, caribou, for your...cooperation."

32

FRIENDS, RODENTS, COUNTRYMEN

Less than an hour after the colonel left them, the cargo compartment's already dim lights went dark. They were too far away for the blinding white flash of the antimatter explosion to reach them, but a gentle tremor shuddered up through the floor.

"And that would be General Slate, fallen into his own trap." William didn't give the words any special inflection, but they cut into Imogene just the same.

A tiny whimper escaped her lips. How many people had been in the general's column? Some of them might have survived the blast, but in her heart, she doubted it. They were all dead.

Because of her.

The lights recovered from the EM pulse, and in their murky yellow glow, Lauren curled her lip at Imogene. "I hope you're happy."

Rocco bared his teeth. "She won't be happy till the tiger gives her a medal."

For a brief moment Imogene met his gaze, then looked down at the deck plates. "What was I supposed to do? Let her kill you all? You know she'd have done it."

The fox's black ears folded in disgust. "So instead you help her torch a whole column? I had a girl in Beta Squad. We were gonna have kits."

An eel of guilt twisted in her stomach. "I'm sorry."

"Like hell you are." Tail bristling, he lunged across the space between them, fist swinging for Imogene's muzzle.

Reflexes from Basic made her raise an arm to block even as she shrank from the anger contorting his face.

Beside her, Bruce shoved the fox away before he could launch another blow. He rose, glowering at Rocco. "Leave her alone. We're all on the same side here."

"You sure of that?" Rocco recovered his balance, tail still twitching. He narrowed his eyes, shooting Imogene a scorn-filled look. "Jared was right: you're nothing but a PAF loving piece of filth!"

Bruce tensed, but she laid a restraining hand on his arm. The last thing she wanted was for him to get hurt on her account. Besides, was Rocco really wrong? She felt like filth.

"I'm sorry," she said again.

The fox twisted his muzzle into a sneer, but he turned away and resumed his seat between Lauren and William.

"I think Bruce is right," Alexei said. "I mean, Imogene messed up bad, but fighting's not gonna help. We gotta concentrate on how to escape." He glanced at William. "You're sure we can't force the door to the crew compartment?"

William waved to the metal mesh door. "Be my guest. But even if we get it open, there's the question of getting away from the convoy."

"Right." Alexei twitched his whiskers and frowned down at the floor. "Still, the door's the first step." He shuffled over and started prodding, then pounding at the door.

Imogene wished he'd give up. It was obviously solid, and if the truck's driver came back while he was attacking it, there could only be trouble.

Finally he did sit down, and perhaps a quarter hour of turgid silence passed before the crew compartment's airlock clanked open. Boots rasped on the deck, but Imogene kept her gaze locked on her hooves. None of William or Alexei's efforts had even wiggled the mesh door, so until it or the cargo airlock opened, nothing outside mattered.

"Imogene?"

Her jaw clenched hard enough to break rocks. She knew that high, clear voice. Knew it, and had hoped never to hear it again.

"Yes, Ming-Xue. It's us." She looked up at the white furred rodent staring back through the mesh.

"And Bruce. Good." Ming-Xue's pink nose twitched. "I am pleased you survived. Although, I might have wished you a better fate than this."

"You and me both." Imogene snorted, then frowned. "I don't suppose you know what's going on?"

The rat shook her head. "Little. And less I should tell you."

Rocco's eyes darted from Ming-Xue to Imogene and back. "That blast just now, where there any survivors? Infantry?" Desperation bled through his voice, and the eel in Imogene's gut twisted a little tighter.

"Maybe a few," Ming-Xue said. "But Colonel Bychkov made sure of the vehicles. No one will follow."

"And you're just gonna leave them out here to die?" Rocco snarled.

Ming-Xue looked away. "It is not my decision." She turned and settled into the driver's seat. "Quiet now; we are moving out."

Imogene tried to sleep as the truck rolled over the dead lunar plains. Her head rested gently on Bruce's shoulder, and his warm, comforting musk washed out the acrid scent of anxious feline and canine sweat.

She tried to sleep, but it was no good. Images poured through her mind. Ryan's shattered helmet leered at her, gray dust swirling around him and changing into thick black smoke. Stars burst amid the darkness, and Jack's voice filled the void: "And they just keep on shining. It's comforting. Comforting..." The frosted globe of his helmet rose amid the dark mist, and deep red blood dripped against the glass. Throbbing, burning blood that belched smoke across the sphere as a once blue world burned itself to ash in the choking velvet night.

She whimpered, nuzzling deeper into the warmth of Bruce's chest. She hadn't wanted any of this to happen. She'd done her best to quench the flames. She told herself that, but deep down something wondered if she'd only made things worse.

"Hey," Bruce murmured. "You doin' okay?"

"No," she said into the fur of his chest. "I'm tired and hungry and locked in the back of a truck going gods know where, and whenever I close my eyes I see Jack, and Jared, and that poor guy's girl in Beta Squad."

"I didn't know you'd met her."

Imogene shook her head. "I didn't, but that doesn't matter. I killed her. And the others. And probably us, too."

Bruce pushed her away far enough to lock his deep brown eyes on her own. "This isn't your fault."

She broke his gaze, staring instead at the grimy gray material of his jacket. "You know that isn't true. If I'd just followed orders we'd be back safe with General Slate now. Every time I try to do something good, it turns out for the worse."

"You did what you thought was right."

"No." She nodded to Rocco. "He's right. I'm a traitor. All I do is keep killing my friends. If that's what's right, then I want nothing more to do with it. A soldier's supposed to kill the enemy, not help them."

Bruce pulled her tighter, murmuring some reassurance she didn't want to hear. If she heard his words, she'd know they were more gentle lies. She squeezed her eyes shut, closing off the world outside and building a dam against her tears. His soft words flowed over her, and she let them, trying to forget where they sat and what exactly he was saying.

The truck came to a stop, but unlike the last three times this occurred, no one brought food for Imogene and the others. Ming-Xue exchanged a hushed conversation with someone over the comm. They spoke too quietly for Imogene to overhear, but the furtive glance Ming-Xue cast back at them when the conversation ended set her fur prickling.

A few minutes later the front airlock opened and admitted a mass of gray-suited soldiers. Colonel Bychkov, and this time a half-dozen armored infantry. The colonel snapped open her visor and grinned at the prisoners while one of her troops unlocked the mesh door.

Lauren sneered back. "So, Colonel Bitch, wasn't it?"

The tiger's whiskers slicked back against her cheek ruffs. "Indeed. I have more questions."

"We're not telling you anything," Lauren spat.

Colonel Bychkov turned a cold blue gaze on Imogene.

Imogene set her jaw and levelly met the colonel's eyes. She was done pandering to the PAF tiger.

"No?" The colonel's lips twitched. "Perhaps I can persuade you." She pulled out a side arm and shot Rocco right between the eyes.

The crack of the chemical propellant pistol was impossibly loud. Imogene's ears flattened. The fox toppled slowly sideways, a stunned expression frozen on his blood-specked face. Her stomach twisted and she ripped her gaze away.

Colonel Bychkov holstered the weapon and let her gaze slide over her captives. "That was to show you I am serious. I will not kill the next one, but you will wish I had."

Her slow survey of the compartment ended on Imogene.

She shuddered, shrinking back from the murderous tiger.

"Given what I have learned from our mutual friend"—the colonel flicked her eyes at where Ming-Xue huddled in the driver's seat—"you must have returned to the Borda fuel depot. Perhaps the fool commanding your unit even used it as a staging area before pursuing us? In what condition did you leave the base?"

Imogene clamped down on her tongue. She'd already helped this vile creature more than she could stomach.

The colonel reached into a thigh pocket and produced a pair of needle-nose pliers. She rolled them back and forth between her hands for a moment, then glanced up at Imogene. "I would rather not get blood on my suit. Tell me, how many troops were left to defend the fuel depot?"

She couldn't have answered if she wanted to. Fear clogged her throat like a lump of rancid field rations. She swallowed, but found her mouth drier than the dust outside.

"As you wish." The colonel turned to her troops. "The stag, I think. Take him to the back. Keep the others seated."

"No!" Imogene clutched Bruce's arm as two of the armored infantry dragged him upright. A third prodded her with his rifle, but she ignored the threat.

"Don't." Bruce shook her off. "It's okay."

The fear in his eyes gave lie to that. She grabbed him again, but they yanked him away. The third guard's jabs found the bruise over her left ribs and she crumpled. Tears of pain and anger burned the corners of her eyes.

The two guards slammed Bruce into the wall, pinning his back against the dark gray metal. Colonel Bychkov strode slowly up to him, stopping with less than a hand's breadth between their muzzles.

"Now, Bruce was it? I think both you and I know this is for your caribou's benefit, but if you value your hide more than she seems to, feel free to answer for yourself. I need cooperation. How or whose does not matter."

She stepped back and gave the pliers a sharp click. "One last time: what defense was left at Borda?"

Bruce tightened his lips, but gave no other reply.

"Hold his head," she said to one of the guards. "I do not want him putting out an eye. Not yet."

The trooper moved up beside the colonel, blocking Imogene's view of what came next. Her view, but not the sound. A horrid wet ripping turned her insides to jelly. Bruce bellowed, something between a curse and a strangled roar. He struggled, and Imogene half-rose, but another jab from a guard's rifle pushed her back down.

Alexei put a hand on her shoulder, but she hardly noticed.

She listened, ears pinned back against her skull as Bruce's cries grew louder. Each new scream seemed to claw at the cabin walls, just as the pain behind them ripped into her chest. And into each panting quiet, the colonel would repeat her question.

Colonel Bychkov and the guard shifted, giving Imogene an unimpeded glimpse. Centimetre deep notches serrated Bruce's ear. Blood oozed from the wounds, matting his fur and dripping from his muzzle.

The tiger took a new grip on his ear, raising the pliers.

"Stop," the word slipped from Imogene's lips before she could restrain it. "Stop, I, I'll..."

Colonel Bychkov turned. A speck of blood marred her white-furred muzzle, and her pale blue eyes gleamed like frozen marbles. "Yes? You have already helped me once. It is too late for honor, but not to spare your friend."

The low growl rumbling in Lauren's throat rose to a yowl. "Don't tell her anything! You help her, it's fucking treason!"

Imogene's jaw worked, but nothing came out. It didn't matter any more, did it? General Slate was dead. And even if she managed to lead their captors into the trap at Borda, she and Bruce would die too. She had to warn Bychkov. It all made sense. But then that's what she'd thought when she threw the detonation trigger.

If she trusted her heart over her duty again, it could only end in more pain and shame and death.

But—

Her eyes darted back to Bruce. His chest and shoulders heaved, jaw locked tight. He was watching her. Everyone was watching her, waiting for her to break. And if she didn't...

Another drop of blood made a low-gravity fall to the floor. She couldn't hear the *plick* as it hit, but her heart still quavered under the impact. She couldn't do this. Not to him.

Her muzzle opened, and Colonel Bychkov leaned forward.

"Bombs," Bruce gasped out. "There's bombs, and a couple wounded guys left to trigger them."

Imogene's mouth snapped shut. Her eyes locked with the stag's, and he managed what might have been a broken smile before the colonel stepped between them.

"What sort of bombs? How many and where?"

Bruce shook his head, sending more crimson droplets off in a slow-moving arc. "I don't know. Just that General Slate couldn't spare the troops to guard the fuel, so he set this up to keep you from getting it."

"And that is the extent of the defenses?" She addressed the question to Bruce, but her ice blue eyes flicked between him and Lauren. Bruce nodded, while the rage seething in Lauren's slitted eyes gave all the confirmation anyone could want.

"So, bombs." The tiger turned to Imogene. "And I suspect you had something to do with them. I saw what they took from your pack."

Imogene gave a slow, reluctant nod.

"Hmm." Colonel Bychkov slapped the still bloody pliers into the palm of her other glove. "I think a lone survivor escaped your general's folly. Escaped, and now returns to her base. Someone who knows enough about the explosives to quickly disarm them once she is inside."

A bitter taste rose up in the back of Imogene's mouth. "And what makes you think I'll help you?"

"I like teeth." The tiger curled her black lips and tapped the pliers against one long, pointed fang. "So useful. So strong, and deeply rooted. Your stag has nice teeth. If you want him to keep them, you will do what I say."

33

RETURN

An abandoned rifle lay in the dust, but Imogene didn't dare stop walking to retrieve it. Colonel Bychkov and one of her men with a sniper rifle were watching from the rim of Borda's crater. No way the flimsy emergency suit they'd given her would stop even a single bullet from that.

The base looked even more bleak than before. Black lines of char and rough sheet metal patches marred the once pure silver dome. She almost missed the entrance Aaron had cut. It was solid now, plated over with scrap from the ruined garage.

General Slate's people had made some repairs, but this was definitely new.

The frozen airlock had been unjammed, and slid open when she thumbed the button. Air hissed in around her. She flipped open her visor and coughed once before slamming it shut again. There might be air, but whatever oxygen it contained was choked with so much soot and filth it hardly mattered.

The inner door opened, spilling dim light from the airlock into the dark corridor.

"Hello? This is Private Haartz, UNA. Anyone here?" She sent the call out over both comms and her suit's external speaker. A distant thump and clanking drifted through the darkness, but no reply came. Picking her way to the center of the dome, she tried again.

"Imogene?" Aaron's voice drawled over her comm moments before the grizzly's blue pressure suit appeared at the end of a corridor. He set down a cutting torch and shuffled towards her. "Didn't expect to see you back so soon."

Dragging Aaron into this added another dozen kilos to the weight already crushing her heart. But protecting Bruce and the others came first.

"Me either," she said. "Is there anyone else here? I need to see about disarming that detonation trigger we left you with."

Aaron's helmet bobbed. "Just me and a skunk with a busted leg. He's got the trigger downstairs."

Two people. Not enough to mount a serious defense. Imogene frowned, reshuffling the half-formed plans she'd worked out on the walk into the crater.

She followed Aaron down and through the second airlock into the lower levels. Their headlamps gave the only light, but the air tasted surprisingly fresh. The dank smell of standing water was gone, and when they passed the stairwell to the power room, only a bathtub ring of oil remained on the now dry steps.

"You managed to pump out all the water?" she asked.

The bear's muzzle pulled into a sheepish grin. "Yeah. Set up a siphon. Stick a hose in the water and throw the other end out the airlock. Sucked it right out clean. I just feel stupid I didn't think of it sooner."

"Any luck with the generators? I assume that's why you did it?"

"Nah. I tried, but everything's still too blurry. I can see to weld okay, but messing with electronics is out."

They turned into the dome's ring corridor, where a pale radiance shone from an open doorway. Aaron stepped into the light "Hey, Norman, relief has arrived."

She followed him into the room where a skunk reclined on a broken office chair. His beady black eyes peered at her over a leg propped up and wrapped from ankle to thigh in yellow thermoset.

"Thank the gods," he said. "About time the general sent someone back for us." He straightened in the chair, arching his eyebrows at Imogene. "How'd the PAF hunt go?"

"We found them, all right." Her gaze darted from his eyes to the cluttered crate-table beside him. She took a step forward. "Do you have the detonation trigger?"

"Yeah." The skunk rummaged in the litter of half-eaten ration trays and pulled out a small matte black box. "Why? The general want us to blow the fuel bunkers?"

"No—" She snatched the trigger from him before his thumb could drift too near the firing button. Her own thumb found the smaller reset button and held it until the remote chirped, signaling the detonation codes were erased. She set down the now useless device and met the skunk's eyes.

"General Slate lied to you. The whole base is rigged to blow, not just the bunkers."

"What?" The skunk's tail twitched. "Why? And where is the general, anyway?"

Imogene shrugged. "He probably wanted you to take any nearby PAF with you."

"But General Slate helped us," Aaron said. "He wouldn't just let us kill ourselves like that."

"Yeah?" She angled her muzzle at a grill on the wall above the skunk. "Why don't you take the cover off that vent and find out?"

Aaron did, sliding his claws through the grate and yanking it off to reveal a block of blue putty explosive. He dropped the grate and backed away. "Damn," he growled. "I'm gonna beat the crap out of him, two-star general or not. Setting us up like that!"

Imogene shook her head. "You won't have to. He's dead. So are most of his troops, and there's a PAF unit up on the ridge waiting for me to defuse the explosives."

"PAF? Waiting for you?" The skunk's muzzle bunched, beady eyes narrowing to slits. "You sold us out, didn't you?"

Rocco had said the same thing. Was it any less true now? She had to hope so.

"Would you really rather have died in the blast? I'm sorry it has to be like this. But I do have a plan." She turned to Aaron. "Is there anywhere you guys can hide?"

Aaron's bloodshot eyes held hers. She struggled to return that red gaze, willing the grizzly tech's amiable nature and logical outlook to keep him focused forward rather than back.

After a long moment, he nodded. "There's a crawlspace under the generator room."

"Perfect." She forced confidence into her tone. "They've got four of my squadmates prisoner too, but there's only ten or twenty PAF soldiers. The rest are medics and wounded. With you on the outside to spring us, we can wait until they settle in and lower their guard, then take them out." She nodded at the skunk's cast. "He's probably out of the fighting, but that's still six of us. Combine that with surprise and we can turn the tables."

She glanced from skunk to grizzly and back. They didn't have time for an argument, and while the plan wasn't nearly as certain as she'd made it sound, at least it was something.

Aaron hitched his massive shoulders. "Better than anything I can think of."

Both of them turned to the skunk.

The white stripe between his eyes narrowed as he glowered at Imogene. "You better make this right. The general might have screwed us, but at least we'd have died doing our duty."

"I'll do my best," she said. He'd probably never believe her, but right now all that mattered was his cooperation.

She sought Aaron's gaze. "Get any weapons you have and whatever else you'll need to hide for a day or two. That goes in the crawlspace. I also want a couple sets of tools and datapads to hide in the most likely places they'll keep us, so we can call you to coordinate, and as a backup. Can you take care of that?"

Aaron nodded.

"Good." She reached up and took the block of explosives from the vent. "We don't have much time, and I've got to pull out enough of the charges to make a good show."

Fifteen minutes later she had an impressive looking stack of blue explosives. Less than two thirds of what she and Jared had deployed in the dome alone, but the PAF didn't have to know that. She helped Aaron move the skunk downstairs, then hurried back up to the surface, barely ahead of the deadline.

She gave the agreed upon signal, and seconds later the Fire Ant crested the crater rim. Dust roostertailed from the skirtless treads as the armored personnel carrier sped down the narrow road to the dome. The crawler stopped and its infantry swarmed out, weapons ready. They flattened themselves against the dome on either side of the airlock, prepping for a hostile entry.

"There wasn't anyone inside," Imogene said over an open channel. "They must have bugged out on their own."

The PAF sergeant's visor snapped towards her, then he waved his troops inside without acknowledging her comment.

Imogene fought the urge to pace. The colonel's sniper was probably still watching her, and if the base was as empty as she'd claimed, there was no reason for her to be nervous.

Her shifting hooves had beaten a small crater into the fine dust before the sergeant reappeared. He gave a beckoning wave to the colonel's position on the rim, then turned to Imogene.

"You, inside."

Another PAF trooper waited in the airlock, and with his rifle held ready, escorted her back into the lower levels. The basement airlock opened, and she saw Aaron being marched deeper into the base. Her hope drained away in a defeated sigh. At least he was okay.

As they approached the power room, a whiff of acrid musk curled Imogene's nose. The trooper prodded her down the stairs, and her stomach knotted.

The skunk's black and white striped body lay in the middle of the corridor, a smeared trail of blood showing where he'd been dragged from the crawlspace. She didn't want to look, but was unable to turn away.

The trooper nudged her with his weapon. "Take him outside. Before the smell worsens."

Hesitantly, she complied, wrapping her gauntlets around those limp, black-furred hands. She tried to avoid the dead skunk's eyes, but his glazed mudpuddle pupils sought her out. Rage contorted his features, and she could almost hear his question: "Why? Why did you betray us?"

With a shudder, she ripped her gaze away. She hadn't betrayed him. She'd done everything she could. Hadn't she?

His dead eyes caught hers again. Silent. Accusing.

No. There was no justification that could ever excuse what she'd done to him.

Outside, she laid his now swollen and rapidly freezing corpse beside the other dead removed from the dome. Amid the pile, Jack's white suit caught her eye. She'd killed him too, hadn't she? A more personal betrayal than the treason she'd delivered General Slate or the skunk, but betrayal none the less.

Colonel Bychkov's crawlers pulled up into a tight huddle beside the dome. Imogene and the trooper watching her stood by as the colonel and a few others entered the base. Minutes later they reemerged, the colonel gesticulating as she issued orders.

One of the supply trucks backed right up to the airlock, while the hospital crawlers disgorged a small swarm of medics. Everyone bore a carton or stack of bedding, all heading for the dome.

The combat vehicles were moving too, the damaged tank settling into a defensive position while the Fire Ant and Komodo rolled back up towards the crater rim.

"Go," the trooper behind Imogene said. "You will help unload." He pointed to where Imogene's companions had appeared beside the waiting supply truck. He followed her long enough to make sure she wouldn't try to disappear, then bounded off to join his squadmates trekking for the ridgeline.

"How did things go?" Bruce asked when he saw her.

"Not great. Aaron's eyes are getting better. He's inside somewhere." She didn't mention the skunk. He could just accrue alongside all her other private guilt.

The truck's front compartment opened and a familiar figure stepped out. "Come on," Omar said. "Door is unlocked. Start unloading."

William and Bruce undogged the cargo hatch while Omar strode closer. He'd picked up a bandolier of grenades somewhere along the line, and hefted an assault rifle. Imogene snorted. With the odds the way they were, he hardly needed a weapon to keep his labor detail in line.

They formed a living conveyor, shifting crates of food and munitions from the truck into the dome's airlock. When the first truck was empty another pulled up to take its place.

While Imogene's group hauled freight, the medics moved wounded into the dome. Some could still walk, while others were carried in coffin-like pressurized stretchers. After the second truck was empty, Omar shifted them over to the coffin-bound patients and medical supplies piling up around the hospital crawlers.

The stretchers were coming back out to be refilled, and on the sixth trip Bruce cast a long look at the blood smeared and much bandaged mongoose inside. He looked up and over at Omar. "You're unloading all the wounded? I can understand a few to make more room, but Borda's no medical center. This guy would be better off in the crawler."

Omar shook his head. "He will be safer here. The crawlers are going north again, to pick up more wounded."

"As if these aren't enough," Alexei huffed from where he and Lauren struggled with a bear-size stretcher. "And where are they gonna find anyone still lively enough to need help anyway?"

The silver tint of Omar's visor hid his expression as he weighed Alexei's question. "Before Ming-Xue and I joined the colonel, several of her vehicles were disabled in a rock slide. And no, I do not know how many or where. Now be quiet and work."

By the time all the wounded were inside, Imogene's arms and legs ached. The low gravity might help, but a convoy's worth of supplies made for a lot of lifting. It had been a long time since she'd had any proper sleep either, and every blink fell with a leaden weight.

A pair of PAF soldiers relieved Omar and herded Imogene and the others into the dome. Her lip twisted in irony when they reached their destination: the very same makeshift cell where they'd held Ming-Xue and Omar. Their processing went about the same, too, stripped of their suits and forced at gunpoint into the small inner storeroom. Aaron already waited inside, and with six of them the room felt crowded.

The door slid shut, and Lauren spat a frothy wad against it. "This just gets better and better, you know that?" Her yellow eyes flashed in the dim light. She turned on Imogene. "You're sure you're on the right side of the door? You were in here alone for almost an hour, and all you managed to do was exactly what Colonel Bitch asked? Pathetic."

Imogene flicked one ear but didn't reply. She knelt and pulled open the service panel beside the door, revealing a handful of tools and a datapad. "There would have been more," she said, "but things didn't work out as well as I'd hoped."

Lauren's eyes widened. She lunged after the datapad, then retreated into a corner, eyes locked on the tiny screen.

A smile twisted its way across Imogene's muzzle, then died. Proving Lauren wrong was about all the pitiful supplies were good for now.

She glanced at Aaron. "What happened?"

His jowls hardened into an unhappy line. "They smelled Norman, and you saw what he was like. Rather die than surrender."

Imogene sighed. Even if Aaron and the skunk hadn't been discovered, the corridors were crawling with enemy troops. How could she have deluded herself into thinking they had a chance of turning the tables?

Bruce knelt to inspect the tools, giving Imogene a good view the crusted blood along the side of his face and the ragged chunks missing from his ear. Her jaw clenched tight and her throat closed. No cache of hidden tools could ever repair the harm she'd done.

The stag returned the pliers and screwdrivers to their concealment. He smiled up at her, warmth struggling to push the weariness from his eyes.

"Good job. This is more than we had any right to hope for." He started to rise, then winced and held his side where the guards had beat him. Sliding back to the floor, he leaned with his shoulders propped against the service panel.

Imogene sat beside him, taking his hand between her own. She took a breath to steady her nerves and instead tasted the growing staleness of the base's overtaxed life support systems.

Her tools might have bought them a chance, but she wondered if the dying base would give them time enough to take it.

The grating sound of the door sliding open roused Imogene from a fitful sleep. The air tasted thicker already. She coughed, then looked up at the door.

Omar stood in the opening, brown fur and rumpled green fatigues replacing his gray armor.

"Bear, stag, come." He waved them to stand. "You are both mechanical. You will help repair the base."

Aaron blew a lungful of the fetid air out in a snort. "Strangely familiar, huh?"

Bruce nodded, then shot Omar a sidelong glance. "Not as easy as it seems being in charge, is it?"

The hare's muzzle tightened. "No. But come. Now the crawlers have gone north, if the base dies, we all die with it."

"And I've got a good idea who'll be first in line if we don't help." Bruce rose to his hooves, and with a quick glance and tight smile towards Imogene, he followed Aaron out of the cell.

Imogene watched him until the closing door cut off her view. With the power room dewatered there might actually be some hope of fixing the generators. That prospect should have lifted her spirits, but they were all dead anyway, one way or another. At least if the air supply gave out she wouldn't have any more opportunities to betray her friends.

She fumbled in her breast pocket and took out her family photo. Dry toothpaste still covered most of it, and with her thick fingernails she scraped off the remaining crust.

Standing under a maple, Josh and their mother smiled up at her. And sandwiched there between them, Imogene smiled too.

Her year-and-a-half ago self stood clean and proud in her pressed-perfect khakis, ready to go out and do what was expected of her. Things had made so much more sense then. Twelve months compulsory service, then back to Helsinki and a settled, stable life where the worst thing she'd have to worry about was a cheating ex-boyfriend. Not whether her boyfriend

364 | Ton Inktail

would be tortured, or if her decisions would condemn dozens of people to death.

The lights went out, then blinked fitfully back to life.

Lauren dropped the datapad into her lap with a growl. "Damn, I was almost in that time." Her eyes flicked up to Imogene's. "Your boyfriend's got a real knack for timing his power cuts. Next time pick a pad that's already got admin privileges."

"At least you've got something to do," Alexei said. "Just sitting here is driving me nuts." He scooted across the floor to where Imogene sat beside the door's service panel. She moved aside as he pulled it open and removed their cache of tools.

He peered into the space beyond for a moment, then turned to Imogene. "Did you get a good look at what Ming and Omar did to jimmy it?"

"Not really."

"Hmm." He looked back into the opening. "What'd Bruce say? A screwdriver stuck in the locking mechanism?"

William edged forward to kneel beside the white rabbit. "Yeah, that would work, but it's better to disable the lock altogether. We've got doors like this at my station. Let me give you a hand."

Imogene watched them with less than half her attention. They were wasting their time, just as much as Lauren with her comms and computers. There was no way they'd get out of the base unnoticed. All they could do was try and suffer as little as possible before Colonel Bitch terminated their existence. Her jaw tightened at the thought of the tiger. She hoped Bruce and Aaron couldn't fix the generators. That the PAF colonel died with the rest of them, choking on her own waste gasses.

William and Alexei finished their work and restored the tools and service panel to their proper places. Lauren continued poking at her datapad, cursing every time the lights flickered. That cursing and the rattle from the ventilation system coughing out an irregular stream of mostly stale air were the only signs of the passing hours.

Eventually Imogene drifted into an uneasy half-sleep where oily black clouds of fear roiled, occasionally curdling into enough coherence for her to worry about where Bruce was.

34

SOLDIER GRAY

They'd been given a stack of field rations at what Imogene's stomach said was dinner time. But that was hours ago, and neither Bruce nor Aaron had returned.

Imogene gnawed a fibrous chunk of plant stem she'd found in the stew. Bruce and Aaron wouldn't have caused trouble intentionally, but Colonel Bychkov and her lackeys weren't the type for half measures. She chewed faster, forcing her thoughts away from what those measures were likely to include. There were plenty of other reasons they might be detained. Working her prisoners past exhaustion fit the colonel well, too.

The door opened, and all that kept Imogene from jumping to her hooves was the fear it might be interpreted as an attack.

Bruce shuffled in and the door slid shut behind him.

Seeing the stag alive and with no new wounds filled Imogene with such relief it took a moment to realize he'd entered alone. The smile she'd stated to give him stuck partway.

"Where's Aaron?"

Bruce sighed. "He's resting with the PAF wounded. One of the transformers slipped and crushed his arm. Bad compound fracture, and he lost a lot of blood before we got it stopped, but he should live. Assuming any of us do." He closed his eyes, and Imogene could feel the effort it took him to open them again. "Colonel Bitch was impressed enough she pulled me off repairs to help the medics instead. How they've kept some of those poor bastards alive I don't know."

He took a few tired steps then slid down to sit beside Imogene. She slipped her arm around him and pulled him close, ignoring the smell of antiseptic and bile clinging to his fur.

Across the narrow space, Alexei stirred. "Lauren's almost into the comm system, and William and I got the door unlocked."

"That's good," Bruce said. "But they're keeping an armed guard right outside, and there's a lot of people moving around the corridors. Things seemed to quiet down towards evening, but not enough."

William reached up and smoothed his whiskers. "So we're gonna need a plan. A good one."

"Yeah." Bruce's eyes drifted shut again. "But I'm dead on my hooves, and clean out of suggestions. Right now throwing open the door and getting shot doesn't sound half bad as long as I get a long, quiet rest afterward."

He shifted against Imogene's side, and shortly his breathing settled into a slow, steady pattern.

Imogene did her best to comfort Bruce as he slept. His head rested heavy on her shoulder, but she didn't mind. She wasn't sure if she dozed off herself, but after what seemed like only a few hours an otter in a blood-smeared medical smock came and roused Bruce for another stint.

"There's a satellite."

Lauren's excited hiss roused Imogene from her contemplation of the glow panel. Hope fluttered deep in her chest, stirring beneath the flood of apathy. She shouldered in beside William and Alexei, peering down at Lauren's datapad.

"Can you call anyone?" Alexei's whiskers quivered with excitement.

"Maybe, but it's in a low polar orbit. We're not gonna have more than a few minutes to try." She pulled up a wide-band hailing channel. "This is Sergeant Lauren Porter to any receiving units, please acknowledge."

She repeated variations on that every few seconds. A dead carrier wave was all the answer they received, and Imogene's hope turned sour. If the satellite was as low as Lauren said, what were the odds of anyone sharing its limited coverage with them? She'd seen firsthand how empty the hills outside were.

A light on the datapad flickered, and General Slate's hard voice emerged from the speaker. "Porter?"

"General!" Lauren's eyes lit up like stars. "You survived?"

"And a handful of others. What's your status? Why didn't you set off the bomb?"

"Imogene fucked it up. We had to surrender. We and the PAF are back at Borda."

"Borda? It's still there?"

"Yes, sir."

"Are the explosives still in place?"

Lauren shot Imogene an inquiring look. She nodded.

"Most of them, yes."

"Then for gods' sake, blow it up! The PAF are heavily overextended. Without fuel they'll crumble. We can regroup and push them out."

"Sir?"

"Do it, Porter." His voice gapped and distorted as the satellite skimmed the horizon. "That's an order. I'm counting on you."

The signal indicator went dead.

Lauren stared down at the datapad, then her yellow slitted eyes lanced into Imogene. "What do you need to set off the explosives?"

Imogene's pulse quickened. The bombs wouldn't need much. Nothing they couldn't easily lay hands on. Assuming of course she was willing to sentence everyone in the base to a fiery death.

Before she could make sense of the emotions swirling through her, the door grated open.

Lauren thrust the datapad inside her jacket, but the only person to enter the cell was Bruce. His hands were clean, but blood specked his forearms above where gloves would cover. He staggered across the cell and collapsed against the far wall.

It broke Imogene's heart to add to the stag's troubles, but he was the one person who could help her see the right way out of this. She opened her mouth, but Bruce beat her to it.

"I put Aaron's kidneys into one of their bears," he said dully.

Imogene's blood turned to ice. "What? But what about Aaron?"

"I don't know. They said he and twelve of the most critically wounded died in the night."

"All together?"

"Yeah." He took a breath of the thick, feted air and coughed. "Probably Colonel Bitch prioritizing who gets to keep burning oxygen. Most of the twelve wouldn't have made it."

Imogene shook her head, not quite able to accept it. "But, Aaron? He was doing okay."

"He was also UNA. Their panda's gonna live now." Bruce grimaced down at his too-clean hands, then crossed his arms, stuffing them out of sight. "So, that's my day. What about you?" He cast a weary look at where Lauren had retrieved her datapad. "Find anyone to talk to?"

"General Slate survived. He ordered us to blow the base."

Bruce's tattered ears twitched, then settled back into their tired slump. "That's not sounding like such a bad idea." He glanced over at Imogene. "Can you do it?"

"Probably. But I'm not sure it's the best thing to do."

Lauren snarled. "Gods! Still? It's a fucking order. You remember what keeps happening when you ignore orders?" She spat on the floor, but curbed her jeer into a more reasonable tone. "Look, if the PAF keep the fuel here, it could cost us the war. What does your bleeding heart tell you about that? Millions and millions of UNA deaths. If you let them keep it, they'll win."

Imogene snorted. As if anyone could win this massacre. But still, what if General Slate was right? She didn't trust him to know any more about the strategic situation than herself, but still, what if? His track record couldn't be any worse than her own.

She looked over at Bruce. The bone-deep weariness in his soft brown eyes, the tattered mess of his ear...

Did it really matter if Colonel Bychkov died of asphyxiation as Imogene had hoped, or was vaporized in a single instant? Either way was no more than the tiger bitch deserved. And with her character and resources, Bychkov might abandon the dying base to save herself. There was no way to outrun an antimatter explosion.

She turned back to Lauren, a planet-size weight settling on her chest. "If we're gonna do this, we need a plan."

The lynx's muzzle split into a tooth-filled grin. "Right. So again, what do you need to set them off?"

"Nothing special. It's all rigged with kinetic sensitive detonators; once one goes the rest will follow. You could probably set the first one off with a hard punch, but an electric short would be better."

"Okay, so triggering them isn't a problem, and we've got the door gimmicked. Where is the nearest charge?"

"Just a few doors down from here. I'll need a screwdriver to open the glow panel it's hidden behind, a power pack from the guard's suit or rifle, and two wires for the short."

William frowned. "Can't you set up a time fuse or something? Our chances of getting away might be slim, but I'd really like to try."

"No," Lauren said. "Even if she can make something like that, the odds of someone finding it are too high. The guard is wearing full armor. Even with surprise on our side he's going to get off an alarm. Then we've got a minute or two before everyone's dead, one way or another."

"We should wait until night, too," Bruce offered. "If everyone's asleep we might get closer to that two minutes rather than one."

William gnashed his teeth. He locked his gaze on Imogene. "You're really gonna fold now? These are still the same medics and wounded you refused to blow up before."

The retriever's words ripped into her like a hail of meteoroids. He was right—a voice buried deep in her heart screamed that he was right. But buried beside that voice was the accusing look in a dead skunk's eyes, and the crushing guilt as a column of UNA troops died in a blast she helped design, and the ragged, blood-dripping edge of a stag's ear.

She lifted her chin. "Yeah, I saved them. And I've seen what saving them cost. We're all dead anyway, and a soldier's duty is to take as many of the enemy with her as she can."

372 | Ton Inktail

35

SACRED DUTY

Waiting was the hardest part of any plan.

They'd picked oh-two-hundred hours to launch their assault, but shortly after midnight the door rasped open. Startled out of her brooding, Imogene looked up at three heavily armed and armored soldiers: Ming-Xue, Omar, and a ferret.

"I am still confused about your orders," the ferret guard said. "The medic I understand, but why the caribou? And why at this hour?"

Omar gave the ferret a patronizing look. "Take a deep breath. Fresh air would be good, yes? The colonel has our best interests at heart. We are taking them outside. For fresh air. We do it at night so questions will not be asked."

The deadly meaning behind Omar's words sent a jolt of panic down Imogene's spine, but it took the ferret several moments to figure it out. His dark brows knotted together, then his eyes shot back to Omar.

"You mean—?"

"Questions are bad," Omar said. "Stag, caribou, come."

Imogene's gaze darted around her allies. Could they launch their plan early? But all three PAF were alert and in full combat regalia. Desperate as she was, she could see the difference between a suicide mission and just plain suicide. Once whatever happened to her and Bruce happened, Lauren and the others might still be able to carry out the plan.

Wordless, Bruce rose slowly and helped Imogene to her hooves.

She cast a last frantic look at William and Alexei. The rabbit's ears folded flat against his skull, while William just watched, brown eyes heavy with pained sympathy.

Lauren gave a tight-lipped nod.

Then they were out in the dimly lit corridors, following Omar with Ming-Xue behind them, her rifle ready.

Imogene's heart pounded. Every step took an eternity, as if the moist, stale air had turned to jelly. Bruce hadn't relinquished his hold, and she clutched his hand. Glancing back, she caught Ming-Xue's eyes.

"Please, you can't do this."

The rat met her gaze, then quickly looked away. "Quiet."

Boots and hooves clicked against the lithcrete stairs. At the top, Omar led them away from the makeshift medical unit and towards the airlock. The airlock, and the fatal emptiness beyond.

Omar thumbed the cheery green open button, then jerked his rifle at the doorway. "Inside."

It took everything Imogene had to force herself into the airlock. Decompression was better, she told herself. Getting shot could drag out. When she turned to look back out of the airlock, Ming-Xue had vanished, leaving Omar alone.

"You don't have to do this," Bruce said, voice low and earnest. "Just give us our suits back and we'll vanish. I swear you'll never see us again."

Imogene's throat tightened. That plea was a grim sort of hope indeed. She'd seen how vast the empty spaces of the moon were. There was no chance they'd survive longer than it took their power packs to run out.

"Unlikely." Omar tugged at the bandoleer of grenades circling his chest. "You two are like moon dust. You get into everything and are impossible to remove."

Ming-Xue stepped back into the corridor and thrust a pair of emergency suits towards Imogene. "We couldn't find your armor. Please hurry." She cast a look over her shoulder. "We must leave now."

Clutching the suits' stiff material, Imogene's hands shook. Her breath caught as the icy block of tension that had replaced her heart began to thaw.

"You're letting us go?"

Omar nodded. "There are...words among the troops. They say twelve patients died last night." He cast a sharp look at Bruce.

"Thirteen, actually."

"And we all know *why* they died." Omar spat onto the deck plates.

Beside him, Ming-Xue's tail twitched. "The colonel may have sold her honor, but we will not. I still have the access codes for the supply truck. We will be gone before anyone knows."

Bruce took one of the suits from Imogene and started yanking it on. "What about William and Alexei?"

"He's right." Imogene paused in pulling on her own suit. "We can't leave without them. And Lauren."

Omar narrowed his dark eyes. "She tried to kill you. And us. More than once."

Imogene crossed her arms. "I don't like her any more than you do, but she's UNA. I won't leave anyone who's that easy of a target for Colonel Bitch."

Omar's lip quirked at their name for the colonel, but he shook his head. "Our bluff will not work a second time. We have delayed too long already. We are leaving. Now."

The command in his tone set her fur prickling. This was one order she had no qualms in ignoring.

"Then go without us. We'll give you a good head start, then try to get our friends out on our own."

He blinked, then arched his brows at Ming-Xue.

She cast him a disgusted look. "No." Her clear blue eyes locked on Imogene. "But he is right about the risk. If trouble starts, do not wait for us. Get out and go east. We will do our best to meet up with you."

Bruce frowned. "Shouldn't we stick together?"

"No. If you return with us, the guard will *know* something is wrong. Stay here. Out of sight."

Bruce glanced at the darkened doorway where she'd gotten the suits.

"Fine." Omar shook his head hard enough the helmet swivels clicked. "We still must hurry." He and Ming-Xue turned to leave, but Imogene caught the white rat's elbow.

"Ming-Xue, I...thank you."

Ming-Xue gave a tight smile. "Thank me when it works."

Crouched in the dark storeroom amid piles of suits, they waited. Imogene gnawed her lip, fighting the urge to check her suit's chronometer. Thirty seconds since the last time? Maybe?

Beside her, in the shelter of a suit-draped desk, Bruce shifted.

She glanced over at his dark silhouette and grimaced. Yet again, her ethics were putting him in danger. But this time she knew she was right. Abandoning your squadmates wasn't an option. Not for any kind of person she wanted to be.

And neither was giving up and committing some sort of glorified suicide. Bychkov might be darkness incarnate, but that didn't mean the wounded under her care deserved to die. How close Imogene had let herself be pulled to that final mistake drove shivers back and forth beneath her fur. Some lines should never be crossed, and if that belief made her weak or a traitor, then so be it.

Claws and boots scraped outside the door, and her muscles tensed. Had it been long enough? Or too long? She sucked in a breath, readying herself to spring at whoever opened the door if it wasn't Ming-Xue.

The door slid open and light flooded in, along with the familiar shapes and scents of Alexei, William, and Lauren.

Ming-Xue followed, rifle clutched tight and whiskers twitching. "Hurry. Please, hurry."

They needed no second urging. William slithered into the nearest suit, Alexei and Lauren only seconds behind him. Ming-Xue and Omar hovered in the doorway, splitting their attention between the escapees and the still empty corridor.

Imogene and Bruce moved up beside them, and with the others close behind, advanced out into the corridor.

A giddy relief rose in Imogene's chest. The welcoming maw of the airlock lay just ahead. She wrapped her fingers around Bruce's glove. They were going to make it out and away. All of them, together and alive.

Lauren shouldered her way between them, breaking their hold.

The lynx stumbled, lurching towards Omar, grabbing at him for support. He gave a muffled exclamation but she was already backing away, a grenade clenched in her fist.

Ming-Xue squeaked. Omar cursed and fumbled after his rifle.

"Don't." Lauren yanked out the pin.

Omar froze.

A feral grin split Lauren's muzzle. "That's right, PAF. Now back up into the airlock. Both of you." Her slitted yellow eyes darted to Imogene. "Those explosives of yours, is there any special trick to setting them off?"

"No," Imogene said tightly. "That grenade should do just fine. But I'm *not* telling you where they are."

"I'll take my chances." Lauren tossed the pin away. "You better get going. I'm not giving you a head start." She backed several metres from the group, then spun and bounded away into the shadowy passages.

Imogene's jaw clenched. After everything, it still came down to this. She turned and drove her fist into the airlock door. "Damn it."

Bruce laid a hand on her arm. "You tried. Who knows? She may not find one before the PAF find her. Right now, we've got to go." His comforting hand turned to an insistent tug, and Imogene let herself be pulled into the airlock.

To hope Lauren might get shot left a bitter taste in Imogene's mouth. But Lauren had made her choice, and better she die alone than adding more names to whatever monument might someday be raised to this madness.

The charges were well hidden. Now she just prayed they were well hidden enough.

Ming-Xue's codes got them into the supply truck and rolling north with every scrap of speed available.

Imogene hunkered on her crate, hand wrapped tight around Bruce's. There was no guessing the blast radius if all the fuel in Borda's bunkers detonated, but every klick of gray, dusty soil they put behind them increased their odds of survival. Just as every second without an explosion decreased the odds Lauren would complete her final mission.

After twenty minutes and perhaps half as many kilometres, the tension in her shoulders eased. She drew a deep breath and gave Bruce's hand a little squeeze.

Then the now-familiar white light of an antimatter explosion seared the landscape.

Bruce grabbed her as the truck skidded to a stop. The vehicle bucked and trembled under an assault of flying rocks and debris, but after the first flash of panic, Imogene couldn't bring herself to care.

She'd failed again.

General Slate had gotten his way. A small mountain of fuel cubes were forever safe from enemy hands, a few vehicles destroyed, and an insignificant lunar valley rendered even less hospitable than it was before. All at a bargain price of noncombatants, enemy wounded, and one loyal lynx.

Her chest collapsed in on itself, and she buried her face in Bruce's shoulder. Tears pressed against the backs of her eyes, but refused her the relief of being shed. There had to be something she could have done better or different. Some way to stop the fires that were consuming everything she'd ever known or held dear. There had to be, but she didn't know what it was.

Bruce held her, smoothing the fur of her head and neck, whispering that everything would be okay.

The truck didn't restart in the wake of the EM pulse. Not until Omar crawled shoulder-deep into the engine compartment to reset a tripped breaker. With the lights back on and ventilation system humming, he spun the driver's chair to face the rest of the compartment.

"I presume that settles any question of pursuit by the colonel. Then what path do we steer?" His dark eyes flicked towards Ming-Xue. "You are more familiar with this region than I."

"Which says little." She flattened one ear at him. "There is the radar site at Bellot. Other bases farther north and east..."

Omar rejected her with a shake of his head. "Those are all UNA bases. We will be imprisoned again, or worse. I say we strike northwest, into the mare. There must be other PAF forces still operational."

Alexei let out a low growl, and Imogene's brow knotted. She leaned forward. "I'm not sure I like the sound of that."

William cleared his throat. "I might be able to suggest something in the middle: my geology station at Goclenius. It is UNA, but we're all scientists. No military." He leveled an earnest look at Omar. "I can't guarantee anything once law and order are reestablished, but until then I'll see you're treated the same as the rest of us."

Omar nodded cautiously, and William continued. "The other big point is that as of two weeks ago the station was still intact. Plenty of food, fuel, and water."

Ming-Xue twitched her whiskers thoughtfully. "Goclenius is north and east, in Fecunditatis, yes?"

"Right. Maybe five hundred klicks, give or take. I know a few small bases that are closer, including Bellot, but I've got no idea what shape they're in now."

She glanced over at Omar. "Goclenius is acceptable?"

The hare shrugged. "I have no better ideas."

"It is decided then. You must show the way when we are close," she said to William.

He gave a weary smile. "Sounds fair."

Imogene half expected them to meet General Slate, or perhaps more PAF stragglers, but there was no one. The kilometres crawled past in an endless procession of empty roads and barren valleys, until late the next day when William led them off the main track and into the hills.

The trail they followed twisted up into the mountains, leading at last to the lip of a small crater. Across the crater's floor spread a tangle of modular housing and laboratory units. There were crawlers too, most of them drilling rigs or old transports like the one William and Louie had driven. Everything was painted reflective white or silver, and fairly glowed in the bright sunlight.

"There it is." William waved one hand towards the viewport. "Goclenius Station. Not much, but right now there's nothing I'd rather see."

Imogene peered forward, taking in the view. "I'll go along with that. Quiet, out-of-the-way, just the kind of place to lie low and let the world sort itself out."

Alexei frowned. "Isn't that deserting, or something?"

"At least we'll be in good company." William reached over and clasped Omar's shoulder. The hare snorted, but didn't shrug off the geologist's hand.

"Besides," Imogene added, "I'm not sure there's much of an army left to desert *from*. And if there is, it's not like we'll be hiding from them. No one could blame us for doing our best to stay alive."

Ming-Xue flicked one ear in agreement, then cast a measuring look down at the base. "That, I suspect, is all anyone will be doing for a long while now. Trying to stay alive."

"We'll manage." Surprised at her own firmness, Imogene glanced around at her companions—old and new alike. Bruce met her eyes with a tender smile. She squeezed his hand, then followed Ming-Xue's gaze down to the shining silver base.

A smile crossed her lips, and she nodded. "Somehow we'll manage. Together."

ABOUT THE AUTHOR

Ton Inktail, AKA Tonin, joined the furry fandom in 2010 and has been writing fuzzy stories ever since. Like all wolves, he enjoys walking in the woods, and has an odd fixation on the moon.

You can learn more about his writing at TonInktail.com or drop him a line at Ton@TonInktail.com

35044698R00216